Praise for Susan S̶l̶e̶e̶m̶a̶n̶'s̶
FATAL MISTAKE

"Sleeman's gritty, high-octane plot will keep the pages flying until the heart-stopping finale. A terrific choice for readers who like their romantic suspense fast-paced and terrifying."

—*Library Journal* (starred review)

"Serial killers, romance and bombs, oh my! *Fatal Mistake* is a thrill ride from page one. Hop on, strap in, and prepare to be entertained!"

—Lynette Eason, bestselling, award-winning author of the Elite Guardians series

"With *Fatal Mistake*, Susan Sleeman has once more crafted a book of romantic suspense that's virtually impossible to put down. This book offers romance set against an exciting search for a mass murderer. The ending will have you frantically turning pages."   —Richard L. Mabry, MD, bestselling author of "Medical Suspense With Heart"

"A delightful, action-packed thriller with unusual detail of research and depth of passion."

—Donn Taylor, author of *Murder Mezzo Forte*

"Sleeman's first book in her White Knights series is a must-read action-packed romantic suspense. Sleeman is a master at keeping the tension high while weaving frequent plot twists seamlessly with an unforgettable romance. Add in a swoon-worthy FBI hero and a strong, sassy heroine and this highly recommended, entertaining romantic suspense will thrill readers!"

—Elizabeth Goddard, author of *Targeted for Murder*

"Tense as a timed detonator, *Fatal Mistake* offers dauntless heroes, romance, hope—and a riveting read."

—Candace Calvert, bestselling author of the Crisis Team series

"Susan Sleeman's *Fatal Mistake* is a taut, well-written, can't-put-it-down thriller. Romantic suspense at its best!"

—Julianna Deering, author of the Drew Farthering Mystery series

KILL SHOT

ALSO BY SUSAN SLEEMAN

Fatal Mistake

KILL SHOT

A Novel

SUSAN SLEEMAN

New York   Nashville

Copyright © 2018 by Susan Sleeman
Reading group guide copyright © 2018 by Susan Sleeman and Hachette Book Group, Inc.

Cover design by John Hamilton. Cover photography by Willie Peterson Photography.
Cover copyright © 2018 by Hachette Book Group, Inc.

FaithWords
Hachette Book Group
1290 Avenue of the Americas, New York, NY 10104
faithwords.com
twitter.com/faithwords

First Edition: February 2018

FaithWords is a division of Hachette Book Group, Inc. The FaithWords name and logo are trademarks of Hachette Book Group, Inc.

The publisher is not responsible for websites (or their content) that are not owned by the publisher.

The Hachette Speakers Bureau provides a wide range of authors for speaking events. To find out more, go to www.hachettespeakersbureau.com or call (866) 376-6591.

Library of Congress Cataloging-in-Publication Data
Names: Sleeman, Susan, author.
Title: Kill shot : a novel / Susan Sleeman.
Description: First edition. | New York : FaithWords, 2018. | Series: White Knights ; 2
Identifiers: LCCN 2017034569| ISBN 9781455596492 (softcover) | ISBN 9781455596485 (open ebook)
Subjects: LCSH: Government investigators—Fiction. | Murder—Investigation—Fiction. | Snipers—Fiction. | BISAC: FICTION / Christian / Suspense. | FICTION / Christian / Romance. | FICTION / Romance / Suspense. | GSAFD: Romantic suspense fiction. | Christian fiction. | Mystery fiction.
Classification: LCC PS3619.L44 K55 2018 | DDC 813/.6—dc23
LC record available at https://lccn.loc.gov/2017034569

ISBNs: 978-1-4555-9649-2 (trade paperback), 978-1-4555-9648-5 (ebook)

Printed in the United States of America

LSC-C

10 9 8 7 6 5 4 3 2 1

For my grandson Jack.
Your creativity knows no bounds and reminds me
to look at everyday things from a fresh
perspective.

KILL SHOT

CHAPTER

1

Atlanta, Georgia
Tuesday, September 12
10:37 p.m.

Murder.

Not a word Dr. Olivia Dobbs took lightly, even if she didn't believe her client's life was in danger. Someone was stalking him, he claimed. Following him. Their sights set on killing. He couldn't give a reason. No explanation. Just a feeling. As his therapist, she couldn't play into his paranoia. It was her job to find a way to get through to him.

She slid closer to him on the park bench to grab his attention. "I know this is a setback, Ace, but we can work through it."

He gaped at her and fidgeted with a bullet strung on a cord that he often grasped during their sessions. "You think I'm flashing back again, don't you? To Iraq. Well, I'm not."

"Please," she said, "don't throw away years of hard work because of one bad day."

"You don't understand. If they find me, they'll kill me." He shot to his feet and ran a hand over the military haircut that harkened back to his service as a marine. He shoved the bullet into his pocket as his gaze roved over Centennial Olympic

Park. Even in the sweltering night air, he shuddered. "I have to leave now, or they'll see us together and think I told you. Then they'll want to kill you, too. I can't let that happen."

"Told me what?"

"Take care, Doc." He saluted, his gaze lingering for a moment as if imploring her to act on his behalf. "I appreciate everything you've done for me."

"Don't go. Please. Let me help you."

He shook his head, the gesture more sorrowful than disappointed, and spun on his red Converse sneakers. Long legs carried him away, his tattered jeans dragging on the brick walkway. He swiveled his head like a searchlight, likely looking for demons he thought real. He ran his fingers through water spurting up from the Fountain of Rings, then scrubbed his hand over his face. At the exit he spun, took one last look, and caught her gaze with eyes pleading for help, then turned up the street and disappeared into the darkness.

She sighed out her disappointment, her breath swallowed by the steamy Atlanta humidity. What a session. If you could even call it that. More like a duck-and-cover exercise on Ace's part.

He'd been jittery and keyed up, unable to focus. She hadn't seen him exhibit these classic signs of PTSD hyperarousal since he'd mastered strong coping skills, and she needed additional time to determine the cause of his regression.

Her first mistake had been to meet him at the park, but she'd had no choice. He'd refused to come to her office. Unfortunately, he hadn't been able to concentrate here. Who could? Not with the sound of gushing water and people lingering in small groups chattering and laughing.

Her second error was letting him take off. He counted on her to help him navigate the scary waters of PTSD, and she'd failed him. Failed big-time. His final beseeching gaze had reinforced that.

What if something happened to him in his delusional state? How could she live with that?

She couldn't. Wouldn't. He deserved more, but what could she do? She reviewed the night, getting lost in her thoughts for how long she didn't know, but finally concluding that she had to go after him.

She headed across the park and slipped past the five Olympic rings, their colorful lights shining through jets of water. Misty spray settled on her face and arms, cooling as it evaporated. At the exit she turned north toward the Salvation Army shelter where Ace often stayed and soon moved into a less desirable and poorly lit area.

Her steps faltered.

Maybe trailing him wasn't safe. Maybe she should go back.

No. She owed Ace her very best. Besides, the shelter was just ahead, and she had pepper spray. Sliding her hand into her purse to cup the cylinder, she rounded the corner. The streetlight's warm glow directed her attention down the way to a man lying on the sidewalk, another man hunched over him. The guy stretched out on his side wore red high-tops.

"Ace?" was the only word she managed to utter as she tried to make sense of the scene.

Was this man in front of her helping, or—

The man swiveled toward her. She searched his face, but his dark hoodie cast thick shadows, obscuring any detail she might have made out. A glint of metal in his hands flashed in the light and caught her attention.

A knife. He had a knife!

She screamed, the sound rolling from her throat and cutting through the silent night. He lurched to his feet. Tall. Over six feet, built and powerful, he started toward her, his knife raised and threatening.

She tried to pull out her pepper spray, but her purse straps tangled around her hand.

The man lunged.

She stumbled back, freed her hand, and heaved her purse at him. It slammed into his face, knocking him off guard.

Run. Now!

She whirled and took off. Running hard. Fast. Rounding the corner and not looking back.

Heavy footsteps pummeled the sidewalk behind her. He was going to use his knife on her. Kill her. Like Ace?

Ace. Poor Ace. Is he really dead?

Her heart clutching, she picked up speed. The street stretched ahead. Deserted, except for a few cars at the next stoplight. She had to reach them.

You can do this.

She pounded forward, moving into a rhythm, but the knife-wielding man was taller, and his footfalls gained on her. She risked a glance over her shoulder.

He'd moved closer. Traveling fast. She kicked into gear. Her legs churned faster than she could manage. Clumsy, awkward, she lost her rhythm, and her foot wrenched in a pothole.

No! Please.

She catapulted forward. Her hands slammed into the unforgiving pavement, and the rough surface sandpapered across her cheek. Pain screamed through her body, but it didn't matter. He would catch her, and she would die.

She listened for the thump of his boots—for him to arrive and stand over her—but heard only a car in the distance behind her.

His footsteps sounded again. Moving fast. Receding.

Lifting her head, she searched. He was gone like a whisper in the night. She collapsed back on the warm concrete to catch her breath.

She was alive! Thankfully alive. But what about Ace? He needed her. She rose to her knees as steps coming from the opposite direction caught her attention.

Had the man circled around?

She shot to her feet, her hands outstretched, ready to defend herself, as she spun.

An Atlanta police officer stood strong and tall, the sight of his navy blue uniform bringing a sigh from deep in her chest. "Are you all right, ma'am?"

"A man. He was chasing me. He had a knife. I think he killed my client, Ace." Her words came flying out, tumbling over each other. She drew in a breath to calm down and make more sense. "He was going to kill me, too. We have to help Ace. Please come with me. Now!"

"Hey, hey." The officer held up his hands. "Slow down, okay? What's your name?"

"There's no time. Ace might still be alive. We need to help him." She started down the street.

The officer's hand came around her arm, stopping her. "Let's not rush into danger, ma'am."

"Look. I'm not a ma'am. I'm Ace's therapist. Dr. Olivia Dobbs." She extricated her arm and quickly caught the officer up on what had transpired.

He eyed her. "I didn't see a man."

"You must have scared him off. Please. We have to help Ace."

"We will," he replied. "But we aren't going on foot. We'll take my car."

She didn't wait for further instructions but started for his vehicle, parked down the street. He trailed her, and she heard him radioing for backup.

At the car he stepped in front of her. "I'm sorry, ma'am, but I have to check for a weapon."

"What? I'm not armed."

"Then you won't mind letting me check so we can get to your friend."

She didn't want to be searched, but she also wouldn't head toward a knife-wielding man without the officer. "Then do it quickly."

She endured the frisking as onlookers ogled her, but the officer made it quick, as she'd requested, then opened the back door for her. She'd never been in the backseat of a police car—never been searched either—but she wouldn't argue with him about these points when they needed to get to Ace.

He slammed the door closed. She noticed the lack of handles in the back, locking her in. He gave her an assessing glance as he slid behind the wheel.

"I'm not crazy," she said. "Ace really is hurt. Just drive and you'll see. But hurry."

"Caution is the name of the game, ma'am." He set the car in motion and ran his gaze down both sides of the street.

Maybe he was looking for the man who'd chased her. She wanted him caught, but helping Ace was more important to her. Finally the car eased around the corner, and she spotted Ace. He hadn't moved.

"There, on the right," she said, her heart plummeting. "See? He's wearing red sneakers."

The officer shifted into park but left the engine running. "I'll be right back."

He grabbed a flashlight and exited the car. She expected him to hurry over to Ace. Instead he made a guarded approach, scanning in all directions. He ran his flashlight over Ace, then jerked his head up to look at the sky. He suddenly bolted back to the car.

"Is Ace okay?" she asked.

"Get down on the floor." He shoved the car into reverse and gunned the engine.

The vehicle shot backward. Her body catapulted toward the seat divider, her shoulder catching it hard.

She righted herself. "What's going on?"

"Looks like a sniper, and we're taking cover."

"Sniper? But the man had a knife."

"Trust me, lady. I've done several combat tours. There's no way your client's injury could be from anything but a bullet. Likely a .50 caliber, and we need to get out of sniper range. If we don't, you'll see firsthand the damage one of those bad boys can do."

* * *

Washington, D.C.
Wednesday, September 13
1:00 a.m.

Nothing good came from a middle-of-the-night phone call. As Agent Rick Cannon stepped into the FBI's airport conference room and spotted top-secret binders waiting for his six-person Critical Incident Response team, dubbed the White Knights, he doubted tonight would be the exception.

Add his team leader Max White pacing the room in long, bold strides plus the stone-faced armed guard at the door, and Rick's feeling morphed into certainty. Something huge had hit the fan. Lives were at stake, and his team would deploy within the hour to minimize the casualties.

Max crossed powerful arms over a massive chest, a scowl drawing down his mouth. A former Army Ranger, Max could intimidate the toughest of guys when he scowled. But not

Rick. At least not on most days. Only because he worked with Max and knew him to be reasonable and fair.

"I'm glad you're the first to arrive." He marched across the room to join Rick. "You'll be taking lead on this incident."

"Weapons or hostage issue?" Rick clarified so he could mentally prepare for which of his team roles he'd be filling on this mission.

"Weapons." Max tapped the nearest classified binder. "I can't read you in until the team is in place and we unseal the documents, but be prepared for your worst nightmare to come true."

Worst nightmare. Likely an even bigger incident than Rick had first thought. After all, Max wasn't one for drama. He was a levelheaded and even-keeled kind of guy.

"Take a moment to get your head in the game so when the rest of the team arrives we're ready to move," he said before stepping up to a large whiteboard.

He picked up a cool-blue marker, and Rick watched him jot each team member's name on the board in square, precise letters. After they unsealed the documents and completed a quick briefing, Max would grab the fiery-red marker and note assignments below their names. This procedure was used to keep from wasting valuable time in planning, so the minute their Cessna touched down wherever they were headed, they'd be ready to take action.

Laughter rang out behind Rick, seeming out of place. He turned to see his teammates, cyber expert Kaci North and hostage negotiator Shane Erwin, stepping through the door. Their focus lingered on the binders as they abruptly stilled their laughter.

Forensic specialist Brynn Young trailed behind them. She stopped to stare at the table. Even in the middle of the night, every hair on her head was in place, but she smoothed a hand over it anyway, the only hint she would ever give of her unease.

Kaci pushed up large black glasses as her gaze drifted to Rick. "Looks like it's going to be a tough one."

He nodded but didn't mention he'd take lead. If Max wanted them to know, he'd say something.

Shane continued into the room, and his long strides carried him across the space. He dropped into the chair closest to Max. "Any chance you'll read us in before everyone gets here?"

Max shook his head. "And there's no use speculating. I'll get started as soon as Cal arrives."

"Right. Cal," Kaci said, referring to the only wayward member of the team, their bomb expert Cal Riggins. "He won't be rolling in until the last minute."

Max checked his watch. "I don't blame him for taking his time, but the minute these long farewells with the wife interfere with an op, he'll be reassigned."

Max often came across as harsh. Not that he had a choice. Their team couldn't afford to be sloppy, and he held each of them accountable. No matter how tight the group was—and Cal was most definitely one of them—Max would follow through and cut him from the team if need be.

"Get your e-mails and texts out of the way now," he instructed as he moved to the head of the table. "Our flight's only about an hour, and we'll spend every minute in planning."

Rick took a seat with his teammates. None of them would touch the binders until Max gave the okay to break the seals, but Rick wanted to rip into his packet to see what Max considered a worst-nightmare scenario.

Not that Rick could name just one scenario when people committed atrocious acts all the time. His stint as a Marine Scout Sniper and five years with the FBI had proved that. He could rattle off dozens, maybe hundreds of horrible things he feared, but honestly, he couldn't narrow down the list to the worst thing.

Let it go. You'll know soon enough.

He changed his focus to his phone until Cal breezed in with a big smile on his face and settled into the nearest chair. Rick wasn't big on smiling, but he couldn't keep his mouth from turning up. Not even with the tension in the room. Since Cal's recent marriage, he'd lost some of his intensity. Not on the job. He was still a guy who had the team's back, and they could count on him. He just smiled a heck of a lot more now, and it was contagious.

"I never knew getting married could slow a guy down so much," Brynn teased.

Cal's smile widened. "Hey, we moved farther away from here is all it is."

Shane rolled his eyes. "Right. Maybe we should start a pool on how long it takes before you call Tara."

Kaci grinned, looking more like a teenager than a woman in her early thirties. "I'll take five minutes after we're airborne."

"Five?" Shane asked. "Nah, he won't make it *that* long."

Max clapped his hands. "Let's get started, but before we do, Shane, put me down for fifteen minutes. Since we're hassling Cal, I figure he'll hold out longer."

Cal shook his head and the team chuckled, but it was a nervous laughter, as Max would soon give the go-ahead to open the binders.

The armed guard poked his head through the doorway and eyed the group, ending the last of the laughter. He was warning them to leave the binders intact and not to remove any of the confidential material. Max gave a firm nod of acknowledgment and the guard closed the door, sealing them in. The minute this briefing ended, he'd check the binders, then put them in a burn bag to be disposed of at FBI headquarters.

"I don't have to tell you that our briefing is highly classified," Max said. "And you'll curtail any discussion of the material to private, secured locations." He let his gaze travel over the group, pausing at each person to make his point.

"Aren't these directions overkill?" Shane leaned back in his chair. "We've been through so many classified situations that the protocol is second nature."

Max pinned Shane with an intense stare. "You haven't been through anything like this, I assure you."

"So let's find out what *this* is," Rick said, hoping to move things along.

"Open your binders, read the intro paragraph, and then we'll review it before getting into a discussion of the mission."

Rick tore through the seal and flipped to the first page. He read only one line before his mouth fell open, and he shot a look at Max. "Self-steering bullets. Our op is about self-steering bullets?"

"Yes," Max said with deadly calm.

"A horrifying bullet that gives a novice shooter the same skills as a highly trained sniper," Rick grumbled. "You weren't kidding when you said this is my worst nightmare."

"Can someone explain, please?" Kaci asked.

"It's simple, really," Rick said, but if the mission involved these bullets, it would be anything but simple. "The EXtreme ACcuracy Tasked Ordnance program, EXACTO, has done what was once thought impossible. Under the Department of Defense's umbrella, EXACTO created a small-caliber bullet with continuous guidance to target. And don't be confused by my 'small-caliber' comment. I mean small only in comparison to a missile. We're talking .50 caliber here."

Cal let out a long, low whistle. Second to Rick, Cal possessed the greatest experience and weapons training on the team, so the self-steering bullets weren't news to him.

"Missile guidance in a .50," Brynn muttered. "You're kidding, right?"

"I wish I was," Rick replied. "And in case you're not up to speed on rifles chambered for .50-caliber ammunition, this rifle is considered one of the most destructive weapons legally available to civilians in the U.S. The bullets will shoot through armor plate and reinforced concrete."

Kaci's face paled. "How does this smart bullet work?"

"The ammo's paired with a custom infrared scope. The bullets have optical sensors in the tips that communicate with the scope and send signals to fins in the bullet to adjust the path to the target. As long as the shooter keeps the scope trained on the target, the bullet will adjust course to hit the target. Even circling back if needed."

"So any yahoo with this scope and these bullets could kill a mark without any training?" Brynn clarified.

Rick nodded. "Takes a special weapon without a rifled barrel, but yeah, anyone on the street possessing these tools instantly becomes a highly accurate sniper and can take out a target at an extreme distance without a lick of training. The record sniper kill for a .50 without the aid of this technology is a mile and a half, and the bullets travel twenty-eight hundred feet per second. Means the shooter would be long gone before anyone figured out where the round originated."

"Whoa," Shane said.

Max scowled. "Exactly."

"Then I'm assuming we have state-of-the-art security for this ordnance," Cal said, using the common military term for weapons and ammunition.

Max widened his stance. "Yes, but—"

"Wait," Rick interrupted as their mission became clear to him. "You're not going to tell us someone stole the self-steering bullets?"

"I'm afraid a rifle, scope, *and* three dozen bullets fell into the wrong hands about three weeks ago."

"Three weeks ago! And we're just being called in now?"

"The Department of Defense tried to retrieve the prototype themselves, but failed."

Rick made strong eye contact with Max. "So our mission is to retrieve this weapon and ammo before someone gets killed."

"Unfortunately," Max replied, his gaze uneasy, "someone has already died, and our mission also includes hunting down the killer."

CHAPTER

2

Atlanta, Georgia
1:30 a.m.

Olivia parked outside the rental bungalow where she lived with her sister Dianna and Dianna's two children. Olivia stared at the warm glow from a streetlight filtering through tall oak trees and trying to wash away dusty shadows clinging to the house. Dianna had been expecting her for hours, but the detective had taken her back to the scene and now the memory of Ace lying in a pool of blood drained her energy and she couldn't move.

Ace. Poor Ace. Gone from this world. Dead. Murdered. How could that be?

Tears pricked her eyes, and she swiped them away. She worked hard not to get emotionally involved with her clients. It took great mental fortitude. Sometimes she failed, and Ace was one of those times. She'd never crossed a professional line with him—or any client, for that matter—but she'd invested much of herself in his recovery these past three years. She'd be lying if she said his care was simply a job, or that his loss didn't cut her to core.

The bright-red bungalow door swung open, and Dianna stepped onto the tiny porch. She shifted her three-month-old baby higher on her shoulder and impatiently curled her arm to beckon Olivia. Baby Natalie's cries tugged at Olivia's heart, so she forced herself out of the car and toward the house. Apparently she didn't move fast enough, as Dianna charged down the steps and across the lawn.

"It's bad enough that you're so late," Dianna said. "But then you just sat there, and I thought I'd have to haul you out of the car."

Olivia bit back her retort. The last thing Dianna needed tonight was for Olivia to share her experience. She had to do what she told her clients to do—put aside unhelpful thoughts. Leave the past behind and live in the present. She'd think of Dianna needing help and no more drama. The morning would be soon enough to talk.

"As I said in my texts," Olivia replied, working hard to keep her tone from sounding snippy, "I was having a bad day."

"*You're* having a bad day! Wylie's been acting out, and Nat's been screaming nonstop. I'm about to pull my hair out." Dianna settled Natalie into Olivia's arms.

"Hi, precious." Olivia snuggled the baby close and hoped the scent of her sweet shampoo would help calm her own nerves. She swayed until the baby's cries turned to whimpers.

Dianna sighed, her breath seeming to go on and on. "I'm sorry for being so cranky, Sis. I really am. I'm exhausted and at the end of my rope. You know I appreciate your help, right? I mean, I've never been a leech like Harrison or Mom."

"No, you haven't."

Dianna once was independent and self-reliant. Strong, positive, and a joy to be around. Until her marine husband walked out on her and their children a few months ago. She'd sunk into a deep depression, so Olivia had convinced her to move back to Atlanta to share a house. Olivia soon saw the extent of Dianna's depression and recommended she see a local psychologist. Thankfully, counseling had helped, but Dianna still needed a sleep aid at night, so Olivia had taken on the responsibility of getting up when Natalie and Wylie needed something. Tonight would be no different. And in fact, Olivia was glad to have the baby to care for when thoughts of Ace kept her awake.

Olivia dredged up a smile for her sister. "Let's get you inside and in bed."

Dianna's flip-flops snapped as she marched across the lawn brown from a dry and sweltering summer. Inside she popped her sleeping pill into her mouth, grabbed a glass of water, and chugged until ice clinked to the bottom.

"Okay, so nothing's different from yesterday. If Natalie gets too fussy and you want to take her for a ride to calm her down, her seat's in my car and here are the keys." She tapped her key ring lying on the counter.

"Got it," Olivia said.

Dianna filled her glass again before trudging down the hallway. Not only was she physically tired, but the loss of her husband and the life they'd been building added to her fatigue. Thankfully, Dianna didn't share their mother's and brother's belief that counseling was pointless. Olivia had argued with her family for years about their misguided opinion of the profession. They thought it a waste of time, but she was committed to helping as many people as she could.

Or she had been until lately, when she'd started to notice the failures more. She'd always been a positive person, so what had changed? Was she just tired from caring for the kids, or was it more?

"I think it's time to face facts, precious," she whispered to the baby as she pulled her close and snuggled. "If I don't get a break soon, I'll burn out, too, and won't be any good to anyone."

* * *

Atlanta, Georgia
3:30 a.m.

Home.

Rick was home, and he didn't much like it. He stepped from the plane well ahead of his team, his feet hitting the tarmac at Dobbins Air Reserve Base in a suburb north of Atlanta. The humidity slapped him upside the head and dampened his clothes.

Yeah, he was home all right. Hard to forget eighteen years of sweltering days even into fall. Playing on the football field and fighting to breathe thick air. Looking up at the packed stands where fans sipped icy drinks. Not his father, of course, but his mother had attended every game when she wasn't on his father's arm at some social event.

He hadn't been back here since his buddy Levi's wedding three years ago, and the steamy humidity felt foreign. Sure, it would have been so easy on that trip for Rick to stop in to see his mother and father, but he and his parents were estranged. Estranged, ha! His dad's fancy word to say they couldn't abide seeing one another and hadn't been together for seventeen years. Rick didn't need his father's fancy language. His money or his prestige either.

Rick had everything he needed. A job where he made a difference each and every day. A small house to call home. His refurbished 1948 Harley Panhead plus enough money to hunt, fish, and mountain climb whenever he had the free time. He'd also kept in contact with Yolanda, the family cook who'd practically raised him. He'd need to make time to see her while he was in town.

That was enough for him. Had to be enough.

The team tromped down the stairs, and Rick shook off his memories to do the job he'd been dispatched to do. He raised a finger to warn two young agents with overly eager gazes to stay put as they climbed from black SUVs near the hold of the plane.

Rick faced the team. "Mind getting the equipment unloaded while I talk to the local agents?"

Kaci swiped the back of her arm across her forehead, then fanned her face. "I think everyone agrees with me when I say we're not much into hauling equipment, especially in this heat. But we're even less into talking to green agents who look like driving us to the crime scene equals taking over the world."

"We were once that eager." Shane chuckled.

"Speak for yourself," Rick replied, earning a laugh from the group as Max came barreling down the steps.

He peered at Rick. "Thought you'd want to know that the autopsy's scheduled at eight."

"Any chance we can push it to a later time so I can calculate the bullet trajectory and interview the witness first?"

"I'm not sure rescheduling is a good idea." Uncertainty clung to his words.

Rick had never seen Max waffle, and he would seize the moment. "The deceased isn't going anywhere, so the autopsy is the only investigative piece that's not time sensitive. Forensics is a different story. Thunderstorms are predicted in the afternoon, as they usually are when the temps heat up in Atlanta. I'll need to locate the shooter's hide before rain or people inadvertently destroy evidence. And with every minute that passes, the witness could change her statement."

"Didn't someone mention that she's a well-respected doctor?" Cal asked. "If so, maybe her observations are more clinical in nature, and she won't have hazy recall like so many witnesses."

"Doctor or not," Brynn said, "trauma like she just experienced could skew her perception."

"And she's not an MD, but a PhD," Max added. "A clinical psychologist specializing in treating trauma and PTSD."

"You're kidding, right?" A sour feeling settled in Rick's stomach.

"No, is that a problem?"

"Problem?" Rick mumbled, trying to wrap his head around the fact that their only eyewitness was a shrink—a profession prior experiences had taught him to be wary of.

Max eyed him. "If it is, let me know now so I can pull you from lead."

"No problem," Rick replied, hoping he was right. "But her credentials won't stop me from having Kaci do a deep background check on her."

"Are you thinking she might not be on the up-and-up?" Kaci asked.

"You know the person who finds a body is always under suspicion for having a connection to the crime," Rick replied. "And the deceased is her client, which means we have to be even more diligent in vetting her. Being a highly respected doctor doesn't change that."

Max stepped closer. "It's going to take time for Kaci to photograph the scene before you can access it. I could try to arrange for you to interview Dr. Dobbs near the scene while you wait for access." He flipped open a thick binder. "Like I thought. Her cell number's in the report. I'll make a call right now and get her down there. Then arrange with the locals to find a quiet spot to hold the interview."

"And if she doesn't agree?"

Max's eyebrow rose. "You doubt my ability to convince her of the importance?"

Rick didn't doubt Max's abilities. He doubted the doctor's willingness to help. "People are unpredictable."

"But if anyone can get her there, Max can," Brynn said.

She spoke the truth, so Rick nodded. "Then let's get to work."

Max shifted the binder under his arm and dug out his phone. The team headed for the hold of the plane, where Rick greeted the agents.

The tallest guy shot to attention and took eager steps toward Rick. He did his best to be accommodating, but when the guy's excitement had him jingling his car keys, Rick snatched them from his hand. "What can you tell me about the shooting?"

"Um...well...just that there was a shooting. Oh, and your team is here to investigate."

"And?"

"And...well...I..." He ran a quick hand over his baby face and shrank back. "My job is to drive you all to the crime scene, but I haven't been read in on the investigation."

"Read in or not, you must have heard some gossip."

He shook his head hard. "I know it's gotta be big if y'all are here, but honestly, no one's even speculating because we don't know enough to start."

The answer Rick wanted to hear. The only way to keep the news of the stolen self-steering bullets from reaching the press was to contain the number of people in the know.

"You can both ride in the second vehicle," Rick said. "We'll need the cars during our stay. Arrange for someone in your office to pick you up at the scene."

The agent sputtered something about being required to

drive, but there was no way Rick would let a rookie drive him in his hometown.

"Take a seat in the other SUV now so you're ready to depart the moment we are." Rick eyed both agents until they complied, then pocketed the car keys and pitched in loading gear.

Max still stood to the side, but Rick hadn't counted on him to schlep equipment anyway. Rick wasn't known for his ability to schmooze and make nice, so as long as Max was on this deployment, Rick would take advantage of it and have him run interference with local officials and obtain any needed warrants from judges.

After the final case was loaded, Rick closed the hatch and turned to the team. "Shane and Kaci, you're in the second vehicle."

Shane rolled his eyes. "Don't much like being a kid who has to sit at the second Thanksgiving table."

"Don't read anything into this. You two simply possess the most patience, and you're less likely to lose your cool and cause an incident with the rookie agents."

"Not sure about that," Kaci said. "But I'm not going to stand out in this heat and argue with you."

The group broke up, and Rick slid onto the SUV's smooth leather driver's seat. He moved the motorized seat back for much-needed legroom and adjusted the mirrors while Brynn and Cal settled in the back. By the time the AC was cranking out cold air, Max had jogged to the car and climbed into the front seat.

"Dr. Dobbs is more than happy to meet us." He clicked on his seat belt. "And the homicide lieutenant offered their command truck for the interview. They've set up a second perimeter where we can park, and they've also pulled all unnecessary personnel from the scene to minimize the number of people getting wind of the ordnance."

He paused for a moment, shifting in his seat to look at Rick. "The lieutenant I spoke with said he'll approve overtime for the team currently in place, so they won't have to bring in others. And FYI, we won't be including any Atlanta agents other than the ERT members in the investigation. Even then, their work will be restricted to evidence recovery, and they won't be read in on the theft."

"Who *does* know about it?" Rick asked as he pointed the car toward the exit.

"The forensic tech who recovered the bullet. Her supervisor, plus the lieutenant I mentioned, and a division captain. I've been assured they'll keep things under wraps."

"Still, that's a big-enough group that we can't count on the word not getting out," Brynn said. "I don't even want to think about the press getting involved."

"What about our local office?" Cal asked. "Has anyone there been read in?"

"When the bullet was discovered, an Atlanta PD captain talked to the special agent in charge, which is actually how we got looped in," Max said. "So he's in the know, but he's the only one."

"I was worried about the grapevine." Rick glanced at Max. "So I questioned the rookie. He hasn't heard a thing."

"Just the way we like it." Max's phone buzzed, and he dipped his head to look at it. "Good. Got the pictures of the scene before the deceased was moved. I'll forward them to everyone's phone."

The thought of viewing the photos put an end to the conversation. Rick concentrated on driving, and the others turned their attention to their phones.

At the crime scene, he was surprised to see so many looky-loos at this time of day hanging close to the yellow tape marking the scene's perimeter. They held cell phones at the ready. Smartphones made working an investigation easier, but they were often used at crime scenes by gawking people hoping to catch anything they could display on social media to spread rumors. Made the Knights' job more difficult. No way Rick would give them or the reporters standing near their vans anything to go on.

He maneuvered the vehicle around in the secured parking area to back into the space. His military training would have had him park this way regardless of the press, but there was also no point in letting the reporters get a look at the team's equipment while they unloaded. The second SUV slid into place next to him, and the team started to unload necessary equipment.

Shane reached for the tote holding supplies to draw a sketch of the scene. He paused to look at Rick, a pensive expression on his face. One he often wore as the profiler on the team. "I spent the drive trying to get in the killer's head and figure out his endgame. We have limited facts right now, but I have to wonder if he plans to use all of the bullets, or if he plans to sell them."

"The time DARPA wasted trying to recover the bullets on their own gave him plenty of time to think about it," Cal grumbled.

The Defense Advanced Research Projects Agency oversaw the self-steering bullet project, or "smart-bullet project" as some called it. A management office only, DARPA contracted with independent companies to actually develop the projects.

Shane pursed his lips. "Here's the thing that's troubling me. If the thief is bent on using all of the ammo, seems like he would have struck sooner."

Kaci hung her camera around her neck. "You don't actually think he'll use all thirty-six bullets, do you?"

"Maybe he plans to fire off a few, or just this one, and sell the rest," Cal suggested.

Rick carefully weighed his next statement so he didn't come off sounding like a jerk. "This might seem callous, but I'd rather he'd use every one of them. That way unscrupulous people can't buy the ammo to analyze the technology and make their own."

"But that would be thirty-six murders," Kaci cried out. "How could anyone decide to kill that many people he knew?"

"Who says he knew the victim?" Rick asked.

Cal frowned. "You mean a random shooting?"

"Sure, why not? Test out the bullets and technology on a homeless guy like Ace Griffin. Or maybe the shooting was a demo for a potential buyer, and they chose the first guy who came along."

"If that's the case"—Max crossed his arms—"then the clock is ticking, and we need to get to work before the ordnance is sold to the highest bidder."

CHAPTER

3

The aftermath of death awaited Rick just a few feet ahead at the crime scene. He'd read Dr. Dobb's statement about Griffin's murder, but he needed to get the lay of the land before heading to the command truck to question her.

He took a deep breath and rounded the corner to the scene lit with large klieg lights. He let the feel of the night, the incident, soak into his pores. Griffin's fear seemed to linger in the thick air, and Rick could easily imagine him running from the doctor who didn't believe him. Wanting to find a safe refuge and slipping past the two-story brick building on the corner. The last thing he'd known was a bullet slamming into his chest. Maybe not even that much, as his death would have been instantaneous.

Rick closed his eyes and thought to pray for those who knew and loved Griffin, but he'd stopped praying after losing his wife, Traci, and their unborn son over five years ago. What was the point of prayer when it went unanswered?

"You ready to do the interview?" Shane asked from behind.

Startled, Rick opened his eyes and spun to meet the gaze of his more laid-back teammate. As team negotiator and profiler, Shane possessed keen instincts when it came to victims and suspects, so Rick had asked him to participate in Dr. Dobbs's questioning.

"Let's get to it." Rick stepped out of the cordoned-off area, ignoring questions called out by curious reporters. They must have caught sight of the embroidered team logo on his shirt, as they started shouting questions about why the FBI was brought in for this murder investigation.

Head down and mouth clamped closed, he eased past them. Shane followed suit and they quickly reached the other side of the street and the truck boasting the Atlanta PD logo came into view. He'd soon be face-to-face with Dr. Dobbs. Unease settled in his gut. Earlier life experiences had left him wary of shrinks and he wasn't eager to question her.

Not that he would let his bias impact the way he treated the doc. As a law enforcement officer, he'd been trained to let go of any prejudices and assumptions before conducting an interview. Otherwise attempts to build a rapport with the interviewee could fail and negatively impact the interview.

But since this was a critical interview, maybe he should let Shane take charge of the questioning. Rick could sit back to observe—a skill he'd honed in sniper training. Snipers weren't simply shooters. They observed, assessed, and analyzed so they could report up the chain of command any problems they were seeing through the scope. Perfect training to prepare him for an observer's role in the doctor's interview.

He slowed so Shane could come alongside him. "I want you to take lead on questioning the doc."

Shane's eyebrow quirked. "Something you need to tell me?"

Rick shook his head.

"Then why put me in charge?" So much for easygoing Shane.

"I'd like to observe."

"You could do that while still taking charge."

There was no legit reply other than the truth, and Rick wouldn't lie to a teammate, so he didn't respond.

Shane shook his head and sighed. "I can usually predict how everyone on the team will act, but not you. There's always something just beneath the surface. Something more to your thoughts, but you only share the bare minimum."

He was right, but Rick didn't think the comment required a response, so he moved on. "I'd also like you to interview Griffin's mother. It'll mean a quick trip to Macon, but your diplomacy skills make you the best guy to deal with a grieving mother."

Shane remained silent for a long time, then finally shook his head. "I'll head out right after I finish sketching the scene."

"Thanks, man."

Shane nodded. "You give any thought to our victim being involved in this?"

"Griffin?"

"Yeah. We all know murder victims often engage in criminal activities with their murderer before they are killed. Ace might have been in on the smart-bullet theft because he blamed the marines for his PTSD and wanted to get back at them. And some PTSD sufferers are prone to getting involved in criminal activities, too."

"I suppose he could be involved." Rick ran his hand over the stubble on his chin and wished he had a shaver for a quick cleanup before the interview. "But any conclusion would be pure speculation at this point."

"True that, but something we need to keep in mind as we move forward."

"Understood." Rick stopped at steps leading to the truck's open door and gestured for Shane to go first.

On the stairway Rick saw Dr. Dobbs standing in the aisle, her back to them. She was tall and slender, with muted red hair falling just below her shoulders. Despite having been called here unexpectedly in the early hours before dawn, she was nicely dressed in a full print skirt of green and turquoise and high heels in a complementary color, drawing Rick's attention to her tanned and shapely legs.

"Dr. Dobbs," Shane said.

She spun, and Rick steeled himself for her impartial, cool, maybe even defensive gaze to land on him. But she didn't even notice him.

Shane extended his hand. "I'm Special Agent Shane Erwin."

"I was expecting an Agent Cannon." Her voice was languid, with a Southern drawl.

"I'm Agent Cannon." Rick climbed into the small space holding workstations, communication devices, and equipment storage compartments.

She looked at him then. A raw scrape covering her cheek, and large blue eyes, washed with anguish, brought his feet to a stop. She'd been hurt. He hadn't heard that. And her response wasn't at all what he'd expected. Not at all.

Nor did she look anything like he'd imagined. He'd seen her in his mind's eye with a clinical appearance, but the woman standing before him was curvy and soft looking. Glossy hair framed a wide face with a narrow chin that he could imagine she raised when tested. But now she bowed her head as if feeling defeated.

"Why don't we all sit down." Shane gestured at a workstation with a chair on each side.

Rick heard Shane, but he couldn't take his focus off Dr.

Dobbs. He was mesmerized by the way she walked. She carried herself with confidence, and yet there was something else in her movements that he couldn't put his finger on. As she settled on one of the chairs, he caught a whiff of cinnamon that matched the warm vibe she was giving off. He had to admit he liked it, and his interest was piqued.

Not a reaction he could have predicted. He didn't like to be caught off guard. Ever. And here? With a suspect, for Pete's sake? One who was professionally trained to hide her emotions if need be and could be putting on a show of grief for their benefit? He couldn't buy into her actions and forget his duty here. He had to keep his focus and look for underlying signs that said she could be playing them.

He signaled for Shane to sit near the doctor while he remained standing to better observe her nonverbal actions. Shane dropped onto the chair, gaining the doctor's full attention.

"Ace was my client," she said, her tone as soft as her curves. "I hope I can help you find his killer."

Shane smiled at the doctor. "Why don't you start by telling us what happened with Mr. Griffin."

Her eyebrows arched. "Mr. Griffin. It sounds so odd to speak so formally about Ace when he was such an informal guy."

"Would you like us to call him Ace?"

"Would you mind?"

Shane shook his head. She didn't look at Rick, so he didn't respond, but he was all for using "Ace" when talking with her if it meant using a name that didn't make her stumble, and, in turn, she was more candid with them.

"Then Ace it is," Shane said. "Go ahead and tell us what happened last night."

She closed her eyes tightly, then blinked several times, flicking away tears that had formed. "Yesterday morning, Ace called my office to cancel our regular weekly appointment. He told me someone was following him, and he couldn't be seen coming to my office."

Shane took out his notepad and pen. "Did he say who?"

She shook her head. "But he was so upset that I was worried he'd lost touch with reality. So I convinced him to meet me on his turf."

"The park is his turf?"

"Sort of. He's homeless, and he often stayed at the nearby Salvation Army shelter."

"So you met," Shane clarified. "Then what happened?'

"He was jittery and hyper. Like in the early days of counseling. He told me if the people tracking him found him, they would kill him. When I tried to get him to tell me who would kill him, he clammed up." She paused and curled delicate fingers into fists. "He was exhibiting signs of hyperarousal, which is common for PTSD, and I'm ashamed to admit I thought he was regressing, and I didn't believe him. So he took off."

"How long did you talk with Ace?" Shane asked.

"Hmm, maybe forty-five minutes or so. I'm not sure if he arrived at ten or not. I didn't look at a clock until after the detective took my statement and I got in my car to go home. The park was obviously still open when I went after Ace, and I know it closes at eleven, if that helps."

Shane jotted the information in his notepad. "And you followed Ace right away?"

She opened her fingers and splayed them on her skirt to stare at them. "I had to think about our conversation first. You know, process before deciding what to do. I'd guess it was five minutes or so before I went after him. That's when I found him. Saw his red sneakers and knew it was him. Then the..." She shuddered. "The man. The one leaning over him. He had a knife, and he chased me until I fell." She lifted an elbow, displaying an angry-looking scrape as if she thought they needed proof of her story.

Proof? Yeah, Rick needed proof. If she really did meet Griffin around ten and talked to him for forty-five minutes, then waited five minutes to go after him, her story didn't jibe with the facts as Rick knew them right now. Preliminary reports said the bullet had been fired from a long distance, and the landscape was such that the shot had to have originated from a tall building. Officer Hazeldale had radioed for help at ten minutes after eleven. If the shooter was at the scene when she arrived, and she waited about five minutes to follow Ace and found him six blocks away, the killer would have had to fire the deadly shot, bolt down a number of flights of stairs, stow his weapon, and then travel a long distance to reach Griffin, all in the span of ten minutes or so. Not likely.

Unless he had an accomplice. Something that might make sense, as he hadn't likely stolen the weapon system by himself. Rick seriously needed to get the MilMed owner to call them back so he could get more details on the theft, but his assistant said he was out of town and they might not hear from him today. Still, accomplice or not, what was the point of the shooter coming down to the body after a long-distance shot? There was no way he needed to check if the .50 caliber had killed Griffin. He couldn't possibly have survived, and the shooter had to know that. Hopefully the doc could shed some light on it.

"Ten minutes," he said, keeping his suspicion from his tone so he didn't raise a red flag and bring up her defenses. "Are you sure about the time?"

She met his gaze for the first time since she'd taken a seat. Large, expressive eyes ran over him, inspecting him as if she'd just realized he remained in the room. Her eyes flared wider, and she scooted back on the chair as if something about him disturbed her.

"The time," he said pointedly.

"Right." She bit down on her lip, her gaze moving away to search the space.

Avoidance? Perhaps looking away because she planned to lie. A common pattern for criminals and people hoping to deceive.

She swung her focus back to him, her chin tilted at a sharp angle. "I'm not sure how much time passed. I mean, I was so worried about him I didn't even think about the time. After I worked things out, I went after him. If I had gone earlier, maybe..."

"Maybe you would have been shot, too," Shane said, and Rick knew his teammate had bought into her story and was trying to make her feel better. "Tell us about this man. Did you get a good look at him?"

She shook her head. "His back was to me at first. Even when he turned, I didn't see his face."

"So let me get this straight," Rick said. "You could see well enough to make out Ace's shoes but not the other man's face?"

"Yes. He wore a hoodie and the light hit just right to leave his face shadowed. And with a knife glinting in the streetlight, I didn't look at his face for long. I just reacted. Took off and kept running."

Rick could see that happening, but he'd be sure the team tested out her statement by reenacting the event.

"What about the guy's build?" Shane asked.

"He was big. Muscular. Scary." She peered at Rick. "Kind of like your size."

Rick noted her statement but took it at face value. Eyewitness testimony was often wrong. Especially when the witness's life was in danger at the time, as hers had been.

"So he was big and strong," Shane said. "Did you catch his hair color or any additional details to help us find him?"

"I didn't see anything else. Sorry." She shifted her focus to Rick. "Just that he was built like Agent Cannon."

So the bad guy resembled him. Not surprising. If a witness had a choice between him or Shane to compare to their villain, they'd choose him. Rick got that. People told him often enough that he gave off a tough vibe, and Shane had a boy-next-door look. Okay, to be fair, Shane had a rugged presence, but his personality was warmer than Rick's, and that made people find him less intimidating. Or she simply liked Shane's personality more and wanted the suspect to look like Rick. Shoot, maybe she was even right and the killer actually *did* resemble him.

"So tell us more about Ace," he said to move them forward, even though he was supposed to be observing.

She crossed her legs and settled back in her chair. "What do you want to know?"

"He was former military, right?"

"Sounds like you already know he was a marine."

Her nonanswer irritated Rick, but then she was right. Kaci's preliminary report had told them about Griffin's stint in the military, but they'd need his service record book to gain more details. "How did he wind up homeless?"

"The same way most people end up homeless."

"I'm not asking about most people. Just Ace," he said evenly, though he was starting to get annoyed with her vague responses.

She eyed him for a moment. Maybe his questions aggravated her as much her lack of answers frustrated him. Or maybe she was thinking of a way to answer without answering again. The only reason he could imagine for either was that she had something to hide.

She picked a speck of lint from her skirt, then looked up. "When Ace returned to civilian life, he worked as a security guard."

"Security guard?" Rick echoed. The smart bullets had been transported by a private security company. Could Griffin have worked for that company and, as Shane had speculated, been involved in the theft?

"Ace's mental health issues kept him from holding down a job," she continued. "So he entered into a cycle of finding employment as a guard with different companies, then quickly losing the jobs."

"Do you have the names of the companies he worked for?" Shane asked.

She shook her head.

Rick struggled to contain his disbelief. "You don't remember a single company's name?"

"He'd been unemployed for a long time and didn't mention company names."

Kaci would likely find Griffin's former employers when she performed her more detailed background investigation, but Rick made a mental note to talk to her about it.

"Can you think of anyone who would want to kill Ace?" Shane asked.

She shook her head. "As far as I know he didn't have any current friends, and he wasn't working, so he didn't have any coworkers."

"Our reports say he didn't have siblings, and his mother is still living," Shane said. "We have no information on a father."

"His father took off when he was a child, and you're right, he didn't have siblings. His mother lives in Macon, where Ace grew up. In fact, she called me after she learned of his death. She wants to know how he died."

"Did you tell her anything?" Rick asked.

"The detective told me not to."

Again with the nonanswer.

"But did you share what you know about Ace's death?" he asked, more insistently this time.

"No, but I want to."

"We need you to keep everything you know to yourself for now."

"I don't like leaving her in the dark." She frowned.

Rick crossed his arms. "Still, I have to insist."

"You'll tell me when I can share with her?"

Rick nodded. "Why didn't Ace move in with his mother when homelessness was his only other option?"

"He wanted to be independent, even if that meant not having a roof over his head."

"Do you think he could be involved in illegal dealings?"

"Ace?"

"Yes, Ace." Rick pressed the wrinkles out of his shirt. He had to do something to keep from going off on her for the way she was making him work for every answer. "I did some reading on PTSD on our flight and saw that nearly a quarter of PTSD sufferers end up committing a crime. So it seems logical that Ace could be involved in crime."

"Your statistics are accurate, but Ace could barely keep his own life straight, let alone participate in something illegal without getting caught."

"Doesn't mean he wouldn't try, right? Especially if he had a partner."

"He was capable of taking directions, so I suppose it's possible."

"Was he trusting of others?"

"For the most part."

"How did he feel about the military?" Rick asked. "Did he resent his service? Want revenge for his PTSD?"

"Look." She met Rick's gaze, her chin jutting out. "I've been forthcoming so far because your questions were pretty generic. But you're starting to get into information protected by doctor-patient privilege, and I can't continue to comment."

"Of course you can't," Rick muttered under his breath as frustration took hold. Doctor-patient confidentiality extended fifty years beyond death, so she was well within her rights to withhold the information, even if Ace had been murdered and releasing his file could help solve the investigation.

She turned the full force of her gaze on him. "I told you I want to help find Ace's killer, and I meant it. I just have to be careful about what I say."

He looked for any sign that she might be lying or withholding information. He found none, but given the seriousness of the weapons theft, he couldn't be too careful and had to push her. "If you really want to help us find the killer, you'll answer all of our questions and more."

She sat up straighter, her shoulders firming into a hard line. She was a tough cookie, that was clear. During sniper school he'd figured out what made people tick. He knew how it felt to be truly tested. To dig to the deepest recesses of his being to achieve a goal. He'd also discovered that few people had what it took to make it through life's most brutal tests. He and his Scout Sniper platoon had faced adversity during deployment. Faced mental and physical exhaustion each minute of the day. There he'd developed firsthand experience that gave him the skills to discover who these exceptional people were.

Most of the time, he could tell if a person was legit or faking it, but he suspected his attraction to this woman was coloring his opinion. She might be all soft and curvy looking and he was having a hard time keeping his thoughts on the interview, but he couldn't let that continue to impact his judgment.

"I'm sorry," she said firmly. "But I've said all I'm going to say. Doctor-patient confidentiality prohibits me from sharing that information without a court order."

Right. She played *that* card. Had he hit on something with blaming the military, or was she simply following proper protocol?

"Ace is deceased, so you really aren't doing him any good by not sharing," he said. "Plus we'll keep any information you share confidential."

"Sorry."

His frustration was turning to anger now, but he managed to contain it. Just barely. "Do you want to find his killer?"

"Of course."

"Really?" He locked his gaze on her. "Doesn't seem that way to me."

She crossed her arms. "You're not a mind reader, are you? You have no idea how badly I want the killer caught. Or anything else I'm thinking."

He pushed off the wall and took his time tucking his shirt in at the waist to reclaim his composure before meeting her gaze head-on. "I'll have that warrant in a few hours, and I'll get the information anyway. There's no point in making us jump through hoops."

Her chin lifted higher. "It's my job. I took an oath."

"To withhold information?" He kept his focus on her, hoping to keep up the pressure.

She simply sat up straighter. "You know that's not what I meant."

He respected her for not backing down. Maybe he'd even like her if she wasn't a suspect. But she *was* a suspect until he could prove otherwise. If his most intimidating stare didn't move her, he'd get nowhere without the legal hoops she was demanding he jump through.

"I'll go request that warrant while you wait." He let his gaze linger for a moment longer, hoping she'd capitulate so she could go home. When she didn't move, he headed for the door.

He felt her eyes on his back, but he wouldn't turn to see what she was thinking. Outside he let out his anger in a whoosh of air. He'd almost let this woman get to him. Almost lost his cool. He'd had to work twice as hard as usual to keep things together.

Not surprising. Childhood issues with his parents and other adults had made trusting people hard for him. But he had no reason to be mad at the doc. Distrustful. Frustrated, maybe, but mad? Nah. His team ran into physicians all the time who refused to share information. If the team had a valid need to know, he simply got a warrant. No biggie. Max would have the document within a few hours, and they'd be good to go.

He'd simply let his unexpected interest in her unsettle him. He wouldn't let that happen again. He didn't want to be attracted to her. To anyone. But a suspect, of all people... ludicrous.

CHAPTER

4

Olivia gaped at Agent Cannon, or more technically at the doorway he'd just stormed through. He was a bully. A big old bully who had an insane need to take charge and get his way. It was there in his tone. In his gaze. Even in the way he looked and dressed. He'd pressed his navy blue polo shirt and khaki tactical pants to military precision, and he continually smoothed out wrinkles. Something she doubted he was conscious of doing. He wore his hair in a popular messy style, but he'd even arranged that to perfection.

And when she didn't cave and reveal privileged information, he'd blamed her and marched out. Crisp steps, controlled and measured. She'd wager any amount of money he was former military. All pressed, starched, and by the book. But there was more. A hint of a rebel that most people would miss. As a professional trained in reading people, she'd picked up on underlying emotions and hated to admit she found that side of him attractive.

"I'm sorry." A conciliatory expression crossed Agent Erwin's face and melted a bit of her frustration. He seemed nice and not at all a bully like Agent Cannon.

"Does he really expect me to sit here for as long as it takes to get a warrant?" she asked. "That could be hours."

"He's talking to our team leader to get the ball rolling, and I'm sure he'll be right back." He offered a tight smile. "If Agent Cannon understood how his questioning upset you, I know he would offer his apology."

I just bet he would.

"He's lead on this investigation," Agent Erwin continued. "Each moment of delay could be catastrophic, so he's under a lot of pressure."

"How could Ace's death lead to something catastrophic for anyone except Ace and the killer?"

Agent Erwin's eyes flashed wide for a moment before a blank expression took over. "That's something I'm not allowed to share."

Olivia thought to argue, but just as she expected the agents to respect her doctor-patient privilege, she had to understand his inability to share about the investigation. She sat for a moment wondering what to do next. The silence with Agent Erwin wasn't uncomfortable, but she also didn't feel like making small talk, so she leaned her head back against the wall and tried to put Agent Cannon out of her mind as she waited. She took several cleansing breaths, but the way he was hulking over her, pushing her with questions she couldn't answer, kept running through her brain.

Wait! Did he think she was involved in Ace's death? Now that would be preposterous. Still, she could see this guy believing the worst in people.

He came back into the truck and sat on the edge of the small workstation to swing his leg as if he couldn't wait to get moving. His attitude should intimidate her, she supposed, but she wasn't afraid of him. She even had to admit she found him intriguing. What made him so focused? Something in his childhood? Had he been bullied?

Sure, she was sounding like a psychologist here, but that's what she did for a living. Besides, analyzing him helped keep her mind off the muscled thigh stretching the seams of his pants. Helped her ignore his handsome face with a wide jaw and a hint of dimples in his cheeks.

Dimples, really? On him. Mr. Grouch. Couldn't possibly be, could it?

"You mentioned talking with Ace's mother." He bent closer, his eyes connecting with hers.

Her heart somersaulted at his nearness, and she moved back, though there really was nowhere to go.

He raised an eyebrow. "I need you to keep all information about this investigation to yourself, and not only with Ace's mother." He paused, and his gaze dug deeper. "Is that clear?"

She nodded, but his over-the-top reaction combined with Agent Erwin's comments suggested there was more to this investigation than just finding Ace's killer. But what, and did it involve her? She opened her mouth to ask, but he got up and stepped away, his powerful strides carrying him to the back door.

He paused at the exit and turned to look back at her. "You can go now, but keep your cell phone on and remain in the area in case I have additional questions."

With that he was out of the truck in a few steps.

Fine. Run away before she could ask any of her own questions. If she saw this over-the-top agent again, she'd do her best to forget about her attraction and wouldn't let him run roughshod over her again.

* * *

Rick banished his crazy attraction to Dr. Dobbs from his mind so he could give his entire focus to calculating the bullet trajectory. On the way to retrieve his equipment, he stopped by Brynn, who squatted near a large bloodstain. She had her field kit next to her and was unpacking supplies. He got his first look at the blood spatter—rusty splotches sprayed over the sidewalk. A large bloodstain covered the cracked concrete, a river of blood trailing away to the gutter, declaring the exact spot where Griffin had crumpled.

Rick pulled up scene photos on his phone and ran through them. "Griffin dropped parallel to the building and was heading east when the bullet struck. That's consistent with Dr. Dobbs's statement. She said he was heading for the Salvation Army up the road."

Brynn shone a light over the area. "Spatter's in agreement, too."

She frowned and grabbed a spray bottle labeled LUMINOL. A highly sensitive blood reagent, luminol detected latent bloodstain evidence. If blood was present, the luminol would reveal a strong, steady chemiluminescent reaction. In this case blood was obviously present, but Brynn would use the luminol to detect the tiniest of splotches to help determine the bullet trajectory.

"Someone kill the lights," she called out.

"Got it," Shane yelled, and jogged to the control box. The klieg lights snapped off, and only a distant streetlight illuminated the area.

Dr. Dobbs had found her client lying in this spot, but where had she stood? Had she been close enough to Griffin to see how much blood he'd lost? Perhaps not, given the way the single

streetlight left the area shadowed. Could she have been telling
the truth about not seeing the man's face, or had Rick's interest
in her left him wanting her to be telling the truth, and conse-
quently missing the obvious?

One way to find out. "Do me a favor, Brynn. Put on the hood
from your suit and stand up."

She didn't question but complied. He backed away until he
could no longer see the details of her face, but could still see her
field kit sitting about where Griffin's shoes would have been.
He moved toward the corner, where he could keep the kit in
focus and yet the shadows kept him from clearly seeing Brynn's
face. So the doc's story could very well be true.

"Thanks." He shared what Dr. Dobbs had claimed.

"With this low light coupled with fear she must have been
experiencing, I can see it happening," she said. "You get a good
feeling from the doctor?"

Good, yeah, but it was all personal. "Not sure what to make of
her yet."

Brynn arched a brow and watched him for a long moment.
"That's unlike you. Maybe you need to talk to her again."

That was the last thing he needed as a man, but as an inves-
tigator, after they processed the scene, he would make a list of
additional questions and get in touch with her. "I need to know
exactly where she was standing when she saw the man with the
knife. Only way to do that is to have her come back down here
and retrace her steps."

"Roger that." Brynn's attention shifted back to her work,
and she sprayed the luminol. Misty drops of blood glowed blue
on the sidewalk and revealed the spatter pattern. "Back spatter's
consistent with a high-force impact from a large-caliber bullet
and a long-distance shot." Brynn got out her camera.

Rick trusted Brynn's assessment, but while she photographed the area, he bent to look at the minimal spatter that the bullet tearing into Griffin's body had created. The low volume and small drops did indeed help confirm that the shot had been taken from a distance.

Brynn moved to the forward spatter on the far side of the stain, which was elongated and more elliptical in shape. In fact, a single satellite had broken off to form a second stain looking much like an exclamation point. All these points told them the shot had come from a low angle of impact, meaning a long-distance shot.

"I'll go ahead and measure these stains and get an angle for you, so after you calculate the trajectory we can compare notes." Brynn rested her arm on her knees. "Once you map out the trajectory then it's a matter of boots on the ground to find the shooter's exact location, right?"

He wished. "It's not quite that simple in this case."

Cal joined them, and Rick took a moment to gather his thoughts so his explanation would be to the point. "Calculating trajectory is actually a math problem. Finding facts to do the math is the real challenge. Especially when the tech has already removed the slug from where it pierced the sign across the street. She might not have taken exact measurements or moved the sign, interfering with my ability to accurately trace the bullet's path. Plus, trajectory calculations are inherently more difficult for long-distance shots, which is what we're dealing with here. Add the self-steering bullet and my distance could be off."

"Why's that?" Cal asked.

"Since these bullets are fired through a nonrifled barrel, they don't spin like typical bullets. They could lose effective range and throw off my calculations."

Cal's eyebrow shot up. "Enough to make a difference?"

Rick shrugged and wished he could be as precise as he liked to be. "We've never dealt with this technology before, so it's hard to tell. If needed, we can ask for specs on the rifle and bullet from the subcontractor, but that will take a warrant and time that we can't afford to waste."

"Do we know which contractor developed the prototype for DARPA?"

"MilMed Systems," Rick replied. "As their name implies, they work with technology involving both the military and medicine. So far their data remains classified. Max doesn't think they'll release it without a warrant to compel them to do so, and he'll get one if necessary."

"Let's hope it's not necessary."

"I'll get going, and we'll soon know." Rick headed for the SUV to retrieve his equipment bag and saw the lieutenant escort Dr. Dobbs to her car. She kept looking back at the scene, but Rick couldn't make out her expression from this distance. He was half-tempted to ask Shane to turn on the lights again so he could get a read on her mood.

But what point would that serve? She was legitimately upset about Griffin's death. That much Rick was sure of, but when it came to her status as a suspect her anguish wasn't relevant. People involved in homicides often felt remorse and sadness over taking a life. Didn't mean they didn't kill someone or that they weren't accessories to murder.

Mad at himself for letting her linger in his thoughts, he jerked his tools from the SUV and turned to leave. Kaci approached the vehicle, likely planning to stow her camera.

He waited for her. "I need you to pull security video for the park and surrounding area. My research says Atlanta has four hundred or so public cameras, and the files are all gathered in a video integration center under the Operation Shield umbrella. That should make finding the right videos easier than normal."

Kaci frowned. "It'll still take a warrant to gain access."

"Max is handling all the warrants, so talk to him about that, okay?"

"I'll get going on it as soon as I put my camera away."

He thanked her and then crossed the street to the sandwich board sign where the bullet entered the first board and exited the second one. For a precise measurement, a bullet only had to pass through two fixed objects. The sign provided those, but the third point, where the bullet had lodged in a metal trash can, would reinforce his calculations. And he was happy to see thick chains holding the sign in place. Potential existed for the forensic tech to have moved the sign a few inches, but the chains at least limited the distance.

He set up his tripod holding a trajectory rod mount and added the inclinometer, a device for measuring angles and slopes. Even with his naked eye, he could tell the shot had come from above, as the holes weren't perfectly circular as a straight-on shot would have created. He passed a fiberglass rod through both holes in the sign and fixed it in place with an O-ring, then added additional lengths of rod to reach the trash can.

He worked slowly. Meticulously. He felt the clock ticking and pressure mounting to find this killer before he struck again, but he resisted the urge to speed up. He checked and double-checked each step and the stats he recorded in his notebook. Otherwise his measurements could be off, and he would waste valuable time sending the team to the wrong building, and then they'd have to start over again.

The rod passed through the center of the tech's measurements.

Yes! Perfect. She'd done her job well.

"What did you find?" Max asked from behind.

Rick spun in surprise. With his focus fixed on the intricate task, he'd missed hearing Max walk up to him.

"I've got the angle." He held out his notebook. "I'll complete my final calculations, and we'll soon have the exact spot where the shooter hunkered down for the kill."

CHAPTER

5

Olivia watched from her living room window as Agent Cannon got out of his SUV. He'd come to talk to her again. Just the thought of having the pushy agent in her home sent Olivia's lunch of fish tacos churning in her stomach. Thankfully, he'd brought his fellow agent to run interference between them.

"Arrgh," she whispered to herself.

She had nothing to fear from talking to this man. She'd done nothing wrong. Not that he seemed to believe that. The longer she pondered the earlier interview, which unfortunately she'd done through a counseling session before deciding to reassign her afternoon clients, the more she believed he suspected her of involvement in Ace's death. That had made her want to say no to his visit, but she wanted Ace's killer found more than her own comfort.

She let the curtain fall and stepped back before he caught her watching. She glanced in a mirror and ran a hand over her hair.

"Stop it," she muttered under her breath. "He's here on business. That's all, and it's not like you want him to be here for anything else."

"What did you say?" Dianna asked from her position in a wooden rocking chair, where she'd finally gotten baby Natalie to sleep.

"Nothing. Just talking to myself."

"You're sounding like you might need to see a counselor, too." Dianna started to smile, but then it fell as if telling a joke was too difficult.

Olivia crossed to her sister and kissed the top of her head. "Nice try, Sis. You'll be back to your witty self soon."

The doorbell rang, and Olivia nearly jumped.

"I'll take Natalie to Wylie's room so you all can have some privacy." Dianna stood and laid a warm hand on Olivia's shoulder, bringing fresh tears to Olivia's eyes. After she'd returned from the interview, Olivia had told Dianna about Ace's murder. Her sister had surprised Olivia by digging her way out of her own despair to offer comfort.

She blinked away the tears and smiled at Dianna. "Thank you."

A squeeze of the hand and Dianna turned to leave.

Olivia opened the door to see Agent Cannon wearing the same clothes as earlier in the morning, but he looked as fresh and put together as he had back then. He took a wide-legged stance, and his shoulders firmed as he met her gaze. If she'd thought he was intense earlier, his sharp focus now was over-the-top and intimidating.

She wouldn't give in to it, though. She stepped back and forced out a smile. "Come in."

"Actually." He shifted a bit, but his focus didn't waver. "I need you to come with us to Centennial Park so we can retrace your steps from last night. We'll start at the park and work our way back to the crime scene."

Her heart lurched, and not in a good way. Gone were thoughts of the man staring at her. Images of the knife-wielding man, his footsteps pounding closer and closer, took over. She'd hoped that after the earlier questioning she'd never again have to go near the place where Ace had been killed. "I can't go back there."

"Seeing the evening through your eyes could help us locate the killer," Agent Cannon said.

"I...I...well..." She swallowed hard.

"Don't worry." Agent Erwin smiled. "You won't be in any danger. The shooter would have to be a fool to hang around an area swarming with police."

He was right and she had to do everything within her power to assist them. "If it helps find the killer, then I guess I can accompany you." She disliked sounding so wimpy and not at all willing to comply, but come on. She'd been attacked just last night in the very spot they were asking her to revisit. How could she not be hesitant?

"Let me tell my sister I'm leaving." She hurried to Wylie's room and quickly informed Dianna of the change in plans. Back in the family room, Olivia grabbed her phone and purse. Each step toward the door felt like quicksand pulled at her feet, but she continued on.

Agent Cannon moved out of the way. "After you."

She exited the house and, after locking the door, started down the walkway. The shower-thick humidity hit her and perspiration dotted her lip. A blanket of sweltering heat had smothered the city for a month now with no sign of letting up. Sure, the usual late-afternoon thunderstorms took the temps down a few degrees, but the added moisture rising from the pavement and sidewalks only made it feel hotter.

Agent Cannon stepped up beside her. "I'm sorry I was so

rough on you this morning. I could have handled things better."

Apologizing? Now that was a twist she hadn't seen coming. She liked his straightforward apology as he took accountability for his actions and didn't try to blame anyone or anything else. She had no choice but to forgive him.

"Apology accepted." She looked up at him and smiled, though that was the last thing she wanted to do.

A strained smile crossed his lips, confirming the hint of dimples she'd seen earlier. Seriously. Mr. Big Tough Guy really did have dimples, and his face was transformed by a youthful charm that made her grin in earnest.

She expected him to look away, but his gaze didn't waver, and her pulse fluttered. Up close she could see his eyes that she'd thought were purely blue held a lot of gray. Thin lines creased the nearby skin tanned from hours outdoors. He really was a good-looking guy if you went for the big, macho type who seemed to steamroll everyone in his path. Okay, fine, she did go for that type, but she wouldn't go for this one or any man right now.

He sucked in a quick breath and snapped his gaze away. Had she somehow offended him? Maybe he was questioning how she could smile when someone had murdered Ace. Maybe that left him more suspicious of her. Maybe he simply didn't enjoy smiling. After all, a man with such intensity might not joke around.

"So you live with your sister?" he asked.

She didn't know if he was making small talk or questioning her, but she had nothing to hide so she would answer. "Dianna's husband recently walked out on her and their children. A three-month-old and a four-year-old. She's depressed and hasn't been sleeping at night. Her doctor prescribed sleeping pills, but they

leave her too groggy to care for her kids, so we got a place together. That way I can be there for them at night."

"That's nice of you."

"It's good for both of us. When she moved all over the country with her husband I didn't get to see my niece and nephew
as much as I'd like, and now I get to see them every day."

He nodded, but she didn't think he really got it.

"Are you close to your family?" she asked.

He stiffened. "Might you know where Mr. Griffin—Ace—
was on August twenty-eighth around six a.m.?"

She tried not to get mad at his refusal to answer and the
change of subject, because, after all, this was the reason he'd
come to see her. "I have no idea where Ace was. His standing
appointment was at ten a.m., and except for last night, I'd
never met with him at any other time."

"You did mention that he often bunked at the Salvation
Army shelter. Is it possible he'd spent the night there?"

"He's been staying there off and on for years, so yes, that's possible." She looked up at him. "Is that night important to his death?"

"Could be." He settled aviator sunglasses on his nose, clearly
ending this topic of discussion.

Of course. She should have remembered that questioning, for
him, was one sided. She sighed out her frustrations. Unfortunately, the sound drew his study again. She sought something
to say, but her mind went blank, so she picked up her speed.

At the car he opened the passenger door for her, earning
brownie points. She climbed in and caught sight of a small *Semper fidelis* tattoo on his bicep. The United States Marine Corps
motto. She recognized it from her work with vets and from
her disappearing brother-in-law, Jason. Too ironic. The slogan
meant "always faithful" or "always loyal," something Jason was
far from being.

"You're a former marine," she stated.

He didn't respond but headed for his side of the car and settled behind the wheel.

"He's a Marine Scout Sniper to be exact." Agent Erwin took the backseat and slammed his door. "So for a jarhead, he's all right."

Agent Cannon arched a brow, but said nothing in return. He clicked on his seat belt, adjusted his shirt, and smoothed out the fabric under the belt.

He embodied the perfectionistic tendencies of a sniper to a T. Ideal as far as she was concerned, as his military affiliation should kill her attraction to him. She'd witnessed her clients' life-altering suffering from their service. Her brother-in-law was a prime example. The day he'd left and destroyed her sister's world, Olivia vowed never to date a guy who'd served in the military or law enforcement. And a sniper? No way. She'd worked with several of them, and they often faced additional challenges.

"Everyone on our team has served in the military," Agent Erwin continued. "I was an army criminal investigations special agent."

As Agent Cannon got the car going and hot air blasted from the vents, she swiveled to face the talkative agent. Younger looking than Agent Cannon, Agent Erwin had blond hair and freckles that made him resemble a beach bum more than an agent. His easygoing demeanor seemed out of character for law enforcement, too.

"Sounds like an interesting team," she said, hoping he'd provide further details.

"There are six members on our team, and we each have a specialty," he said. "I'm the negotiator and criminal profiler."

Made sense. He appeared to know what made people tick, giving him the skills to negotiate. Fit perfectly with the warm, open personality he'd been displaying.

"Agent Cannon's our hostage rescue, firearms, and ballistics expert," Agent Erwin added. "We also have experts in forensics, cyber crimes, and explosives on our team, and, of course, a team leader."

"You're obviously proud of your team."

"We're the best at what we do," Agent Cannon replied. "What's not to be proud of?"

"We're modest, too." Agent Erwin grinned.

Agent Cannon glanced at her, but she couldn't read his eyes behind the mirrored glasses. "In all seriousness, we're just guys doing our job."

"Somehow I doubt that."

"We can't help what others think, but that's how we think of ourselves," he said.

People often believed snipers were cocky, but in her experience the "cockiness" was more often self-assurance from surviving one of the most challenging training courses in the military and meeting high expectations on the job. They had no time to fail. Each shot had to be precise. If they missed, fellow soldiers could lose their lives.

He didn't elaborate, so she moved on. "How long have you been on this team?"

"Five years, give or take."

"And you?" she asked Agent Erwin.

"Three years."

"How did you hook up with the FBI?"

"You mean besides the lengthy interviews and crazy background checks." Agent Erwin laughed. "Seriously, none of us are the kind of people who can sit around. We need to be in the action, so joining an FBI Critical Incident Response team is the best thing next to the military."

"We're always faced with a new challenge and a ticking clock spurring us on to work faster," Agent Cannon added.

"But wouldn't being a patrol officer be more exciting?" she asked.

Agent Cannon frowned. "Don't believe everything you see on TV. A lot of their job is routine."

"Our jobs are basically heaven for us." Agent Erwin smiled. "We stand ready to deploy from D.C. within four hours, anytime and anywhere, to mitigate the highest-priority threats facing our nation. What's not to like about that?"

What in the world had Ace been part of if a team that deployed only for high-priority threats had come to town to investigate his death? She knew they wouldn't tell her and she would need to keep her eyes and ears open to figure it out.

She turned to look out the window, and silence settled around her. Not comfortable silence. Not with the ongoing tension sizzling off Agent Cannon. She tried to ignore it but continued to be aware of him sitting next to her.

She forced her attention to the scenery as it flew by. It wasn't long before they were inching through traffic by the park. Atlanta traffic was known for being bad, particularly near tourist attractions such as the Georgia Dome, the Georgia Aquarium, and the World of Coca-Cola.

Agent Cannon moved seamlessly through it and pulled to the side of the road by one of the park entrances. He shot a look over his shoulder at his teammate. "Take the vehicle back to the scene. We'll be there shortly."

"Roger that."

Agent Cannon exited as if the car were on fire, and Olivia considered asking Agent Erwin to remain with them, but she suspected one of the reasons he'd come along was to take care of the car. She stepped outside, and, despite Agent Erwin's assurance that she'd be okay, scenes from last night played in her head and her unease ramped up. To distract herself, she concentrated on the heat that hit her full on after the cool air in the car. She'd lived her entire life in Atlanta, but after the last few weeks of unusually steamy weather, Alaska seemed like a better place to live.

As she joined Agent Cannon on the sidewalk, her brother Harrison's ringtone sounded from her phone. He had the worst timing. She loved him, but he could be challenging. Her sister and most of her friends considered him a leech, sponging off Olivia's generosity, and she had to admit they were right. Despite it being the worst thing she could do for him, she enabled him by providing the money for his and their mother's living expenses.

She knew better than to let it continue. Boy, how she knew better, but her father was a PTSD sufferer, and when he'd divorced her mother, she'd fallen apart, leaving then-twelve-year-old Harrison to fend for himself. Dianna had moved out by then and was attending college on the West Coast.

Though only eighteen, Olivia felt called to make up for the loss of both parents, and she doted on him. But then she'd started college herself and couldn't be there for him as often. So guilt set in, and she gave him extra grace for his mistakes and problems. They'd developed a pattern, and now cutting him off seemed to be the only solution.

But how could she do that? She feared he'd end up homeless and their still-fragile mother wouldn't be able to handle it.

What a mess. She was a psychologist, for crying out loud. How could her family be so dysfunctional?

Lost in her thoughts, she hadn't noticed the phone had

stopped ringing, but she didn't put it away. Why bother? Harrison would call right back and continue to call until she answered. As if on cue, the phone pealed again.

"I need to take this." She answered before Agent Intensity took over again. "I'm kind of busy, Harrison. Is this urgent, or can I call you back?"

"The rent's overdue, and Mom doesn't have the money. The super is threatening to kick us out."

Olivia sighed. "How much do you need?"

"A thousand should do it."

"A thousand dollars. You're kidding, right? Your entire rent is only twelve hundred."

"What can I say? Mom had a hard month."

"If you would get a job, you could help her out with the rent."

"I'm looking, but no one's hiring." His whiny voice grated on Olivia's already-raw nerves.

"Come on, Harrison," she said. "There are plenty of jobs out there. You just don't want to do them."

"Would *you* want to work in a minimum-wage job?"

No. That's why I didn't bail on getting my college degree. "I don't have time to get into this right now."

"That's good, because we've had the same conversation like a zillion times."

And maybe after a zillion and one times you'll listen.

"I'll transfer the money to Mom right now. Talk to you later." She disconnected before he could ask for anything else. She thumbed to her banking app, but could feel Agent Cannon's gaze on her. She looked up. "I'm sorry. My mother needs money right away."

"No problem," he replied, and she was surprised at the understanding in his tone.

Her gut churning, she quickly made the transfer. If she did decide she was burned out on counseling and made a career change, she could end up making less money and her family would have to become self-sufficient. Not only had she supported her brother and mother for years, but now Dianna needed money, too. Olivia didn't want Dianna to give up on her dreams of staying home while Natalie was a baby. Her needs were legitimate and Olivia gladly helped support her. Her mother and brother after all these years, not so much. Still, Olivia couldn't solve this problem standing in the sweltering heat with an FBI agent waiting on her.

She exited the app and stowed her phone. "Okay. I'm ready."

He gave that clipped nod again, something she was coming to believe he often did in lieu of speaking. "Take me to the spot where you met with Ace."

She eased through laughing children and adults snapping group pictures and selfies in the park. She approached the bench where she'd sat with Ace and found herself irritated by the visitors' cheerfulness. Irritated at life going on as if Ace didn't matter. He did. He mattered, and if for no other reason, she would put aside Agent Cannon's gruff exterior and do whatever he required of her.

She turned to face the agent and gestured at the bench. "We talked here."

"Go ahead and have a seat."

She rested on the edge. He joined her, sitting far closer than she would have liked.

"What do you remember about the night?" His voice was soft and compassionate, like that of a psychologist working with a client, and for the first time she also detected a hint of a Southern accent and couldn't help but wonder why he kept that under wraps, too.

"Was anyone watching you?" he asked.

"I never took my focus off Ace, so I didn't see anyone else. Plus if the killer was here last night, wouldn't Ace have seen him and taken off?"

"Possibly. So fast-forward to when Ace walked away. You said you watched him go. Did you see anyone then?"

A vision of Ace striding away immediately popped into her mind. She saw his jeans dragging on the brick. His gaze pleading when he looked back at her. Then he quickly disappeared around the corner. That was it. Everything she'd seen. "Sorry. I was too focused on him to see anything else."

Agent Cannon got up. "Let's walk the route you took when you went after him."

She stood, and the strap of her purse slid from her shoulder. Frustrated at not being able to provide any helpful details, she jerked the strap back into place.

"Looks like you want to kill that thing," Agent Cannon said.

"Kill?"

"Your purse. Ever since you got that call you've been shoving it around."

"I didn't even notice." She was probably taking her frustration with Harrison, and over Ace's loss, out on her purse. "It saved my life last night, so I'd rather not kill it off."

His eyebrows rose over the rims of his glasses. "Saved your life how?"

"When the killer started for me with the knife, I couldn't get my pepper spray out, so I threw my purse at him."

He ripped off his sunglasses and hung them around his neck, his sharp gaze landing on her. "The purse you're holding. That's the one you threw at him?"

"Yes, why?"

"Did the fabric actually touch him?"

"Yes."

"And you told the police that last night?"

"I didn't have to. They recovered my purse and gave it back to me."

"Didn't the forensic staff process it for evidence?"

"All I know is the police gave it back to me before I left last night."

"Of all the sloppy work." His eyes narrowed. "It should have remained in evidence."

"But why?"

"If the purse made contact with the suspect, then the canvas likely contains touch DNA, and we can run that for a match in the system." He dug out his phone and tapped the screen. "Brynn, I need a large evidence bag at the park now!" He listened to whatever this Brynn person was saying, his focus razor sharp, giving Olivia a glimpse of how he might look with his eye fixed on a rifle scope.

"We'll be waiting, so make it double time." He disconnected and shoved his phone into his pocket. "Our forensic expert is on her way to collect your purse." He gestured at the bench. "Take a seat and keep it on your lap to prevent additional contamination."

"I'll gladly do as you say, but I watch *CSI* and—"

"Make sure you don't say that when Agent Young gets here."

"Why not?" Olivia sat and rested her purse on her knees.

"The *CSI*-type shows aren't anywhere near reality. People who watch them expect minor miracles in forensics that don't really exist. When these people are seated on a jury and Agent Young's forensics don't contain flashy bells and whistles, they doubt the evidence. Drives Agent Young crazy."

"I had no idea." Olivia peered at the expensive designer handbag she'd splurged on after she'd obtained her counseling license. "So forget my comment, but I still have to ask. If my purse is already contaminated, how will taking additional samples help?"

He dropped down next to her. "If we're able to lift DNA or fingerprints and locate a match in our database, we'll have a suspect and direction to proceed."

"I see." Olivia sat back to wait for Agent Young to arrive, her mind going to the recent interview.

She still had so many questions about Ace's murder. Like why had he been killed, and why were top-notch agents investigating his death?

She swiveled to face Agent Cannon. "Don't get me wrong here. Ace was a wonderful man, and he deserves the very best investigators on his case, but I highly doubt agents with your skill sets would be here for that reason alone."

"Our reason for taking on this investigation is on a need-to-know basis."

Cryptic, but she took his statement as confirmation that he was hiding something from her. "If you'd fill me in on what's really going on, maybe I could be of more help."

"Trust me, Doc." He stared across the park and slipped his sunglasses on. "You really don't want to know the details and are far better off dropping your line of questioning."

CHAPTER

6

Rick disconnected his call with the manager at the Salvation Army shelter and worked hard to hide his disappointment from Brynn as she talked to Dr. Dobbs, still seated on the park bench. The guy insisted on a warrant before he would tell them if Griffin had stayed there the night that the self-steering bullets were stolen. Not surprising. Crime shows on television had changed the way people reacted to law enforcement, and they often pulled the warrant card. The minute Rick got back to the scene, he'd get Max started on requesting one.

Rick shoved his phone into his pocket and turned his attention to Brynn, who was opening a large evidence bag. He'd hated to pull her away from the shooter's hide to collect the purse, but it was their best lead right now. Before picking up the doc, they'd followed his coordinates to a high-rise office building. A jimmied door lock on the rooftop said they were in the right place. Brynn confirmed the location by lifting gunshot residue and hadn't finished processing the scene. But priorities often changed in a flash, and it was almost a given that they would lift touch DNA from the doc's handbag.

Dr. Dobbs dropped the purse into Brynn's evidence bag, then sat back, her legs crossed, a bright-pink pump dangling from her foot. She asked Brynn logical questions about the investigation, but Brynn remained closemouthed. Not only did she know the importance of not sharing about the smart bullet, but social interaction came hard for her, and outside the team she was often shy.

"Okay, I get it," the doc said after Brynn ignored another question. "Stop asking for either of you to explain."

"And there's no point in questioning other team members either," Brynn added.

Dr. Dobbs frowned, and Rick couldn't believe it, but he actually felt bad for her. He'd never had a hard time keeping things confidential. After all, if he limited how often he spoke, even with people close to him like his team, he couldn't reveal anything he shouldn't. Yet oddly enough, he had an urge to share the magnitude of their investigation with the doc.

Craziness. Pure craziness. She had zero clearance, much less the top-level permission needed to possess such highly classified information. Plus, an average citizen like the doc would freak out at hearing such a bullet actually existed. Even someone who seemed as well-adjusted as she did.

Brynn closed the bag. "By the time you get to the crime scene, I'll have removed the contents of your purse. You can take those items with you, but not the bag itself."

"I paid a pretty penny for that designer brand. Was one of my favorites, actually. But after this I don't care if I ever see it again."

If she expected Brynn to comment on the big-name designer bag, the doc would be sitting here for eternity. Brynn had never shown evidence of caring about expensive girlie things.

Brynn tucked the sealed evidence bag under her arm. "I'll jog back to the scene and get the evidence logged in."

Olivia swiped a hand over her glistening forehead. "You're going to run in this heat?"

"Do a stint as a soldier, and you learn to run in every kind of weather." Brynn smiled and the doc smiled back, her eyes lighting with a genuine warmth that fanned Rick's interest even more.

He felt Brynn's eyes on him, so he pulled his gaze free and focused on her.

"Okay, then." She'd clearly noticed the vibe flowing between him and the doc. "I'm off." Her tactical boots, the kind they all wore for duty, thumped on the pavement as she jogged away.

"I like her," Olivia said.

"Agent Young's one of the best." He ignored the thought pressing at his brain that the doc didn't much like him. "You lead the way back to the crime scene and feel free to stop when needed if you want to explain or tell me more about when you followed Ace."

She marched down the street, her shoulders pulled back, but he'd seen fear settle in her eyes before she'd turned away. A half mile down the road, she paused to stare ahead. She nodded at a large pothole in the middle of the road and wrapped her arms around her stomach. "This is where I fell last night when I was running away from the man with the knife."

Rick might be oblivious to other people's emotions at times—okay, a lot of the time—but his gut told him to offer comfort, and he started for her.

What in the world are you planning to do?

He'd thought to rest a hand on her shoulder, when only a few hours ago he'd grilled her like a big T-bone steak. And now what? He suddenly trusted her? Believed she was on the up-and-up? But why?

He came to a stop and watched her. He got that her pain was real, but that didn't mean she wasn't part of this murder plot. It just meant she had residual fear from last night. The man who'd chased her could be a person she'd partnered with who had turned on her.

"Did the man with the knife get as close to you as I'm standing?" he asked.

"No."

"And you're sure you didn't recognize him or know him?"

She tilted her head, a question on her face. "Like I've told you, I didn't see his face."

He'd expected her to ask another of her questions, but she turned and started down the sidewalk, moving quickly as if fleeing from the man. She didn't stop until the crime scene came into view. Rick glanced ahead at the people still hugging the barricades and reporters lingering by their vehicles. The moment they noticed him, they perked up and jumped into action, cameras rising to shoulders and microphones jutting out.

He faced Dr. Dobbs. "The reporters recognize my uniform and are bound to rush us. I need you to stay calm and not respond to their questions. Can you do that?"

"No comment." The side of her mouth quirked up in an unexpected smile.

Despite the reporters watching him, and his distrust of the doc, he couldn't help returning the smile, and he had to admit his lighthearted response felt good. Real good. He considered taking her arm to protect her from the mob, but this being her second visit to the scene today, reporters might misconstrue his gesture and declare on the news that she was a person of interest or a suspect under arrest.

"Move at a quick clip. Keep your head down and stay by my

side," he said to keep that protective instinct at bay. "I'll do my best to shield you."

They headed into the throng. Microphones were shoved in their faces, and Rick swatted at them as he would at an irritating fly. He also made sure he kept Dr. Dobbs moving forward. She heeded his directions and didn't look at, much less talk to, a reporter.

"Is there really a sniper on the loose?" a slender man asked Rick, but he brushed past him.

A woman in a neon-yellow dress stepped in front of him, and he had no choice but to stop to avoid bowling her over. "Why has the FBI been called in to investigate the homicide of a homeless man?"

"Please excuse me." He started forward, forcing her to move out of the way.

The doc fell behind, and he didn't care if the press got the wrong opinion. He circled his arm around her waist to tug her close and help her move forward. She gave him a grateful smile, and he had to work extra hard not to forget he had a job to do.

The female reporter rebounded and darted in front of them again. "Can you tell us your name, ma'am?"

Rick paused and fired her a testy look. "I asked nicely for you to let us through. Don't make me ask again."

She seemed to mull over his request, then bent and swept out her arm with a flourish.

"By all means, Mr. High and Mighty Fed," she whispered so only Rick could hear.

She was trying her hardest to bait him into responding. Instead he picked up speed and escorted Dr. Dobbs through the barricade held open by the officer of record.

"Vultures," the officer muttered as they passed.

Rick nodded his agreement and directed the doc around the

corner to where Griffin had died. Being in full view of the crime scene was likely more painful for her than battling the reporters, but at least she could relax after their aggressive behavior.

"Thank you." She sighed. "Obviously you've had experience with the press."

"I have," he said. "But I didn't handle that well at all."

"I don't understand."

"Agents are trained to be cognizant of the way we're perceived on a local level. It's the only way the general public can form an opinion of the agency, and my body language told whoever watches this broadcast that agents are pushy and self-involved."

"But that last reporter was asking for it."

"Doesn't matter." He didn't add that if anyone at headquarters saw the broadcast, his tough-guy behavior would get him a slap on the wrist. Max would go to bat for him, but there were only so many times that Rick could upset the locals before the powers that be would want him pulled from the investigation. Still, he wasn't about to let a possible reprimand stop him from doing his job.

"So," he said, moving along. "You came around the corner and spotted Ace. How far did you get before seeing them?"

She took a few steps forward. "This is where I saw his red sneakers and the other man squatting over him."

She'd moved to nearly the same spot Rick had landed on when he'd tested her earlier statement with Brynn. He'd like to conclude that the doc's statement was truthful, but in fact, she could have gotten a look at the shooter's face and just gotten lucky that her denial panned out. Most investigators would take this as a confirmation, but he wasn't like most investigators, and he'd probe for additional details. "Tell me more about the other man."

"I can't tell you anything more than I did at the station."

"Try closing your eyes. Think about stepping around the corner. How did it feel? What did you see?"

She looked up at him. "You've obviously had interview training. I'd likely have said the same thing in my counseling practice."

Another nonanswer. "Then I'm sure you're willing to try it."

Her eyes closed, her long silky lashes settling on high cheekbones covered in freckles. Her shoulders shot back as if she was trying to make herself appear larger for whatever was coming. "He wore a camo jacket with a hoodie underneath. But the sleeves were pushed up. He raised the knife. Came toward me. There was something on the inside of his wrist."

"What?"

"A tattoo. I think, anyway. But it was dark so I can't be sure."

"Left or right side?" he asked, ignoring her doubts so she would, too.

"His left. He was holding the knife in that hand."

"Then he was left-handed."

"Yes, I suppose he was."

That was something new. Not much, but little things often added together to build a solid suspect profile.

"Could you make out the tattoo's design?" Rick asked.

She shook her head.

"What about his pants? Were they camo, too?"

She scrunched her eyes tighter. "Maybe. I'm not sure."

"Was the jacket a dark or light green?" he asked, as soldiers wore lighter-colored army combat uniforms at the local national guard center.

"It was too dark to tell."

So he might have been in full uniform or not, or he could simply be a civilian who liked camo jackets. Or a hunter, as they often favored military wear. Either way, his clothing meant the team should check with local shooting clubs and firing ranges for a man who might have served in the military and had a wrist tattoo. With Cal's extensive knowledge of weapons, he'd be right at home with that crowd, so Rick texted him a request to get started on compiling a list of locations.

Dr. Dobbs opened her eyes and blinked a few times before meeting his gaze. "It's odd that he wore a jacket in this heat."

"He was likely concealing a weapon."

A delicate brow arched. "His knife, or do you mean he could have had a gun, too?"

"Maybe both."

"If so, then why didn't he shoot me?"

"Maybe he isn't our shooter."

She sighed. "Then who was he, and what was he doing with Ace?"

"He could simply be a guy who happened upon the body and was looking for money."

"But why chase me, then?"

"He might think you got a good-enough look at him to ID him, and he wants to keep you from sharing that info with us."

She met his gaze solidly. "Then the risk to me is over, because I've told you everything I know."

If only that were true. "He doesn't know what you've told us and might still be thinking about locating you."

"But at this point he could assume I told you everything, right?"

Rick shook his head. "Witnesses often remember things as time goes on. Like you did just now. Maybe he's afraid you'll continue to remember. Or he wants to make sure, if he's caught, that you won't be alive to testify against him."

She shuddered, but said nothing. Rick had to wonder again

if she was keeping something from him, but he wouldn't dig deeper at this point. To do so would reveal she was a suspect, and that could close her down even more.

Brynn crossed the street and handed the doc a small plastic bag filled with items from her purse. She clutched her belongings to her chest as if searching for a lifeline, and he felt bad about having to continue to question her.

"Thank you," she said, her focus on Brynn. "I hope you can find something of value on the purse."

"If touch DNA exists on the bag, I'll find it." Brynn shifted her focus to Rick. "Can I talk to you alone for a minute?"

"Don't move from this spot, Doc," he warned, then stepped out of earshot, but kept her in view in case she ignored his directive and decided to wander. "You have something new?"

"I recovered a partial McDonald's receipt at the hide. Only the bottom half, showing a Sausage McMuffin was purchased."

A burst of excitement brightened Rick's outlook. "Do we have a credit or debit card number for the purchase?"

"No, sorry. It's a cash receipt, and I don't have a date or time of purchase either."

His excitement bubble burst. "You keep saying it's hard to lift prints from receipt paper, so I don't see how this will help."

"Wow. You really do listen when I share technical details." She grinned. "You rarely comment, so I figured you were zoning me out."

"Don't get a big head." He gave her a wry smile. "I tune you out plenty of times, too."

She rolled her eyes good-naturedly. "Well, the good news is there's a fingerprint expert in Nebraska who's recently refined the technique for lifting prints from receipts. And McDonald's receipts are the easiest to process. She isn't sure why their paper yields better results, but thinks it's related to the thermal layer."

"Then you may get a print."

"Yes, but this all assumes that the shooter dropped the receipt instead of some random person who ate breakfast on the roof."

"Odds are good that few people have breakfast on a rooftop where access requires a key."

"True." She furrowed her brow.

"What's wrong?"

"Takes a calculating guy to coolly sit on the rooftop and down a Sausage McMuffin, then plug a guy with a .50."

"Good for us, though, right? If he really did eat a McMuffin up there, then he had to get it from a twenty-four-hour location. We can request security footage for all twenty-four-hour McDonald's in the general area around the time of the shooting."

"It's possible I could lift DNA from the receipt, too."

"Then process it," he said, and even as he spoke, he was disappointed with the lack of evidence at this point. "Like ASAP. We need a strong lead. We've been moving like snails today. Shoot, even snails could move faster."

"It's early on. Give it time."

"Normally I'd agree with you. Even tell everyone to chill out, but our shooter could be setting up right now for a sure shot to end someone's life. Or maybe he's trying to sell the technology. Either way, people will die if we don't speed things along."

She gestured at the street. "Max is headed your way. Maybe he's got a solid lead for you."

Rick turned to see his boss slip under the yellow crime scene tape cordoning off the inner perimeter.

"I need to get back to work," Brynn said.

As she walked away, Rick had to wonder if she was bailing to avoid Max, who didn't look happy about something.

He stopped in front of Rick, and his gaze shifted to the doc. "Dr. Dobbs, I take it."

Rick nodded.

"You get any information from her other than the purse?"

"The shooter wore a camo jacket with hoodie underneath and potentially has a tattoo on his left wrist. She couldn't make out the tattoo design because of the darkness. He held the knife in his left hand."

"Every little bit helps." Max pulled a folded document from his back pocket.

"The warrant for her records?" Rick asked hopefully.

He nodded. "I'll be happy to slap it in her hand if you'd like."

"Let me," Rick said, surprised that the idea of Max slapping anything in the doc's hand left him uneasy.

"Who am I to take the joy of serving a warrant away from you?" Max gave Rick the document.

Rick told him about the Salvation Army shelter. "The manager said they have records for that night, but he needs a warrant to show them to us."

"The local PD hooked me up with a judge willing to work with us, so it should be easy to produce one within an hour or so."

At least something seemed to be going their way today. "I'd like to head over to the doc's office to get her files. Could you assign someone to question the manager?"

"If her files are electronic, she can simply transfer them to you."

"At her convenience, yes. But I'm sure I'll get faster results if I'm standing over her waiting for the files."

"Good point," Max said. "You head out. I should have time to get the warrant and question the manager."

Max conduct a routine interview? Rick's jaw nearly dropped

at the thought, but he managed to keep his mouth closed. "I assume Brynn told you about the receipt."

Max nodded.

"I'll also need someone to run down the twenty-four-hour McDonald's locations in the area and get security footage."

"Grabbing video is pretty straightforward. I'll hand it off to the locals and light a fire under them."

"Thanks," Rick said. "Every bit of help will move us forward faster."

Max stepped away and Rick returned to the doc, who narrowed her eyes. "Who was that man you were talking to?"

"Our team leader, Max White."

"I thought you were intimidating, but him? Sheesh." She mocked a shudder. "He gives off a crazy vibe."

Rick didn't bother denying that both of them came across as intimidating. But in Rick's case, in addition to his size, the sharp sense of focus he'd acquired as a sniper often left people thinking he was trying to intimidate when in reality he was just appraising a situation.

Still, his take on the situation didn't matter when he needed the doc's help. "I've been told that before. I'll try to keep it in check."

"No need to change who you are for me."

"Spoken like a true shrink." She grimaced, not at all the reaction he'd expected. "What's wrong?"

"I don't like that term."

"Duly noted." He handed over the warrant and made a mental note not to say *shrink* again, as antagonizing her wouldn't help the investigation.

She unfolded the paper, her gaze fixing on the first page. He wanted to get moving, but she had every right to digest the details.

When she looked up, he forced a professional smile to his face. "I need to get my hands on the records ASAP. Do you have electronic files with remote access, or do we need to go to your office?"

"I once kept files online, but then I was a victim of identity theft and my bank accounts were emptied. Now I don't trust even the most secure networks."

Interesting. "Tell me about the identity theft."

She eyed him. "I fail to see how my personal business is relevant."

"You never know what might be related to Ace."

She crossed her arms. "I doubt my stolen money has anything to do with him. My personal accounts were breached, not my professional ones."

"Did you contact the police?"

She nodded. "They haven't been able to figure out who stole the money."

Bank fraud fell under the FBI's jurisdiction. That combined with her status as a suspect gave Rick a legit reason to investigate her theft, and he wouldn't dismiss it as easily as she seemed to be doing. After the doc's evasive answers, he'd make sure Kaci followed up on the missing money to determine if it was one more area where the doc shouldn't be trying to evade his questions.

CHAPTER

7

A mere ten minutes from the murder scene, Rick followed the doc up wide stairs to a converted lemony-yellow Victorian home located on a tree-lined street. The building served as her office and fit the warm and welcoming vibe she continued to give off. Tall trees and thick underbrush lined the far side of the street, likely to keep down the noise from the busy road behind them.

They passed through a grand foyer with rich wood floors and banister leading up a winding staircase. She took the stairs up to a long hallway, her full skirt swishing in front of him and grabbing his attention.

How could he let a simple sway of her hips make him forget about his reason for being here?

His phone chimed, and he checked the text from Cal in response to Rick's earlier message. *Glad to look into hunting associations and shooting ranges.*

"Thanks," Rick replied while she unlocked and opened a squeaky door painted bright blue. He trailed her into a room just big enough for two chairs and a table with a lamp. Neat stacks of magazines lined the table. With her clientele, he wasn't surprised to see titles like *G.I. Jobs* and *Military Spouse*, but the fashion magazines surprised him. Likely the doc's own collection. She stepped toward another door, this one with a box containing a buzzer and small camera mounted beside it. Her clients likely rang the buzzer to let her know they'd arrived.

She entered the other room, a hint of vanilla air freshener filtering into the waiting area. He followed her into an office that was bland. Neutral. A beige sofa took up one wall, the windows covered with darker beige curtains that she flung open. A leather easy chair sat to the side, a tiny glass table nearby. Not much of a hint to her personality, but the space looked the way he'd expected a shrink's digs to look.

She crossed the room to a small desk in the corner. On the wall above, she'd hung her diploma and Georgia counseling license, reminding him that he really didn't know much about her, and he wanted details that the initial report Kaci had provided didn't include. "Did you go straight from school to private practice?"

She shook her head and clicked on a crystal desk lamp, the only hint in the room of what he was coming to recognize as her very feminine tastes. "I fulfilled a required year of supervised internship, then worked three years at the local VA before I started my practice."

"Is that how you became interested in PTSD?"

She shook her head and sat, but didn't speak, raising another red flag.

"What made you become a shr—What should I call you? Counselor? Therapist?"

"Technically I'm a psychologist, but *therapist* or *counselor* works." She opened a laptop with a shiny silver case and focused on the screen.

He pulled a wooden chair closer and straddled it. "So why did you want to become a counselor?"

Her head popped up, and she blinked a few times. "From your tone, I'd say you have something against counselors."

They were here to talk about her and her practice, not his issues, but he suspected that if he blew her off, she wouldn't give up, so he had to answer.

"Not counselors with ethics, no," he replied, purposely not sharing the bad experiences he'd had with shrinks.

"You're questioning my ethics?"

Okay, he wasn't going there and risking offending her more. "Your interest in PTSD. How did it come about?"

She pressed her lips together for a moment. "Is this small talk or something I need to answer for the investigation?"

Her touchiness surprised him, and yet it didn't. In his experience, shrinks got touchy when you turned the tables on them. "Does it matter?"

"Actually, I'd rather not discuss my motivations for the job. So if you're not requiring me to answer, then..."

Griffin's death easily connected her counseling practice to the investigation, but odd as it might seem, he found himself wanting to get to know her. Even more now that she didn't want to talk about her motivations. "It could be helpful to the investigation."

She sighed, sat back in the chair, and laid her hands on her skirt. "My interest started with my father, who was career army. He served tours in the Gulf War and Afghanistan. Each time he came home, he was less and less like himself." She recited the words as if they were just facts, but she kept twisting her hands, telling him she was bothered by sharing this story. "I was six when he went to the Persian Gulf. That fun-loving, caring guy never returned. I got a sour, unhappy father instead, and I just wanted my daddy back."

Rick didn't want to force her to talk about something so personal, but now that she'd mentioned a military connection, he couldn't let it drop. "Did he get treatment?"

She shook her head. "Back then PTSD was recognized by the AMA, but it still wasn't being treated effectively. I remember my mom saying Dad was a faker and telling him to snap out of it. Over time he improved some on his own. Still, he wasn't the same. And then...then he deployed to Afghanistan for two more tours before retiring, and his symptoms got progressively worse. He came home the week of my seventeenth birthday. He was barely functioning and started drinking his days away. He was totally wasted the day of my party and made a scene. As a teenager I was mortified, but mostly I was horrified that my dad was struggling so badly. I vowed that day to figure out how to help him."

"And were you able to do so?" he asked, completely wrapped up in her story now.

Her lips trembled as if tears were imminent, but she sat quietly, and he didn't press. Just waited and fought the urge to offer comfort by holding her hand. To tell her everything was okay, when that was a lie. Life rarely turned out with storybook endings. He'd seen far too many lives torn apart over the course of his military career to believe that.

"Sorry," she said. "I wasn't able to help him. Still haunts me."

"What happened?"

"He kept drinking to drown out his issues. He managed to hold down a job, so he didn't think he needed help. He was such a stubborn man. So stubborn that my parents split up." She fidgeted with a delicate gold chain she wore around her neck. "He died one night from a self-inflicted gunshot."

Rick's heart went out to her. He might not want to connect with this woman, but her father's fate mirrored Traci's, except that his wife's death hadn't officially been ruled a suicide. "I'm sorry for your loss."

"Thank you." Her gaze lingered on his. "He died just before I received my license. Not that I would have been able to help him just because I had my credentials, but I hadn't given up on him and would have kept trying."

He nodded. "Sounds like you feel guilty for not helping him."

"Guilty? No. I know better than that. No one can be responsible for another person's actions. Sure, you may fight or argue and the other person takes off and does something dumb as a result, but even then, *they* are the ones who chose the action. Not you."

Rick's thoughts went to his wife. He imagined holding the baby, his son. The softness of his newborn skin. The sweet baby smell. Feeding him. Changing him. Watching him grow up. Playing together. Bonding over sports and just being present for his son in a way his father hadn't been. Loving this child. His family complete. His heart full.

But what did he have instead? Emptiness. A hollow hole he couldn't erase. Maybe if he'd seen that her therapist, Dr. Fox, wasn't helping Traci enough. Maybe then he'd have found a way not to deploy as often and leave her alone so much of the time. And maybe then he would believe Dr. Dobb's theory.

"It's different if you neglected someone, though," he said.

"I suppose that depends on your definition of *neglect*."

"Not being there when someone needed you."

"You mean choosing not to be there for someone?"

"No. Just not physically being around."

"In that case, it's still the person trying to take responsibility for someone else's actions." She leaned forward, her gaze remaining on his. "Are you by any chance a man of faith?"

He nodded.

"I'm a believer, too, and a Christian counselor. One thing I often remind clients of is that nothing happens that God doesn't allow. I mean, take Ace for example," she continued. "Even if I failed to do all I could for him, God was still watching over us and was in control."

"Isn't that an easy way of letting yourself off the hook?"

Her eyebrow arched. "So suppose a person stepped off the curb when a car was coming. The driver does everything he can to stop, but doesn't succeed and the person is killed. Should that driver feel guilty?"

"No. They did everything they could."

"I did all I could do at the time for Ace. Sure, in hindsight I can think of better ways to have handled the situation, but I acted with the information I had at the time."

Was she right? Could he let himself off the hook for Traci's and the baby's death? After all, short of going AWOL, he couldn't have left the marines. Nah, it didn't work that way. The doc was just trying to justify not believing Griffin last night. Still, Rick had an insane urge to tell her about Traci. Get the doc's opinion. He opened his mouth, but thankfully she waved a hand, stopping him.

"Listen to me," she said. "I didn't want to say anything, then I go on and on like we're best friends."

Best friends? He doubted they'd ever be that. Not unless he learned to trust again, and that was about as likely as reconciling with his father.

* * *

Agent Cannon's expression shifted, but he continued to eye her. Olivia hadn't a clue what he was thinking. Not when he'd closed down and taken on that blank look he seemed to favor. The psychologist in her wanted to dig into his past. Especially after his comment about neglecting someone. She would have to be an idiot not to realize he was thinking about someone in his life or even himself, but no matter if she prodded, he wasn't the kind of guy who would open up.

So why did he keep staring at her? Perhaps he didn't care for her comment about going on as if they were best friends. She could solve that.

"Don't worry," she said, keeping her tone casual. "I get it. Just because I shared about my private life, I know we're not friends nor likely to become friends." She turned her attention to her laptop. "Let me print a copy of Ace's records for you."

"Print? But you said you didn't have electronic records."

At his accusing tone, she met his gaze. He really didn't trust her. Not one bit. And it hurt.

"I said I don't have my records stored online or on a network computer that can be accessed from a distance," she said. "This computer isn't connected to any networks or the Internet. So it's as safe as the paper files I keep here in my office."

He didn't comment but continued to stare at her.

She didn't care. Okay, fine, she cared about what he was thinking, but he'd proved his unwillingness to share, so why ask? She returned her focus to the screen and sent Ace's fifty-page record to the printer, then crossed the room to watch it spit the pages out. She felt the agent's gaze remain on her, but she didn't bother to turn.

She might be skilled at reading nonverbal cues, but this man managed to control his emotions enough to stay behind a thick wall he'd erected and wouldn't let her or likely anyone else

through. Which was telling in itself. If he needed to live behind such a big wall, then he had something to hide. The last
thing she needed in life was to ponder following her interest in
a man like that.

"So now that we have our warrant," he said, "you can share
Ace's opinion of the military."

She faced him. "He said there was no such thing as a former
marine. Once a marine, always a marine, he'd claim. His pride
and respect for his service and the service of others was so obvious."

"Most marines, including me, would agree. So he didn't let
the PTSD and the loss of normal life change that perspective?"

"Never."

The printer stopped, and she grabbed the pages to deliver
them. She expected Agent Cannon to take them and leave. Instead he tapped the paper on the desk and kept tapping until
the pages were perfectly aligned.

He looked up. "Do you have a clip I can use to keep these
organized?"

She dug a binder clip from the desk. "If you'd like, we can
talk about your need for perfection. I've had great success with
helping other snipers work through those issues."

"What makes you think I want help?" He clipped the papers
at the top, then slowly lifted his head to meet her gaze. "I happen to prefer things orderly."

"Orderly, yes, but you seem obsessed."

He didn't respond but turned his attention to the report and
started reading. He certainly didn't plan to sit here and read
every page, did he?

She had a life, and he could read anywhere. "If you don't
mind, I have work to do, and I'm sure you don't need me to
read the file."

He coolly assessed her. "I might have questions that only you can answer."

"You could call me."

He sat back and rested the report on his lap. "You don't seem to get the urgency of my investigation."

"Perhaps if you told me what you're keeping from me regarding Ace's death, I could better understand."

"As I said before, I'm not going there. So make yourself comfortable. I won't take long." He bent his head and flipped a page.

She curled her fingers in frustration. Large and in charge, that was what this guy was, and she disliked his behavior as much as she liked seeing his commitment to finding the killer. He reminded her of her father. Of many of her clients. Their self-assurance and belief that they were always right made working with them a challenge.

She watched his intense focus, the pages turning at a rapid rate and with swift strokes, as if she didn't exist. She suspected she didn't exist for him right now with his focus fixed on the report. He ran a hand through his hair, disturbing it, and she had the urge to smooth the wayward strands back into place. To touch him.

"Watching me won't make me read any faster," he said without looking up.

She should have known he would be aware of her every move. Snipers had to know their surroundings at all times while still focusing on their rifle. She wouldn't underestimate him again. "I'll make some coffee. Would you like some?"

"Please."

She crossed the room, chastising herself for thinking of him as anything other than an FBI agent. She might find him attractive, but that didn't mean she had to act on it. For one, he lived in D.C. Two, he was likely a "love her and leave her" kind of guy. No thank you to that. She'd wait for her ideal man. A guy who was open and honest about his emotions. One who thought of others before himself. Who could commit without being overbearing. Sure, she'd never met that kind of guy, but she hoped one existed. And three, the big one—he was former military.

Three huge strikes against him. Any guy with three strikes had already struck out in her life.

At a small refreshment bar in the corner, she put a K-Cup into the machine and pressed the power button. Water dripped through the grounds, and the nutty scent of coffee filtered into the air.

He looked up. "Tell me about PTSD. I know guys who have it. Others simply have issues with readjusting after deployment. I'd like a clinical perspective."

"I'm glad you asked," she said, and she really was. "People think they know what PTSD is, but there are a lot of mistaken ideas out there." She rested against the refreshment cabinet. "First, it doesn't only affect soldiers who've been in combat or police officers who've been shot. Anyone can experience PTSD after witnessing or being involved in a life-threatening event. So natural disasters, car accidents, assaults. They all count. Even learning about a violent death of a loved one can be the cause."

He tilted his head and studied her. "After last night you fit that bill."

"Almost."

He sat forward, clearly interested. "Why almost?"

The coffee maker beeped. "Do you take anything in your coffee?"

"Just black."

Right. Plain. No frills. No way to mess it up. She started a cup for herself and then delivered his.

"Thanks." He wrapped long, slender fingers around the mug, but his focus didn't waver, leaving her feeling self-conscious.

She returned to the snack bar to put distance between them, but knew his gaze tracked her. When she turned, he was sipping his coffee and watching over the rim. Always watching. If only she had an inkling of what he might be thinking.

"About the PTSD," he said. "How are you different?"

"It's normal to feel on edge or have trouble sleeping after a traumatic event," she replied, thankful for the redirection of her thoughts. "You can have trouble doing daily things, like working or spending time with others. But most people start to recover after a few weeks. Not people with PTSD. The feelings don't go away on their own."

"Okay, so not enough time has passed for you to know how you'll deal with your trauma."

She nodded and retrieved her cup of coffee.

"Then when I see in Ace's records that he didn't come to you for years after returning from combat, you probably had no doubt that he had PTSD."

"I suspected it, yes, but had to confirm as I do with all clients. You'll see the assessment I use in the first few pages." She gestured at the file. "It might also be helpful for you to know that PTSD is more common than most people think. One in ten men and two in ten women will react to trauma this way. And having very intense or long-lasting trauma, getting hurt, or having a strong reaction to the event makes you more prone to it. Which is why combat and abuse are so prevalent in PTSD clients, as these types of trauma are ongoing."

"And the symptoms are?" He lifted his mug and sipped.

"Reliving the event over and over. Avoiding things and people who remind you of the event. An increase in negative thoughts and feelings. Feeling on edge all the time. The last was particularly true of Ace, but he'd improved a lot. Then last night." A vision of him lying on the sidewalk surfaced, stealing her breath for a moment. "Last night he was so unsettled. I wish it would have turned out differently, but..."

"Trust me. I get it, Doc."

He'd finally given her an opening to ask questions about his past, and she wouldn't miss it. "I suppose you have plenty of stories from your combat days where you wish you could have helped."

A vulnerability clouded his eyes before he dropped his gaze to the printout.

"Agent Cannon?" she asked, not willing to let his evasion go this time.

He lifted a finger—his DO NOT DISTURB sign, telling her to butt out.

Fine. She would, but at least his avoidance told her he wasn't some robot with firm control over everything, as he'd first appeared to be. He was human after all and wasn't invincible. She'd touched a nerve—a deep one, she suspected—and now she was even more interested in figuring out what drove this infuriating, closemouthed man.

CHAPTER

8

The afternoon was nearly gone by the time Rick arrived at the two-story brick building housing the Fulton County Medical Examiner's Office. Fortunately, the place was located less than ten minutes from the murder scene, and Rick didn't have to waste valuable time stuck in traffic.

He worked his way down the hall and prepared himself for what he was about to see. He wasn't squeamish, but his visit meant a life had been lost at the hands of another person, and that cut him to a quick. Some people might think that an odd reaction for a former sniper, but he didn't kill for the thrill of it. He'd taken lives to save others. If he hadn't been on overwatch for the other troops, many lives would have been lost. Especially in the early days in Iraq. That was very different from brutal murder.

In the autopsy room, he found Dr. Elena Idoni bent over the table, holding a ruler over Griffin's wrist and dictating into an overhead microphone. "A five-millimeter scar—"

"Sorry I'm late, Doctor," Rick said.

She looked up, her dark eyes behind the face shield locked onto him. With the back of her hand, she batted at a strand of black hair peeking from her cap as if frustrated. She had olive skin and that, coupled with her name, left him thinking she was of Italian descent.

He displayed his ID. "Special Agent Rick Cannon. I think you were expecting me."

"You're late." She returned her attention to the table. "Have you experienced an autopsy before?"

"Many times."

"Then you don't need me to explain the procedure, but I have no idea if anyone ever reviewed it with you or if they followed proper protocol, so I'll do so." She picked up a scalpel, then looked at him. "Thus far the body has been photographed, fingerprinted, and weighed. I've reviewed his hair and nails and inspected for moles, scars, et cetera on my external exam. I found nothing remarkable, just a minuscule scar and a tattoo on his forearm. I also found tinea pedis, which is common for a homeless man. Though I have to say his hygiene was far better than most of the homeless population who come through here."

"What's tinea pedis?"

"Athlete's foot. Also remarkable is that he had no syringe marks, meaning he wasn't a user like much of the homeless population." She lifted the scalpel. "And now I'm about to begin my internal exam with a Y incision."

Rick needed more information about the tattoo before he moved on, as it could very well tie Griffin to the shooter. "I want to take a photo of the tattoo if you don't mind."

"I don't mind." She turned Griffin's right arm over to display a small tattoo in the shape of a wheel with eight arrows pointing out from the center.

"Ever seen a tat like this?" he asked.

She shook her head.

He snapped several pictures from different angles, then looked up. "Mind if I have a look at the bullet entrance and exit wound before you make the cut?"

"So you're a doctor now?"

He shook his head. "Former sniper, and I've seen my share of damage done by a .50, but I've completed my ballistic trajectory estimation and wanted to confirm the angle in the body."

"You're not guessing at the caliber from the injuries, are you? Because if you are, you can stop right now." He opened his mouth to speak, but she rushed on. "You can't accurately tell the caliber from the wound. Drives me nuts when law enforcement tries to do that. I've seen large wounds caused by small-caliber bullets and small wounds caused by fragmented large-caliber projectiles. The only accurate way to determine caliber is to recover the bullet at the scene. And as I told the officers on site, the bullet passed through the body. Studying the wound is pure speculation, and you should be at the scene looking for the bullet instead of hanging out here."

"We—" he started.

"And FYI, not that it applies here, but for future reference so you don't annoy another ME, I have never recovered a rifle bullet in anyone, because they either perforate or completely fragment in the tissue."

"We recovered the bullet," he finally got to say.

She frowned. "Why didn't you say so?"

Rick thought it best to keep his answer to himself and bent low to get a good look at the wound. "Can we turn him for the exit wound?"

She lifted the body, and Rick confirmed the downward angle. "Thank you."

She made the Y cut, and Rick went from thinking of Griffin

as the doc's client to thinking of him as a murder victim who was going through an invasive procedure to aid in finding the killer.

After splitting the ribs, she inserted her hands in the cavity. "As expected, there's a good deal of internal damage." She continued her exam, removing organs to study, weigh, and set aside. With the stomach in hand, she looked at him. "Are you interested in the gastric contents?"

"Interested? No. But it could tell us what Griffin did before he met with his therapist. So yeah. I'd like to know."

She dumped the contents into a bowl and poked around in the liquid. "I see pieces of chicken, cheese, and half-inch-long sections of bacon."

"Normally bacon would say breakfast to me, but since he died at night are you thinking a chicken sandwich with bacon?" he asked.

"Could be. Especially with the partially digested french fries I'm seeing. I'd estimate the food was consumed within an hour of his death, and he didn't chew well." She scooped something into her hand. "One of the fries is nearly whole."

Rick looked at the tiny waffle fry. "Chick-fil-A."

"They're not the only restaurant to serve waffle fries."

"Yes, but they're the only fast-food place that does, and a homeless man might have scrounged up enough money to eat there."

"Sounds plausible." She went back to her work, and Rick used his phone to search the Internet for a Chick-fil-A in the area. He located one within walking distance of the park. Close enough for Griffin to have eaten there. If his claim of being followed was true, the restaurant's security camera could have captured the guy tailing him.

As Rick started to pocket his phone, he received a text from

Kaci. *Retrieved park security footage. Don't have a secure connection to email the files. Hotel room #208. Stop by and bring your computer if you want to review them.*

He thumbed in, *Be there ASAP.*

He stood patiently for the next two hours while Dr. Idoni concluded her work without locating any other remarkable items, and then he headed to Chick-fil-A to request their security videos. The good news was they had footage from last night and cameras in various locations, so the odds of recording Griffin and the man he'd claimed was tailing him were good. The bad news was the manager insisted on a warrant to produce the files.

Rick fired off a text to Max asking for the warrant, then stepped outside to heavy gray clouds and thunder rumbling overhead. He hurried to his car before the typical summer afternoon downpour soaked him through. He'd barely gotten behind the wheel when the sky let loose with a deluge, making his trip to the suburban hotel far longer than he'd hoped.

By the time he pulled into the lot, his muscles were tight from squinting at the road, but at least the rain had tapered off. In the lobby he waited for the clerk to complete his check-in and glanced around the place. He often thought of his parents' palatial home as a hotel, but not a drab place like this one. If he'd chosen to let them know he was in town, he thought his mother would insist on him staying with them. She would cater to his every whim, and their cook, Yolanda, who'd been more of a mother to him than his actual mother had been, would serve sumptuous meals. He wanted to see Yolanda while in town, but he wouldn't go to the house.

"Here you go, sir." The clerk slid the keycard across the counter.

In his room he dropped his bag on the floor and dialed Yolanda's cell phone.

"Ricky? Is that you? Really you?"

Her voice wrapped around him, reminding him of her warm hugs when he was younger. "Yeah, it's me. Sorry I haven't called lately, but I'm in Atlanta for work and want to get together."

"You're here?" Her voice rose like an excited teenager's. "Oh, my stars, that's the best news I've had in months. Your mama will be so glad to see you."

"No. Wait," he said. "I thought we could meet somewhere away from the house."

Silence filled the phone, so unlike Yolanda.

"Yo?"

"You need to see your mother, Ricky. Your absence is hurting her. Not that she'd tell you. She's too proud to reach out to you, but it's high time you reconcile with her. I won't push it with your dad, but your mama is another story. So I'm putting my foot down." She took a deep breath. "If you want to see me, you need to come to the house."

"I can't do that, Yo. You know that."

"Then I suggest you think about it and call me back when you come to the right decision."

"I—" he said, but she'd disconnected the call.

In all the years they'd been talking, she'd never hung up on him. Sure, on each call she'd encouraged him to visit his parents or at least call them, but she'd never been this adamant. He probably deserved the hang-up, but he could do nothing about it, so he stowed his phone and tried to swallow the pain of her refusal to see him.

Unfortunately, as he picked up his computer to go to Kaci's room, Yolanda's rejection continued to sit like a lump in his gut. For some odd reason, Dr. Dobbs came to mind. What would she tell him to do in this situation? Did he really care what she thought? Seriously, how did she worm her way into his mind like this?

Work. He needed to focus on work, just as he always did. He headed to Kaci's room, three doors down a dark hallway with swirly blue carpet. She quickly answered and stepped back.

"Did you look at the footage?" he asked, glad to have his mind on business again.

She shook her head. "I've been too busy working on the other things you assigned."

He crossed the room to a small round table with two chairs. Kaci's laptop sat near the closest chair, so he took the other one and set down his computer. "Your background checks turn up any info?"

"We've only done the basics, but they check out on the doc." She dropped into the chair by her computer. "No criminal record. Good credit score. No ongoing debt. No violations on her driver's license. Same is true of Officer Hazeldale and Griffin."

"FYI, his mother didn't have much on him either. She told Shane that after Griffin's first deployment to Iraq, his communication was sporadic. Even then she believed he was showing signs of PTSD but wouldn't admit it. Ace told her about his therapy with Dr. Dobbs and authorized her to communicate with the doc on a regular basis. His mother figured if she kept checking to see if her son was showing up at his appointments, she'd know he was still alive."

"That's so sad." Kaci frowned. "His poor mother."

"Agreed," Rick said, but after his recent call with Yolanda he couldn't help but see the similarity to how he was treating his own mother. He could choose to see her or not, but Ace's PTSD had robbed him of such a choice.

Rick hated to see a fellow vet suffer. He'd seen it so many times. Too many times, and yet each one broke his heart all over again. He had to admit to respecting the doc for taking on and helping clients who suffered from PTSD. He just wished he knew if she was being honest with him about her involvement in Griffin's death.

"Do you really think Griffin was mixed up in the theft?" Kaci asked.

Did he? Rick wasn't sure. "Max said Griffin alibied out for the night of the theft. He'd checked into the shelter and spent the whole night, but that doesn't mean he wasn't in on the planning."

"Then I'll have the team keep digging."

"The doc told me Griffin used to work as a security guard. Can you have your analysts gather a list of his former employers?"

"Will do."

"What about the doc's identity theft? Any progress there?"

"Like she said, the locals are investigating, but the case remains unsolved. I've requested the files, and I'll keep after it to see if it's relevant." Kaci gestured at his computer. "Log in, and I'll transfer the video files."

He signed into his laptop. She connected a cord from her computer to his. The tip of her tongue poked out of the corner of her mouth as her fingers flew over the keyboard. She had such a single-minded focus that he enjoyed watching her work. Enjoyed in an older-brother kind of way, not the way he'd liked watching the doc earlier. That was a whole other ball game.

Kaci unplugged the cord and quirked a smile. "I put the park videos on your desktop so they're easy to find."

He didn't waste his breath denying her implication that his

computer skills were limited, as they were, but he *could* play videos. He turned the computer and saw fifteen security files labeled by location and time stamp sitting on his desktop, as she'd promised.

He clicked on the first file. Griffin stepped through the park entrance at three minutes after ten, his movements cautious. He checked over his shoulder every few feet. He drew the stares of park visitors, but that was likely due to his unkempt and jumpy appearance, not because any of them were tailing him. Griffin soon disappeared from view, and Rick let the video run, watching for any suspicious person entering the park. Three minutes later a man who resembled Rick from a distance stepped into view.

"I have a guy matching our suspect's description. He's wearing camo trousers and a sand-colored T-shirt."

"Military?" Kaci asked.

"Video's not clear enough to tell if the uniform's official, much less which branch. If official, he's in violation of his uniform code by not being in full uniform." Rick tracked the guy. He walked with assurance, his hands shoved into his pockets. Another violation for a man in uniform. Hands were never allowed in pockets while in uniform, unless retrieving something.

Rick paused the video and swiveled his computer. "You should take a look at this."

Kaci peered at the screen. "Dr. Dobbs described the shooter wearing a camo jacket and hoodie. This guy's not wearing or carrying them."

"He could have had them with his rifle and put them on then."

"If you want me to run a facial recognition scan, I'll need to enhance the picture."

"Run it. Too bad the military doesn't have a database that we can search so we could figure out if he's an active duty soldier."

"If they did, you know I'd be all over it." She grabbed a notepad and jotted down the video file name and location. "I'll have my team in D.C. work on the file, but it might already be clear enough for the doc to ID him as our suspect."

Rick nodded his agreement, then started the video rolling again and kept his eyes open for a wrist tattoo, but the man soon walked out of camera range. Rick continued to watch until the time when Hazeldale radioed for help then he moved on to the second park video. At five after ten, Griffin arrived to talk to the doc. His back was to Rick, but he could clearly see Griffin's hands and legs constantly moving as he talked. Thirty minutes later, he took off and stepped off screen. He'd departed ten minutes before the doc had thought. That changed her original timeline, giving the shooter additional time to take Griffin out and get down to his body. A much more believable scenario, and she might be telling the truth. That made him unreasonably happy. But why? It didn't clear her of a connection to the murder. It only told him that the man with the knife could be their shooter.

Rick moved on to additional videos shot from other angles. On the last one, he spotted the guy in camo trousers exiting the park shortly after he entered. Rick checked the time stamp. Forty-nine minutes before the estimated time of Griffin's death, meaning the man had plenty of time to leave the park and take a stand at the hide to take Griffin out.

Rick zoomed in on his footwear. "He's wearing military boots, but I can't make out the style. And there's a shadow by his sleeve. Could be something or not."

Kaci looked at the screen. "We can probably improve the picture."

"I'll have the doc watch the footage, too. Maybe she'll see someone or something I missed."

"Right." Kaci met his gaze. "*After* you run each file a hundred more times tonight."

He fired a questioning look at her.

"Hey, I know you."

"What's that supposed to mean?"

"Mr. Obsessive. You won't take a chance that you're missing anything, and you'll look at these files until you fall asleep at the computer."

She was right. He'd keep watching until the wee hours of the night. And then? Then, tomorrow, he'd visit the doc again, something he could say wasn't a hardship. No hardship at all. He didn't want to admit that to himself, so he surely wouldn't discuss it with Kaci.

"Okay, then, clam up as usual." She shifted her gaze to her computer. "I'll just go back to my darknet search for anyone trying to sell the ordnance."

She didn't need to explain the darknet to him. He was all too familiar with hidden computer networks living beneath the Internet that everyday users accessed. The deep web came first and wasn't accessible by a typical search engine. That layer included some libraries, government sites, and members-only sites. Then came the darknet, intentionally hidden even deeper so both website owners and users were entirely anonymous, making them virtually impossible to track and giving them the freedom to engage in illegal activities.

"Find anything of interest?"

"Not yet." She looked up. "Which surprises me. I should have found something by now. Maybe our suspect doesn't plan to sell the technology."

"Or he already has a buyer."

"You mean he stole the bullets for someone in particular?"

"It wouldn't be far-fetched to think he'd secure a buyer before taking the risk of stealing it."

"You could be right." She sat back and frowned. "If we're talking about an experienced arms dealer, they likely have contacts and don't need the darknet. And if this was a crime of opportunity, our thief isn't likely familiar with darknet resources."

"I doubt we're dealing with a crime of opportunity," Rick said. "With all the security protocols in place by DARPA, the theft had to be planned. If I ever get to talk to MilMed's CEO, maybe we can figure this out."

"He. not cooperating?"

"His admin says he's traveling and unreachable. I hope to talk to him in the morning."

"Might be a good idea if I sat in on that interview in case a hacked network has compromised MilMed's security."

"You think that's a possibility?"

"Sure. Hackers from other countries have infiltrated most of our nation's networks, so why not this one?"

Rick eyed Kaci. "Isn't that a bit of an exaggeration?"

She shook her head, sending her ponytail swinging. "Our Cyber Task Force is up against businesses with the same mistaken impression all the time. Businesses often downplay the persistent threats they face. The actor—the guy who actually goes in and steals data—infiltrates the network in a stealthy manner and—"

"Wait," Rick interrupted. "How can they infiltrate without the companies noticing them?"

"The actor targets employees of the company they're trying to hack. A favorite ploy is to send a message with a link that, if clicked, gives the actor access to the company's network."

"Don't most business e-mail programs filter out this kind of spam?"

"Most do, but the actor also uses social media, where the person least expects a threat. Or he can simply drop a thumb drive in the company's parking lot. Most employees who find a drive plug it into their computer to locate the owner or look at the contents. Then bingo, the drive runs a script that gives the actor access to the network."

"So they get in," Rick said. "Wouldn't the network administrator notice their activity?"

Kaci shook her head. "The purpose of the infiltration is to harvest and exfil data, not inflict harm. They wait for prime network traffic time to make a move, and because many businesses don't believe they've been infiltrated, their security staff is watching only incoming traffic. They don't even look at the packets of data that leave their network. These companies have no idea they've been hacked until one of our Cyber Task Forces discovers the hack on another investigation and informs them." She took a breath. "The biggest threats come from state-sponsored actors out of Asia looking to gain product information."

"Let's hope the investigation doesn't take us overseas," Rick said.

"Max can reach out to the CIA to learn if we have any exposure there."

"God help us if we do," Rick said and refused to even imagine the chaos that could ensue if a foreign country gained access to this deadly technology.

CHAPTER

9

At six-thirty the next morning, Rick looked up as Kaci stepped into the small conference room on the hotel's first floor. She was yawning and sipping coffee, as if channeling his fatigue from a sleepless night.

"So the MilMed guy won't talk to us, and suddenly his only slot is before any sane person gets out of bed," she grumbled as she set her coffee and laptop on the table.

"We're often pulled out of bed at all hours of the night."

"Then maybe we're not sane." She chuckled and dropped into a chair.

"I hear you, but we really need to talk to Erickson, and you'd be down here in thirty minutes anyway for our morning status update."

"Yeah, but I wouldn't have to look presentable like I do for a video call. I mean, it takes time to look this stunning." She grinned and plumped her hair.

Rick chuckled. Even grouchy she was fun to work with. He opened his computer and connected the call, then arranged the camera so they were both in the picture. When Wallace Erickson answered, his gruff hello set the tone for the interview, and not in a good way.

Rick put the guy in his fifties, and he had a receding hairline, a graying goatee, and deep wrinkles near his eyes. His tight expression and rigid posture said he wasn't any happier than Kaci about the early-morning call.

Rick introduced himself and Kaci. "Thank you for meeting with us."

"Sorry for the delay on getting together," Erickson said, his tone flat and his apology forced. "We had an issue with another technology we're perfecting."

"Not something else stolen, I hope," Kaci said.

"No, no." A strained smile crossed his thin lips. "So what can I do for the two of you?"

Rick sat forward. "The details we were given on theft of the self-steering bullets are pretty sketchy."

"I apologize for that. What do you need to know?"

"Everything."

"Oh, I see." He rubbed a hand over his forehead and then massaged as if he had a headache. "Since the technology was stolen during transport, I suppose you'd like to know about our arrangements. We chose to move it covertly. No big vehicle convoy or additional armed guards. Our theory was the fewer people who knew about it the better. Just a security guard hired from a trusted company and the van driver, who is one of our researchers and would have handled the prototype demonstration."

"You're talking about a demo at the Marine Corps Base Quantico," Kaci clarified.

"Yes. We planned a route that avoided the major thoroughfares. The technology left our facility in Fort Meade at 0400.

The transport vehicle should have arrived in Quantico by 0700 but was stopped by a large-caliber bullet through the engine block at 0636."

"Do you know the caliber?" Rick asked.

"A .50 but not one of our bullets." He continued to massage his head. "This occurred near Dale City. The guard and our employee said that two armed men wearing ski masks approached the vehicle and tied them up."

So they'd been right. More than one man was in on the theft. "And you discovered the theft when your employee didn't arrive on time."

"Right. We called him, but when he didn't answer we tracked the route backward until we located them."

"Who knew about the transport?" Rick asked.

"The driver and guard, of course. And, let's see . . . " His hand dropped. "The head of the security firm and our head of security were in the know. And of course, so was I."

"That's it. Just the five of you."

Erickson tilted his head, his eyes narrowing. "The military big-wigs attending the demo were aware that the technology was en route, but weren't read in on the transport method or time."

"Who investigated the theft?" Kaci asked.

"My security staff."

Rick's mouth almost fell open at his response. "So an outside investigation wasn't conducted?"

Erickson crossed his arms. "DARPA reviewed my findings."

That didn't constitute a thorough investigation. Far from it. "Please tell me you at least had an outside company administer lie detector tests to your employees and the outside security staff."

Erickson nodded. "They were all cleared."

At least the guy had done one thing right. "I need copies of those reports along with all of your investigative files."

Erickson sighed. "I'll check with legal to see if we can provide them."

Rick wanted to snarl at the man, but he stifled his frustration by curling his hands into fists where Erickson couldn't see them. "I can provide a warrant if needed."

"I expect you'll need one." Erickson drew in a long breath and let it out slowly, like a leaky tire.

"Were there any written communications about the transport?" Kaci asked.

"Like e-mails or memos, you mean?"

"Yes."

"Sure, yeah."

"Has your IT department evaluated your network for any intrusions?"

"That goes without saying."

"What doesn't go without saying is if any intrusions were located." Kaci sounded as aggravated as Rick felt.

Erickson jutted out his chin. "We have a clean bill of health."

Kaci leaned forward, looking as if she wanted to climb into the screen and get in his face. "Are you saying you have a clean bill now because you rectified any intrusions, or you're saying there wasn't an intrusion?"

He didn't respond.

"Look, Mr. Erickson." Her firm tone made the man cringe. "Just give me a yes, the network was compromised or no, it wasn't compromised."

"I would need my IT people to answer that for you, but I can tell you our network is impenetrable."

"Then you're naïve." Kaci slapped her hands on the table and leaned even closer. "Every network can be penetrated, and I'll need to audit yours."

"I'm afraid that's not possible."

Kaci shot a pointed look at Rick, asking for help.

"You don't want to make us go over your head, do you, Mr. Erickson?" Rick asked.

"There's really no one above me in the company."

"I'm sure if you don't comply with our requests we could work with DARPA to pull your contract," Rick said, though he had no idea if Max had that kind of influence.

Erickson crossed his arms. "I can't give you access to the network."

"Then expect a warrant soon." Rick met Erickson's gaze. "I'm getting the feeling that you don't want this technology found."

"Of course I do."

"But not by having anyone review your files and network," Kaci said.

He sat up higher. "You can hardly blame me for following protocol and checking with legal."

"I can, Mr. Erickson." Rick stifled a sigh and moved on. "How do you think word got out about the transport?"

"Our investigation turned nothing up, so I honestly don't know. That's why you all were called in." His tone said he wasn't too happy about it.

"Do you have any thoughts on who might have done this?" Kaci asked. "Like maybe an ex-employee with a grudge?"

"I'm not aware of any former employee who would want to steal anything."

"Just what *are* you aware of?" Rick snapped.

Erickson crossed his arms. "I don't need to sit here and be insulted when I have important things to do." He reached for his computer as if he planned to disconnect the call.

Fine with Rick. They wouldn't get anywhere with this man, and their best bet was to get the warrant for his records and the network, then come back at him with facts.

"You'll be hearing from us soon." Rick held the man's gaze a moment longer, then severed the connection.

"Sheesh." Kaci crossed her arms. "Aren't we on the same side?"

"He's hiding something," Rick said. "We could be dealing with an inside job."

"Or it's simply that his security isn't up to par, and he's afraid he'll lose his contracts."

"If he's been lax, he deserves to lose them. I'm sure Max will make these warrants a priority."

"Go ahead and get them so we can review the files, and I'll hack their network to show Erickson how easily it can be done."

Rick eyed her. "Are you sure it's a good idea to attempt the hack?"

"Good idea? No." A mischievous grin lit her face. "Necessary? Yes, if we want him to see reality and cooperate."

"Do you want me to tell Max about your plans, or do you want to?"

Her grin fell. "The less Max knows the better."

Rick would go along with her for now, as Max often gave the team flexibility and freedom, allowing them to bend and break rules in a crisis to get the job done. Something Rick appreciated. But on the other hand, Max didn't accept screwups and was a tough disciplinarian. If her hack backfired on them, Max would hold Kaci accountable. Still, Rick agreed that Erickson needed to be taken down a peg if they were to gain his compliance, not to mention prevent similar thefts in the future.

Rick closed the video window, revealing the photo of Griffin's tattoo that he'd left open the night before during his research.

"What's that?" Kaci asked.

"Griffin's tattoo. It's a symbol called 'chaos.'"

She pulled the computer closer. "Which means what exactly?"

"My research says there are a bunch of meanings, but the most common one is that a small cause can have large effects."

"Interesting," she said, staring at it. "Any idea why Griffin chose this particular tat?"

"He was a sniper, so I'm thinking one shot from a sniper can significantly change the course of events, and perhaps that's what it meant to him."

"Too bad Tatt-E isn't up and running or I could upload it there."

The Tattoo Recognition Technology–Evaluation software was being developed by the FBI and the National Institute of Standards and Technology. The database, similar to the facial recognition database, held one hundred thousand images of tattoos from prison inmates and felons.

"What about ViCAP?" Rick asked. The FBI managed the Violent Criminal Apprehension Program database that held details of violent crimes such as murder and sexual assault. "A detective could have mentioned it in another crime."

"I'll do a quick search." Kaci opened her computer and started typing, her focus riveted to the screen.

While she worked, Rick went to his e-mail and read a message from Max date stamped late last night. The local police had located six twenty-four-hour McDonald's within ten miles of the park and collected the videos of people who had bought Sausage McMuffins near the time of Griffin's murder. Max had attached still shots of four buyers. None matched the description of the knife-wielding man, but Max had asked locals to interview these men just in case the doc hadn't been accurate in her description. He also asked the locals to widen the McDonald's search area.

"No references in ViCAP." Kaci shoved her computer away.

She was frustrated. Rick got that. Man, he got that, but he tried not to show his own frustration with all the dead ends. The sun hadn't even come up, and they'd already struck out multiple times. Rick wished he still believed in the power of prayer, as it seemed they were going to need all the help they could get to find this killer.

10

Three hours later, Rick found the doc's inner office door closed. Not a surprise. He'd gotten a look at her calendar the day before and noticed she had back-to-back counseling appointments scheduled, but he wanted to be in the waiting room the moment she was free.

Too antsy to sit, he paced the tiny space. His phone rang, and when he saw Yolanda's name on the screen, he quickly answered.

"I told your parents that you're in town," she said straightaway.

Rick's gut clenched. "And?"

"And if you heard the tone of your mother's voice when she asked if you were going to visit, you would already have stopped by. Now I want you to think long and hard about coming to the house for a proper visit."

He didn't like hurting Yolanda and his mother, but seeing his father was out of the question. "I'll think about it. Okay?"

"Guess that's better than a flat-out no, but Ricky, you've got to do your best to reconcile with your mother."

"I'll do my best."

"You don't sound convinced."

"I'm not, but I'll do my best to think about it."

"Promise?"

"Promise."

The doc's office door opened, and he was thankful for the interruption. "I gotta go."

"Call me back as soon as you make a decision, you hear?" Her tone was reminiscent of the times she'd scolded him when he'd gotten in trouble as a kid.

"Yes, ma'am," he said, and disconnected.

A tough-looking guy wearing an army T-shirt and jeans marched out of the office and to the exit as if a drill sergeant had dismissed him. It looked like the session hadn't gone so well, and Rick hoped the doc wasn't in a bad mood. He poked his head in the doorway and spotted her sitting behind her desk, her fingers poised over her computer keyboard.

He knocked on the doorjamb. "Got a minute, Doc?"

Her head popped up. "Agent Cannon. This's a surprise."

Her narrowed gaze said it wasn't a pleasant one, and he had to admit that her lack of enthusiasm at seeing him stung. He held out his laptop as he crossed the room. "I have videos from the park, and I hoped you would take a look at them."

She drew in a sharp breath and watched him carefully. Her genuine angst touched something inside, and before thinking about it, he took a seat next to the desk and placed a hand on her arm. "You're strong, Doc. I saw that yesterday. You can do this."

Her mouth fell open. Had he left her yesterday thinking he had no compassion?

"Look, I'm sorry if I was a little intense yesterday. I sometimes get that way when I'm working a case."

"Sometimes?"

"Okay, you're right. I'm usually pretty intense, but I'll try to do better at curtailing it today."

A nice promise, just like the one he'd given Yolanda, but could he follow through on either one? Did he even want to? It would mean trusting the doc. Letting go of his issues with his mother. Running the risk of seeing his father. He'd only said he'd try. That he could do with the doc. The others he still wasn't sure about.

He gestured with his laptop again. "Are you up to it?"

She nodded and crossed her legs. His gaze was drawn to her black-and-white-checked pants hugging her body. He didn't need to imagine her long legs that seemed to go on forever above strappy and very feminine sandals. She'd added a lime-green sleeveless sweater, her tanned and toned arms taking his mind in a very different direction.

"Did you want me to watch that video?" she asked.

Shocked at how easily he'd let his interest carry him away, he set up the computer and stood behind her to watch. He caught a whiff of her scent, a mixture of cinnamon and some flower he couldn't place, but he forced his mind to remain on the video. Griffin appeared on-screen, and she reached up to trace his movements with her finger.

"I'm sorry, Ace," she whispered. "So sorry. I wish..." A sob took her words.

It was as if she'd forgotten Rick was in the room and let her feelings pour out. Or she was playacting to turn suspicions away from her. Great. Less than a minute had passed and he'd let his distrust color his thoughts. When the man dressed in camo appeared, Rick reached over the doc's shoulder to pause the video. She recoiled.

He moved to her side and squatted to minimize the intimi-
dation his size often caused. "Do you know this guy?"

She continued to stare at the screen and shook her head.

"You're sure?"

"Positive."

"Could he be the man who chased you?"

She leaned closer to the computer. "Could be, but like I keep
saying, I didn't get a good-enough look at him to be sure. Do
you know who he is?"

"No."

She turned her focus to him. "But you think he might be the
killer?"

Rick shrugged. "The camo trousers suggest military, and we
know Ace was a marine, so that might suggest a connection. So
do this guy's boots, but he isn't wearing or carrying the jacket
you mentioned. And I didn't see a wrist tattoo. He could also be
a soldier wannabe, bought his gear online, and has nothing to
do with the investigation." Rick stood. "I want you to look at
the other videos, too. Just in case you see something I missed."

"You've studied these, then."

"Most of the night."

"No wonder you look so tired."

He hadn't thought he looked *that* bad in the bathroom
mirror, but he'd obviously been wrong. He started the video
playing and watched again, this time trying to see it through
her eyes.

"There," she said. "Stop the video."

He clicked pause.

She stabbed her finger at the camo man in the background.
"That's the same guy. Can you zoom in?"

Rick was glad she'd taken the viewing seriously and watched
carefully enough to catch sight of this guy again.

"See his tattoo? The bottom, peeking out of his T-shirt? It's like Ace's tattoo."

"All I see is a shadow."

"But look." She traced her finger on the screen. "See the arrow? It's darker."

"Maybe." In actuality, he still didn't see any detail. "Kaci's team is working on improving the video."

Her eyes narrowed.

"What's wrong?"

"Either he has a tattoo on the inside of the wrist that we can't see plus one on his arm, or he's not the shooter."

"It's not unusual for a guy to have more than one tat."

"I suppose." She still didn't sound convinced.

Discussing it any longer wouldn't be fruitful, as this was pure speculation. He moved back to her side to make eye contact. "Tell me about Ace's tattoo. Did he ever talk about the reason behind it?"

"He said in the marines he followed one path—the path his superiors put him on—but the tattoo meant there were many possibilities in life. That if people would take an open-minded approach to life, they would see that people doing the same job could take many different paths to success."

"Did Ace often philosophize this way?"

She shook her head. "He was a no-nonsense guy, and I always found the tattoo to be at odds with that. He was like you—like a lot of soldiers I work with. Single focus. Get the job done and move on. So his tattoo came out of nowhere, and I often went back to the subject to get him to open up more."

"And did he?"

"He only ever mumbled a few things about it, and they made no sense. I reread his file last night and highlighted passages on this very topic for you. I left the file in my car, so when you leave, I'll walk out with you to get it."

Rick was thankful she'd gone out of her way to help. The question was, was she really helping, or was this a way to shift his focus away from his suspicions of her?

He might be warming up even more to her, but he'd have to continue to keep his eyes open for potential deceit. "If this guy's tattoo matches Ace's, the odds are very long of him being in the park at the same time as Ace and not being affiliated with him."

"So what do you do now?"

"Wait for the enhanced video and, if it's clearer, hope you recognize him."

She shot a panicked look his way. "You think if he's connected to Ace, that means I might know him, right? Know the killer?" She circled her arms around her waist. "Oh, man. I could know the killer. Really know him."

"We never want to think anyone in our circle is capable of such violence, but as a shr—counselor, you ought to know people do unpredictable things all the time."

"True, but I prefer to think of people as basically good."

Rick hadn't had that rosy outlook since before his mother started agreeing with his father's unreasonable demands.

Dr. Dobbs peered up at him. "It's clear you don't share my opinion."

He wouldn't get into a personal discussion about how his parents had failed him and those rose-colored glasses had come off at a young age. "Let's go ahead and watch the remaining footage."

She frowned at his response, but he moved them back to the topic at hand by starting another video. They watched the remaining ones without the doc pointing anything out.

Rick closed the computer and picked it up to leave. "If Kaci is able to improve the images, I'll come back to show them to you."

"I'll walk you out and get that file." She retrieved a key ring from her desk drawer.

After she locked up the office, he followed her down the hallway, her spiky heels clicking on the wood floor. He didn't know how women could handle wearing such torture devices, but he sure didn't mind looking at them. Or her. She'd been right in the office yesterday. He could have read Griffin's file without her. And he'd been right, too. He'd made her stay because of the urgency of finding the suspect, but if truth be told, he didn't mind having her around for company. Him. Rick Cannon. Mr. Solitary, as his team often referred to him, liked having this woman around.

He hadn't wanted or considered having that kind of companionship in years. Even before Traci died. Back then he'd come home on leave, and for the first few hours everything was like it had been when they'd married in their early twenties. But then things quickly became strained between them, and they didn't communicate anymore.

His fault. He might have been on leave, but he'd learned to compartmentalize his feelings and keep them buttoned up to prepare for what he might see or do on his next deployment. He didn't recognize his behavior back then, but after Traci died, he'd done some deep soul searching and discovered he'd been distancing himself from her when she'd needed him.

What would the doc make of that if he told her? Or make of his estrangement from his family? It would be hard to put her sunshine-and-rainbows spin on it, that was for sure.

She stepped out the door before him. The oppressive air hit him hard, but she didn't comment or even seem to notice.

"It's even hotter today than yesterday," he said.

She looked back at him. "That's Atlanta in the summer for you."

"The temps seem higher than I remember growing up here."

"Kids handle heat better than adults. Plus it's been an unusually hot summer."

"I hear you there." Okay, seriously. Who was this guy engaging in small talk? He never talked about the weather.

The doc was good at her job if she could keep getting him to do things outside the norm. Like almost revealing Traci's death yesterday when the doc talked about neglecting others. He'd even thought about telling her that he believed that if he'd been stateside, Traci would be alive. That he'd have a son. Crazy as it sounded, he still wanted to tell her. Pathetic, when he didn't know what her role was in this situation.

"I should get going." He gestured at his car and waited for her to move toward her own vehicle.

A soft breeze played over the area, and his gaze drifted to swaying trees across the street. A flash of light caught his attention. He homed in on it. Another glint, like the sun hitting a wristwatch. The barrel of a rifle poked through the leaves.

"Sniper," he yelled and lunged forward to take the doc down and out of the line of fire.

CHAPTER

11

A rifle report drowned out any sound of a bullet whizzing overhead, but Rick was certain it had been close and was intended for the doc. He curled his body around her, putting his back to the shooter and bracing himself for a second wave.

"They shot at us," she cried out and tried to free herself.

He tightened his grip before she took off running. He drew his handgun and cocked an ear to listen for movement.

Leaves rustled, but from a distance he couldn't be sure if it was the wind or the shooter taking off. From the sound of the rifle report, he was sure that the shooter wasn't putting .50s downrange as the report wasn't that of a large bore. A good thing. They wouldn't be safe anywhere from an armor-piercing bullet. But they also weren't safe from *any* rifle while they remained out in the open.

"We'll move behind your car for protection," he said. "Stay behind me."

"But I—"

"No time to talk. Let's move." He jumped to his feet and tugged her with him.

Holding his handgun at the ready, he scanned the woods and moved in front of her for protection. They sidestepped to her car, and once they moved behind it, he urged her to sit, then squatted next to her.

"Do you think he's stopped shooting?" Her eyes were wide and terrified.

"Looks like it, but we can't let our guard down yet. You call 911 while I get my team out here. Make sure to tell them where we're located and that I'm an armed FBI agent."

He watched her for a moment to make sure she followed directions. Her hands trembled, but she dialed. He got Max on the phone and elicited a promise to join them in less than five minutes. By the time Rick hung up, police sirens already screamed in the distance.

"If the shooter hasn't taken off yet, he'll be in the wind now." He popped up to assess the situation. He saw no movement. No flash of light. Nothing. He dropped down again.

"Shouldn't you go after him?" Her voice was borderline hysterical.

"I'm not wearing any protective gear, and I'd be an open target. Besides, I need to stay with you."

"Right. Sorry. I didn't...I mean...you're doing your job. And I'm thankful for your protection." Her face paled, and she gulped in air.

Touching her could complicate things, but he threw caution to the wind and took her hand. "It'll be okay."

She stared at their hands, then looked back at him, fear consuming her gaze. "Okay for now, I suppose, but then what? The cops will arrive. The shooter...Ace's killer, I bet...will be gone. But he wanted to kill me, right? I mean, that shot wasn't for you."

"That would be the logical conclusion to draw." He firmed his hand over hers. "But don't worry. I'm here to protect you."

"But you won't be. All the time, I mean. You have a job to do. I'll be alone, and he'll still be out there." She tried to free her hand.

He held tight. "Look at me, Doc."

She swung her gaze his way. Her lingering fear sent his anger boiling. Suspect or no suspect, she didn't deserve to be terrorized. No one did.

He realized he was gritting his teeth, and he relaxed his jaw to give her a comforting smile. "I won't let anything happen to you. I promise."

"How can you promise such a thing?"

"I just can." *Right. Exactly how are you going to do that?*

A siren wound toward them, making it impossible to continue talking, so he simply held her hand and waited for the patrol car to stop near her vehicle. He let go of her hand and raised his credentials over her car's hood. "Special Agent Rick Cannon here. We called in the shooting. No one was injured. The shooter fired a rifle from the woods about thirty yards to the east."

"Stay in position," the officer replied. "We'll let you know when we've cleared the area."

Patrol officer on the scene or not, Rick held fast to his weapon and wouldn't let down his guard before his team arrived and pronounced it safe.

"You should also know my team is on the way driving a black SUV," he called out to the officer. "If you barricade the road before they get here, you'll need to let them through. The shooting is part of an ongoing investigation."

"Roger that." The officer radioed in an update before another siren screamed toward them.

Rick stowed his creds and leaned back against the car to wait. The doc pulled her knees to her chest and picked at a large tear in her pants. Tears glistened in her eyes, and it took every bit of Rick's willpower not to pull her into his arms.

Was he simply reacting as any man would in this situation, or was he actually letting her get to him?

Fortunately, he didn't have to think about it any longer, as his team arrived, and he focused on the action until Max declared they were in the clear.

Rick stood.

"Dr. Dobbs all right?" Max asked as he approached the car.

Rick nodded. "In shock, though."

"Let's have the medics look at her."

"I'm sitting right here and can speak for myself. I don't need a medic." She started to get up.

Rick offered her a hand, and she clasped his with icy-cold fingers, proving she was far from all right. "It's protocol in a situation like this to be checked out."

She watched him carefully for a moment, then nodded.

"Let me walk you over there," he offered.

She sighed out her relief, but kept darting her gaze around as they walked. She was still afraid, but unwilling to admit it.

"You can relax now," Rick said. "There's no way the shooter would hang around with all of these officers on scene."

"But Ace was shot from a long distance, right? Why can't that happen here?"

"The geography doesn't allow the shooter to take a nearby stand without revealing himself. Only a fool would do that."

"Then let's hope it's not a fool who wants me dead."

Rick doubted they were dealing with a fool, but with someone very cunning, so he didn't bother responding and left her with the medic. Each step he took away from her filled him with regret over leaving her unprotected. He believed what he'd said—the shooter couldn't find a close-up hide, and he didn't have a long-distance shot. So why the angst? Maybe he was reliving his issues over not being present for Traci. True or not, it was easier to think that than to consider that the doc was starting to mean something to him when he was no closer to trusting her.

Whatever the reason, he had to make sure she wasn't in ongoing danger, and that meant putting her in a safe house ASAP. But where and how? Olivia wouldn't go into hiding without her sister and her sister's children, that was for certain. So how did he handle that? It would be extremely hard to find a large-enough home for all of them that was close enough for his comfort. A hotel wouldn't be safe at all, and putting her with friends would endanger the friends, so neither was an option.

So where, then?

A picture of his parents' house, more like a compound with their state-of-the-art security, flashed in his brain.

No. Not there. No way.

Shaking his head at such a crazy idea, he crossed the road to his team and tried to come up with another location. Tried and failed. So what about his parents' house? Could he actually go back there? If Yolanda was right, his mother desperately wanted to see him, so if he made his visit contingent on their providing a safe haven for Olivia and her family, he was certain his mom would agree. Plus if the entire team, Olivia, her sister, and the kids stayed on the property, they could create a buffer. His parents would be less inclined to get into any arguments with him if the house was filled with other people. They were all about not making a scene in front of others.

Yeah, this was a perfect solution. He could alleviate his guilt over not visiting Yolanda and actually get to see her, all the while avoiding confrontation and having to delve into his issues with his parents. And at the same time, he'd provide an extremely secure place for Olivia. The only thing left was for Olivia and her sister to agree and for him to get the team on board with the idea.

They stopped talking when he joined them, so he started with a quick rundown of events. "You'll find the slug near the building entrance, Brynn, and it won't be a .50."

"You sure of that?" Max asked.

"You fire off enough .50s in your life and you know the sound."

"So maybe this shooter isn't the suspect we're hunting," Max said. "Otherwise, why not use the weapon system that's a guaranteed kill?"

"Maybe he didn't want us to connect the shooting to Griffin's death," Brynn suggested.

"But Griffin was only killed last night," Shane replied. "Wouldn't the shooter have to know we'd see a connection?"

"It might not be connected," Max said. "The doc could be involved in something else where someone wanted to end her life."

"What about the identity theft?" Kaci asked. "The police haven't made any headway on that investigation. The shooting could be connected to that."

Rick liked Kaci's suggestion a whole lot better than Max's. "That sounds more likely than her being involved in anything illegal."

"Doesn't have to be illegal," Shane said. "This could be one of her clients going ballistic on her."

When Traci died, Rick had been mad enough to want to kill, so the idea wasn't far-fetched. "I'll ask the doc about that."

"These are valid suppositions, but they're just that," Max said. "We need some hard evidence to make a determination."

To a person, they peered at Brynn.

"Thanks, guys." She stared back at them. "Put all the pressure on me, why don't you?"

"You do always say forensics is the key to solving a case." Kaci chuckled.

Brynn rolled her eyes. "Then I guess you better let me get started on processing the scene."

She departed, and Max held a folder out to Rick. "The MilMed warrant. The only way I could get it through the judge was by limiting the scope. So it's very narrow, and you'll need to review the details carefully before proceeding."

Rick wanted MilMed's files, but after this shooting there was no way Rick was leaving town to serve a warrant. He passed the file to Cal. "I know you won't complain about heading back to D.C. to serve this and gather the approved records from MilMed."

A big smile slid across Cal's mouth. "I'll be glad to take care of it for you."

"And while you're at it, I want you to interview the security guard and MilMed employee who were transporting the ordnance when it was stolen."

"Understood."

Rick faced Shane. "That means you'll take over visiting the shooting ranges and gun clubs."

"No worries," he replied. "I'll handle it so lover boy can go home to the wife."

Cal groaned, but the smile remained in place. "I finished making a list of local hunting associations and shooting ranges in the area. I'll e-mail it to you, Shane."

"Perfect," Shane said. "I can take the picture of Ace's tattoo and the one of the suspect from the park video with me. Guys don't always remember details of another guy's face, but a tat like that will stand out. If someone has seen it, they're bound to remember."

Rick moved his focus to Kaci. "I dropped my computer back there, and I'll need you to take a look at it."

"Of course."

"Anything new on the doc's background?" He felt as if he was starting to sound like a broken record.

She shook her head. "She's looking as squeaky clean as she appears. My team's running with the identity theft data provided by the local cops. Maybe if we're able to track the thief, that will get us somewhere."

"I wouldn't give up on the background check either," Rick said, despite his gut's telling him that the doc was a victim only. "Everyone has something they don't want others to know about, and I want to know her something."

Shane raised an eyebrow. "This is starting to sound personal. Like you're going above and beyond to find some dirt on Dr. Dobbs."

"Just doing my job." The moment the words came out, Rick knew they weren't completely true. His drive to vet her likely had more to do with wanting to trust her. But could a background check really let him do that? There weren't dings in a personal history for being two-faced. The only way to ensure she was who she appeared to be was to get to know her better, and that *so* wasn't happening.

"I'll keep digging," Kaci said. "But don't hold out hope for some deep, dark secret. We haven't uncovered a concrete motive for her involvement in the shooting. I think she's who she presents herself to be and nothing more."

"Or not." Max moved in closer. "One scenario we didn't

mention is that Dr. Dobbs could be the shooter's partner, and he's afraid she'll talk, or he wants all the money for the bullet sale for himself, so he turned on her."

Rick glanced at the doc. She'd left the medic, a large bandage on her elbow, and stepped toward her office. Her eyes were dark and unreadable. "Shrinks do have to be good at hiding their true emotions."

Shane flashed him a questioning look. "You make that sound like a bad thing."

"Maybe not. At least not while in session with a client. But it's problematic if they use it to deceive law enforcement. Or even if they try to hide things from people who need to know what's going on with one of their clients."

Shane lifted his sunglasses and stared at Rick. "Sounds like you're speaking from experience, bro."

Rick wasn't about to continue this discussion, so he moved on. "Anyone consider that she could be using her ability to hide her true thoughts to get her clients to reveal military secrets?"

"That's an interesting take," Max said. "Let's request her client list to see if she's treating any officers who might have sensitive details to share."

"Our current warrant for her records loosely covers this, so I'll see if I can get her to comply." Rick let his gaze follow the doc as she approached the front steps and settled on one of them. She pulled up her legs and circled them with her arms, her chin resting on her knees. The gaping tear in her pants spoke to her brush with death.

She met his gaze for a brief second, then shivered and shifted to stare across the street. He'd like to think her reaction to the latest incident meant she wasn't involved, but she'd also be in shock if a partner tried to kill her. Rick would continue to reserve judgment on her trustworthiness, but with a shooter gunning for her, she still needed their help to stay alive.

"I'm most likely to believe the shooter thinks she got a good-enough look at him and can ID him," Rick said. "So he's trying to take her out before she can do so or testify against him when he goes to trial. Either way, she'll need protection."

Max gave a firm shake of his head. "Not from us. Not with a deadly shooter running free. We don't have time to babysit. I'll try to get a local to take on her detail."

"What are the odds of that with the way city budgets are cut to the bare minimums?" Shane asked.

"I have an idea about that, but everyone will have to agree," Rick said, not believing what he planned to say.

"We're listening," Max said.

"My parents' house is about as secure as Fort Knox, and I thought she could stay there."

Max shrugged. "Go ahead and arrange that if you want, but I don't see why we all need to weigh in."

Uncertainty plagued Rick, something foreign to him. "If we all stay there, too, we can take turns keeping an eye out for her safety. And at the same time, we can watch for signs that she's connected to the shooter."

Max eyed him. "I'm not sure it's a good idea for all of us to be cramped in a house for the duration. We need some alone time, too."

"We won't be cramped. The house is twelve thousand square feet with eight bedrooms."

"Seriously?" Shane's tone rose. "Your parents must be loaded."

Rick didn't respond, as it went without saying. "There's a pool, tennis courts. Theater. An excellent cook. So staying there won't be a hardship." *For anyone but me.*

Kaci grinned. "As long as they have Wi-Fi, you can count me in."

"With those amenities, I'd be a fool to say no," Shane said. "Though the Wi-Fi is optional."

"Then it sounds like a plan," Max said.

Rick nodded. "I'll check with Brynn, then call my mother to make arrangements and text everyone the address."

"You think your mom will agree to a bunch of people hanging out at her place?" Shane asked.

"She'll agree." No question about that. She'd do just about anything to see him for the first time since he'd taken off on his eighteenth birthday.

CHAPTER

12

Olivia looked up to see Agent Cannon approaching the outside stairway where she waited for instructions on her next move. His steps were quick and decisive, and he soon stopped in front of her. She couldn't miss his narrowed eyes and his pressed-together lips. *Great.* He had more bad news to share. Didn't take a rocket scientist to see that.

He squatted down, closer than she'd like when she was all teary-eyed and emotional and might reach out to him. She expected an intense locking of gazes, but he stared over her shoulder. *Right.* The news was so bad he couldn't look at her.

Could she take any more?

She lowered her head to her knees and practiced the deep breathing exercises she taught her clients to use when life over-whelmed them.

He sucked in a sharp breath and settled on the step next to her. His leg touched hers, the heat warming her as much as warning her that he sat far too close for her comfort.

"How are you coping?" His soft and gentle tone was as warm

as the touch of his leg and totally out of character for the man she'd seen this far.

Not good. She scooted away. She felt him watching her, but if she looked at him and saw his pity or concern she really would fall apart. "I've been better."

"Like I said before, you're far stronger than you're giving yourself credit for, Doc. You'll come out the other side of this just fine."

She twisted her hands together. "Are you sure you're not the psychologist here?"

"Me? A shrink? No way."

"Guess that would be a nightmare job for you."

"Besides the fact that it involves sitting inside all day, I wouldn't have the patience for such a job. But this isn't about me. I want to talk about your safety."

Safety? "You think the shooter will try again?"

"Yes."

A single word, one that had the power to make her lose control of her emotions if she let it. Really lose it, as she had the night her father died alone in his car.

"Might a disgruntled client be behind this?" he asked.

She finally met his gaze and, thankfully, found a neutral expression. "Sounds like you don't think the shooting is related to Ace's death."

"The bullet that was just fired is a smaller caliber than the one that killed Ace. Could be a different shooter or the same shooter with a different weapon. We don't know, so we'll investigate all options."

"That does make you think, doesn't it?" She sighed. "I'd have to be a very bad psychologist if I didn't notice that one of my clients wanted to kill me."

"Still, it would be a good idea to review all of your cases."

"With the police and your team swarming the area, I'll have to cancel my appointments anyway, so I can get started on that right away." She not only wanted to help figure out if the shooting was related to her practice, she was also thankful for something to keep her mind occupied.

He cleared his throat, and her defenses shot up in preparation for his next comment.

"There could also be a connection to your identity theft."

"My theft?" She swiveled to face him. "But why? The hacker already has all my money. Why kill me?"

"The hacker could be afraid you're onto him, he'll be arrested, and you'll testify against him."

"But the police told me that most identity theft is perpetrated by faceless hackers in other countries."

"That's true in many cases, but not all. It could be someone you know, and that's the connection we need to focus on."

"No." She shook her head hard. "I don't believe it. It's not someone I know. The people in my life wouldn't steal my money. Let me help support them, yes. Steal my money, no. I told the police as much, and I know they checked it out because they talked to my family and friends."

"We'll have to dig deeper, so be aware that an agent will be pursuing the theft, and that could mean interviewing them again."

She sighed. "I hate that more people have to suffer because of my personal issues."

"It can't be helped." He braced his legs on the step, the muscles in his thighs coiled and ready, as if he thought he'd need to spring to his feet. "What about Ace? Anyone in his life who might blame you for his death? Maybe think you had a part in it and want to get revenge?"

"Like I said, he doesn't have any friends that I know of. I

imagine he has buddies from his military days, but he didn't mention keeping in touch with anyone. Besides, they wouldn't know about his death yet anyway, right? Unless his mother contacted them."

"Agent Erwin talked to her yesterday, and she mentioned letting extended family know." He met her gaze. "In any event, until we can figure out who took the shot at you, I want to put you in protective custody."

She didn't like the sound of that. "What exactly would that entail?"

"Usually it means a safe house and an officer or agent on duty 24/7, but in this case I think it would be best if you stayed at my parents' house."

"Your parents?" She gaped at him. "Why on earth would you want me to stay there?"

He held up a hand. "I'm not explaining very well. They have a large compound in Buckhead with state-of-the-art security that will ensure no one can get to you. My team will also stay there, so we can look out for you."

"Me? Stay with *you*? In the same house?" she asked and didn't have the presence of mind to question the fact that his family lived in one of Atlanta's wealthiest neighborhoods.

He winced. "I'm sorry that's so repulsive to you."

"No, wait," she said quickly to cover up having reacted as a woman, not a witness. She didn't want him to think she had any personal thoughts about him. "I didn't mean it like that. I'm just shocked. It feels like a personal connection, and I assume that as a professional you have to keep your distance. Won't my staying with your parents blur the line?"

"Not for me. I don't have a strong connection to my family, and the house is almost as big as a hotel, so it's like staying in one."

Interesting. The psychologist in her wanted to ask for details, but his tight look of resolve showed that her questions wouldn't be welcome.

"It's in your best interest to do this." He'd gentled his tone again.

"I'd be happy to comply, but I can't go into hiding and forget about my sister and her kids."

"I knew you'd say that. My parents have a guesthouse on the property. Perhaps your sister would be open to staying there."

His generosity continued to surprise her. "Are you sure your parents will be up for hosting all of us?"

"If it means I spend time with them, I'm pretty sure my mother will host a marauding army." He fisted his hands.

"Sounds like there's some bad blood between you."

He quirked a brow and stared at her. "I get that you want me to tell you all about it. To lie down on your couch, so to speak, and let it all out, but leave it alone, Doc. For both our sakes."

"Okay," she said, but telling a psychologist not to try to help was like telling an alcoholic like her dad not to drink. Still, she'd do her best.

"You can review your files," he said. "And then we can stop by your place to pick up a few things."

"Thank you for your consideration, Agent Cannon."

"It's Rick," he said matter-of-factly as he stood.

This second indication that he was lowering his professional barrier left her gaping at him again.

"Don't waste time analyzing it, Doc. There's nothing there. We'll be spending a lot of time together, and 'Agent Cannon' will get tiring for both of us. That's all."

She nodded, but didn't get the sense that he meant what he said. It didn't matter, though. As he'd said, they'd be spending time together, and she'd like to dispense with the formality, too.

"Then call me Olivia." She started to rise, but her legs wob-
bled, and she had to grab on to the railing to stay upright.

Agent Cannon—Rick—slid a hand under her elbow. A
flurry of emotions fired at his touch. She wanted to free her arm.
To be strong and not need him or anyone else. Be the psychologist she'd been a day ago, when she didn't feel so lost inside.
But she *did* need him. Just for now. For today. Once she recovered from the latest incident, she'd be herself again. She had
to be, before she couldn't find the resolve to work this out on
her own and gave in to these feelings for a man who was oh so
wrong for her.

* * *

Two hours later, Olivia sat on her suitcase to close it. Since coming home she'd explained the plan to Dianna, doing her best to
convey the seriousness of the situation without making her sister too worried or scared. She told her she was helping the FBI
as a witness, and that the agents were concerned for her safety
and also wanted her nearby for the sake of the investigation. She
left out the part about being shot at. Dianna was dealing with
enough stress already. But Olivia did tell her that though there
was no reason to think Dianna or the children were in danger,
the FBI wanted Dianna to be careful until the killer was in custody.

Olivia had then arranged for colleagues to handle her most
pressing appointments and remain on call for her patients until
the situation was resolved. With Rick waiting in the family
room, she'd changed her torn pants for shorts and added a casual knit top that would be comfortable in her time off, then
started packing. Thankfully, Dianna had finished packing and
taken the kids to the doctor for a routine check-up, so her sis-

ter didn't have to make small talk with a man who had proved chatting was a challenge for him. One of the other agents had agreed to escort Dianna and the children to the house later.

Olivia swung the suitcase to the floor and dragged it out to the living room. Rick sat on the sofa, his long legs stretched out and crossed at the ankles and his head resting on a cushion, his eyes closed.

They suddenly opened, and he lurched forward before his gaze cleared, and he relaxed. "Ready to go?"

She nodded and chose not to comment on his response that displayed the uneasiness he and many law enforcement professionals and soldiers lived with.

He took her bag and carried it to the car in silence. He'd said very little since they'd left her office. Sure, he wasn't a very talkative guy to begin with, but maybe he was silent because she'd disappointed him when she didn't come up with even one client unstable enough to fire a shot at her. He'd kept after her, asking question after question until she was ready to scream. Finally he'd given in and asked her to provide Agent North with a list of her clients so the young agent could investigate them. He'd promised neither the clients nor their families would be approached without her knowing about it first, and she hoped North would follow through on that promise.

"You never told me about the notes you highlighted on Ace's file," he said once they were cruising up the highway toward Buckhead. "Now would be a good time to do so."

She reached for the file in her briefcase and flipped to her first highlighted passage. "Most times when I circled back around to the tattoo, Ace said nothing. But one time he said, 'The guys. We voted.'" She flipped a few pages. "Another time he said, 'Tank deserves it.' Both times, I asked him what he meant, but he wouldn't elaborate. When I saw the entries again last night,

I wondered if Tank was a nickname for someone Ace had served with. So I reread the file looking for any mention of a Tank and didn't find one."

"Unfortunately, we don't have a way of obtaining a list of the people he served with, much less one with nicknames."

"What about his military records?"

"We've requested his service record book, which is basically his marine personnel file. It'll include locations where he was stationed, his assignments, et cetera, but not the men he served with."

"And you can't even begin to look for a guy with only his nickname to go on." Frustrated, she stared out the window and watched the lushly manicured lawns, green from regular watering, and the stately houses pass by. When he swung the car into a gated driveway, her mouth dropped open at the sight of the impressive estate. "You said there was plenty of room, but this—"

"Is completely over-the-top," he finished. "House is twelve thousand square feet, if you can believe that."

The drive opened to a wide clearing and circled back again. The two-story Tudor with stone facade sprawled in the clearing, putting-green-smooth grass and perfectly manicured shrubs surrounding it. She'd grown up in small rental houses, and she felt like Cinderella arriving at the ball. Except she wasn't dressed for the opulence. Her khaki shorts and knit shirt weren't of the Neiman Marcus quality this house cried out for.

Her usual confidence fled. "I can't imagine growing up here."

"I didn't. At least not in this house. In the late nineties, my dad had our house razed and built this one. I only lived in it for two years before I took off for the marines." He parked the car in front of the double front door with wrought iron accents, climbed out, and grabbed the suitcases from the back.

She hadn't even set foot on the driveway pavers when the door swung inward and a woman came charging out of the house. She wore pointy-toed pumps and designer jeans that she'd paired with a fitted white blouse. She stopped shy of Rick and tucked a strand of chin-length blond hair behind an ear, revealing a pearl earring.

"Son," she said on an exhale. She took another step, then halted to look up at him.

"Hi, Mom," he replied, but he made no move toward her.

She kept staring at him as if memorizing everything about him as tears dampened her eyes. She suddenly pressed a hand over her mouth and shook her head. "Where are my manners? Your guest will want to come in."

Rick turned to Olivia, and her heart ached over the pain and confusion she found in his eyes. She closed the car door and, hoping he'd give her a clue about the discomfort between him and his mother, didn't take her gaze off him as she moved forward.

"Mom, this is Dr. Olivia Dobbs," he said, his tone devoid of emotion, proving once again his ability to hide his feelings at a whim.

His unease made Olivia forgot all about her own, and she offered her hand. "Please call me Olivia."

His mother smiled and firmly gripped Olivia's hand. "And I'm Grace." She stepped back and sent a nervous smile in Rick's direction. "I had Yolanda prepare your favorite iced tea."

"I stopped drinking sugary tea years ago," Rick replied.

Grace's smile fell, and Olivia wanted to sock him in the arm, then rush over and hug the woman who appeared desperate for her son's affection.

"I suppose if Yolanda already made it I'll have a glass," he said. "I don't want to hurt her feelings."

Grace gave a tight nod as Rick often did before she turned and strode up to the house, her narrow heels clicking on the brick drive. She stood back at the door, allowing them to enter the foyer.

Hoping to cut the tension, Olivia smiled at Grace, whose name fit her to a T. She was trim and elegant, but not in a showy way, and she moved with a self-assured glide.

She closed the door behind them. "Let's go to the drawing room for tea, and then I'll have Upton take the bags to your rooms."

She stepped across the gleaming wood floor where Rick set down the suitcases, but Olivia couldn't get her feet moving. She simply stared at a sparkling crystal chandelier hanging in the two-story foyer before letting her gaze follow the winding stairs and wrought iron banister leading to the open second floor.

"I know it will be hard to feel comfortable in such a place, but think of it as a hotel," Rick said. "That's what I do. Then maybe you can accept that the money sunk into this house would feed thousands of starving children." Rick followed his mother.

So he didn't enjoy the pretentious lifestyle. Was that his grievance with his parents? He might have a different philosophy of life, but was that enough to put a rift between him and his mother?

Olivia really wanted to know the answer, but with Rick's unwillingness to share anything personal, she might never know. She trailed him into a room with cream walls, thick crown molding, and a coffered ceiling. Two very formal camelback sofas faced each other in the center of the room, a long glass table between them.

"Please take a seat." Grace gestured at the sofa facing three sets of French doors to the outside. "You can see the gardens from here."

Olivia sank into the plump cushion, but before Rick could sit, a chubby woman bustled into the room carrying a tray. She had frizzy short hair, reading glasses near the tip of a wide nose, and remnants of red lipstick. She wore a white uniform with a striped apron over the top. She bounced across the space and stopped in front of Rick. "Upton wanted to bring the tea up, but I had to lay my eyes on our little Ricky."

"Yolanda!" Rick's rigid expression melted into a smile of warm affection.

Olivia was shocked at his soft response, but even more shocked that the big hulk of a man allowed Yolanda to get away with calling him *Ricky*.

He took the tray from her to set it on the coffee table. "It's good to see you."

Yolanda held out her arms. "Come here and give me some sugar."

Rick didn't hesitate but put his arms around her and gave her a fierce hug. Olivia saw his contented smile, and for the first time since she'd met him—which, granted, hadn't been very long—he seemed at peace.

Yolanda eventually pushed back and touched Rick's cheek. "Seventeen years is too long, Ricky. Your mama has about expired waiting for you to visit."

Guilt spread across Rick's face, but he didn't respond. Olivia could hardly imagine what was going through his head, what with returning home after a seventeen-year absence and doing so with her as his audience.

"Let's have some of Yolanda's famous tea," Grace said, further proving she was appropriately named.

"I need to get back to the kitchen anyway," Yolanda said. "I'm making all of your favorites while you're here. Tonight it's pulled pork, collards, spaghetti salad, and my candy apple pie."

"My tastes might have changed a bit."

She waved a hand. "Nonsense. You grew up on my down-home cooking, and no one ever loses a taste for the solid food that'll put meat on your bones."

She faced Olivia and stood with her hands on her hips. "Where are your manners, Ricky?"

"Sorry." He introduced Olivia.

Yolanda's eyebrow shot up. "A doctor. Now aren't you improving in your taste in women?"

"No, wait. I'm not his...his woman," Olivia said.

"We're colleagues," Rick explained, a hint of a smirk on his lips.

"Start doing some fancy talking with this one, Ricky. I can tell she's a keeper."

"We're just colleagues," Rick said again.

"Um-hum." She winked at Olivia, then waddled out the door and closed it behind her.

Grace poured tall glasses of tea over ice. "Yolanda's been with us for so long she's like one of the family."

"Not like family. She *is* family." Rick sat on the sofa next to Olivia, his face wearing that adamant expression she often found there. If the comment bothered Grace, she didn't show it, but handed a lovely crystal glass to Olivia.

"Thank you." Olivia smiled at Grace. "Unlike Rick here, I love my tea sweet. The sweeter the better."

"Then you'll love Yo's tea," Rick said. "She can fatten up a person just by looking at them."

"You and your mother haven't succumbed."

"Thanks to our gym, which you're all welcome to use while you're here. Rick can show you where it is." Grace passed a glass to Rick, her hand jerking back when they touched fingers.

From the look of things, the strain wasn't from a small rift, but an all-out family feud.

"And I got away before my metabolism slowed down." He took a long drink of the tea.

Olivia waited for him to grimace, but he took another drink, so she figured he was sending a message to his mother.

Grace took her tea and sat on the edge of the other sofa, her posture perfect. "Will your team arrive in time for dinner?"

"Depends on what they uncover at the crime scene. We'll have to play it by ear."

She nodded.

"I'm sorry, Mom," he said, sounding sincere. "I know you don't know how many people to plan for and that puts you and Yo in a tough place, but our work is very unpredictable."

"Don't worry about it. It sounds like you love your job."

"I do."

"At least now I don't have to worry about you being deployed to war zones." Her voice caught, and she made a production of taking a sip of the tea.

"Will Dad be home for dinner?"

"Unfortunately, he's out of town on business."

Olivia saw Rick's posture visibly relax.

"He'll be home tomorrow, though."

His shoulders firmed again. Perhaps not noticeably to his mother, but Olivia could spot nonverbal cues others missed, and Rick had been tossing them out since they'd arrived as if lobbing grenades in a war zone.

His phone chimed, and he quickly looked at it before frowning. "I have some work to do, and Olivia could probably use a rest before her sister and the kids arrive. So if you don't mind, we'll go to our rooms."

He was right. She would be happy to rest, but she didn't want to leave Grace with a crestfallen look on her face. She and Rick set down their glasses at the same time and came to their feet. Olivia took another long drink, then added her glass to the tray.

Rick crossed over to his mother and rested a hand on her shoulder. "I am glad to see you, Mom. I don't know how to...what to..." He glanced at Olivia, then back at his mom. "We can talk later."

"Of course we can." She pressed her hand over Rick's but quickly let go. A genuine smile claimed her face, her dimples, like Rick's, showing.

He faced Olivia. Raw, unfettered pain darkened his eyes, and she gasped. At her response he erased the pain with the blank expression he seemed able to call up at a moment's notice. "I know you'll want to spend the night at the guesthouse, but I've asked Mom to set aside a room for you here so we can keep a better eye on you during the day."

Grace peered at Olivia. "Let me show you to your room."

Olivia nodded, but wished they could all stay in the drawing room so she could use her counseling skills to help them eliminate the awkward formality between them and find the words they both wanted to say.

Grace stepped out of the room, and Rick shouldered his computer case. He gestured for Olivia to precede him. She caught his gaze and held it, and a million things were transmitted in his look of vulnerability.

It hit her then. Hard. She didn't want to help him as a psychologist. She wanted to help him because she was starting to develop feelings for him. How had she let that happen so quickly? She knew better and had to be careful not to fall for him. That thought scared her almost as much as the bullet outside her office that had nearly taken her life.

CHAPTER

13

Rick wouldn't let the butler carry up their suitcases, so he grabbed them as his mother led the way up the winding staircase, and he tried to remember how it felt to live in this mausoleum of a house. All that came to mind were the daily, sometimes hourly fights with his dad and the unhappiness they'd brought. Not only for him, but his mother suffered with each argument, too.

And now, if Olivia's look a few moments ago had meant anything, she was feeling the ongoing tension. His fault, of course. His mother had been open and welcoming. He'd been a jerk, and he'd hurt his mom. Maybe that was what he was trying to do. To pay her back for all the years she'd hurt him when she'd taken his father's side even though it wasn't in Rick's best interest. Still, rudeness like that wasn't reflective of the man he tried to be.

What must Olivia think? Surprisingly, he cared about that.

She paused in front of him and gestured at the opulent foyer below. "It takes a lot of commitment to your cause to want to leave this luxury to serve your country." Her voice wasn't much more than a whisper, and he appreciated her keeping her tone down so his mother didn't hear.

"We all have to do our part for our country," he replied, but when he caught sight of his father's portrait on the ancestors' wall, Rick knew his statement was a lie. Not everyone did their part. His father and his cronies didn't. They were too busy socking away money.

Olivia met his gaze. "Still, I'm impressed with your sacrifice."

Rick's heart puffed up under her compliment. *Stop it.* He didn't need anyone's approval. He'd decided that at eighteen when he'd given up on his parents and walked out the front door. He'd lived without needing approval ever since. So why suddenly care about what a woman he didn't really know thought about him?

"Are you two coming?" His mother peered down on them from the top of the stairs.

Rick nodded, and his mother led them to a guestroom she'd painted a soft green and furnished with a king-size four-poster bed sitting on a large wool rug. She'd been so excited to purchase the bed after the house construction was finished. She loved to decorate. Could spend hours or days on it. He liked things to be nice, but he hated ostentatious displays of wealth and could only think of how the money could have been better used.

"What a lovely room." Olivia went to the window to look outside.

"I'm so glad you like it." His mother preened. "I'll leave you to get settled, and I'll let you know when your sister arrives."

Olivia turned. "Thank you so much for letting all of us disrupt your life."

"It will be nice to have the house filled with people, and of course, having children around is always a treat."

She headed for the door and stopped near Rick. "Dinner will be at seven. It's just a casual thing, so come when you like."

"Thank you." Olivia offered another smile.

Rick was thankful for her kindness, as he doubted his mother got many genuine smiles in her life. He needed to make an effort to be a better son while he stayed with her.

The moment the door closed Olivia faced him. "Why are we here?"

"I told you. It's the safest place for you right now."

"I'm sure there are plenty of safe places for me. You're clearly uncomfortable here and haven't been back for seventeen years, so why choose it?"

"It seemed like a good idea at the time."

"And now?"

"Now I'll go to my room so you can rest."

She arched a brow. He'd disappointed her, too. He honestly wanted to tell her about his past, to explain, but he didn't want to be analyzed by her—by anyone. He turned to leave.

"Your mother seems nice," Olivia called after him.

"She is," he replied, not willing to take the bait.

"And yet you don't talk to her."

His steps faltered, and he looked over his shoulder. "And I don't talk about her either. My room is three doors down on the left. Let me know if you need anything. Otherwise I'll see you when your sister arrives, and I'll help them get settled in the guesthouse."

He stepped into the hallway and firmly closed the door. His mother stood at the end of the hall, her eyebrow raised. He forced out a smile and headed in the other direction before she started asking questions, too.

In case she considered following him, he quickly entered his room and closed the door. Look at him. A grown man and he was running away from his mother as he had as a kid when she'd disappointed him.

He ran his gaze over his teenage room, waiting for the space decorated in navy blue and taupe to evoke any feeling within, but he was numb. He slid his gaze to his football trophies, sitting on built-in shelves right where he'd left them. He'd loved football. Loved the concept of team that had been missing in his family. But he still felt empty. No emotions. Nothing. No, that wasn't quite true. Bitter bile rose up in his throat at the thought of the teenager who'd desperately wanted love from his dad. To be seen for who he was and what he wanted in life, not what his father wanted.

Enough. Self-pity never got him anywhere. Forget the past. He'd done it for years. He was an adult, for crying out loud. He didn't need to let a visit to this place entice him into wallowing in self-pity over his childhood.

He went to his desk under the window looking over the backyard. Right. Backyard. More like groomed park. His computer hadn't survived the damage from when he'd dropped it, but Kaci already had a new replacement for him. He put it on the desk and turned it on. His phone rang, and when he saw Brynn's name, he grabbed it in hopes she had a lead.

"What's up?" He tried to sound casual, but he heard the tension lingering in his own voice.

"I struck out on lifting a fingerprint on the receipt. I did recover DNA from both the receipt and the doc's purse. No match in the database, but the two profiles match."

"So our shooter and Olivia's attacker are the same guy, and he *did* go to McDonald's. Just not one close by."

"We really need to get the locals moving on the expanded search."

"Agreed." He thanked her, then hung up and texted Max to push the locals on the videos. He moved to his e-mail, the first one from Kaci. She'd enhanced the park video and run the suspect through facial recognition to no avail. She attached several images of the park suspect she'd sharpened and enlarged and also included the surveillance video from Chick-fil-A that she'd received after Max had served a warrant.

Rick started with the shot of the guy in the park that was now precise enough to show his camos weren't regulation. Rick sent the picture to his phone so he could show it to Olivia later, and then moved on to the shadow on the shooter's arm, now clear enough to prove Olivia's theory that he had a tattoo there that matched Griffin's tat. This guy had to be connected to Griffin. Rick switched to the boot photo. The Marine Corps emblem of eagle, globe, and anchor was embossed on the heels of boots that Rick recognized as the marines' authorized Belleville 590 hot-weather boot.

With the guy not wearing an official uniform, even with official Marine Corps boots, Rick wouldn't jump to the conclusion that this guy was a marine. The boot could have been bought online, but Rick had to admit that with the tattoo connection to Griffin, the guy in the video was most likely a fellow marine.

Rick started the Chick-fil-A surveillance video. The parking lot camera caught Griffin heading inside, and a few minutes later a guy wearing jeans and a camo jacket hopped down from the cab of an older flatbed truck. The license plates were too low for the camera to record, but "GMC" was displayed in large letters on the grille, and it appeared to be a two-ton model. This guy also wore tan boots, but only a flash of them were visible as his feet dropped to the pavement out of camera range.

He shifted his jacket, giving Rick a glimpse of a holster and handgun on his left side. So the guy was carrying. Could be trailing Griffin, too. He strolled toward the restaurant and rubbed the back of his left arm over his mouth. He revealed a tattoo on the inside of his wrist. Excitement over the lead building, Rick froze the screen to zoom in.

Semper fi. Really? The guy had a *Semper fi* tattoo? Meant odds were good that he was a marine. Had one of their own stolen the weapon that had killed Griffin? A weapon that would likely be used against marines in the future?

Angry, Rick slammed a fist on the desktop with baseball cards displayed under a layer of glass. He wanted to punch the wall, too, but he started the video playing instead. The camera caught a clear shot of the guy's face.

"What the..." Rick zoomed in, then his mouth fell open.

The man in the camo jacket, the guy facing him on the camera, wasn't the man in the park video. Was he the shooter's accomplice, confirming that two men really were in on the smart-bullet theft, as Erickson had claimed? If so, that meant not one but two men could possess the lethal ordnance and end a life with every pull of the trigger.

* * *

Rick chased Olivia's nephew Wylie, then picked him up and swung him around. The four-year-old's giggles rang through the air, and Rick let go of the investigation for a moment to laugh along with the redheaded, freckle-faced boy. He didn't take after his mother in appearance. Rick had only caught a quick look at Dianna when she'd entered the guesthouse, but her haggard expression and the dark circles under her eyes told him she was stressed out. Wylie didn't look like his baby sister either, so Rick figured the boy resembled his wayward father.

Rick twirled the child one last time. Wylie giggled again,

his mouth splitting into a big smile, his eyes going wide. Rick didn't remember such childhood fun, and he doubted that such joyous laughter had ever been heard on this property.

He couldn't resist hugging the boy one more time before setting him down. He raced across the lawn as fast as his chubby legs could carry him, tumbled onto the grass, then picked himself up and took off again.

Rick's heart lifted with rare joy. "Seems like he never stops."

"Only when he sleeps. Even then, he's a wiggler." Olivia peered up at him. "You're so good with Wiley. Do you have a lot of experience with kids?"

"Me? No."

"So no brothers and sisters?"

"None. Not even cousins." He worked hard to keep the loneliness that his secluded childhood had brought from his tone. His lost son came to mind, and he forced himself to ignore the thought, as he was already facing way too much turmoil from being here. He turned his thoughts to his friend Levi and his son instead.

Levi was still an active-duty sniper, but had served as Rick's spotter for the last five years of Rick's military career. Rick had texted his buddy from the plane and learned Levi was deployed but due back later in the week to visit his family before heading back to Camp Pendleton in California, where he was stationed. Three years was too long not to see a guy he'd basically been connected at the hip with for five years. If the team completed its mission before Levi's return, Rick might ask for a few days off.

"I *am* godfather to my buddy Levi's son. I know you have a brother and sister. Any other siblings?"

She shook her head and shifted sleeping Natalie higher on her shoulder, looking like a natural herself.

"Do you want children of your own?" he asked.

"Someday. Yeah. But I'd actually have to be in a relationship for that to happen, and I don't even have time to date, so . . ."

He was irrationally happy to hear she wasn't dating. "Job taking up all your time?"

"Yes, and for the last few months, it's been Dianna and the kids. And even if she didn't need me, with the way Jason bailed on her, I'd be hard-pressed to get married and have children."

For some reason her viewpoint on marriage bothered him, and he wanted to give her hope. "Not all marriages split up."

"I get that, but I also know people who leave the military have a much higher rate of divorce."

"So Jason was military?"

"A marine. Like you." She shook her head. "I don't blame him. Not really. He's another living casualty of war."

"You mean PTSD?"

"He never sought treatment and is a totally private guy, so I can't be sure, but he's had a difficult time since reentering civilian life." She shook her head. "One good thing about my practice is I know never to get involved with a man who has a military background. Odds aren't good for that kind of relationship to work out."

"Ouch." He mimed sticking a knife in the chest because that's exactly what her comment felt like. Not that he'd do anything about pursuing a relationship with her, but he wanted to be the person who ruled it out.

"Sorry, but that's how I feel." She continued to rub the baby's back. "How about you? Do you want kids?"

He didn't know how to answer her.

She cleared her throat. "Is that a tough question?"

"No. I'd like kids. But it's not gonna happen for me."

Her eyebrow quirked up in that shrink sort of way, her counselor stare trying to dig deep. Just as he'd predicted.

Time to move them on. "We probably should get these guys back to Dianna if we don't want to be late for dinner."

"But your mom said it was an informal meal and to arrive whenever."

"Trust me when I say there is nothing informal in my family. My dad always demanded we have dinner on time. Even if he was out of town, my mom enforced the rules, and despite saying otherwise, she'll expect us at seven."

Wylie came buzzing at them, his arms outstretched, mimicking an airplane, and Rick whisked the boy onto his shoulders. "Time to go, bud."

"Aw. I wanted to see inside the castle."

"Castle?"

"Over there." He jabbed a stubby finger in the direction of the main house. "I've never been in one."

"I'll make sure you get to visit the castle before you have to go home."

Wylie planted his hands on the sides of Rick's face and pulled his head up to look at him. "Promise?"

"Promise."

The four of them turned toward the guesthouse. Wylie chatted on and on about the size of the yard and the castle and asked where the drawbridge was located. Olivia answered his questions, but Rick simply enjoyed the chatter and joy of a child's wonderment. The peace and calm he felt with Olivia walking beside him. The soft breeze chasing away the humidity for once.

He'd always wanted kids so he could be the parent he'd never had, but marrying again was a pipe dream. One that at this very moment he wished could become a reality.

Back at the guesthouse, it took twenty minutes to get Natalie into her portable crib, to convince Wylie that he needed to stay with his mother, and to promise to have dinner delivered to them. As Dianna put it, she wasn't up to mingling with the crowd.

They were stepping out the door when Dianna called out, "I almost forgot, Sis. Harrison called. He wants to know why you didn't invite him and Mom to stay here."

Olivia spun. "Why would I?"

"He said since I was getting a free vacation, he should, too."

"This isn't a vacation," Olivia replied, a sigh in her tone. "You know why I'm staying here, and if I'm to help you out with Natalie, so do you."

Dianna held up her hands. "You told me not to tell him about your situation, so don't shoot the messenger."

"Sorry. I . . . " Olivia shrugged. "I'll call him and explain."

Outside she marched down the sidewalk and onto the stone path leading across the estate. Man. She could move fast when she was irritated.

As much as Rick enjoyed seeing her long legs moving below her shorts, he caught up to her and tugged on her arm. "Hey, slow down. You'll get overheated at that pace."

"I'm worried about Dianna, and I burn my worry off with movement," she said. It surprised him that she could be thinking about her sister after hearing about her brother's selfish ploy. "Plenty of women do well as single mothers, but Dianna doesn't really have the fortitude to handle it."

"She could surprise you." His thoughts turned to Traci, who couldn't handle being a single parent either.

"She could at that, but if she doesn't, I'll pick up her slack."

"Like you do for your brother and mother?"

She shot him a testy look. "You have no idea what's going on there, so leave it alone."

"You're right. I don't." He wanted to ask for details, but it had nothing to do with his investigation, and he'd given her the silent treatment about his life, so turnabout was fair play. He kept his mouth shut and walked by her side.

If only when Traci was alive, she'd had a caring sister like Olivia—any living relative, for that matter—things might have been different. She'd be alive. He'd have a nearly five-year-old child of his own. A boy racing across the grass as Wylie had done. A son to lift into his arms and hold close as every child deserved.

"Sorry." Olivia's steps slowed. "I didn't mean to snap at you, too." She sighed. "Promise me that you won't tell anyone that I have such crazy drama in my family. No self-respecting psychologist should allow such dysfunction in their life."

"I suspect you're human, too." He chuckled.

"Gee, thanks. I think." She wrinkled her nose before a full-fledged smile brightened her face, stealing thoughts of everything but how remarkable it would be to kiss her.

Seriously. He wanted to kiss her. Right here, right now. Out on the lawn in front of anyone who might be looking out a window or gawking from the patio. A woman he barely knew. A suspect, for Pete's sake. One he still couldn't prove had told him the truth about her involvement with Griffin's death.

He jerked his gaze away, and they walked for some distance in silence before she looked up at him.

"This property is amazing," she said.

"It is."

"You said the house was built when you were in high school, right?"

He nodded. "The original house was much smaller and far less formal. Most of the grounds were wooded, and I used to spend a lot of time hanging out in them." Time when his parents were too busy climbing the social ladder to pay much attention, and when he'd come to depend on Yolanda.

"This place never really felt like home," he added, but at the widening of her eyes, he wished he'd kept his mouth shut.

"And that's why it was so easy to leave for the service?"

"Partially." He left it at that. He'd already discussed more of his personal business with her than he'd wanted to.

The patio came into view, the team sitting in lounge chairs, laughing and boisterous, providing him with a change of subject. "I should warn you that my team is a force to be reckoned with, and they might be a bit overwhelming."

"No need to worry on my account. I deal with soldiers and law enforcement professionals all the time. I can handle myself."

He glanced at her to see whether she was putting on a show for him or truly believed what she'd said, and he found confidence in her gaze. She was so not like Traci. Olivia was a proud woman, standing tall and strong, while Traci had been shy and submissive. The type of woman he believed he best fit with. A complement to his strong personality.

Maybe he was wrong. Maybe he was best paired with a strong woman who could take care of herself during his deployments and not depend on his presence to keep her going. He could be onto something here.

So what? He wasn't going there with her or anyone. He couldn't risk putting another woman through his frequent absences only for her to buckle under the pressure.

CHAPTER

14

Olivia kept on their path toward an interlocking-brick patio the size of a small house. Grace had arranged lawn furniture with orange cushions in intimate conversation groups, and a teak dining table and twelve matching chairs sat under a massive pergola outlined with glittering lights. An array of colorful flowers and greenery spilled from pots to complete the resort look.

"Wow," she said to Rick. "This setting is beautiful."

He nodded, but the guy who'd almost opened up to her on the walk was long gone and locked down tight. His gaze was fixed on his mother standing by the patio doors, where she talked with Yolanda. Grace had changed into a long linen skirt with a white blouse and chunky necklace. She'd pulled back her silvery blond hair with a clasp, and sparkly earrings dangled from her ears.

Olivia glanced down at her very casual shorts and T-shirt and instantly felt out of place. Her footsteps faltered.

Rick glanced at her. "Everything okay?"

"Your mother. She's so nicely dressed for a casual dinner. I wish I'd worn something else."

"My mother always dresses formally. Besides, look at my teammates. You fit in just fine."

She ran her gaze over the team members, minus the forensic expert, sitting on plump furniture. Olivia had met all of them earlier when they'd arrived, but they'd changed clothes and now wore an assortment of tactical pants and polo shirts resembling their work attire, and, for that matter, resembling Rick's, too. A style of dress often favored by law enforcement and military personnel, if her practice told her anything.

"Before we join them, I need to show you two pictures."

"Of?"

"Kaci improved the park video, and we have another video from Chick-fil-A that might be of the shooter." He dug out his phone, tapped the screen a few times, then handed it to her. "This is the guy from the park. Swipe left to see the guy at Chick-fil-A."

She carefully studied both pictures and handed the phone right back to him so she didn't have to continue to look at the men. "They do look alike, but I still can't say if one of them is the creep who chased me. And I definitely don't know either of them."

"Okay," Rick said, sounding disappointed. "Let's join the team."

He set off, and she followed at a much slower pace. She'd told him she could hold her own with his team, but the stern expression on Agent White's face as he ran his gaze over her, measuring and testing, left her uneasy.

Agent Erwin rose from a chair and offered his seat. Olivia smiled her thanks and sat, perching on the edge to keep from relaxing and saying something she shouldn't. Rick stood next to her as if he needed to protect her. She appreciated his concern, but she really hoped she'd be able to handle herself.

"Did your sister get settled in, Dr. Dobbs?" Agent North asked.

"Yes, and it was very considerate of Rick's parents to let them stay here, too." She smiled at the young agent, who'd put her hair into pigtails and looked more like a teenager than a woman old enough to be an agent. "And please call me Olivia. All of you."

"Since we'll be spending a bit of time together, I think it's easiest if we use first names." Rick turned his gaze to his boss and held it there.

Olivia had no idea it was such a big deal to dispense with this formality, but apparently it was.

"Agreed," he said, but his attention moved to the door.

Still wearing her team uniform, Agent Young—now Brynn, Olivia supposed—marched over to them, then plopped down on the sofa by Max.

"Nice digs, Cannon." She propped her feet on the table, and Olivia had to admire her for not caring about the formality surrounding them. "You kind of downplayed the place."

Rick opened his mouth as if planning to speak, but suddenly stiffened, and his face blanched. Olivia followed his gaze to see a man stepping out the patio door. He was tall, with silvery hair, and, besides laugh lines and a small paunch, he was the spitting image of Rick.

"Your father?" she asked.

He nodded. "He was supposed to be out of town."

"What's the meaning of all this?" His father waved his hand over the crowd and approached his wife.

Olivia was too far away to hear their conversation, but Rick's father suddenly shot a look at the group. His gaze locked on

Rick, and if Olivia thought Rick had paled earlier, his tan now disappeared completely.

Their family feud was worse than she'd believed. Far worse, and her heart ached seeing how much the situation pained Rick. He was helping her with a place to stay and she could repay him by getting to the bottom of his family strife and working through it. He couldn't continue to live with an estrangement like this eating away at him. At least not live fully, and after getting to know him better, she'd begun to want happiness for him more than anything.

* * *

Rick swallowed hard and waited for his parents to approach. They strolled arm in arm across the brick, their public persona of the perfect couple in place, but he knew that behind closed doors they barely talked. At least that was the way it had been when he'd lived with them.

"Son," his father said.

Rick waited for him to offer his hand. Thankfully he didn't. If he had, Rick didn't know if he could have brought himself to shake it. The last time his father had touched him was on Rick's eighteenth birthday, when the old man's anger had exploded and he'd punched Rick in the nose. Then the mouth, breaking Rick's jaw. That was the night Rick left home.

"Please introduce me to your team." His father offered his pearly white smile that Rick wished he'd struck and damaged that night.

Rick gritted his teeth for a moment, then made the introductions. He provided each team member's specialty, and his father had a snippet of a story to share with each one of them to establish a connection. His dad believed the team was buying into his superficiality, but Rick knew his teammates. They weren't buying it at all. And Olivia? She wore her counselor face and gave nothing away.

"Dinner is ready," his mom said the second there was a break in conversation. "Our cook has asked for Rick to go first, since she always loved to spoil him. I know it's not proper etiquette, but Yolanda has been with us for so long we wouldn't want to hurt her feelings. I hope you understand."

"After you, Son." His dad gestured at the buffet set up by the house.

Rick wished he'd quit calling him *Son*. He might call the man standing before him *Father* or *Dad,* but Rick didn't much think of him that way. Sure, he'd fathered Rick, but the beating and lack of apology had long ago erased all bonds.

"I'll go first," Rick said. "But y'all come on, too." The Southern accent he'd worked so hard to eliminate to break that tie with his past resurfaced, making him even more uncomfortable. Still, he forced himself to wait for Olivia and the team to stand, then headed for the buffet.

As usual for his mother, even a spur-of-the-moment dinner was laid out with panache and fanfare. Crisp white tablecloths and polished silver along with fresh-cut roses from her garden covered a dining table large enough to seat everyone. Flowery china that had been passed down from his grandparents was stacked on the end of the buffet table, and large silver dishes were lined up like soldiers in perfect formation.

"This is a casual dinner for your mother?" Olivia whispered from behind. "I can't imagine what she'd do for a formal one."

Rick glanced back. "Crazy, right?"

"Now Ricky, give me your plate, and I'll heap it full of your favorites." Yolanda stood behind the table, spoon in hand.

Rick cringed at her use of *Ricky.* He didn't mind it, not

really, but he wouldn't live it down with the team. He hoped they hadn't heard her, but he saw the smirks. They were just too polite to say anything in front of her.

Rick handed over his plate, and Yolanda dished up the promised pulled pork, collard greens, and spaghetti salad. She'd also added plump biscuits that she hadn't mentioned making. "I left the pie in the refrigerator, but the minute you're ready, I'll whip up the cream and have it out here pronto."

Rick would get more razzing from his team, but he stepped around the table, took the plate, and set it down, then gave Yolanda a big hug.

"You're the best, Yo," he said, and he genuinely meant it. She was the closest he'd ever come to having family, except Levi, and he wanted her to know how much she meant to him.

She blushed and knuckled him on the cheek. "Oh, you go on now."

He picked up his plate and lifted it up for his team. "Enjoy every bite of your dinner, but remember to save room for the best pie you'll ever eat."

His dad was eyeing him, but he avoided eye contact while heading for the table. He put his plate at a setting on the side. His dad would take the head, and Rick didn't want to sit anywhere near him.

Rick didn't take a seat, but waited for Olivia to join him. For some odd reason, it seemed as if she was his date, and he shouldn't have gotten his food before her. When she came to the table, he pulled out her chair.

"Ah, manners," she said. "I guess your mother did rub off on you some." She wrinkled her nose.

He wanted to linger in his bad mood and didn't want to cheer up, but he had to smile at her cute expression. He sat next to her. "I think you're good for me, Doc."

She shot him a surprised look. "How so?"

He shrugged. "You just are."

Embarrassed at sharing his feelings, he dug into the cold spaghetti salad with Italian dressing, onions, green peppers, and tomatoes plus a special red spice mixed in. He groaned.

"Good?" Olivia asked.

"Try it." As his teammates came to the table, he leaned closer to Olivia. "Yo used to tell me it was fairy dust sprinkled on the noodles to get me to eat it. Tell anyone that, and I'll deny it."

She grinned and then took a bite. "Fairy dust or not, it's really good. I wonder what the spice really is."

"She's never said, but if you ask, I'm sure she'll tell you."

Once everyone was seated, his mother came to the table. "Can I get anything for anyone?"

"Please, just join us," Max said. "The team isn't used to first-class service like this, and I can't have you spoiling them. Now me—" He grinned. "Spoil away."

Even as Rick's dad took the expected seat, Rick laughed at Max's joke. It was a rare day when Max lightened up, and Rick wouldn't miss out on it.

"No need to spoil him, Mom," Rick said. "He's the boss and sits in his ivory tower while we all do the grunt work, so I'd say he's already spoiled."

Laughter rang out around the table, and Rick could say he was honestly enjoying himself.

"You know, Son," his dad said when the laughter died down "it's not all fun and games in ivory towers. We work hard there, too, don't we, Max?"

Max shot his dad a confused look, and Rick cringed at how quickly his dad had ended the good mood.

"I was kidding," Rick said. "Max doesn't work in an ivory tower. He's a government employee like the rest of the team, working untold hours for little pay. But he's making a difference in the world and saving lives, so isn't that the most important thing?"

His dad clenched his jaw.

Olivia raised her tea glass. "To everyone on the team. Thank you for your service."

Rick appreciated her saving the dinner by ending a discussion that was bound to go downhill fast. He clinked glasses with her and took a long swallow. The others started conversations, easing the awkwardness.

"Thank you," Rick whispered to her.

"You're welcome, but now you owe me." She faked twisting the ends of a mustache.

"And what do you intend to collect as payment?" he asked good-naturedly.

"You'll tell me exactly what's going on between you and your parents."

"Now?"

"Later. When we're alone. And don't think you can get away with your usual clamming up. There's no way I'll let you off the hook."

* * *

Fredrick Cannon smiled from the head of the table, his gaze running over the group as if he felt superior to them, but it was his little secret. Olivia doubted his feeling of superiority was a secret to anyone here. Rick's personality couldn't be more diametrically opposed to his father's, and she was thankful for that. Though his father was talkative and animated, all of it was superficial. She much preferred Rick's stoic behavior, because when he did say something, there was substance to it.

A squeaking noise caught Olivia's attention. She turned to find Yolanda pushing a silver trolley holding dessert plates and two pies piled high with whipped cream. She'd swirled caramel sauce through it and sprinkled nuts over all.

"Dessert," she announced.

"I won't complain about being the first one to have a piece." Rick pushed back his chair to face her.

The red-cheeked Yolanda cut and served Rick a thick piece of pie with a graham cracker crust, apples, and cream cheese filling, all of it dripping with more caramel sauce.

She rested her hand on his shoulder, and he peered up at her. Olivia wished she could see his expression, as she knew it would tell her a lot about him. He took his plate, dug in, and didn't seem as if he was coming up for air soon. When Olivia took the first bite of her slice, the sweetness exploded in her mouth and she was in dessert heaven, soon to be in a sugar coma. Others started eating, and silence fell over the table, moans of appreciation the only sounds.

"It's just a sugary dessert, for Pete's sake," Fredrick said, but no one paid him any attention, and they all continued eating.

Kaci's phone dinged, earning her a sharp look from Rick's father. "We don't allow phones at our table."

"Our work doesn't stop for anything."

Olivia was impressed with the young agent's ability to stand up to Fredrick.

She glanced at the text, then looked up and met Max's gaze. "Will you and Rick join me for a minute?"

As they got up, the joy of the evening evaporated from their faces. Olivia lost all interest in her pie and sat back to watch them. They chatted for only a moment before returning to the table.

Rick stopped by Grace's chair. "We need a private meeting space. Can we use the library?"

"Of course," she said. "Would you all like some coffee?"

Rick shook his head.

"I'll be glad to powwow with you if I can be of help," Fredrick offered.

Rick's mouth fell open for a second before he snapped it shut. "Let's go, team."

"Can I bring the pie?" Shane asked.

"You won't want it once you hear the latest," Max warned.

Olivia's stomach tightened against the delicious meal she'd consumed.

Rick bent down. "If you wouldn't mind waiting here, we might need to call you into the meeting."

"Of course." She tried to sound calm but couldn't help wondering what could be so dire and at the same time be connected to her.

He hurried to catch up with his teammates, who were stepping in through the patio doorway. She watched his powerful strides, his body tense with a sense of urgency, and she suddenly felt alone. It was hard to believe it hadn't even been two full days since she'd wished he would leave her alone. How had she gone from wanting that to wanting him to sit next to her?

"Can I get you some coffee, sweetheart?" Yolanda asked.

Olivia swung her gaze to Yolanda. "You mean me?"

"Why, of course. I can tell you're about as sweet as my pie."

Olivia forced out a smile. "Coffee would be great."

She didn't want it, but she also didn't want to hurt Yolanda's feelings.

"I'll put the pie away and grab some." She loaded items onto her cart. "Land sake, but I didn't expect the night to end this way. Our boy Ricky has a mighty tough job."

Fredrick harrumphed, and Grace fired him an irritated look.

So Grace wasn't all prim and proper. It was looking more and more like Rick took after her.

"Can I help you get the coffee?" Grace asked Yolanda.

She waved a hand and disappeared with her cart.

"Why don't the two of you join me in more comfortable seating?" Fredrick asked, but it was issued as a command.

Olivia followed him to the seating area where the team had earlier lounged. She took one end of the sofa, and he sat on the other end, Grace in the love seat facing them. Olivia hadn't wanted to go with the team, but there might be less turmoil in the library than she would experience in the tension that existed between Grace and Fredrick Cannon.

15

Rick waited to speak until everyone was seated on the nail-studded leather chairs and sofa and Cal had joined them via phone.

"This better be worth it," Cal said over the speakerphone. "Tara and I were settling in together, if you get my drift."

"TMI, man," Brynn said, and tight laughter broke out.

"So what's going on?" Cal asked.

"Kaci just received a text from one of her analysts. She had him continue regular searches of ViCAP for crimes similar to Griffin's murder and for the chaos tattoo."

Shane sat forward, his eyes riveted to Kaci. "And they found something?"

She nodded. "A police detective just input a murder, and we think it could involve a smart bullet."

"Where?" Cal asked.

"Mobile, Alabama. The former marine, a Cesar Santos, was plugged from a long distance walking down the street at night. The bullet went clean through him and lodged in a fence post."

Rick didn't correct her by saying marines never thought of themselves as former. Being a marine was a mind-set. A lifestyle. Nothing ever changed that.

"When was he murdered?" Brynn asked.

"Six days ago, but the detective only entered it in the database in the last hour."

"Are we certain it's related?" Shane asked.

Rick shook his head. "But there are too many similarities not to consider them."

"Name them," Cal demanded.

"The victim has a matching chaos tattoo and served in the marines," Rick said. "He was killed early in the morning on a deserted street. He died from a large-caliber wound from a gun fired at a distance. Single shot. Experts say the shooter used a knife to remove the bullet from the fence. Because the police didn't recover the slug, we can't be certain it was a .50 or even a smart bullet."

"Sounds like the shooter didn't want law enforcement to discover the smart bullet," Cal said.

Rick nodded. "That's what I'm thinking, and we have a shooter with a knife like the guy seen lurking over Griffin."

"Exactly," Max said. "As if he planned to recover the bullet at that scene, too, but Olivia interrupted him."

"The real kicker is that the victim is also . . ." Hating to utter these next words, Rick paused for a moment. "Olivia's former client."

As he'd expected, conversation erupted among his teammates.

Brynn cleared her throat, and the conversation stilled. "It can't be a coincidence."

"Could be," Rick said trying to dispel the look of doubt in Brynn's eyes, but he didn't honestly believe it. "And we can't limit our investigation to the connection to Olivia."

"Perhaps both victims were involved in the ordnance theft," Shane suggested. "And the shooter turned on them to cut them out of the money."

"Sounds plausible," Max said. "Though we still don't have any evidence to suggest Griffin was in on the planning, and we do know he didn't execute."

"We need to discover the whereabouts of this Santos fellow on that night," Shane said.

"Speaking of the theft, where are you with MilMed, Cal?" Rick asked.

"I've reviewed all of the internal correspondence." Cal's voice carried across the room. "No one other than the five people Erickson told you about were included in communications. I also interviewed the staff and have a potential lead with the security guard. Turns out he has a drinking problem, and he's known to brag about his work. He's a police academy washout and wants to feel more important. I'll be interviewing him in the morning to see if he told anyone about the delivery."

"Keep us informed," Max said.

"Now might be a good time to tell you I lifted a boot print from the woods," Brynn said. "Size eleven, I'd guess. Looks like the tread from a military or combat boot. I took high-resolution 3-D images of the print and sent them off to an expert for evaluation."

"The guy in the park video was wearing Belleville 590s with the USMC emblem embossed on them," Rick said.

"I'll text my expert so he can run a comparison." She took out her phone and started tapping the screen.

"I wish I could say the print helps us narrow in on one suspect," Rick said. "But after talking to Erickson and seeing the guy in the Chick-fil-A video isn't the same guy from the park, we now know that at least two men are involved in the theft. The guy in the park has a chaos tattoo matching Griffin's. The odds of them not being connected have to be astronomical."

Kaci's eyes lit up. "I could actually plug it into an algorithmic and give you the exact odds, but they are long indeed."

If Rick didn't know that Kaci was an extreme geek, he would think she was joking at a time like this.

"The guy at Chick-fil-A had a *Semper fi* tattoo on his left wrist," Rick continued. "And was wearing a camo jacket like the one Olivia witnessed the night of Griffin's murder. He also was strapped, carrying on his left side."

"A lefty, like the guy with the knife," Brynn said.

Rick nodded. "I showed both photos to Olivia, and she didn't recognize either guy."

"Or at least she claims she doesn't know them." Brynn eyed him as if waiting for him to admit his interest in Olivia that Brynn had witnessed in the park. She was a strong team player, and as such she often felt she needed to protect the others from anyone with questionable motives.

He didn't acknowledge it, though. "I stand corrected."

"I've run the second guy through facial recognition, too," Kaci said. "No match. Just like the other suspect."

Shane tapped his chin. "So we're dealing with thieves with no prior record. Stealing the smart bullet is pretty brazen if they're novices."

"Maybe they just haven't been caught," Brynn said.

Max's forehead creased. "Either way there's no doubt we're looking at two suspects now."

"Anything else in the video to help our cause?" Shane asked.

"The guy drove a two-ton GMC truck. Flatbed. White. It had something strapped on the back and covered with canvas. Looked like motorcycle handlebars—a pair of bikes side by side—under there, but that's my gut feel. Still, the truck is something to go on."

"I can return to the ranges and clubs I visited today with the new suspect's picture," Shane offered. "Plus I now have the *Semper fi* tat to share and the truck picture, if you'll send it to me. Like I said yesterday, other guys might not remember a face, but will be all over a tat and a truck."

"I'll e-mail you a list of the people Griffin worked with in the past so you can ask about them, too," Kaci said.

"I've tasked the locals with interviewing them," Rick added. "But they might miss a connection to a shooting range or gun club, so it's a great idea to check it out while you're at it."

"Okay." Brynn sat forward, her eyes narrowed. "I'll mention the elephant in the room. Are we all still thinking that Olivia might have something to do with the theft and shooting or not?"

"I admit it looks bad that Santos was also her client," Rick said before anyone else could weigh in. "But we haven't uncovered a motive for her to be involved. Plus I've spent more time with her than the rest of you, and I don't see it."

Shane eyed him. "You could be getting too close."

"I concur," Brynn said.

Rick shook his head, but wondered if they were right. No. He hadn't gotten too close to make solid decisions, but he'd lost a bit of his edge.

"So what's the plan?" ever-practical Cal asked.

"Not that I've had a chance to work out any details, but I need to talk with the detective in Mobile, review evidence, and view the crime scene." Rick looked at Kaci. "Once I have Santos's time of death, I'll be asking you to confirm that Olivia was here in Atlanta. I highly doubt that she's the shooter, but—"

"You're assuming she wasn't here?" Max interrupted.

Rick shook his head. "I'm assuming she'll provide us with an alibi for the time of the murder, and we'll need to verify it."

Max nodded, but he was holding something back, and Rick didn't like the look. Max likely had the same opinion as Shane and Brynn, that Rick was getting too close to Olivia. If Rick saw a teammate go to bat for a suspect without any proof of their innocence, he might have the same opinion.

"The murder occurred on a public street, and the crime scene has likely been compromised by now," Brynn said. "There's no point in me tagging along. I'm available via virtual reality if you need me."

Rick nodded and thought it might be worth not having Brynn on site for the rare chance to use their Google Glass display with the virtual reality app. "Unless something else comes up, I'll leave for Mobile first thing in the morning."

Rick's mind was barreling ahead a million miles per hour and he needed more information and time to make sound decisions. But one thing he did know, the next step was to question Olivia. "It's time we find out what Olivia knows about Santos."

Max ran a practiced eye over Rick.

"I'll go get her." Rick took a step to leave.

"There's one more thing I need to mention before Olivia joins us," Kaci called out. She chewed on her lip, telling Rick she didn't want to bring up whatever she was planning to say.

"Out with it," Max said.

"I hacked into MilMed's network, and you won't believe what I found."

"You did what?" Max shot to his feet.

"Erickson was being such a doofus telling us that their network was impenetrable. I wanted to prove him wrong to get him to take us seriously and cooperate."

Max spun on Rick. "Did you know about this?"

"I knew she planned to try, but not that she succeeded." He shifted his focus to Kaci. "What did you find?"

"There were other technologies in the van carrying the self-steering bullets, and they were stolen, too."

"Technologies like what?" Max asked.

"I don't know yet, but if they didn't tell us about these items there might be other things they haven't mentioned, and we need to know about them."

Max scowled. "Or we don't have the security clearance to be read in on the other technology."

Kaci closed her computer. "Um...well...if that's the case, I've really messed up."

"Meaning you've been poking around in their network," Max said.

"Well, yeah, I mean I am a nerd after all." She grinned. "And not looking deeper would be like telling one of you not to get excited about the latest weapon to come on the market."

"Fair point," Max said. "But we wouldn't hack into a site to read about a weapon's prototype."

"Because you can't, but—"

"But nothing," Max snapped. "You better hope when we tell MilMed about the hack that they don't press charges for going beyond proving they're hackable." Max mumbled something under his breath, then faced Rick. "Get Olivia."

As Rick headed for the door, he couldn't help but smile over Kaci's hack. She'd simply done what any of them would have done in the situation—gone the extra mile to try to end a very volatile situation.

On the patio Rick found Olivia seated near the fire pit with his parents. Guilt over leaving her to fend for herself had him hurrying across the space. She looked up and met his gaze with a thankful one.

"We'd like to talk to you." Rick made sure to keep any angst over the latest killing out of his tone.

She was out of the chair so fast he had to stifle a chuckle over her desire to leave.

"Would you all like some coffee now?" his mother asked.

"We're good, but thanks."

"I'm still available to help," his father offered.

"Law enforcement isn't in your wheelhouse." *Getting arrested for punching your son's lights out is.*

Rick gestured for Olivia to precede him.

Once they were out of earshot, she leaned closer. "I thought you were a force to be reckoned with. And Max, too, but I have never met a man as intense as your father. In a completely different way, though."

"Different how?" he asked.

"His confidence isn't real like yours and Max's is. So he has to prove himself all the time. He's afraid that someone will see through him and find his true insecurity, so he defends that soft underbelly even if it means becoming aggressive and disrespectful."

Rick stopped walking in the large lower-level rec room to look at her. "You got all of that in what, thirty minutes or less?"

"I'm trained to read between the lines."

"And your between-the-lines reading says my confidence is real, huh?"

She laid a hand on his arm. "If you're worried that you're like your father, you can let that go right now."

"I'm not worried about that. Trust me."

She nodded, but he could see she didn't buy it. Shoot, maybe he *had* been harboring the belief that he acted like his dad and had been a tyrant and bully to Traci when he'd come home from deployment. He'd tried to adjust to civilian life as quickly as she'd wanted, but he'd just lost friends, mentors, saw others being blown up, losing limbs. So sliding back into the minutiae of everyday tasks like taking out the trash, fighting traffic, even showering seemed pointless when he would deploy again and see the same terrible things, maybe lose his own life.

"But your mom is a real sweetheart," Olivia continued, jerking him free from his thoughts. "Once you get beyond the social superficiality." Olivia smiled. "She told me stories about you growing up, Ricky."

He groaned. "I wondered how long it would take for someone to use that name."

"You mean I was the first?" She wrinkled her nose, the freckles connecting into solid spots. "Then you all must be dealing with a huge problem, as I can't imagine your teammates not ribbing you about that right away."

Exactly.

"Can you give me a heads-up on what to expect?" she asked.

"Sorry. I need to wait until the entire team is present."

She nodded, but her face took on the same hurt expression Traci had always worn whenever he'd failed her. He couldn't do anything about it, so he started walking again and escorted Olivia upstairs.

"I'm impressed with the way your entire team works together," she continued. "I sense that there's some strong egos in the group, and the fact that you all can put that aside and work as a team speaks to your skills."

"*Some* strong egos?" He laughed and shook his head. "We're all guilty of that, but we have the same goal. Right the wrong and do so expediently. Plus we're all former military and can draw on our ability to follow when needed. Gives you a sense of brotherhood like nothing else can."

He opened the glass library doors and waited for her to enter, but she stopped to look around the room. He wondered what she thought of the heavy furniture his father had chosen. Or the many bookshelves his mother had packed with first editions and other expensive leather-bound books. All books his father never took a moment to read. Fiction, he said, was for the lazy. Self-help and entrepreneurial books were for the successful man.

At a small round table, Rick pulled out a chair for her. She sat and clasped her hands in her lap. "Okay. I'm ready. What is it?"

"Do you know a Cesar Santos?" Kaci asked.

"He was my client. Don't tell me he's involved in this."

"Did he know Ace?" Max asked.

"Not that I remember, but I worked with Cesar long before I knew Ace, so it's possible." She shifted in her chair. "They were both marines. I suppose they could have met there."

"With the size of the marine corps, the opposite is also possible," Rick said, but he doubted his own statement.

Olivia sat forward. "If it's important, we can check my records first thing in the morning to see if they ever mentioned each other in a session."

"What about your other clients? Might they have known Ace or Cesar?" Rick decided to follow the same tack they'd taken with Griffin, using his first name to keep Olivia more relaxed and open.

"Again, not that I know of, but I mostly work with PTSD clients, so it's possible." She shifted in her chair, sitting up higher.

"How are clients referred to you?" Brynn asked.

"I can't receive official referrals from the VA because I'm a Christian counselor, but there are a few doctors on staff there who send patients my way. And doctors in private practice who don't handle PTSD refer, too, as do clients."

"Do you keep a record of how a client is referred?" Brynn asked.

"If a doctor or the VA refers them, yes, as I also request records. If they self-refer or another patient refers, no."

"There was nothing in Ace's file about Cesar referring him, but might he have done so?"

"I don't remember that happening."

"When's the last time you spoke with Cesar?" Rick asked.

"At his last appointment. Right before he moved back to Mobile. Again, it's been years, so I'll have to check my records to be certain, but I don't recall having a reason to talk with him after that."

Rick watched her carefully for any disingenuousness but found none. But then, how could she be so uncertain about a former client? Didn't sit right with him, as if he'd been wrong about her, and she really didn't care about her clients.

"So he moved, and that's why your counseling relationship ended?" he asked.

"That and he'd finished his treatment, so it would have ended soon anyway." She rubbed her palms over her shorts.

He hated seeing her so nervous, but couldn't let that stop his questions. "Do you know why he moved?"

"Cesar and his wife reconciled during counseling, and they moved back to her hometown." She cocked her head. "Why all the questions about him anyway?"

"He was killed six days ago by a large-caliber round," Rick said.

She gasped, and her hand flew to her chest. "Like Ace, you mean?"

"We don't have details, but there are some similarities."

"Then you have to look into it. Find out why anyone would kill him." She bit her lip and seemed to be processing the news when her eyes suddenly widened. "Oh my gosh. Do you think someone is targeting my clients or former clients? But who? I mean that's crazy, right? Wait. This killer *is* crazy. Okay, fine, that's not a word a psychologist should use. So unstable, then. Demented. Either way, he's a killer."

She drew in a deep breath and panted as if heading for an anxiety attack.

Rick sat in a chair next to her and made eye contact. "Breathe, Olivia. Just breathe."

She shot a look around at the team members. "I'm sorry. I'm not usually this unsettled, but he killed two of my clients." She shot out a hand and gripped Rick's arm. "Could this be why he shot at me today? Because he has some grudge against me, like you said? Maybe something related to Ace and Cesar?"

"Or he has an unhealthy attraction to you," Cal said, and Rick knew he was thinking about the man who'd targeted his wife not too long ago. "He might want to eliminate the men in your life."

"The only man in my life is my brother, but I suppose if the killer had lost touch with reality he could see my clients as something other than clients. Still, I can't think of anyone who displayed such an attraction."

"But you can't totally rule it out?" Max asked.

She shook her head.

"Would explain why someone tried to kill you outside your office," Rick said. "But with no contact with Cesar for years, it wouldn't explain why he was murdered."

"Then let's push this thought to the back burner for now," Max said.

Rick regretted having to say his next thought aloud, but it was best coming from him. "We'll need to know where you were at Cesar's time of death."

"Me? You suspect me?" He hadn't thought her voice could

go higher, but it was as shrill as a bottle rocket screaming into the air. "You think I killed him. That's ludicrous. I've never even held a gun, much less shot one. I hate them. Ever since my dad...I would never own one. The police even checked at Ace's murder scene to see if I had a bruise from shooting a gun. I didn't then. I don't now." She pulled aside her shirt to reveal a bruise-free, creamy shoulder.

"We'll take that into account." Rick wished not having a bruise proved she hadn't fired the M82A3 rifle that had been modified for smart bullets. The weapon had a significant muzzle suppressor that helped reduce the recoil, thus reducing bruising. Also it was heavy, and the resulting recoil wasn't bad. If she'd fired this bad boy and hadn't wanted a bruise, she'd have had to pull it tight and make good contact between the weapon's shoulder stock and her shoulder.

He tried to imagine her lying behind this weapon, one of the girlie skirts she liked to wear splayed out. Her sky-high-heeled pumps lying flat. Her finger with the brightly polished nail dropping down to the trigger.

Nah. She was a girlie girl. All feminine and seemingly without the least interest in firearms. True, that was a superficial, maybe sexist evaluation, but his gut said he was on target. So if she'd never shot a gun, hated them actually, that would make her a prime candidate for not holding the weapon correctly and sustaining a bruise. Still...

"Our background check on you will continue," he said.

"It's a waste of time looking into me. I could never...I never." She sighed. "I wouldn't hurt Cesar or anyone else."

"Doesn't mean you don't know the shooter."

"But I don't." Her eyes filled with anguish. "Have you all been thinking I was the killer all this time?"

Rick wanted to assure her that he didn't think she was the

shooter, as he really didn't, but he couldn't speak for everyone in the room. "The person who finds a body is always suspected of a connection to the murder until we can rule them out, and you found Ace."

She pinched the bridge of her nose, and it cut him to the quick to have to keep her on his suspect list, but like it or not, he had a job to do here. "If there's anything you think I should know, you should tell me now."

"Like what? That I'm a secret serial killer? That I have an arsenal of weapons hidden in my home?" Her voice rose with each statement, and her gaze cut wildly around the room, her crestfallen expression making him feel even worse. He wished he could let go of his distrust, but he couldn't until clear-cut facts proved her innocence.

"We have to do our due diligence," Max said. "And that means knowing where you were when Cesar died."

"Okay." She clasped her hands together. "I keep a detailed schedule. If he was killed during the day, I'll be able to give you my exact location and my clients can vouch for me. Weekends and evenings I spend with Dianna."

Rick nodded and refrained from saying that with her sleeping pills, Dianna was in no position to provide a nighttime alibi for Olivia. "Once we have the details on the investigation, we'll let you know."

"I don't want that suspicion hanging over my head, so how long will that be?"

"I'm heading to Alabama tomorrow to talk to the detective for Cesar's investigation, and maybe that will shed light on the subject."

"Wouldn't it be faster to request his reports by e-mail?"

"Perhaps, but I want to visit the crime scene and talk to any witnesses."

She nodded absently, seeming lost in her thoughts, before her eyes widened. "Can I come with you? I'd like to pay my respects to Cesar's wife. My friend Patsy lives in Mobile, so I can stay with her if we need to spend the night. You could, too, if you want."

Rick nodded and caught the look in his teammates' eyes. They were thinking the same thing he was. She might have made her quick request to accompany him because she was a special person who really did want to offer condolences to a grieving widow, or because she had other motives. The very reason he would make sure she remained in his sight at all times.

16

Friday, September 15
8:12 a.m.

Olivia and Rick headed up to the stairs to Olivia's office, where they planned to review her records to see if Ace or Cesar ever mentioned each other. Key at the ready, she rounded the corner to her office and came to a screeching halt. "The door's open."

Rick pushed past her and drew his weapon. "Stay out here and call 911."

She reached for her phone, but Rick's smooth movements mesmerized her as he eased up on the door and flattened his back against the wall, reminding her of a sleek panther seeking his prey. He shot a quick look inside, then back at her. "Make that call."

His pointed look had her dialing while he disappeared inside.

"FBI," he called out. "Show yourself."

The 911 operator answered the call, and Olivia reported the break-in while trying to listen for any indication that Rick was in danger. She heard only silence from her office. She moved closer to the door to listen.

"Is anyone injured?" the operator asked, making Olivia jump.

"I don't know about injuries. I'm with FBI agent Rick Cannon, and he's gone inside the office to check things out."

Rick stepped into the hallway, and Olivia barely heard the operator promise to send a patrol officer before she hung up.

He holstered his gun. "The office is trashed." He gestured at her phone. "Are they sending an officer?"

She nodded and pocketed her phone. "But what's the point when you're already here?"

"Break-ins don't fall under the FBI's purview, so you'll want a local officer to take a report for insurance purposes."

She glanced at the doorway. "Can I take a look?"

"Yes, but be careful not to touch anything."

She entered the waiting room, thankful to see it was undisturbed. She approached her office, and her heart fell. Sure, Rick had told her it had been trashed, but seeing folders and reports that she'd carefully filed strewn across the floor, along with books from her shelves and items from her desk, sliced through her heart. When she spotted her favorite crystal lamp shattered in pieces, she could barely contain her tears.

She clamped a hand over her mouth to keep from sobbing and took breaths in and out through her nose. Rick stepped up behind her. Even if she hadn't heard him, the warmth of his body told her he was there. Warmth that gave her the courage not to flee. Not to turn tail and run from the invasion of her privacy and all the other disasters in her life right now.

"Does your waiting area camera record or just let you see the visitor?" he asked.

"No recordings."

"Too bad. We might have gotten a lead from it." He paused, remaining completely still behind her. "Your computer is gone. Means your files are gone, too."

She spun to look at him. She could clearly see the pores on his face and realized she was standing way too close. She stepped back rather than give in to the temptation to lean against him for support. "Why would anyone want my files?"

"As far as I see it, there are a few possibilities." His gaze darkened, telling her she wouldn't like what he had to say.

"Like?"

"Like the person who emptied your bank account believed you might have something to incriminate him on your laptop and so he took the machine."

"Then he's out of luck. I have nothing but client files on that computer."

"It could also be that Ace and Cesar's killer is worried you have something in their files that will incriminate him."

"That makes sense." She pondered other reasons to take the computer, setting her breakfast churning in her stomach.

She glanced at Rick and found him watching her, the same suspicion lingering in his eyes that had been there last night.

"With the way you're looking at me," she said, "I'd think you believe I had someone steal my computer so you couldn't request the rest of my files or calendar to prove my alibi."

His eyebrow went up, and he didn't deny her claim.

She stared at him for a long moment, trying to make sense of the fact that he seriously believed she was a criminal. "How can you think such a thing after getting to know me?"

"It's my job. I don't have to believe everything I speculate on, but I *do* have to follow up."

Disappointment radiating through her, she lifted her chin. "I'd thought...I mean..." She shrugged.

"What?"

"I don't know...I guess...I thought we connected and there was something going on between us."

He watched her as if trying to decide what to say. "I can't deny I'm very attracted to you."

"So it's just a physical attraction?" she asked, hating that she needed to know the answer to that question.

"No."

Her heart warmed at his admission. At the same time, it cooled at the implication. "Then how can you not trust me?"

"I just can't." He folded muscled arms over his broad chest, resembling a solid wall that would never budge. "Can we leave it at that?"

"I don't want to, but you've proven how unwilling you are to talk about your life or your emotions, so I know I won't change your mind." An ache from his attitude added to her distress from the break-in and tears pricked again, but these were angry tears. Frustrated tears. She wished he would open up, but in reality she was too tired and emotional to continue this discussion right now.

She was far better off focusing on the implications of the computer theft. "This also means someone has my clients' files and their contact information. I protected my computer with a password and protected the individual files, too. If they crack the main password and actually get into my computer, they shouldn't be able to get into the files."

"You didn't use 'password' or '123,' did you?"

She shook her head. "The identity theft taught me the value of using strong passwords—it was one of several reasons the bank cited as to why they weren't responsible for replacing most of the stolen money. Now I always create random ones."

She paused to meet his gaze head-on. "And before you accuse me of involvement in the break-in to stymie the investigation, I back up my files to an external drive every

Friday and take it to my safe-deposit box. That drive holds the records we're looking for, plus my schedule for the dates in question."

Rick's scowl eased. "Assuming you're telling me the truth, which I think you are, not only can we retrieve your files, but it shows that you had nothing to gain by the computer theft."

He smiled. The charm she'd been powerless to resist replaced his intensity. Thankfully, footsteps sounded in the hallway, snapping the moment between them, and she let her brain take over for her heart.

She was such a fool. How could she be attracted to a man who believed her capable of consorting with a murderer? She studied human nature for a living, for goodness' sake, and yet here she was falling for him. Ridiculous. She needed to shrug off her crazy interest in him. Concentrate on the investigation and prove that she had nothing to do with the killer. Study her records. Find that link between Ace and Cesar so the killer could be found. That was where she needed to put her focus. Only there.

"The sooner we get a look at your files, the better," he said, echoing her thoughts.

She glanced at her watch. "The bank doesn't open until nine thirty."

"So much for our early start. I'll give Brynn a call to take over here so we can leave as soon as possible."

Olivia nodded, but the last thing she wanted to do right now was drive for four hours with a man who not only didn't trust her, but believed she could be a criminal.

* * *

Mobile County, Alabama
12:15 p.m.

Rick glanced in the rearview mirror. He'd done so for hours to make sure no one was tailing them. He was eager to get to Mobile, so he kept the speedometer hovering over the speed limit. Due to the break-in, he'd already had to change his appointment time with Detective Skinner, and Rick didn't want the guy to get mad over another change. Or maybe his lead foot was all about his conversation with Olivia. An attempt to lessen the time he was alone with her. She'd made it clear that she wanted him to open up, and shrinks couldn't resist a challenge when they saw one. He had a messy life, ripe for analyzing. Complicated issues with his parents. With Traci's loss. The loss of his child. Things he planned to keep to himself.

As if sensing he was thinking about her, she closed the computer, stretched her arms overhead, and yawned. "I'm looking forward to a good night's sleep tonight. These late nights with Natalie are exhausting."

She leaned her seat back and crossed her legs. She was wearing white capris and a black striped knit shirt with sensible flat black shoes. He couldn't help but compare her to Traci, who had been the polar opposite of Olivia. Traci had loved to wear flashy clothes and draw attention. He'd found it attractive when he was younger, but now? Now he preferred Olivia's modesty, which left far more to the imagination. A simple kiss with her would send his senses reeling. The very reason he shouldn't be alone in a car with her.

"It was nice of your mother to stay with Dianna tonight," Olivia continued, totally unaware of his wayward thoughts.

"It was at that," he replied. "Surprised me."

"Why's that? She seemed eager enough to help."

"I've never seen her with babies, so I didn't know she liked them. When I asked her to help, I figured she'd hire someone."

"But she had you, and I can't believe I'm about to say this, as I can't imagine it at all, but you were once a baby."

He glanced at her to find her grinning, and despite his best effort, he couldn't stop himself from smiling along with her, bringing Cal to mind. Since he and Tara married, he'd been annoying with all the smiling, driving the rest of the team nuts, especially Rick. There was no way he was acting the same way, was there? If he was, he needed to stop it now. He wouldn't have Max pull him off lead, and he sure wouldn't let himself fall for Olivia.

"Your mother seems very warm and compassionate," Olivia continued. "I'll bet she was a good mother."

"She's warm and compassionate," he replied and left it at that.

"But not a good mother?"

He shrugged and focused on the road, hoping Olivia would give up.

"Oh no you don't." She grabbed his arm. "No clamming up. You owe me from last night when I changed the subject, and you knew talking about your life would be the payment."

"I thought you'd forget about that."

"I won't, so you might as well tell me now and get it over with." She let go of his arm, but swiveled to face him.

He had no clue how to have a conversation with her that he'd only ever had with Traci and Levi. Better to try to avoid it again. "I'm not used to talking about my family."

"You're not used to talking about much other than the job, from what I can see. And even then it's like pulling teeth to get you to talk."

"Good point," he said, and continued to hope she'd drop the subject.

She didn't speak, but he felt her focus on him. He felt her disappointment, too. Either he could drive for their final hour with her gaze burning holes in his side, or he could answer. "I don't know where to start."

"Maybe it would help if you pretended you were on a scope, dialing in your target and putting everything else aside to focus on only one thing and start there."

"What?" He shot a quick look at her, his suspicions running rampant and telling him he was right in not trusting her. "Who taught you about dialing in a target?"

"My sniper clients said it all the time." She eyed him. "What? You still think I partnered with the shooter who took Ace out?"

That was exactly what he'd thought. "I'm sorry, but I never hear anyone but shooters talking about dialing in a scope, so when you said it...I...my mind went there."

"I wish it didn't. I wish it said, 'I can trust you and not jump to conclusions.'"

"Honestly"—he met her gaze—"I wish it did, too."

"So why can't it?"

"We had that discussion at the office."

"No, *I* had that discussion, but you clammed up."

"I didn't promise to talk about that."

She sighed. "You're right. You didn't. So let's move on. I won't use any terminology that will set you off, and we can stick to your family. Tell me about your mother."

He didn't think it was a good deal, but he tried to be a man of honor and that meant honoring his promises. "She was a great mother when I was a little kid. But when my dad started advancing in his career, she got caught up in making a name for them in top social circles. She was out of the house all the time. Luncheons. Fund-raisers. Dinner parties. I spent most of my time with Yo. Except Sunday mornings when we all attended church, I never really spent time with both of my parents. Not even holidays."

He shook his head. "Mom's a believer, but Dad went to church because it looked good to the public. He kept trying to get me to think like him—humor Mom and not buy into the whole church thing. Then, when I got old enough to develop a worldview, his need to keep raking in money no matter the consequences bothered me."

The memories hit hard, and he paused to take a cleansing breath. "We started arguing about it all the time. I was at fault, too. I did things to get under his skin. Started attending church more often. Joined the youth group. Funny thing is, what started out as rebellion ended up being good for me. I became a believer. That's when Dad really lost it. Forbid me from going to any church events outside our Sunday-morning service. And you know what? All this time my mom went along with what he wanted. Even when he said I couldn't go to church."

"What did you do?"

Olivia's attention remained fixed on him, but he couldn't look at her or he might lose it. "I went anyway and lied about it. Didn't even tell Mom because she kept siding with Dad. She never considered me in her decisions, and took his side on everything to keep up appearances at all costs."

"Parents need to present a united front."

He shot her a look then. "Even when your father breaks your jaw? Should your mother support that?"

"Your father hit you?"

"A fierce jab to the nose and uppercut to the jaw on my eighteenth birthday. I asked Mom to intervene. To take me to the ER and have him arrested. She refused. After all, we couldn't ruin the social giant Fredrick Cannon's reputation with an allegation of abuse. So I left home that evening. Haven't spent a night under their roof until last night."

"Not that there's an excuse for him hitting you, but why did he do it?"

Flashes from the altercation came racing back, and Rick tightened his hold on the wheel. "He'd made a development deal that displaced two hundred low-income families who would likely end up homeless. All to line his pockets, when we had more than enough money. I couldn't stomach his greed anymore. So I told him my life would count for something, and I was enlisting in the marines."

"And he didn't like that."

"I don't think the fact that I was going away bothered him, but it wasn't socially acceptable for the son of a powerful businessman to enlist in the service. It would embarrass him."

"But service to our country is honorable."

"Sure, maybe if I'd gone to college first and gone in as an officer. But a grunt? No way." He shook his head. "But I didn't care. I wanted to make a difference, and I couldn't do it living with them. So I stood up to him, and that's when he went off on me."

"So this is why there's such a rift between you all?"

He nodded.

"I'm not at all condoning either of their actions, but don't you think it's time to put it behind you?"

"It's so far in the rearview that I don't even think about it anymore."

"Except when you're with your parents."

"Apart from last night, that hasn't happened since the day I left. Won't happen again once we leave town, so it's not an issue."

"It's still eating away at you."

He looked at her. "I'm not forgiving them, so don't even try to convince me to do so. There's nothing you can say that will erase their betrayal."

She held up her hands and faced the window.

Right. He'd disappointed her. Of course he had. He'd been doing it all along, and that's why he didn't want to talk about his life. She couldn't understand his position. Plus she was a shrink. Wanted to fix things. Meddle. Not that it mattered. She could sit there for the rest of the drive and not say a word, and he wouldn't reconsider. Not now. Not ever. Besides, the two of them needed to stick to the investigation.

He grasped for the first thing that came to mind and gestured at his computer. "I have to admit I was surprised that you're having a hard time remembering information on former clients."

"I doubt I'll ever forget an actual client," she said, not looking at him. "But my caseload prevents me from remembering all the details."

Thankfully, she readily moved on with him, and he'd keep the discussion going, as that was far better than having the air filled with her disappointment. "How many clients do you have?"

"Typically I have about forty active clients at one time. Since I don't see them all every week, I have about twenty-five appointments in a week."

"More than I thought." Had he rushed to judgment when he'd thought not remembering former clients meant she was bad at her job or hiding something?

"I know a few psychologists who see forty people a week." She shook her head. "I don't see how they can handle that many clients. If they aren't putting in extremely long hours, it's irresponsible. Even then, that many appointments, plus the record keeping and billing, would take a toll on the doctor, and that can't be good for their clients."

"Did Cesar suffer from PTSD, too?"

She nodded.

"How long does a typical PTSD client see you?"

That question must have piqued her interest, as she glanced at him. "Typical treatment with cognitive behavioral therapy, if there is such a thing as typical, lasts for three to six months. That's the most common treatment, but other therapies can take longer. And some PTSD clients have other mental health issues, so their treatment could last for one to two years. Or even longer, as was the situation with Ace."

"So in the time since you've seen Cesar, you've had hundreds of clients."

Her eyebrow quirked up. "Why all the questions about my client load?"

"Honestly?"

She nodded.

"Like I said, I was surprised that you didn't remember the details of treating Cesar. I thought maybe you were withholding information or maybe you didn't really care about your clients."

She swiveled in her seat, her gaze never leaving him. "And you think I'm doing that because I'm guilty of something to do with Ace's death?"

"I did, yes." She opened her mouth, and he held up a hand. "I don't believe you fired the rifle, but until we figure out the shooter's identity, we can't completely rule out that you're involved with him."

"What you're saying is, I will remain a suspect until the real shooter is caught."

He nodded. "I hope you understand that it's not personal."

"Not personal! Seriously. It's very personal." She crossed her arms and looked away.

He took a moment to gather his thoughts and phrase his words carefully. "I want to believe in you. I'm trying, but I've been through too much in life to take things at face value."

She met his gaze again. "That's a sad way to live. A very sad way, and one of these days, you'll wake up and wish you hadn't built a wall around yourself. That you'd lived the faith you profess and believed the best of people. Loved them like Jesus, because love always expects the best in others."

Her disappointed tone left his gut aching. She was likely right. He was too jaded. For as long as he could remember, he'd expected the worst in others. And as she'd said, if he didn't change, he'd live a very lonely life. Problem was, he couldn't find a way to forgive his parents, and as long as he was unwilling to try, she would be powerless to help him, no matter her willingness to try.

CHAPTER

17

Mobile, Alabama
2:30 p.m.

Detective Skinner was an earnest-looking guy with mounds of case files stacked on his desk. Rick hoped his investigation would also close Santos's murder investigation, thereby lessening Skinner's heavy workload.

He gestured at a metal side chair by his desk and plopped a folder in front of Rick. "Your copy of our records. I don't have the time to review each page with you. So I'll give you an overview, then we'll visit the scene. You can read the file on your own time and call if you have questions."

Rick took out his notebook and pen. "Before we start, mind telling me why you used ViCAP before you had time to run down all the possible leads? It's often a last resort."

"This one is odd."

"In what way?"

"For starters, we don't get many long gun killings in the city. And as far as I know, we've never had a large-caliber shooting from such a distance. Couple that with the slug being removed from the fence, and I knew we had something else going on."

He steepled his fingers. "Seems I'm right, as the entry brought a fed running to my door within twenty-four hours."

The guy was looking awful smug, but Rick wouldn't comment. "Go ahead and give me that overview."

"Dispatch received a 911 call from a bread truck driver on his morning route. He passed the deceased lying on the street, but thought nothing of it. Not with the high homeless population in that part of town. He made three deliveries, then doubled back to another stop at the end of the block near the deceased. That's when he noticed that Santos was nicely dressed, so he went over to investigate and, upon discovering he was dead, called 911."

"You check out the delivery schedule to confirm the driver's story?"

He gave Rick a well-duh look. "I caught the case at seven a.m. on Friday morning, and the ME placed time of death two hours prior."

Olivia's schedule showed back-to-back appointments that day starting at eight a.m. She couldn't have been in Mobile and gotten back to her office for that appointment. Still, they would confirm her alibi with the client.

"As the ViCAP report says," Skinner continued, "we didn't recover a slug, but one had embedded in a fence and was removed with a knife. We called in an SBI ballistics expert who placed the shooter at about eight hundred yards."

Rick respected the staff at Alabama's State Bureau of Investigation and had no reason to doubt their accuracy, but he would still check it out. "Your thoughts on who might want to kill Santos?"

Skinner leaned back in his chair and clasped his hands behind his head. "Not too many shooters who can make that kind of shot, so we're looking for a very skilled marksman."

Rick wished he could tell Skinner that he was way off base here, as his theory was likely driving his investigation, but Rick wasn't free to mention the smart bullet.

"You'll see in my files that Santos had no connections to the local gun community," Skinner continued. "And he was well loved. I haven't located any one who has a grudge against him."

"Obviously someone does."

"Or he was in the wrong place at the wrong time."

After Griffin had died the same way, Rick sincerely doubted that, but he couldn't mention his reasoning, as he wasn't about to lead Skinner to the team's investigation. "What about financial issues? Gambling, et cetera. He have any problems?"

"Nada. He was clean and responsible." Skinner snapped forward and glanced at his watch. "I have a meeting in an hour, so let's continue this at the scene."

Rick nodded his understanding, but he wasn't moving before confirming the completeness of the report. A detective was only as good as his report-writing skills, and Rick wanted to know if Skinner had covered all bases.

"Give me a sec." In the folder he found witness statements. Clear photographs of the scene. Detailed evidence lists. Documentation of the scene and an evidence log. Missing were any video files and Santos's service record book. Santos had separated from the marines years ago, meaning Skinner wouldn't think military at this point, so the missing SRB made sense. Questioning it would only raise a red flag.

Rick thumbed through the last pages. "No autopsy report."

"ME isn't finished with it, but I attended the autopsy and my notes are in the file. Nothing remarkable other than the bullet removal and the tattoo that was in my ViCAP report." Skinner got to his feet.

Rick didn't budge. "Still, I'll need the complete autopsy report."

"I don't know how it usually works for you, but around here the ME is on his own timetable."

"I'm sure a little prodding will speed him up."

"You haven't met our ME." Skinner held up a hand. "But before you go all demanding fed on me, I'll give him a call to see if I can get a report today and e-mail it to you."

Having gained Skinner's offer to help, Rick stood. "Thank you."

"Don't thank me yet. I may strike out." Skinner started for the door. "Maybe now would be a good time for you to tell me why the feds are interested in my case."

Rick kept in step with Skinner. "As I told you on the phone, it has similarities to an investigation I'm working."

He glanced at Rick, his eyebrow quirked. "I'm going to read between the lines here the way we always have to do with you feds and assume you're working a murder investigation."

Rick didn't deny or confirm it.

"If we have two deaths that are related, then we might be talking serial."

"I don't know that our cases are related yet, so don't jump to conclusions."

Skinner pressed open the exit door to the lobby where Olivia sat waiting. She'd have been far more comfortable at her friend's house, but Rick couldn't leave her on her own for safety reasons. Or for his team's peace of mind while she was still a suspect.

"Ready to go?" he asked.

She got up and, thankfully, didn't ask about the investigation. He'd warned her in advance not to share any information about Griffin. It was nice that she complied while they walked to the elevator, where Skinner left to get his own car.

Rick had the address for the murder scene and would use GPS to find his way.

In the car he waited for Olivia's questions, but she didn't speak. She hadn't said much since their discussion on the way to Mobile, so he had to believe she was still frustrated with him. He didn't usually stew over other people's feelings, but Olivia's silence for the drive to the crime scene bothered him more than he cared to admit.

He parked behind Skinner and turned to her. "I'm sorry to make you sit in the car, but—"

"I have no business hearing what the two of you discuss."

"I would have phrased it a little nicer, but yes." He reached for the handle. "I shouldn't be long."

Folder in hand with diagrams for the crime scene, Rick made sure to keep Olivia in sight as he met Skinner on the sidewalk near a telltale bloodstain. It was brown now and scuffed from foot traffic, and the average passerby wouldn't have a clue that a murder occurred here except for an impromptu memorial holding flowers, stuffed animals, and candles.

"Santos was facing south." Skinner pointed at a fence due north of the stain. "Bullet lodged in the fence post. Or at least we're assuming the damage was caused by the slug and removal."

Rick quickly estimated the distance and wasn't surprised the bullet had traveled so far before lodging.

"Of course, with it pried out of the wood, we can't confirm caliber and had to rely on the ME's evaluation. Which he readily admits is a guess."

"But you did confirm a knife made the pry marks in the fence."

He nodded. "According to the SBI expert, anyway."

"You doubt it?"

"Nah, I don't have the expertise to comment on the findings is all."

If there was any question about the bullet and removal, Brynn would put it to rest.

"And the shooter's location?" Rick asked.

Skinner jabbed a thumb over his shoulder. "We believe it's the parking garage. Fifth floor. Address is in the report. At least that's what the—"

"—SBI expert said."

"Right. The details are all in my report." He glanced at his watch again. "You'll also note we swabbed a wad of spit found on the concrete in the garage. Was a good distance from where the shot was fired, and we doubt a shooter would leave saliva as a calling card, so we're not thinking it's from him."

Rick was skeptical about their conclusion, but there was no point in saying so. "Has it been sent in for processing?"

He nodded. "But the lab's backlogged, so it could take some time."

Rick flipped through the file. "Says here your tech took several swabs and only one has been sent off. I want our lab to process one as well."

"I'll check with my LT and get back to you."

Rick nodded. "Are there any witnesses?"

Skinner shook his head. "Not many people out at that time of day, and in this neighborhood, those who are don't make for good witnesses."

"Then thanks for your time, Detective."

"My cell number's in the report if you have other questions."

They shook hands, and Rick backtracked to the car. He opened Olivia's door. "How would you like to take a short walk?"

"It would be good to stretch my legs."

"Let me grab a few things from the back." He opened the hatch and took out his tote holding necessary supplies.

Back on the sidewalk, she joined him. "I assume the bag means you have a purpose for our walk."

"I want to see the shooter's vantage point." He started off.

She didn't comment, but when they reached the impromptu memorial, her footsteps faltered and she looked up at him. "You see death all the time. How do you handle it?"

"Compartmentalizing."

"Classic defense mechanism." She continued down the street. "But you should know, sometimes those compartments fill up, and when things overflow . . ." She shrugged.

"I'll be sure to keep an eye out for that."

"Problem is, you often can't see it in yourself."

"Is this a pitch for the value of counseling?"

"Doesn't take a psychologist to see it. Just someone who cares about you."

She was so on target, he felt like a .50 had slammed into his chest. He'd cared about Traci, and it hadn't been hard to see the problems she faced. Fat lot of good it had done her.

"Is it a blessing to be able to recognize someone's issues or a burden? Like with your father when you couldn't help?"

"Both, I guess, but I'd say the blessing outweighs the burden, as most of the time I'm able to help."

He paused to look into her eyes, finding her sincerity and honesty refreshing. "You're a special person, Doc."

Embarrassed at putting his feelings out there, he started off again.

She caught up to him and took his arm. "You're an exceptional man, too. You just have to let people see it. Like with your parents."

He groaned. "I'm not going back to that topic."

He picked up speed and heard her nearly running to keep up, so he slowed. At the garage he turned. "We're headed to the fifth floor. I doubt our shooter would risk being trapped in an elevator, so I want to take the stairwell. You can ride up if you want."

"Lead on. The exercise after sitting all day is good for me."

He strode to the steps, and at the third floor he looked back. He expected she might be breathing hard, but she was holding her own.

"I can keep up," she said. "I may sit most of the day, but I counterbalance it with yoga and running."

Rick continued to the fifth floor and exited. He opened the folder and studied the diagram, then located the shooter's supposed firing location. Rick dropped the folder and his tote bag. "The folder is off-limits."

"I hadn't even considered looking in it until you told me not to. But now..." She grinned.

Shaking his head, he dug out his spotting scope from his tote.

"What's that?" she asked.

"A spotting scope." He put it to his eye and focused. "It's used by a spotter who partners with a sniper. When the sniper takes a shot, the spotter tracks the vapor trail so if the bullet goes wide, the spotter can help readjust the sniper's position or aim. I'm using it to confirm the shooter's location. I can do that by lining up the spot where Cesar was hit with the fence where the bullet lodged."

"Interesting."

She actually sounded interested. He looked up from the scope to find her rapt attention on him. "Would you like to see?"

"Sure."

"Okay, let me get the scope lined up, then step in front of me." He moved back from the half wall so she could slip into place. Keeping his arms locked in position, he said, "Come on."

She eased in front of him, his awareness of her nearly over-whelming. He felt her body heat, and her scent seemed to heat up, too. Or was it his imagination? She scooted around, brushing against him, firing off senses that had lain dormant for years. This was a bad idea. Very bad.

"See it?" He choked the words out.

"I do. It's like..." She excitedly swiveled, and they came face-to-face, mere inches separating them. Her gaze met his, and interest flared in her eyes.

She was close. So close. Her eyes darkened. He lowered the scope and cupped the back of her head to eliminate the distance to kiss her. Her eyes flashed wide, panic flooding in. She planted her palms against his chest. Shoved hard. She wasn't strong enough to move him, but he wasn't about to force himself on her, so he stepped back. She smoothed a hand over her hair and looked away.

Great. She was trying to eradicate his touch. She felt like he'd assaulted her, and he hated the way his gut twisted. He should say something, but what? He'd read her wrong. Crossed a line she clearly didn't welcome. A mistake. Big one. He wouldn't further compound it by speaking. He tucked the scope back in the bag and moved away from her to closely inspect the top of the concrete wall.

"What are you looking for?" she asked, her voice breathy.

Interesting. Their nearness had affected her, too. Didn't mean she wanted his attention, and she was determined to act like nothing had just happened. Fine with him. "I'm trying to find physical evidence that confirms the shooter put the bullet downrange from this location."

"Didn't the local police tell you that he did?"

He nodded.

"But you can't trust their assessment."

He glanced at her. "I can, but it would be foolish to do so."

"Because you don't trust anything, or because you possess expertise that they likely don't have?"

"Expertise." He ignored her other comment. No point in leading them back to the discussion in the car. He examined the wall, looking for what, he didn't know. Maybe a hint of rubber from the tips of a bipod.

"Mind sharing what you're looking for as you search?"

He froze. Was she trying to get information on the case, or was she really interested in investigative procedures? As she'd said, trust didn't come easily to him, and as he stood there thinking about the shooter taking Santos out, he knew in his heart that she wasn't involved in the murders.

He still didn't know if she was using her skills as a psychologist to put on an act with him—an act like the one Traci's psychologist was so good at—or if Olivia was being earnest and really cared about him. Maybe sharing something simple like this could help him to trust her with more important things in the future.

"I'm looking at the scene from an experienced shooter's point of view to determine the best way to make the shot," he said. "A large rifle is needed for a .50 caliber bullet, so the guy most likely used a bipod to hold the weapon and could have rested the bipod on the wall. But the most accurate shot comes with a shooter lying down. This stance naturally aligns your body with the target, putting you in a relaxed position for a better shot."

She moved closer to the wall but kept her distance from him. "But that couldn't happen here because of the wall."

"Not necessarily."

"Explain, please."

He dug out his tape measure and rolled it out over the concrete wall. "As I suspected, the wall is about the average height of a truck's tailgate. If it was me taking the shot, I'd open a tailgate, back the truck up to the wall, and lie in the truck bed." He stepped back from the wall and looked at it for any missed evidence.

"There." He pointed at a black smudge on the concrete, then squatted to get a better look. "Paint."

"From a truck?"

"Maybe. Looks about tailgate height."

"But couldn't it be from any car that parked here?"

"Not likely. A bumper would protect the vehicle. The car would have to sideswipe the wall to actually leave paint, and the parking block would prevent that from happening."

"So the paint could be from the shooter's truck."

He nodded because he couldn't share details about the Chick-fil-A guy's having a white truck. Besides, they didn't know if that guy was their shooter or if he owned more than one truck. He might even have borrowed one.

Rick grabbed the folder to check the evidence list. "They took a sample of the paint, but they didn't think it was related, and it was never processed."

"But you can get them to do so."

"With lab backlogs, it's easier for me to take a sample and get Brynn to run it." He grabbed his bag and withdrew a knife, envelope, and tape to collect the paint.

"Let's say you do get this to Brynn. What good will it do?"

He started working on the wall. "The FBI maintains a paint database called the National Automotive Paint File. It contains over forty thousand samples of automotive paint used by manufacturers on their vehicles. So Brynn can compare the sample here to the database, and if we're lucky we'll learn the make and model of the truck. Then we can look at traffic cams, store surveillance footage in the area, et cetera, and talk to witnesses to see if that make and model truck was spotted in the area on the day of the shooting."

"Which I suppose could give you a license plate number."

"Exactly." He pocketed the paint sample, then reviewed the evidence list again and noted the location of the saliva. He measured it out, then used chalk to mark the average size of a pickup with open tailgate for reference, while keeping in mind that the shooter could have been driving a bigger truck.

"What are you looking for now?" she asked.

He explained the saliva mentioned in the report. "Detective Skinner doubts it's from the shooter."

"But you don't."

"I'm keeping an open mind. My chalk line simulates a full-size truck with tailgate open. I want to see if the saliva was found in a logical location for our shooter if he'd used a truck."

"You know the size of a pickup off the top of your head?"

"Along with many car sizes. You'd be surprised how often that information comes in handy." He closed the folder. "If my angle is right, and the truck was full size, the driver could have spit when he got out of the cab."

"Why didn't the locals figure this out?"

"Because their ballistic expert must have overlooked the fact that the shot could have been taken lying down. Thankfully, it's the first thing I thought of." And more importantly, it suggested an experienced shooter who knew to lie down for the shot.

"Now what?" she asked.

"Now I look to see where they recovered gunshot residue."

He picked up the file and stepped to the location where the residue had been recovered. "When a weapon is discharged, residues are expelled from the barrel onto nearby surfaces," he said before she asked. "It can travel three to five feet, and gets progressively lighter the further it travels. The report shows a minimum amount of residue collected from the wall, which adds more credence to my findings."

"Wouldn't they have questioned that?"

"They chalked it up to wind and timing." He closed the folder. "Time to go back to the fence post and call Brynn to give her a look at the post through our virtual reality software."

"And that's important why?"

"I need her to confirm the bullet was removed by a knife. If she can't do it from the shots I provide with Google Glass, then I'll work with the property owner to allow me to remove the post and bring it back to her."

Olivia shook her head. "If I ever doubted that your team would find this killer, I don't doubt it anymore."

"Oh, we'll find him all right."

Question was, would they find him before he killed again? Or before he sold the state-of-the-art technology to the highest bidder, who would use it to kill any person of his choosing?

18

On the sofa in Patsy's living room, Olivia was completely out of sync with the big strapping guy sitting next to her. No doubt she was developing feelings for Rick. Or maybe the psychologist in her wanted to help him, but now, as the thought popped into her head, she didn't believe that. She was attracted to him. Pure and simple. A woman for a man. Nothing professional in her feelings for him at all. Sure, she'd be glad to help him reconcile with his family, but that was the end of her desire to act as his psychologist when so many other possibilities kept barreling into her brain.

"And where do you live, Agent Cannon?" Patsy asked, thankfully grabbing Olivia's attention again.

"Rick, please," he replied. "In D.C."

As Patsy and Rick exchanged facts, Olivia looked around the living room. She hadn't visited Patsy since she'd purchased her house, and Olivia loved the homey vibe of the wide front porch, the historic brick fireplace painted white, and the many original built-ins from the late eighteen hundreds. Olivia had always wanted to own her own home, but any money beyond her emergency fund that she could have saved for a down payment had gone to her family. Now even her emergency savings were depleted due to the identity theft.

Rick's phone rang. He glanced at the screen and frowned. "Excuse me. I need to take this call."

He stepped out the front door, and Olivia saw him, phone to ear, pacing past the window. He appeared to be getting bad news, and if it was bad for him, it was likely bad for her, too.

"He's kind of intense," Patsy said.

"Kind of?" Olivia laughed. "He's over-the-top."

"Just your type."

"Not hardly."

"Yes hardly. You pretend to like the sensitive, share-your-feelings type, so you end up dating the wrong guys, and that's why you're still single."

"Dating? What's that? I haven't been on a date in years. I don't have time to find the 'sensitive' man of my dreams."

"Right. Keep telling yourself that."

The door opened, and Olivia held up a finger to shush Patsy.

Rick pinned her with his gaze as if he'd overheard their conversation, but she waited him out, and he finally changed his focus to Patsy. "I need to take a video call. Would you have a room where I could do so in private?"

"Sure. My office–slash–guest room where you'll be bunking." She got up. "Right this way."

Rick grabbed his laptop case and an overnight bag that made Olivia's suitcase look like she'd packed for an ocean voyage a decade long.

He glanced at her. "We can grab some dinner when I'm done if you like."

Alone. As in a date-like environment. Not hardly. "I'm sure

Patsy would be happy to share dinner with us at a local place of her choosing."

"Um, I'm busy tonight." Patsy looked over her shoulder. "But I'm glad to recommend a few places for the two of you."

Patsy hadn't mentioned being busy before now, and Olivia suspected the business she mentioned had more to do with her comments about Rick. When Patsy returned, Olivia told her as much.

"He might want to talk about the investigation," Patsy said. "And I wouldn't have any reason to be there for that."

Olivia's phone rang. "Saved by the bell."

Patsy laughed. "I'll take your things to your room for you."

Olivia answered the call from her sister. "Everything going okay there?"

"It's great." Dianna's voice was the most upbeat and cheerful Olivia had heard it since Jason walked out. "Grace is so amazing. She spent the entire night here last night and didn't wake me once. Then she had breakfast delivered for all of us. We ate this incredible feast while she went home to change. She came right back and stayed with the kids so I could go swimming and sit in the hot tub. Oh, and she had a massage appointment this afternoon, and she insisted I take it instead. She even paid for it."

"Wow." Olivia wondered what Rick would make of his mother's generosity. "So did you call to brag on Grace, or did you need something?"

"It's Harrison. He said you didn't call him back, and he's insisting on coming over here."

"I'm sorry. With everything that's been happening, I forgot again."

"Maybe now's the time to tell me why you had to race out of town so fast."

Olivia hadn't wanted to worry her sister with a second murder and so had avoided providing details. "Like I said. It's a work thing."

"Right, like you had an emergency counseling session in Mobile that required the help of a dreamy FBI agent."

Olivia sighed and finally understood the frustration Rick felt when she kept after him for information about the investigation that he couldn't share with her.

"I can't talk about it, but I *will* call Harrison." She quickly said goodbye before Dianna asked additional questions. She dialed her brother, who would quiz her even more.

"About time you called." He launched into an explanation of how slighted he felt over Dianna's free vacation and listed the reasons he was more deserving.

Not once in their ten-minute conversation did he even ask about her or why she was in Mobile. Of course he didn't. He considered only himself, and she knew deep in her heart that when they caught the killer and her life returned to normal, she had to deal with her family's unhealthy dependence on her.

After ending the call, she wandered down a narrow hallway to a small bedroom with a plump bed covered in Patsy's great-grandmother's quilt. Patsy was Olivia's first college roommate, and Olivia would never forget the day she'd arrived on campus to find Patsy spreading out the quilt on her bed. She'd immediately warned Olivia that it was priceless to her and Olivia better not spill anything on it or otherwise ruin it.

Patsy hefted Olivia's suitcase onto a small bench at the foot of the bed. "I see you still don't travel light."

Olivia smiled. "And I see you're still using the quilt. I'm surprised you trust me with it."

Patsy swatted a hand at her and headed for the door. "Go ahead and get settled in, and I'll make that list of restaurants for you."

Olivia didn't feel like unpacking, so she plopped onto the

bed and leaned back to close her eyes for a minute. For some reason the parking garage came to mind, along with the feel of Rick's hand sliding into her hair, her scalp tingling at his touch. She didn't even have to close her eyes to remember the emotions that had raced through her. To remember the color of his eyes up close. The warmth emanating from his body, his musky and very masculine scent.

As Patsy had said, he was the kind of guy she was attracted to, but that meant nothing. It had to, didn't it?

* * *

Rick set his laptop on a small desk against the wall opposite the Murphy bed that Patsy had demonstrated how to operate. He opened their secured video conferencing program and waited for the rest of the team to log in for a status update.

"We're all here," Max announced.

Rick explained his visit with the detective, the trip to the parking garage, and a second visit with the detective to pick up the saliva sample. "I'm bringing the paint and saliva to you tomorrow, Brynn. Can you process immediately?"

"Sure, if the local lab will give me access again."

"I plan to review the case file in detail tonight. If I find any additional evidence that's taking its sweet time to be processed, I'll try to fast-track that as well." He caught a breath before continuing. "And per your request, I'm bringing back the fence post where the bullet was removed. I hope you and maybe the Toolmarks guys at Quantico can confirm the theory of the slug removal." Brynn worked closely with the FBI's only forensic lab that was located in Quantico, Virginia.

"I won't even ask what you had to do to get the owner to saw off the fence post for you." She grinned.

"Just a bit of Southern charm."

"You, charming?" Kaci shook her head hard. "No way."

"My mama taught me how to work it," he said, using his thickest drawl, which he'd never done with the group, and wondered why he'd chosen now to loosen up.

They chuckled, and he felt something akin to friendship that he'd only really experienced with Levi. He hadn't reached out to the team for the same reason he'd been closemouthed with Olivia. He didn't want to get close to them, or anyone else for that matter, as that would mean revealing all his baggage. But this felt good. Right. Maybe trusting Olivia had opened the path for more in his life.

"I do want to point out," he continued, "that if the shooter taking a prone position in the garage is correct, it could further cement that our shooter's active or former military, but it could also say he's an experienced shooter."

"Which means my visits to the gun clubs and ranges are even more important," Shane said. "It was a bust today, but I still have a number of places on the list."

"Keep me informed," Rick said.

"Will do," Shane replied. "How goes it with Olivia? Any better feel for her involvement?"

"I've seen no evidence of it," he replied, trying to sound impartial. "Perhaps it's time for us to take a more inductive approach to our investigation in regards to her."

Shane arched an eyebrow. "You mean stop thinking she's involved, as it could be coloring our opinions? Instead analyze her credibility as a witness?"

"Exactly," Rick said.

"Speaking of credibility, I've concluded her background screening, and I haven't found anything to suggest she's anything other than an upstanding citizen. And her client list revealed she hadn't treated an officer for years, so she couldn't be using her job to get sensitive details."

Max's forehead creased. "We've uncovered no motive for her involvement either."

Rick nodded. "Based on that, there's no reason to suggest we keep her on our suspect list."

"It does remove any emotion from the equation and replace it with analytical elements," Shane said.

Brynn frowned. "But it also removes our gut feel, and that often leads us to our suspects. So I don't think we should be so hasty."

"Doesn't take away *my* gut feel," Rick added, but had to wonder if he was letting emotions dictate his response. "I just don't see her as being in on this and have given her a thorough evaluation."

"Then let's drop all efforts to connect her as a coconspirator," Max said. "But by all means, we need to determine why two of her clients are now lying dead."

"I'll be talking to the bread truck driver and Santos's wife in the morning. Maybe she can shed some light on a connection. And the ME promised the autopsy report in the morning as well. Not that I expect any big revelation, but it might contain something of interest."

"Any other updates?" Max asked.

"I contacted the last of my sources in our field offices," Kaci said. "No one has a lead on any actors who could have targeted MilMed."

"I've gotten a similar response from my CIA contacts," Max said. "We'll back-burner the foreign sales for now."

"Except for monitoring the darknet," Kaci added. "If there's any chatter about foreign sales, it'll show up there."

"Understood," Rick said, hoping this deadly weapon system didn't reach foreign soil.

* * *

Rick strode past an Iraqi tank at USS *Alabama* Battleship Memorial Park on Mobile Bay. He'd come here to see the Fallen Heroes Memorial honoring those who'd lost their lives in Iraq and Afghanistan since the 9/11 terror attacks. He'd lost his buddy Hank Vose from Alabama, and Rick wanted—no, needed—to pay his respects.

The wind whipped across the park, and Olivia struggled to keep her hair out of her face. Still, she remained in step with him, her spiky heels clicking on the concrete path.

"You sure know how to show a girl a good time," she said.

"Everyone should be interested in military history," he replied quickly. "Might help keep us from repeating it."

"I was joking, Rick." She wrinkled that cute little nose, and despite the purpose of their visit to the park, he smiled.

"I promise dinner will be more..." He almost said "romantic," but they weren't on a date. They were on a business trip, and they'd both best remember that. "I'm surprised Patsy didn't join us for dinner."

"That was her attempt at matchmaking."

"Us?" His voice croaked like a middle schooler's.

"I know, right? She says you're my type."

He stopped dead in his tracks and faced her. "And am I?"

"Let's see." She tapped her finger against her chin. "You're very good looking, which I suspect is any woman's type. You're decisive, and I like that. Extremely confident."

He couldn't tell if she was joking or serious, but he had to find out. "I hear a *but* coming next."

"But," she replied, drawing out the word, "I'd rather be in a relationship with someone who's more open and willing to share."

"Right. That. I told you about my parents."

"After I nagged you to death."

He wished he could tell her that it had been a fluke and that he'd be more open, but history didn't support that. "I've told you more than most people."

She gave him a tight smile. "You're very private. I get that. But that's what I'm talking about. I want more in a relationship."

"And yet." He paused and met her gaze. "There's something— a connection—between us, and it seems to be getting stronger."

She nodded, then held his gaze. "Doesn't mean I'll do anything about it."

He didn't want a relationship, but her continued rejection stung, and he turned to stare over the choppy water. "I can't change who I am. Not for you. Not for anyone."

"You can, actually. For yourself. You have to decide it's worth it to share and get to know someone. But don't work on it on my account. For a possible relationship, that is. You're also former military, and I won't go down that path."

He swung his focus back to her. "Path?"

"You may not show the classic signs of military stress, but I see it in you. Who knows, maybe that's why you keep everything bottled up. You want to keep a tight control because you're afraid if you let go, whatever happens might sink you."

He had his share of demons from the war, but they weren't controlling his life by any means. Not something she'd want to hear. She'd already made her mind up about him. "Sounds like you have me all figured out."

"No. Just speculating. Besides, I get the feeling that you're not interested in a relationship either."

He looked at her. "What makes you think that?"

"You said you wanted kids, but it wouldn't happen. Either

you have a physical reason you can't have children, or you don't see yourself getting married."

She was trying to dig deep again, and he didn't like it. He shifted his weight and widened his stance. "No health issues, and I'm not getting married again."

Her eyes widened, shock at his revelation obvious in the darkening of her eyes.

"You were married?" She whispered the words as if she'd lost her voice.

He nodded and decided to share the bare minimum with her. "Traci and I got married in our early twenties. While I was still in the marines, her car hit a tree. She died instantly, and so did our unborn son."

"How awful for you." She took his hand between hers. "I'm so sorry."

It had been a long time since he'd had a woman's comforting hand in his, and the warmth was amazing and reassuring. Encouraging, drawing him physically and emotionally closer to her, so he continued. "I didn't know Traci was pregnant until the autopsy. I was deployed in Afghanistan when she died. Had been for months, with limited contact. Turns out Traci had told her therapist that she was conflicted about the pregnancy. She was depressed and could hardly handle taking care of herself. She figured with me gone so often, she'd be a single parent, and she couldn't deal with that. So she was considering terminating the pregnancy."

"Oh, Rick."

Her sympathy was nearly his undoing. Nearly the thing to release the free fall of emotions she'd predicted. He stared at their hands. "The police think Traci might have ended her life. If she'd only told me about the baby, I would have left the marines. Come home."

She squeezed his hand, but he still couldn't look at her.

"Such a stress is hard to recover from, and it makes perfect sense that you think you'll never be a father." She stepped closer, bending forward to make eye contact. "Have you ever considered talking to someone about it?"

Right. She was a shrink. Always a shrink. Not the woman he'd come to care for more than was good for either of them. He pulled his hand free and stepped back. "Talk to someone like a shrink, you mean."

"Yes, a therapist or psychologist."

"See, here's the thing, Doc. Traci was seeing a shrink. Dr. Fox. She knew Traci was struggling and could have gotten in touch with me, but she chose not to."

"Doctor-patient confidentiality."

He fired her a testy look. "No. Don't use that excuse. At least not in this case. Traci gave Dr. Fox permission to update me on her condition. Shoot, I'd even attended counseling sessions with Traci to help her work things out. But Fox wanted Traci to be able to make up her own mind about the baby without any undue pressure from me, and she told Traci that in a session. After that appointment Traci was so conflicted about what to do about the baby that she couldn't concentrate on driving and crashed her car into a tree. And like I said, the police suggested she'd taken her own life." He shook his head. "Dr. Fox admitted that when she was young she'd been forced to make a similar decision under great duress. She didn't want any of her clients to go through the pressure she'd faced. So she let her personal feelings make her professional decision with Traci. Chose not to get in touch with me. Warned Traci not to do so either."

Olivia's eyes widened with understanding. "No wonder you were leery of me."

"She's not the only reason. I had a bad experience with a

shrink when I was a teen, too. My dad hired her, and she was his puppet, telling me all the time in my sessions what my father wanted, and that if I didn't comply I'd be causing myself unhappiness. I knew her behavior was wrong then, and I know it now. So no offense, Doc, but I'm still leery. The only thing that's really changed between us is that I'm letting our interest or connection or whatever you want to call it between us color my opinions." He crossed his arms. "I need to stop that. For the good of the investigation."

"The investigation. Right." Her expression tightened.

He'd been tactful in his response, and he hadn't expected his comments to bother her so much. "You make it sound like focusing on the investigation is a bad thing. We have a killer running free. I have to stop him before he strikes again."

"Of course." A bitter smile slid across her mouth.

Okay, she was upset. Nothing he could do about that. He wouldn't take back anything he'd said. Besides, the divide between them was better for both of them, as he still didn't know who she was. Was she the caring woman he saw now or a counselor putting on a good front? His gut said she actually cared, but then his gut also had once had him agreeing with Traci that Dr. Fox was a wonderful doctor. Proving that on this subject his gut could be wrong and until he knew for sure who Olivia was, he couldn't get involved with her.

He glanced at his watch. "The park is closing in a few minutes. I should get to the memorial."

He gestured for her to precede him across the lawn brown from the dry summer, and he followed. He was almost grateful to reach the concrete circle surrounding the marble monolith, as it took his mind off the way he kept disappointing her. A trio of women stood to the side of the monument engraved with a soldier in a navy uniform, but otherwise he and Olivia had the area to themselves. He stepped up to the eight-foot-tall tower, first fixing his gaze on the top, where combat boots with a rifle and helmet were mounted.

He was choked up by memories of fellow soldiers, all branches, who'd lost their lives on the battlefield and by memories of past deployments when his platoon had displayed a lost soldier's boots, helmet, and rifle in the same configuration. With the humidity he could hardly breathe, but he stepped closer until he located Hank's name. Rick ran his fingers over the lettering. A jagged razor of pain cut through his core. All this thinking about his past and the visit to his parents had his emotions raw, and he thought he might drop to his knees.

Olivia joined him and took his hand, twining her fingers with his. Here she was mad at him or disappointed in him, and yet she had enough compassion to put aside her feelings to offer comfort. She could very well be the only thing that kept him from collapsing.

"Tell me about your time in Iraq," she said, her tone encouraging.

He'd never wanted to talk about his deployments. Actually, he'd never spoken about them with anyone outside the sniper platoon. So why the pressing need to speak now? Maybe to acknowledge Hank's sacrifice. All the sacrifices.

"My first tour was in '05. I'd just finished sniper school and deployed to Iraq. When we first rolled into Ramadi, we were faced with around a hundred IEDs a week. Our platoon was tasked with locating the people placing these IEDs and taking them out. Our missions started with overwatching other companies to make sure they weren't targets."

"And how did you do that exactly?"

"We couldn't help others if we were killed, so we chose our hides with a good view of the area, but also had to have a good escape and evasion route. Just in case. One particular time we were made by the Iraqis. Ambushed. Couldn't get out without taking fire. That's when Hank died." The memory sent a shudder through his body.

Olivia moved closer. "So the other soldiers. You watched over them from these hides?"

Grateful she'd moved him forward, he nodded. "Sometimes that was an easy task. You'd catch a look at a guy in a ski mask in Iraq. Screamed 'bad guy.' But other times they hid, and the people protected them. Even the local police. But we did the best we could to distinguish good from bad. Most of the time you got it right. But sometimes...sometimes...you'd get it wrong. Fire on an innocent. Or a shot goes wide and your target gets away."

"And what about those you did hit? Do they haunt you?"

He shook his head. "Our protocol helped with that. We took body shots just under breastplates. That keeps you from seeing who you're shooting."

"You must have been worried you'd be shot, too."

"Yeah, in the close-in engagements, but if we did our job right, the range of our rifles was our safety. The majority of sniper engagements are single target at three hundred to a thousand yards. You can't see me with the naked eye at that distance. Means you can't hurt me. And the sniper's cardinal rule says never to fire more than two shots from one position, which kept their snipers from placing us, too."

"Still, the pressure must have been off the charts."

"Yeah, I guess." He sighed. "You screw up as a sniper, and you'll be on the news, because a screwup means you've been killed."

She stepped in front of him and met his gaze. "Are you ever bothered by nightmares?"

"This is starting to sound awful clinical, Doc."

"No, I'm just curious. I want to know you. Know how deeply you carry this with you."

He shrugged, intending to blow her off, but at her crestfallen look, he couldn't. "Sure. Yeah. I have nightmares now and then, but not about a hit. They're always about the misses. Whenever a shot went wide and the target made it out of there alive, I knew fellow soldiers would die at his hands. I'll wonder for the rest of my life who was killed because I missed my shot. That's what keeps me up at night."

She squeezed his hand. "Thank you, Rick. For your bravery and service. And giving up so much for our country."

He'd been thanked in the past, but never before had it meant so much to him. He let go of her hand and drew her into his arms. Her head against his chest, he tightened his arms and stared at Hank's name. The pain, the anguish of a moment ago was gone, and peace settled over him. Something he hadn't experienced since his childhood. And it was all because of the strong woman wrapped in his arms. He could no longer deny she'd found a place in his heart. If only he could be sure of her motives and find a way to change his life to include her.

Father, he prayed, as he hadn't in years, *I've been banging my head against a closed door long enough. Please open another one so I can find my way through the mess of my life once and for all so if Olivia is who she professes to be, I can see her as You do.*

CHAPTER

19

Mobile, Alabama
Saturday, September 16
10:20 a.m.

The morning sun overhead, Olivia stepped onto the concrete walkway leading up to Cesar's modest brick bungalow. A chain-link fence open to a dirt driveway surrounded the property. The grass was perfectly manicured, not a common sight for the lower-income neighborhood. Totally normal for Cesar. He, like Rick, had retained those perfectionistic sniper tendencies. She had gotten the feeling at the memorial, though, that Rick was thinking about his life and considering the value of letting go of some of the perfectionism and letting go of his past. Maybe, anyway.

She approached the front door, and her thoughts turned to Luna. Olivia's heart was almost too heavy for her to keep moving forward. Her training included how to handle grief, and she'd seen it firsthand too many times to count, but for some reason today seemed especially hard. She'd chosen to wear her favorite summer dress, a blue-and-white gingham check cinched at the waist, to help keep her spirits high. She smoothed down the full skirt and glanced back at Rick. She was probably looking for reassurance that she shouldn't need. She was coming to rely on him too much.

At the door he stepped up next to her. His expression was grim, his jaw clenched.

"Before we go in," she said, "you should know Luna has very little information about Cesar's military experiences. He wanted to spare her the pain of hearing what he'd gone through. In fact, that's why they'd split up for a time. She knew he was troubled and wanted to help, but he wouldn't share."

"Sounds familiar," he said. "Most of the guys I know haven't shared deployment details that they were cleared to reveal to their loved ones. Why take them through that hell, you know? I didn't tell Traci much for that very reason."

At first she'd thought he meant her, but he was talking about his wife. Made much more sense than thinking of her in such a capacity. "Let me do the talking at first with Luna. Your direct manner might not be well received."

His head dipped in a quick nod before he knocked.

Luna soon opened the door. Only a few inches over five feet, she'd been delightfully cheerful the last time Olivia had seen her, but today dark circles hung under her eyes. Her hair that had once been glossy and perfectly combed was messy, as if she'd just climbed from bed.

"Dr. Dobbs." Tears filled her eyes. "I'm so happy to see you. If you came to talk to Cesar, he..." A sob took her words.

"I know." Olivia pressed a hand on Luna's arm. "That's why I'm here. To offer my condolences."

"That is very kind of you."

"I was very fond of Cesar, and I know how deeply your family feels his loss."

Luna nodded, and from her pocket she produced a lace handkerchief to dab at her eyes and nose as she stepped back. "Please. Come in."

Olivia wasn't certain how or when to introduce Rick, so she stepped through the door and hoped he would follow and allow her the opportunity to find the right timing.

The entrance opened to a small family room with terrazzo tile flooring and one wall painted a blinding orange. The room held an easy chair and a sofa covered with a brightly woven blanket. The wall above was filled with happy family photos, pictures of Cesar in his uniform, and small shelves holding religious figurines and candles. Olivia sat on the sofa and gestured for Rick to join her. Luna collapsed in the chair as if she couldn't hold herself upright any longer.

"How are you doing?" Olivia asked.

"It is hard, but my faith gets me through." She picked up rosary beads lying on a Bible on a small ceramic table next to the chair and kissed them. "And, of course, my family, but I am not quite as resilient as the children."

Olivia heard them giggling from another room, and she wished adults could heal as easily and naturally from grief as young children often did. "Is there anything I can do for you?"

Luna shook her head. "Your visit is enough." Her gaze moved to Rick, and she sat staring at him.

"This is Rick Cannon," Olivia explained. "He's with the FBI."

Rick offered his credentials.

Suspicion flared in her eyes. "You are here about Cesar?"

Olivia hated to see the sweet woman suffer more, so she scooted off the sofa and knelt next to Luna to take her hand. "Rick wants to ask you some questions, but I'm here solely for you. Whatever you need, just ask."

A fond smile claimed her face. "You were always so good to Cesar and our family. We owe our last years together to you."

"Not to me. It was Cesar who did all of the hard work to get back together with you."

Her chin quavered. "I almost wish he hadn't. Then he wouldn't have been in Mobile and would still be alive."

"I'm sorry, Ms. Santos, but I don't think that's the case," Rick said.

Her smile evaporated. "What is it you know that I do not?"

"I'm investigating a death similar to your husband's, and I think the same person killed both of them."

"You mean the bullet wasn't random but was meant for Cesar?" She shook her head hard, her limp hair swinging over stooped shoulders. "But the detective. He could not explain why someone would want to do this. He suggested that Cesar was in the wrong place at the wrong time."

"My gut says he's mistaken, and Mr. Santos was purposefully targeted."

Luna dabbed her eyes. "Do you think that's why his HOG's tooth was taken that night?"

"HOG's tooth." Rick's voice rose. "Your husband was a sniper?"

Luna nodded. "And very proud of it."

Rick shot Olivia a suspicious look.

"I thought you knew that," Olivia said. "Otherwise I would have told you."

He eyed her. She hated that his first reaction was always to think she'd hidden something from him, but she also got that trust didn't come easily to him and that it would take time to overcome that.

"A HOG's tooth is a bullet on a cord, right?" Olivia asked.

He nodded. "Specifically it's a projectile portion of a 7.62 round—the part that most people think of when they think *bullet*. It has a hole drilled through the wide end, and is usually strung on paracord to be worn around the neck. It's given to every Marine Scout Sniper when they graduate from the Schoolhouse."

Olivia knew Schoolhouse was slang for sniper school. "Ace had one that he held during most of our counseling sessions, but he didn't really discuss it. What's its purpose?"

"It's symbolic only. A marine who graduates from sniper school is called a HOG—hunter of gunmen, i.e., hunter of enemy snipers. The bullet represents the bullet meant for the sniper, and since he has it in his possession and it can't be fired, he's invincible."

"Ace probably held onto his to ward off his anxiety."

"I didn't notice it in the list of his personal effects at the autopsy. Do you know if he had it with him the night he died?"

"Yes. He kept turning it over in his hands."

A knowing light came on in Rick's eyes.

"Cesar wore his all the time," Luna said. "I was so sad to hear that it had been taken. It meant so much to him."

Rick nodded. "Means a lot to every sniper."

"Cesar was glad to have his to prove he wasn't a PIG," Luna said.

"Professionally instructed gunman," Rick said before Olivia could ask. "Other members of a Scout Sniper platoon who didn't graduate from sniper school and are often less skilled snipers."

"Why would someone want to take it?" Olivia asked. "And do you think Ace's was taken, too?"

He flashed a warning look her way telling her to hold off on that line of questioning, then faced Luna again. "Do you know anyone who might have wanted to hurt your husband?"

"No, and I have told the detective this."

"What about in Mr. Santos's past? Did he communicate with old friends?"

"He did occasionally talk on the phone to some men he served with, and one or two times he went to Atlanta for something to do with them."

"Did you hear what they talked about or know why he traveled to Atlanta?"

"He always talked in the bedroom. It would have been rude of me to listen, so I did not do so. And he did not want to talk about the trips. He was troubled by something, though. Very troubled." She sighed. "Now I wish I had pushed him to tell me about it. Maybe he'd still be alive, but I was not raised to question my husband."

"I don't think even if you pushed that he would have shared much," Olivia said, thinking of Rick's unwillingness to speak of his past. "He didn't want you to have to think about the things he'd seen while an active soldier."

"That was my Cesar. Caring." Her gaze took on a faraway look before clearing and focusing again on Rick. "Do you have any other questions?"

"Did Mr. Santos make the calls you mentioned on a cell phone or landline?" Rick asked.

"We have chosen a life of simplicity so we do not have cell phones. We do not want to be on call whenever anyone wants to contact us. We have no television or computer either."

"How about e-mails or written letters? I know you don't have a computer, but he could've used one at the library or a friend's machine."

"No, and Cesar did not write letters."

"Do you know where he was on August twenty-eighth around six a.m.? It was a Monday morning, so that might make it easier for you."

That date again. Olivia made a mental note to search for it on the Internet to see if anything important came up.

"He would have been at work. He never missed a shift."

Rick gave a clipped nod, and if Olivia was right, he looked relieved, too.

"Do you recognize the name Archie Griffin? Your husband might have called him Ace."

"No. This is not a name I recognize."

Rick sat back for second, and Olivia knew he was trying to make sense of all that he'd heard and be thorough about his questioning. "Could you tell me Mr. Santos's last unit?"

"He was attached to the 1/5."

Olivia had learned enough about the marines to know she meant he was attached to the First Battalion, Fifth Marines Regiment.

"The 1/5 is out of California. Did you return here after Mr. Santos separated from the marines?"

"We lived in Atlanta. I'd moved there during his service to make travel easier for both of us." She frowned. "Then we split for a while, and I came back home to be near my family. That's when Dr. Dobbs helped Cesar, and then he joined me here."

"So one of his specialties was sniper. What was his other top MOS?" Rick looked at Olivia. "I imagine you're familiar with military occupational specialty codes."

"I know each marine carries two specialties that remain at the top of their record, but over the course of a career they may have several different MOS codes," Olivia said.

"Cesar only had two," Luna said. "He was a sniper and primary marksmanship instructor."

A quick frown flashed on Rick's face, but he quickly eliminated it. Olivia wouldn't ask him what was going on in front of Luna. The moment they stepped outside, however, she'd be all over it.

"One more question, if you don't mind," Rick said.

"Go ahead."

"Did Mr. Santos have a tattoo?"

"Yes. He came home from a deployment with one on his shoulder."

"Might you have a picture of the tattoo?"

"No. We have no photos of Cesar without a shirt."

"Then can you describe it for me and give me a better time-frame of when he got it?"

"It was a bunch of arrows in a circle. He said it was to honor a fallen marine, but he didn't tell me the soldier's name. I could tell losing his friend bothered him, so I did not pry." She paused and tapped a finger on her chin. "This was the year our daughter was born, so about five years ago."

Rick came to his feet. "Thank you for your time, Ms. Santos. I know my questions have been hard for you."

She tipped her head in a somber nod.

"Rick was a Marine Scout Sniper, too," Olivia said.

Luna's eyes flashed up to his, and instead of suspicion, they now held respect, as Olivia had hoped they would when she revealed his service. She hugged Luna and handed her a business card. "Call me if you need anything. Even if you just want to talk. I'm here for you."

"You are as special as Cesar always said," she murmured, then escorted them to the door.

Rick stopped at the threshold. "I'm so sorry for your loss, Ms. Santos. Your husband sounded like a wonderful man."

"Thank you." She clutched Rick's hand for a moment before stepping back.

On the sidewalk Olivia peered at Rick. "Why were you so disappointed when Luna told you Cesar only had two MOS codes?"

"Instructors interact with a large number of marines. If Cesar had done so for years and our killer is a soldier, Cesar could well have trained the guy who killed him."

"That's horrible."

Rick nodded and started for the SUV.

She hurried to keep up with him. "And Cesar's last unit. Why did you want that?"

"Max has run into a wall in getting Ace's records and could have the same problem with Cesar's SRB. They're supposed to be kept in a national archive for six years after date of enlistment, but in case they're not available there, his last unit could potentially have them."

He opened the passenger door, but she ignored it. "I suppose you'll need a warrant for that."

"Actually, no. Service records are now basically public information."

"Public, really?"

"Not public in the sense that anyone can get them. The requestor has to have a justifiable reason for asking."

"Which you do."

He nodded.

"But what are you looking for?"

"I have to believe, with Cesar having a tattoo matching Ace's, that they served together at some point. Perhaps in the same sniper platoon. Luna said the tat was inked for a friend, and you said Ace mumbled, 'The guys. We voted,' and 'Tank deserves it.' Like you said, Tank could be the guy who died, and the friends are part of his former platoon."

"I can give you a list of my clients who were former snipers, too, so you can check for a connection to others."

"I appreciate that," he said flatly.

His lack of eagerness baffled her. They were searching for a shooter. One who could make difficult shots. So why wasn't a list of snipers helpful?

"I would think it would help to know which of my clients were snipers and could have made those long-distance shots."

He leaned on the car door. "I never said the shooter was a sniper."

"Didn't you?"

He shook his head.

"Then I guess you didn't, but the officer who came to my rescue did." She met his gaze head-on. "So *is* the shooter a trained sniper?"

"We have no proof that he is."

"And you haven't said he wasn't. Means you can't talk about it." She slid into the car, her thoughts racing. So maybe the shooter wasn't a trained sniper, but how could a shooter who wasn't a sniper shoot so accurately? Maybe it was his weapon. A special one, perhaps, and one that had a connection with the August date that Rick kept mentioning. Perhaps her Internet search would turn up the answer.

Before she could ask Rick about it, he slammed her door and walked around the front of the vehicle. When he climbed in, she hoped he would elaborate, but he simply cranked the engine.

"Don't worry, I get it," she said. "You can't share details."

He shot her a surprised look. "Thank you for respecting my position."

"Finally, right." She chuckled. "I mean you've had to mention a few times that you can't share."

"You're tenacious. I like that." His gaze connected with hers, and that heat, that emotion that was growing between them crackled in the confined space.

She wouldn't linger in such dangerous territory. "Tell me about the HOG's tooth. Did you wear yours?"

He shook his head.

"Why not?"

"It was more of a symbol of having achieved a goal when so many others fell short, not something I really believed would protect me."

"How many men were in your class?"

"We started with forty and sixteen graduated."

"Less than half. I can see why the HOG's tooth is important to you."

"And that's why I didn't wear it. I wanted to keep it in a safe place. And like I said, I didn't believe it had any power to protect me. Only God can do that."

"Did most guys wear them?"

"A lot of them didn't. They respected the fact that it had to be earned like a medal and put theirs away for safekeeping, too."

"Not Ace or Cesar, and now the killer's collecting them. Why would he want to do that?"

"You're talking about the psychological reason he might be taking them. Like taking a trophy."

She nodded. "The killer has to know all about the HOG's tooth and what it signifies to have any reason to want them. Which could help show the shooter is military or former military himself and why he can make such long shots."

Rick's face went blank. Stony. She'd entered another area he wouldn't discuss.

"Unless of course the weapon he's using makes him a better shooter," she continued, not taking her gaze from him. "That's it, isn't it? He has some kind of weapon that makes him a supershooter."

No response.

"Okay, you can't talk about it. So I'll simply recap what I

know. We may or may not be dealing with a trained sniper as the shooter. Regardless, you and your team were brought in on what seemed like a simple murder case. And that occurred before we knew two men had been murdered. So it wasn't because of a serial killer. You won't confirm the guy is a sniper, but he's killed two people, both times with one shot from a great distance. So if he isn't a sniper, he must have some sort of special weapon."

She cast him a look and waited for a response. He didn't move. Not a fraction of an inch.

"A special weapon it is, then," she continued, and when he didn't deny it, she dug out her phone to check on the August date in hopes of seeing a reference to some sort of special weaponry. One that would make a superteam like the White Knights hop a plane and give their unbridled focus to a basic murder investigation.

Rick got the car onto the freeway heading back to Atlanta and hoped Olivia would stop asking questions. She was tenacious, he'd give her that, reasoning out the problem and figuring out the killer had a special weapon. He didn't want to keep the information about the smart bullets from her and considered telling her. But that would be a violation of his security clearance, not to mention promises he'd made to the team. He'd never had a problem holding things back from a witness or suspect. But she wasn't just a witness anymore, was she? She'd become so much more to him, and he couldn't let that connection continue to grow, or he'd wind up hurting her. When they got back to Atlanta, he'd try to find a way to spend less time with her while making sure she was safe.

She faced him. "We got off track when we were talking about the reason this shooter might be taking the HOG's tooth."

He nearly blurted out his thanks for bringing up a topic he could discuss. "I think the shooter is targeting snipers as an act of revenge and taking the HOG's tooth to thumb his nose at their training or service."

"Revenge for what?" she asked.

"Maybe Ace and Cesar were part of the same platoon and they were supposed to provide cover for the shooter or for his unit. But the snipers failed in some way, the shooter was injured or someone he cared about died, and he's seeking revenge. Or could be a soldier's family who blames these guys."

"Say that's true. Why suddenly kill them when they've been out of the military for so long?"

Because they now have the weapon to do it. "I'm guessing the timing has never been right. Or if a loved one died, perhaps the family didn't know the details until now. The real key here is finding out if Ace and Cesar knew each other and how. And the SRBs, once we get them, are a good place to start."

She nodded, then fell silent, and miles passed beneath them before she spoke. "Thank you for bringing me along to see Luna. I know it was inconvenient, but I appreciate getting to offer my condolences and to see Patsy, too."

Her sincerity had him swallowing hard. He had additional reasons for letting her come along, and she needed to know that. "I wanted you to be able to see Luna, but I also figured that if you were with me, I could keep an eye on you."

"Oh," she said, the single word laced with sadness. "You still think I'm part of this somehow, and you can't believe what I tell you because you're still leery of people in my profession."

He knew he shouldn't let his experiences keep him from trusting people, but he was no closer to letting it go now than he had been when he'd met her, and he doubted the prayer he'd uttered at the parking garage was going to change that. He was embarrassed to tell her about that, so he kept his mouth shut and his eyes on the road.

"Let me share something I tell my clients," she said. "If you keep believing the lies you tell yourself, you can't move on. Only when you let go of the lie can you move forward and find what God has in store for you."

"You think I'm lying to myself?"

"Come on, Rick. You're a smart guy. Do you really believe all counselors are unethical? Granted, you've had several bad experiences and have every right to be distrusting, but you can't apply your experiences to all counselors. I would never believe all soldiers are a bad lot from the few soldiers I worked with who were. That's not fair to your former profession, and you're not being fair to my profession."

"I . . ." He heard her, got her, knew she was right, and yet . . .

"Some of the hardest issues we have to overcome stem from our childhood," she continued. "We're in a formative state where we naturally trust adults and authority figures. We embrace what they say. If they say we're worthless, then we embed that into our personality and live our life looking for things that prove it out. You were told in counseling that you were wrong to feel the way you do. To trust your father and do as he told you even when you knew it was wrong. If you didn't comply, you'd be to blame for your continued unhappiness, but all you saw was that another adult let you down. Then your father hits you and your mother supports him. Let down again. When Traci has troubles, your only way of dealing with it is to chalk it up to more people you should be able to trust letting you down. In a way you even think Traci let you down because she considered aborting your child, and then may have ended her life."

She paused, maybe waiting for him to speak, but he didn't know what to say.

She continued to hold his gaze. "And now you find you have

feelings for me, so to stop yourself from being let down again, you make the decision that I can't be trusted." She took his hand as he met her gaze. "You can trust me, Rick. I may not be ready for a relationship, but I won't betray your trust. I won't expect more from you than you can give. I won't expect you to be anyone but who you are."

"Won't you?" he asked, hating that he was still suspicious. "Aren't you asking me to be something else right now?"

She didn't speak for a long, awkward moment. "I'm asking you to think about your life. Because whether you know it or not, you're an amazing man who deserves all the peace and happiness you can find. That's what I want for you, Rick. That's what I want."

* * *

Atlanta, Georgia
1:45 p.m.

While Rick delivered the evidence samples and the fence post to Brynn and drove the two of them to his family home, Olivia thought about her advice to him. She deserved the same happiness and peace that she wanted for him. Everyone did. And she wouldn't find happiness or peace by putting limitations on her life and not being open to what God put in front of her. By saying she wouldn't get involved with a man in the military or who had served in the military, she'd acted like Rick.

She'd told him to let go of his issues. To stop lying to himself, when she was embracing her own lie. Worse yet, she was a psychologist, and she knew better. And as a Christian, she knew trying to make any major decision without God was foolish and stressful. Peace only came when she put her life in God's hands.

Rick pulled up to the main house, and she made a promise to herself. She'd trust God. Trust Him to show her how to move forward. Not take things into her own hands. And that included her growing feelings for Rick.

He got out and carried their suitcases to the front door. Once she stepped inside the blissfully cool foyer, he closed and carefully locked the door behind them, then double-checked it. His cautiousness reminded her that right now her feelings weren't important. Not when a killer who Rick was certain would come after her again was still out there. She had to keep her focus on that.

"Mom," he called out.

Olivia waited for a response from Grace or for her to join them, but they were met with silence.

"Maybe she's gone out." His stomach rumbled. "Guess it's easy to tell I'm hungry. How about you?"

"It *has* been a long time since breakfast."

"Then let's go to the kitchen to scrounge up some lunch."

"What about our bags?"

"Leave them here, and we'll take care of them after lunch."

Olivia looked around the spotless foyer. "Are you sure that's okay?"

"Sounds like you're starting to get my point about living in a showplace." He took off across the foyer without waiting for her to answer. He led her to the back of the house and into a large kitchen that resembled a restaurant kitchen more than one in a home. A spicy aroma filling the space set Olivia's mouth watering.

"Ricky, you're back!" Yolanda bustled across the room to embrace him. She bumped into him hard. A Mack Truck came to Olivia's mind, but he took the collision in stride, returning her hug, a contented smile on his face.

Olivia loved seeing his worry evaporate and the tension in his face ease. She'd told him to get over his past, but he had quite a past to get over, and if he decided to try, it would be a hard road.

Another reason not to get any more involved with him. *Right. Putting up your own limitations again.* But she had to this time, didn't she? Her professional experience told her he might never get over his past, and she'd be a fool to get involved with someone carrying so much baggage. But if that was what God willed...

"What's that amazing smell?" Rick asked.

Yolanda pushed back and smiled up at him. "Rosemary chicken. Remember when you used to have fun stripping the leaves off the stem for me?"

He nodded. "More than that, I remember how amazing it tasted."

"Does my heart good to hear that." A wide smile revealed a missing tooth on the bottom, but somehow it fit her personality. "I suppose you discovered that your mother's gone out."

He nodded. "We skipped lunch, and I was hoping I could rustle something up for us."

"You? Of course not, but I'll be glad to plate up the seafood salad I served for lunch. Won't take but a minute." She pointed at stools by a long island that was big enough to be called Long Island.

"I can help," Olivia offered.

"I know you can, and thank you for offering, but it's my pleasure."

Olivia slid onto a padded stool, and Rick joined her. She hoped he would start a conversation, but instead he took out his phone.

"Got Cesar's autopsy report from the ME," he said.

"Now that's not something you should be talking about over food." Yolanda looked up from piling lettuce on chilled plates she'd removed from a refrigerator about the size of Olivia's entire kitchen. "No wonder you're not married."

Olivia tried not to laugh, but she couldn't stop it.

Rick gave her a funny look and set his phone on the counter. "Not that I'm saying you're right, Yo, but what do you suggest we talk about?"

"Oh my, it's worse than I thought. You have a beautiful woman sitting next to you, and you need an old lady's advice on what to say."

Rick gaped at her for a moment, then tossed back his head and laughed. It was deep and melodic and what Olivia would have expected if he ever fully relaxed. And it drew her to him like a tugboat pulling her emotions.

"See." Yolanda pointed her tongs at Olivia. "All you had to do was lighten up, and she's smitten with you."

Rick's smile fell as he swiveled to look at her. Their gazes met, and she felt a physical pull. She fought it off but remained locked on his gaze. The sound of plates clanking onto the counter in front of them was the only thing that kept her from kissing him. She jerked her gaze away and found Yolanda smiling at them.

She patted Olivia's hand. "I'm so glad you can see in him what I know he tries his best to hide."

"Yo, don't—"

"Don't what? Tell her what a compassionate, caring man you can be? I don't need to. She's already figured it out."

He glanced at Olivia again, and she nodded her agreement with Yolanda.

"See," Yolanda crowed. "I'll get your tea and utensils."

"I told you as much in the car," Olivia said.

"You did, but I thought it was your counselor-speak."

"Trust me," she whispered so Yolanda didn't hear. "I'll tell you when I'm talking to you as a professional. Otherwise you can assume anything I say is coming from Olivia the woman."

* * *

Rick was enjoying lunch with Olivia until his phone dinged, reminding him of his responsibilities. He glanced at the text from Max saying he'd e-mailed the SRBs for Griffin and Santos. Rick quickly confirmed the files waited in his e-mail account, then pushed to his feet, albeit reluctantly. He might be feeling comfortable in this big mausoleum of a house for once, but he couldn't sit at the counter and bask in the warm fuzzies when he had work to do. Sure, he liked being with Yolanda. Liked being with Olivia just as much. But he had a killer and lethal bullets to find.

He peered at Yolanda. "I'd love to keep chowing down on your amazing food, but I have work to do."

As if confirming his need to leave, he received a text from Cal. *Security guard lead didn't pan out.*

"Thank you for the delicious lunch, Yolanda." Olivia stepped down from her stool.

Yolanda waved a hand. "Shoot, I'm happy to feed you anytime you want."

Rick gave Yolanda a quick hug. "I'll be waiting for tonight's dinner."

She smiled up at him, her broad cheeks rising as a sigh of happiness escaped. Her contentment had always drawn him to her. No matter her life situation, no matter her turmoil, the only way he ever knew she was having a problem was that he would find her reading her Bible more frequently than for her usual daily devotions. Reading the Bible, along with regular church attendance, was something he'd given up when Traci died. Maybe he was blaming God. Could that be part of his problem?

"Now you two come back anytime," she said, and planted a big kiss on his cheek.

He hugged her tight again, maybe clinging to the one solid rock he'd had in his life other than God. He'd clung to neither of them in so long, and he was adrift. He needed to anchor himself again, and then maybe he'd figure out the mess of his personal life.

Olivia studied him as if she could read his mind. Shoot, maybe she could. She was a shrink, after all. A good one, he suspected. Especially since she'd told him she was a Christian counselor. As she'd stated, not all counselors were bad, and being an ethical Christian counselor had to make a world of difference.

He smiled at her and received a surprised look and shy smile in response.

"Now aren't the two of you cute as can be." Yolanda clapped her hands. "They're singing in heaven over this connection, Ricky. Now don't mess it up."

Rick rolled his eyes and gestured for Olivia to go ahead.

In the hallway she turned to Rick. "Yolanda's quite a lady. Her family is very lucky."

"She never married."

"So you're like a son to her."

He frowned.

"What did I say?"

"She always meant a lot to me." He ran a hand over his head, messing his hair, then tried to right it but without a mirror had to give up. "But honestly, I didn't realize until this visit that I was as important to her. I should have tried harder to visit her more often over the years."

"You can change that."

"I can at that." Before they could get sidetracked again, he held out his phone. "Max e-mailed Ace and Cesar's military records. Maybe you could help me find a connection between them."

"Sure."

"We can print the e-mails in my father's office." He led the way even deeper into the house to an office with paneled walls, a heavy mahogany desk, and dark leather chairs.

Thankful he had the wireless network password so he could print from his phone, Rick went straight to the printer. After Griffin's report finished, he tapped the pages to order them, then found a clip and handed them to Olivia. She took the report to the table while he waited for the remaining pages of the other SRB to finish printing along with the autopsy reports.

"Where do we start?" she asked.

He joined her at the table. "At the beginning. Both Ace and Cesar were infantry and may have gone through boot camp together. Find Ace's enlistment date and location of training."

As she scanned the file, he quickly located Santos's information. "Cesar enlisted in 2000."

"Ace was 1998."

"Okay, so they didn't go through either School of Infantry phase together. Move on to their assignments." Rick ran his finger down the page and called out Santos's assignments, but Olivia shot each of them down.

"Ace attended sniper school at Camp Lejeune."

"When?" Rick asked, his excitement building.

"October 2003."

"Bingo!" He pumped a fist high above his head. "They were in sniper school together."

"And we know they both graduated."

Rick sat back, thoughts burning through his mind. "Wait...
'03. That was Levi's class."

"Your friend," she said. "The one whose son is your godson."

"Yes. Levi was my spotter for my last years of enlistment.
He'll know the names of the other guys who graduated from his
class."

"Do you think the shooter's in that class, and for some reason
he's killing off his classmates?"

"Could be." The thought of his best friend, the only person
besides Yolanda who gave him a sense of family, taking a .50 to
the gut sent a cold wave of fear over him.

She grabbed his arm. "We have to warn him."

"He's deployed right now, and I know that no soldiers from
his class are in his platoon, so he should be fine until he returns
stateside." At least that's what Rick prayed.

"When will that be?"

"A few days," Rick said, suddenly realizing that when he
next talked to Levi, he would have to tell his bud about the
death of two guys who would have meant the world to him.

"Can you call him? To get the names of the other snipers in
his class?"

"I'll text him and ask him to call. He's traveling, though, so
he may not be able to respond quickly."

She chewed on her lower lip. "What about other ways to get
the information?"

"I'll put Max on it, but it took days to get SRBs. Could take
as long for the list of the '03 class graduates."

She tightened her hold on his arm. "Then we better pray that
Levi's somewhere he can take the call. Because without that information, we might be looking at another sniper losing his life."

CHAPTER
21

Levi's reply to Rick's text came at one a.m., when everyone else had gone to bed. Not Rick. He couldn't sleep until he'd heard from his friend and warned him of the danger. Rick opened the text and read. *32 in the class. 8 guys graduated. 1 died in the line of duty.*

Eight of thirty-two snipers was lower than the ratio for a typical class. Levi could never murder a fellow marine. Griffin and Santos were gone, as was this other member Levi mentioned in the text. That left four possible suspects in their graduating class. A very manageable list to run down. But was he thinking too narrowly?

Also possible was that one of the men who hadn't graduated held a grudge against the graduates and was killing them. He hadn't killed before because he couldn't make such a long shot unassisted. To qualify for the Schoolhouse, he'd have to have earned a marine corps rifle qualification badge, meaning he'd repeatedly hit targets from five hundred yards. The odds of getting caught at that range were greater, but smart bullets gave him sniper abilities. And if he was a washout, he'd never received a HOG's tooth, so he could be taking them as a souvenir to prove that even without one he was superior to the graduates.

Levi would have a feel for the entire class, but he wouldn't know the washouts as well as he knew his fellow graduates. Rick would focus on the smaller group and have Kaci gather information on the nongraduates, then widen his circle as necessary.

He typed into his phone, *Can you talk?*

I'll call you, came the immediate reply.

Rick moved to his desk and dug out a pen and notepad. Engraved at the top of the paper was the logo for the Saint Francis High School Knights. *The Knights.* His former football team was called the Knights, too. Odd that he hadn't thought of that before now, but then he rarely thought of his life in Atlanta. He had fond memories of the football team, but attending the posh private school where they groomed students to emulate people like his father? Not so much.

He woke up his phone and stared at the device, willing it to ring soon. When it did, he punched talk. "Give me their names."

"Hello to you, too." Levi chuckled.

"Sorry. Can you please give me the graduating snipers' names?" He used the diplomatic tone he had been taught at Saint Francis, and that made Levi laugh even harder. "C'mon, man. Don't keep me in suspense."

"Okay, let's see. There's Dirk James, Marcus Floyd, Jim Patton, Archie Griffin—Ace to us—Philip Neal...he's a senator now." Levi snorted. "He never had a political bone in his body. Now he's serving on the Senate Committee on Armed Services and making the decisions you and I once complained about. I would *never* have seen that coming."

Rick jotted down the names and underlined Neal's. Could these murders have to do with the guy's political office, specifically the Committee on Armed Services? Maybe the other killings were meant to cover up an assassination attempt planned for Neal.

"And the other guys?" Rick asked, as he only had five names on paper.

"Cesar Santos. And then there was Karl Little. He was this humongous guy, and we called him Tank. He's the one who died. Happened about five years ago. We all got tattoos in his honor."

That clarified what Griffin had told Olivia and matched Luna's dates as well. And if they'd gotten the tats five years ago—right after Rick left for civilian life—it explained why he hadn't known about Levi's tattoo.

"Tell me about the tat," Rick said.

"It's called a chaos tattoo. It has—"

"Eight arrows coming from a circle."

"Hey, man. How'd you know?"

Despite a gut tight with emotions, Rick told Levi about his friends, trying to soften the blow, but there was no way around saying two of the guys he'd gone through hell and back with had died, too.

"Man. Oh man...man...Like wow. That's rough." Levi fell silent.

Rick gave him time to process and didn't push the conversation, but sat back to wait for Levi to speak again.

"You're running this investigation, huh?" he finally asked.

"Yeah."

"Then promise me this. You'll get this jerk, and you'll do it before he hits anyone else."

"I can promise I'll get him and do it as fast as I can."

"That's all I can ask, I guess." A long sigh filtered through the phone. "What else do you need to know?"

"Have you ever heard of a Dr. Olivia Dobbs?"

"Sounds familiar, but I don't know why."

"She's a counselor who specializes in PTSD."

"I know Ace and Cesar got help for that. Maybe that's where I heard the name."

"You stay in touch with these guys?"

"Ace not so much. We all tried, but he ended up on the street and was hard to find. Cesar kept an eye on him, though. Cesar credited Ace for getting him through the Schoolhouse, and he mentioned a few trips to Atlanta to check up on Ace."

That explained the trips Luna had mentioned. "Do you think Santos might have referred Griffin to Dr. Dobbs?"

"Sure, yeah, if she really was Cesar's doc. She got him back on track, and I know he was grateful. So yeah...sure...he'd give her a good recommendation."

Rick made a note to tell her about Santos's appreciation of her help.

"So *was* she Ace's doc?" Levi asked.

"Yes."

"Obviously you think these killings are related to my class," Levi said. "You worried the rest of us are in danger?"

"I am," Rick said. "And I also think someone from the class is doing the killing."

"No way," Levi snapped out. "No. No way. You know how it is. Going through the Schoolhouse together. We'll be brothers forever. Even with the guys who didn't make it. We'd never turn on each other, and you might as well stop thinking that right now."

"Yes, but—"

"But you won't listen to me," he shouted. "You've forgotten

how it feels to be part of our family and started to act like that straitlaced lawman you've become."

Rick detected a level of frustration far deeper than the situation called for. Or did Levi think Rick was turning his back on him? "This isn't personal, man."

"Isn't it? You're bad-mouthing my bros."

Rick could see Levi's point, and if the situation were reversed, Rick would be protesting, too. "Then tell me about them so I can clear their names faster."

"What's to tell? Marcus met a mine with his name on it in Afghanistan, and he's living off disability. Dirk and Jimbo are still serving. Dirk's attached to the 1/7 and Jimbo the 2/4."

With two of the guys still in the marines, their whereabouts at the time of the shootings could easily be determined.

"If you had to vote one of your remaining classmates most likely to turn killer," Rick said, "who would it be?"

"You gotta know it's not me."

"Of course it's not." Still, Rick would have Levi investigated as protocol dictated. "So who would you pick?"

"Dude, don't even make me guess." He sighed again. "You'll be all over the person I name, and I won't do that to one of my guys."

"I'll make sure he's treated fairly."

"Not happening, so leave it alone."

He respected Levi's commitment to his brothers, but Rick had a job to do. He glanced at the notepad and zeroed in on the suspect who'd been wounded and might have an ax to grind. "Tell me about Marcus."

"Okay, but we need to be clear that I'm not saying he did anything."

"I'm clear."

"The loss of his leg really changed him. He lives in Nevada

out in the desert in a compound. He hooked up with some lib-
eral antigovernment groups, but other than that, he keeps to
himself."

"Did he blame the marines for his injuries?"

"He has some issues there, but if he went postal because of
it, the guys on the team are the last ones he'd take out."

"Still, I'll have to send someone to question him."

"And warn him, right? I mean, if this is about the team, he
could be in danger, too."

"Right," Rick said. "You're sure one of the guys who washed
out wouldn't want to kill you all?"

"C'mon, man. We settled that. I'm not ratting someone out."

"Okay, then how about outside of the class? Can you think
of a reason anyone would target you all?"

"Man, I don't know. I mean it's been a long time since
we were together, and I'm guessing this situation is recent,
right?"

"Maybe. Maybe not." Rick hated to be so vague with his
buddy, but he couldn't tell Levi about the smart-bullet theft.

"You know, you could be wrong about everything. So what if
two of the guys from our class were killed? Doesn't mean it has
to do with the class at all. Could be something Cesar and Ace
were involved in."

"True, and if so, our investigation will reveal that, but I want
to get your gut feel on who could be targeting your class. Did
any of you serve together after graduation?"

"Cesar and Dirk did, and so did Marcus and Ace."

"But never Santos and Griffin?"

"No, and I don't know about the other guys. This is bizarre,
isn't it? We survive the war and then this? Seems unfair. Will
you keep me updated?"

"As much as I can," Rick promised. "And you can be sure

we'll check in with all the guys to make sure they're safe and provide protection for them."

"Then be aware that Marcus doesn't like visitors and won't take too kindly to you suits showing up there."

Rick ignored the suits remark. "You stateside yet?"

"Still en route."

"When you arrive in Atlanta, I'll have a fed waiting to protect you."

He groaned. "You gonna send someone back to Pendleton with me, too?"

"Yes, if we haven't found the shooter by the time you're ready to leave," Rick replied. "I get that you don't think you need anyone by your side. Especially not some FBI agent. But don't fight me."

"At least make sure the fed you send can handle a weapon as well as I can."

"No can do. The only person like that is me, and as much as I'm glad to save your butt like I did so many times downrange, I have something else I need to do."

A big belly laugh rumbled through the phone. "Seems to me you've gone soft in the head. It was totally the other way around. *I* was the one saving butts."

"Whatever." Rick closed their conversation by reiterating his warning to take care. He grabbed the notepad and rushed to Max's room.

Max answered his door in a flash and didn't bother asking what was going on, just stepped back to let Rick enter. Rick headed straight to the chairs by the window, but decided he was too antsy to sit. He handed the list of guys to Max and told him about the call.

"We also need to consider the soldiers who didn't graduate," Rick said. "But that's a long list. Twenty-four guys, to be exact.

I'd like to start with the short list of graduates, and have Kaci run checks on the ones who washed out. Then, if need be, we dig deeper into them."

Max nodded as he peered at the notepad. "The graduating class started with a total of eight guys. Three are dead, leaving five men in that group who could be our killer."

Rick nodded. "Subtract the senator and my friend Levi from the group, and that leaves only three possibilities. Marcus Floyd, Dirk James, and Jim Patton. Patton and James are still active marines stationed out of Pendleton. They can't move about freely like civilians can, so getting an alibi for the night of the theft and the murders should be easier."

"And this Floyd guy?"

"From what Levi said, I think he might be our guy." He shared about Floyd's injury and living conditions.

"I'll get local agents out to the base and to Floyd's house. We'll bring all three guys in to question them. Might hold them for their own protection, too." Max eyed Rick. "I'll also assign an agent to your buddy once he hits the States."

"Already told him to expect a sidekick after he lands. We need to warn the senator, too."

Max glanced at his watch. "He won't like the late-night call, but it can't be helped. I'll impress upon him the importance of going to ground until we can get a detail on him."

"You planning to tell him about the smart bullet?"

"Can't do that yet."

"Then how will you get him to hole up somewhere?"

"I don't know, but warning him that a sniper is after him should do the trick."

"If he's like every other sniper I know, he'll think he can handle the situation on his own."

"After working with you, I totally get that." A wry smile crossed Max's face. "Do you have a better idea?"

"Better? . . . Not sure, but Neal serves on the Senate Committee on Armed Services, and I'm thinking Griffin and Santos's deaths might be a ruse to cover up an assassination attempt on Neal. Means he could be the next on the list and deserves the best team for his detail. We should head to D.C. to watch his back." Max frowned, so Rick rushed on. "We need to interview him anyway. We can take care of both things at one time. If he's the next target, we'll be in place to capture the shooter."

"True." Max narrowed his eyes. "What about the local leads we haven't run down?"

"Like what? The employees Griffin worked with or the shooting ranges? We can turn them over to locals, and you can follow up on collection of the McDonald's videos via long distance."

"And what about Olivia? We can't leave her unprotected."

"Simple. She comes with us."

Max eyed Rick, his gaze mining for any hidden agenda. He could be looking for a personal reason Rick wanted to bring Olivia to D.C., so Rick put on his best poker face and didn't argue his case to further inflame Max's suspicions.

Max looked at his watch. "We go now so we're camped on the senator's doorstep before he gets out of bed in the morning."

"Understood." Rick headed off to wake everyone so the team could be in position before the sniper struck in D.C. and claimed the senator's life.

CHAPTER

22

Washington, D.C.
Sunday, September 17
5:00 a.m.

On the D.C. Beltway with Olivia beside him in the car, Rick tapped his thumb on the steering wheel. He was antsy and impatient. Too much time had passed without information on the senator's safety. Max had left Neal a voice mail before they'd left Atlanta, but they hadn't heard back. No way Rick's concern would abate until Max called in an update.

If only Rick had been able to continue on to D.C. with the team, but due to her lack of security clearance, Olivia couldn't land at the team's top-secret airfield there. So they'd made a stop at Turner Field at the Marine Corps Air Facility in Quantico, Virginia. While there, Rick dropped off the fence post at the FBI lab for the Toolmarks team to review. The rest of the Knights had continued directly to the senator's condo, and Rick and Olivia were driving to D.C.

"Come on, Max," Rick muttered. "Call."

Olivia faced him. "Relax, or you'll burn out before we even get to our destination."

"Something's wrong. Max should have called by now." His

phone chimed in Max's ringtone, and Rick picked it up to answer. "About time."

"You sitting down?" Max asked.

"In the car," Rick replied, his gut tightening. "Almost to the office."

"You'll want to detour to the senator's condo. He's been killed. Same ammo. Found him on his balcony."

Just as Rick had predicted. Worse, even. "When?"

"ME puts Neal's time of death about the time I left a message to warn him."

"Do you think the call woke him, and he stepped out there?"

"If it did, he never listened to the message, as it was still displaying on his phone as a new voice mail when we arrived. Looks like he went out for a middle-of-the-night smoke, which his wife said wasn't uncommon."

"Text me the address, and I'll be there as soon as I can." Rick ended the call and slammed a fist against the wheel. "Senator Neal's been murdered."

"Oh, how awful." Olivia clutched her hands together and rested them on her denim skirt.

His phone dinged, and he activated the address from Max in the phone's GPS. "We're rerouting to the senator's condo. I won't have time to find an alternate safe location for you. You can't stay in the car, so you'll have to come with me. I'll try to find a quiet place for you to wait."

"Don't worry about me. Since I had to miss church today, I'll find an online service or devotional on my phone."

He nodded, but honestly, he couldn't think about missing church right now. He hadn't been attending, but at least he now realized he should start going again. He'd rectify that after they had their killer behind bars and returned the ordnance to MilMed.

"I need to caution you," he added. "We know the shooter was in D.C. as late at 0130. Means he could still be in town and watching."

Fear flashed in her eyes. "I hadn't considered that."

"As we move from the car to Senator Neal's building, you'll need to follow my every instruction even if it makes no sense to you." He tried to smile, but failed. "No questioning. Just do as I say as quickly as you can."

"Of course." She fell back on the seat, her hands tightening even more.

He'd scared her, but he'd had no choice. A healthy respect for the danger would ensure she reacted quickly, and maybe he had a chance of protecting her from the same fate as Neal.

Rick made a quick U-turn and followed the route into the heart of D.C. to the senator's high-rise condo. Local police had cordoned off the street crowded with early-morning pedestrians pausing to gawk.

Rick found a parking space on a side street. He turned off the engine and faced Olivia. "On the walk to the building, I need you to remain on the inside and close to me. No stopping or getting ahead. Okay?"

"Yes. Yes, of course."

"I'll scope out the area first, and then I'll come around to open your door." He didn't wait for her to respond, but stepped into the refreshingly cool air. At only sixty degrees, it was easier to breathe here than in Atlanta, but apprehension still tightened his chest.

He searched the street lined with tall buildings where a shooter could easily hide on a rooftop. He honestly doubted their suspect would be hanging out in the area after killing a senator, but killers could be unpredictable. Especially a serial killer who'd gotten away with multiple crimes. The more lives they took without getting caught, the bolder they became.

Rick checked both sides of the street, but there was no way he could see the extreme distance a smart bullet could travel. He had to believe in his skills. And in God, he supposed. He was the only one who could really protect Olivia from these deadly bullets.

He opened Olivia's door and stepped back. She moved to the inside of the sidewalk as instructed. With a hand on her lower back, he urged her even closer to the buildings. The senator's high-rise soon came into view, and Rick scanned the floors to the top, not surprised to see lights glowing in most windows and occupants watching the action. Thankfully, Neal's balcony wasn't located at the front of the building, in view of onlookers.

Rick displayed his credentials to the officer manning a barricade, and then to the officer of record at the front door. He took down Rick's information, and they stepped under the wide portico to enter a spacious foyer with pricey furniture and decor. Not surprising when a one-bedroom condo sold for over half a million in the sought-after Penn Quarter.

Rick directed Olivia across the foyer and away from the windows. He let out a long breath, releasing his stress over moving her safely inside. He displayed his credentials for the uniformed doorman, who stood to the side gnawing on his lip, then arranged for Olivia to wait in a small office on the main floor.

Once she was settled, Rick started for the door, hating with every step that he had to leave her behind. He paused and looked back at her. "You sure you'll be okay here?"

She held up her phone. "Going to church, remember?"

"Right." He forced out a smile. "You can reach me by cell. Don't hesitate to call if you need anything, okay?"

"Don't worry about me. Just go do your thing."

"Promise me you won't leave this room for any reason without me by your side."

"Even to go to the restroom?"

"Even then. Call me. I'll come down to escort you and wait by the door." He could tell by her look that she believed he was overreacting, but there was no way he could go overboard in his efforts to keep her alive.

At the lobby elevator, he selected the seventh out of nine floors, and the nearly silent car took him to the senator's condo. Rick slipped on disposable booties and gloves from the box at the doorway before entering the condo. The small foyer opened up to a large combination living room, dining room, and kitchen with pricey artwork filling white walls. A slight woman sat on a small sofa, her arms crossed and her head bowed. No doubt the senator's wife. She looked up, her eyes swollen and red.

"If you're looking for the others, they're on the balcony with Philip." A sob wrenched from her throat.

"Thank you, ma'am," he said. "I'm sorry for your loss."

A clipped nod, and she dabbed a tissue at her eyes.

He moved past her to the sliding door and onto the balcony. Max and Shane stood to the right, an area directly outside the room Rick thought to be the bedroom. Neal lay in congealed blood in front of them. Dead. Murdered.

Rick ground his teeth together. How had he failed another marine? Three dead now. How many more before Rick figured out the shooter's identity? How many?

Guilt tried to overwhelm him. He wanted to grab the turquoise owl figurine from the patio table to smash it on the concrete, but balled his fingers into fists instead. What good would it do to destroy something? It wouldn't eliminate his guilt or frustration. He could far better serve the senator by focusing, figuring out the shooter's hide location, and bringing in the killer.

He looked at the body again. Neal's position told Rick that the senator had been facing east, and that the shot had come from the same direction. The building was one of the tallest in the area, so Rick's view to the east stretched as far as the eye could see. He turned to find a concrete privacy wall on the west side of the balcony with a fairly round bullet hole in it, meaning the shot had come from a similar elevation. Rick looked for the slug but didn't see it. Either it had lodged too deeply in the thick concrete wall to see, the team had already recovered it, or it had passed through. Max would have the details.

Rick joined him and Shane. "Since you mentioned Neal was killed with a smart bullet, does that mean you recovered it?"

Max nodded. "Passed through the wall behind you and into the adjoining neighbor's balcony. Brynn's over there now."

"Anyone besides the team see it?"

Max shook his head. "We got here before anyone else was up and moving. We had the doorman call up, and he woke Mrs. Neal. When we found the body, we immediately went next door and woke the neighbor so we could recover the bullet."

Rick peered into the distance. "Looks like the shooter's escalating."

"How's that?" Shane asked.

Rick moved his focus back to Shane. "He took a kill shot where he had no hope of recovering the bullet or taking the senator's HOG's tooth. If the guy even wore his."

"Since the shooter didn't recover the bullet that killed Griffin, he probably didn't worry about keeping things under wraps anymore," Shane said.

"Then I'm right and he's getting reckless and escalating quickly," Rick warned. "A deadly combination."

* * *

"We're almost there." Kaci glanced at Olivia from behind the wheel of her compact car.

"Thanks for driving me." Olivia yawned after a long day of doing nothing.

"With our shooter in the wind, we couldn't very well have you riding on the back of Rick's Harley."

Thinking of his excitement when he'd left to pick up his bike from the airport made Olivia smile. "He really seems to love that bike."

"I don't think *love* is a strong-enough word." Kaci wrinkled her nose. "It was a rusty old thing when he bought it. We all thought he was crazy, but wait until you see it. He's restored every inch, and it's real pretty."

"Should I tell him how pretty it is when I see him?"

Kaci shot a horrified look in Olivia's direction. "Not if you want to live."

"So he loves the bike, *and* he's touchy about it."

"Yeah, I mean, it's a real guy's bike, you know. At least that's what he says when he says anything."

"Kind of the silent type."

Kaci scowled. "I'll say."

Olivia heard the low, throaty rumble of a motorcycle from behind, and she didn't have to look to know Rick had caught up to them. He roared past and saluted. He wore a worn leather jacket and black helmet, and sat on the motorcycle with such confidence, Olivia's interest in him rose even higher.

He disappeared ahead on an exit ramp, his bike leaning into the curve, and Olivia worried he might wipe out. A shudder rolled over her body.

"What's wrong?" Kaci asked.

"I have a fear of motorcycles."

"Bad experience?"

Olivia nodded. "With my dad. He was kind of a daredevil."

"Rick seems pretty responsible as far as I can see."

"Honestly? I think he'd be the kind of guy to take risks."

"He doesn't have a death wish, if that's what you mean."

"No, he's just a guy who likes the thrill of risky things."

"You could be right." Kaci took the exit, and they moved into a residential neighborhood with trees and grass, a pleasant sight after Olivia's day of confinement.

She'd sat in the windowless office at the condo until lunchtime. Then Rick had picked up takeout and, despite its being Sunday, he'd transported her to FBI headquarters, where she again sat alone in an empty office while a young agent babysat her and the team frantically searched for a lead.

Kaci turned onto a dead-end street. A garage door sat open in a traditional bungalow with brick siding. The house and landscaping were neat, not a surprise given Rick's personality. Kaci pulled into the driveway, and Rick stepped out of the garage. He'd removed his helmet and wore the same peaceful expression Olivia had seen when he was with Yolanda, but there was something else lingering in his eyes. Boyish charm oozed from him, and her heart tripped again.

Oh, man. She was in over her head with him, and the last thing she should be doing was spending the night at his house. Not because she was worried anything improper would happen, but because she would learn more about him, and undoubtedly fall even further for him. She might be open to the fact that God had put Rick in her life, but he had so many unresolved issues. Surely God would want her to use the common sense He'd given her and be leery of those issues, right?

She turned to Kaci. "What are you doing tonight?"

"Working, why?"

"I wondered if you could join us for dinner. Maybe hang out for a while."

Kaci appraised her for a long moment. "You're safe here with Rick, you know. He won't let anything bad happen to you, and you don't need another agent around."

It wasn't her safety she was worried about. At least not the safety of anything more than her heart.

"Thanks for the ride." She grabbed her tote from the back, then joined Rick.

Kaci departed without talking to Rick, but he waved and eyed the street, his tranquility disappearing. "We should go straight inside."

In the garage she turned her attention to the motorcycle. The large bike had a red gas tank and fenders, shiny chrome detailing, and a rich black leather seat that resembled an oversize bicycle seat.

"Kaci warned me to keep quiet, but I have to say, your bike is real pretty." She grinned at him and waited for his response.

"If you repeat this to anyone else I'll deny it," he said solemnly. "But she *is* real pretty, isn't she?" His grin held a bit of devilment, and his gaze locked on her.

He moved closer, his focus riveted to her. She waited, breath held, and he seemed to move in slow motion. The moment when she'd thought he planned to kiss her came rushing back. She'd stepped back then, but now she was powerless to move. He stopped close enough for her to catch his musky scent. She filled her lungs with air. Her heart open. Waiting. Hoping. Anticipating.

He reached out. Expecting the softness of his touch on her face, she closed her eyes. The strap for her bag was lifted from her shoulder. Her eyes flew open.

Rick stood watching her. "I'm getting hungry, how about you?"

"For food," she squeaked out.

"Yeah, what did you think I meant?"

"Nothing."

A knowing look crossed his face, and he colored a deep red. Mr. Big, Strong, Fearless Agent and Sniper was blushing. Oh, man, that was even more tempting, but she had to leave it alone. Focus on food. "I suppose you won't have much in the refrigerator."

"I can scrounge something up. Worst case, I keep meals in the freezer that I prepared earlier so I know I'll have food to come home to."

"You cook?"

"Yeah, I find it relaxing." He smiled. "You can close your mouth now. It's not that shocking, is it?"

"Um, yes, it is."

Chuckling, he headed inside the house, and she followed him down a hallway to a large living space. She'd expected closed-off rooms in the older house, not a contemporary space with vaulted ceilings. The open kitchen sat to the right, and a wall of windows at the back displayed a large deck and big yard.

"Your home is beautiful. I expected..." She stopped before she offended him.

"What? A bachelor pad filled with big leather furniture and a huge TV?"

She nodded.

"Nice to see I can surprise you so many times in a few minutes." He set her bag on the floor. "And you were sure you had me all figured out."

"I'll admit your house is totally not what I expected."

"Guess my mom's taste rubbed off on me more than I thought."

"And Yolanda's in the kitchen, I hope?"

He chuckled and opened the refrigerator. "I've got soda, juice, and water."

"Water, please. I feel parched after this day."

"I'm sorry you had to sit and do nothing. That wasn't in the plans."

She waved off his concern. "Did you learn anything that will help find the killer?"

His eyes creased, a hint of despair coloring them. "That's the thing about long-distance kills. The shooter doesn't leave evidence behind at the crime scene. Sure, we can find his stand, but by the time we get there, it can be contaminated by people who had no idea they were trampling evidence. Today's spot was a perfect example. Another public parking garage."

"But you found the saliva and paint at the garage in Mobile. And you have the fence post, too."

"Yes, and I'm still hoping they'll produce a lead." He opened the freezer. "Since it's so warm out, why don't I grill? I've got some great chops."

"Sure, if you're up to it."

"Like I said, it relaxes me. Same reason I like riding my Harley."

"You do seem different here."

He took out a packet wrapped in white butcher paper and set it on a plate. "Different how?"

She slid onto to a bar stool. "Softer. More talkative."

He popped the plate into the microwave and tapped buttons to send it whirring into action. He leaned back on the counter, crossing his ankles and placing his hands on the countertop behind him, drawing her attention to his powerful chest. "Guess this is where I feel the most comfortable. Not like at my parents' house. I want my place to feel like it should be lived in. Not a showplace."

"It's very warm and inviting. I like it." *And you.*

He pushed off the counter. "Why don't we head outside? There should be some lettuce, tomatoes, and cukes in the garden if Cathy hasn't picked it all."

"Okay, wait. A garden? That's too much for me to believe."

"Since I'm gone a lot, my neighbor does most of the work, but she reaps the rewards, too. After multiple tours overseas and more MREs than I care to mention, I like knowing where my food comes from."

Olivia rested the back of her hand on her forehead and pretended to faint. "You can't keep springing these surprises on me. I might not make it until morning."

He laughed hard, and after grabbing a colander, he came around the island to peer at her. "Would you like to see my garden or my cooking apron?"

Her mouth fell open again.

He crooked a finger under her chin and closed it. "Just kidding about the apron."

Laughing, he headed for the patio door, which he slid wide open to let the lovely breeze fill the stuffy house. She traipsed after him over a wide deck and down stairs to three raised garden beds. He circled each bed, his fingers dancing over the leaves, and she expected him to start humming any moment. He stopped at towering metal cages holding tall plants with red, yellow, and purple fruits.

"All tomatoes?" she asked.

"Yep." He handed her the colander. "Here, hold this."

"You might be relaxed, but you're still bossy in your garden."

That devilish grin returned, but he didn't say a word.

He plucked large red and yellow tomatoes from the vine and placed them in the colander. Next came a few purple ones and a few handfuls of cherry tomatoes. "The cherries are for snacking on while we wait for dinner." He snapped a few branches from a lower-growing plant that she recognized as basil and dropped them in the colander.

"Mmm, basil." The sweet scent made her taste buds stand up and take notice. "How did you learn to garden?"

"Traci." His smile disappeared. "She loved it, so I decided to find out why."

"And did you find something besides knowing where your food comes from?"

"I guess more of that peace that I mentioned." He moved to another bed with a trellis covered in vines and started picking green beans and dropping them in with the tomatoes. "The lettuce has bolted in the heat, so we'll have green beans."

"You keep mentioning peace. If you reconciled with your family, you might find it more often."

His head snapped up, and gone was the good humor. "Now you've gone to meddling."

He turned his attention back to the vines and forcefully tossed beans into the colander.

She'd spoiled the mood. She opened her mouth to apologize but then snapped it shut. Maybe a bit of tension was a good thing, as it would keep them both from giving in tonight to feelings they had no business giving in to.

CHAPTER

23

Seated in a comfy chair at the patio table, Rick sliced into his thick chop grilled with honey barbeque sauce, but his usual joy in dining outside was missing. He wanted to relax and enjoy the meal with Olivia. Take a few moments away from the investigation to regroup and clear his head so that when he got back to it, he'd have sharper focus. Even more, he wanted Olivia to enjoy herself. She'd seemed to be having a good time until he'd blown up at her in the garden. She'd hardly said a word since then. He had to make things right.

"I'm sorry," he blurted out. "I was rude before."

"It's okay. I understand." She forked a bite of the basil tomatoes.

"No, it's not okay, but thank you for understanding." He lifted the chop toward his mouth but held off on biting. "You may not think I get it, but I do. You think I'm broken. As a counselor you feel a need to fix me, so you keep trying."

Her head popped up. "I don't think you're broken and in need of fixing."

"But you..." He shrugged.

"I suggested you try to make things right with your parents, but do I think that if you don't, you'll lead a miserable life? Fail to be all that you can be? No. I don't. I simply think you'll feel better if you made the effort. That's all." She took a long sip of water. "And FYI, I don't think people are broken in general. There's no one right way to be—one perfect and actualized human being to strive for. God made each of us uniquely gifted and endowed. Just be that person."

"I'm not sure I agree. I see some pretty broken people in my job."

"Right. There are social deviants who I agree are broken. Or people with serious mental health issues. But overall, most of us are trying to get by and enjoy life."

"What about your clients?"

"Broken? Not most of them." She leaned closer. "They get up each morning. Go to work. Deal with day-to-day issues. They don't act out in aggressive ways. Some self-medicate with alcohol or drugs, creating additional issues in their lives, but by and large they go on." She frowned. "Ace was not one of those clients, but he also had other mental health issues going on."

Rick slowly chewed a bite of green beans and savored the flavor as he thought. "You said the other day that unless otherwise stated, your opinions are from Olivia the woman, not from the doc."

"That's right."

"But isn't it hard to separate? I mean, I look at people through my law enforcement point of view all the time. So how is it different for you?"

"Because I make a conscious effort not to shrink people, as you would say. Sure, I form an instant impression of people, the way most everyone does, but I try my hardest with those I care about to be just a person."

"You care about me, then." He winked and expected his teasing would bring out a smile. Instead she frowned.

"I guess I do." She sounded reluctant to admit it.

"And it's clear that you don't much like the idea."

"I don't want to talk about it."

"Ha! How's that fair?"

"I suppose it's not, but that's how I feel right now." She took a bite of her chop and chewed.

He couldn't very well expect her to talk when he'd been so closemouthed, so he moved on. "Isn't it hard not to want to help people all the time? You have a wonderful education, and you're a very compassionate woman. I'd think when you see them going down the wrong path, it would be hard not to try to help."

"Yes." She set down her fork. "And based on my relationship with my family, it's clear I err by stepping in."

"But is that helping them?" he asked, hoping she didn't take offense at his comment.

"No, but it's also not making them resent me for shrinking them."

Realization hit him. She was exactly as she'd seemed from day one. Caring. Kind. Committed to her work. Nothing like Dr. Fox or the shrink from his teen years.

And she was everything he would want in a life partner. Where Traci had been dependent and needy, Olivia was strong and independent. She wouldn't fall apart when he deployed, but could easily function on her own. That thought had him falling back in his chair. How could he keep his mind on protecting her when all he wanted to do was kiss her until they were both breathless?

A quizzical expression claimed her face. "Is something wrong?"

Boy howdy, was it. "We should finish up here so I can get to reviewing files."

"Can I help with them?"

"The files?" *No* came to his mind right off the bat, but maybe her clinical education could be helpful. "I assume you've had human anatomy classes. You could look at the autopsy reports for Ace and Cesar and might see something I'm missing."

"Sure." She sat back.

"It's not urgent," he said. "You can finish eating."

"I've eaten enough, and if I hadn't, the talk of autopsies stole my appetite."

"Sorry. Autopsies are a routine part of my job, so I don't think anything of them. Besides, after the marines, I can eat under most any conditions."

"Then by all means." She gestured at his plate. "Eat away, and I'll sit here and enjoy looking at your yard." She stared into the distance but soon shook her head.

He swallowed his bite. "What?"

"You. A garden. Cooking. Next thing you'll tell me is you sew, too."

"If mending things in the marines and sewing up a wound count, then yeah, I'm a regular seamstress."

She laughed, and he was glad to see her good mood return. As he finished eating, she asked questions about the garden and his neighbor, sounding a bit jealous. Or maybe he wanted her to be jealous.

"Cathy is going on eighty," he said. "But she's very spry, and she loves tending the garden."

Olivia nodded as if he'd offered sage advice, telling him she really did have misgivings about Cathy. He wiped his mouth with his napkin and pushed to his feet. "For dessert I have ice cream and raspberry sauce I froze this summer. We can have that later, long after we put the reports away."

"Do you want to work inside?"

"Normally I'd say yes because I'd get distracted out here, but you'll keep me on track, right?"

"Yes, sir." She saluted.

He stacked her plate on his. "I'll be right back with the files."

In the kitchen he stopped to look back at her sitting in his garden. At his home. Someone to talk to other than Cathy. This was how his life would be with a woman in it again. He could easily get used to it. Very easily. But even if he could get past not trusting Olivia, he didn't want another person to lose their life because he'd given in to his feelings and spent the night enjoying her company when he had a killer to find.

He slung his backpack over a shoulder and grabbed a pitcher of water. On the patio he refilled their glasses before rummaging through his bag for Griffin's and Santos's file folders. He extracted the autopsy report from each of them and handed them to Olivia.

He then opened Kaci's background reports on Floyd, Patton, and James to look for any similarities or red flags. He started with Floyd's file, and he had to admit the guy was a strong possibility for their shooter. He had ties with Aryan Nations and other white supremacy groups, and his violent behavior at protests had resulted in numerous arrests. Those facts alone didn't provide a motive for killing his fellow snipers, but they did show that he believed violence could solve problems.

He flipped to Floyd's picture, and his jaw about hit the floor. He turned the folder to face Olivia. "You recognize this guy?"

Her eyes widened. "He's the man in the park video."

"No wonder the Nevada agents haven't found him."

"Since he didn't appear to be the guy following Ace, maybe he just happened to be in Atlanta."

"But why? And why in the same park as Ace?"

"What if he knew about the murders and came to warn Ace?"

"Only way to find out is to ask him." Rick grabbed his phone and typed a text for Max. *Marcus Floyd is the man in the park video. I need an APB put out on him.*

Max quickly replied. *You got it. We should wrap up here ASAP and head back to Atlanta in the event Floyd is picked up.*

Agreed, Rick replied. *I can be finished tomorrow.*

"What do you make of these scars?" Olivia asked.

Rick set down his phone. "What scars?"

"Both of the MEs found a five- to six-millimeter scar."

"So about a quarter of an inch. It's not unusual to find small scars during an autopsy."

"In the exact same location on both of them?"

"Let me see."

She handed over the reports and pointed at the sentences noting the scar on the interior of each man's left wrist.

"Interesting, but I don't know what to make of it." He stared at the report. "I'll have the ME check for a scar on the senator, too."

His phone rang, displaying Kaci's picture.

"I have to take this." He slipped inside and quickly answered.

"I finally got through the hard drive on the senator's laptop," she said. "I found something interesting."

Her dire tone raised his concern. "What did you find?"

"Ransomware."

"Ransomware? Someone locked his computer?"

"No."

"Isn't that the point of ransomware? A hacker invades your computer and locks it so you can't get back in until you pay the ransom demand, and they give you access again?"

"You're basically right. But hackers can personalize their demands, choosing to lock any item they think will get them the best price. Could be a whole computer. A file. Even something as small as a picture or a single document."

"What are they holding for ransom on the senator's machine?"

"Nothing, now, but at one time they'd locked a hidden drive. I found remnants of their hack in the root directory. He paid fifty thousand dollars to free that drive."

"What's on it?" he asked, hoping for that strong lead they so desperately needed.

"That I don't know yet. I have to crack the password."

Rick blew out his frustration. "Then how does this help us with the murder investigation?"

"I have the date and time the hack occurred and tracked it back to a coffee shop in Atlanta. If they have surveillance cameras, we may be able to ID the hacker."

"And you think the hack is related to Neal's death?"

"I don't know without seeing the drive's contents, but we have the Atlanta connection. Surely not a coincidence. And paying fifty grand to get access to the file again says it has to be important and might be a compelling reason to commit murder."

CHAPTER

24

Monday, September 18
7:58 a.m.

On the fifth floor of the Consolidated Forensic Lab, Rick's phone buzzed just as he reached the door to the District's morgue. He glanced at the text from Max. *James and Patton in custody soon. APB on Floyd a bust so far.*

Rick fired off a quick confirmation text, then stepped into the large room with a long stainless sink on one wall and several metal tables spaced throughout the area. Rick joined the balding ME at the table and introduced himself.

"Before we get started," Rick said. "Does Neal have a small scar on the inside of his left wrist?"

"Found one in my initial exam." The ME adjusted the overhead light and displayed the tiny scar.

"What do you make of it?" Rick asked.

"Make of it? You mean is it remarkable?"

Rick nodded and snapped a few close-up pictures of the scar.

"I suspect that since you asked about it, it must be, but it certainly didn't contribute to his death." He tapped the senator's bicep. "But if you're interested in scars you might be interested in this one. Much larger."

Rick saw nothing, so he bent closer. "What am I looking at?"

"As you can see, the skin is darker than the surrounding area. A clear example of hyperpigmentation from laser removal of a tattoo." He ran his gloved finger down a faint line. "If you look hard enough, you can still see the outline of the tattoo. Plus there's scarring from the initial tattoo."

Rick got even closer and saw the arrows in the circular chaos shape. So Neal had his tattoo removed, as if trying to remove himself from a connection to his sniper buddies, but why?

"I've added the removal to my notes." The ME peered at Rick through thick glasses behind his mask. "Though again, it has nothing to do with his cause of death."

Common sense told Rick the tiny scar could be a tattoo, or... "Could the wrist scar be from a tattoo removal, too?"

The ME ran his finger over the scar, then lowered the light above the wrist. "Removal. No. It could be from getting a tattoo, but there's no ink and it's awfully small for a tattoo." He looked up. "Are you ready for me to proceed?"

Rick didn't need to ask about the gunshot wound. Not when they'd recovered the bullet and he'd noted the wound's location the prior day.

"Go ahead." He stepped back to watch the doc make the Y cut, but Rick's mind remained on the small scar. It had to mean something, but what?

Maybe Levi had the answer. Rick texted his buddy, though knew he might not answer until he arrived in Atlanta.

The ME took hours to conclude the autopsy, after which his only note was that the senator's lungs were consistent with his being a smoker, and he cautioned Rick not to smoke. Not at all helpful to the investigation.

Rick hurried to the break area to join Olivia. He hated that she'd been sitting there for hours. Just like yesterday. But she couldn't stay at his house alone, and he didn't feel safe leaving her in the lobby, so he'd arranged for the break room. She'd taken it all in stride and was being a real trooper. At least that morning she'd selected a mystery from one of his shelves and had something to do.

She sat at a round table, her focus on the book. She'd crossed her legs, the usual pump dangling from her foot. She might be wearing plain khaki slacks, but the red gauzy blouse cinched at the waist with a thick leather belt was ultrafeminine, as were the spiky red shoes. Her clothing was never suggestive, and yet she looked crazy sexy. How she did that, he didn't know.

He approached her, his grumbling stomach announcing his arrival.

She looked up. "I know you said you can eat anywhere, but how you can be hungry after watching...well, you know?"

He felt bad about his ability to consume food after such an event, but it wasn't something he could control. "We'll be spending the day at my office, so let's grab some food on the way."

They picked up Chinese takeout and ate together in an employee break area before he escorted her to a small conference room where Agent Walden would watch over her. He'd rather not abandon her again, but office visitors required an escort at all times, and he couldn't take her to the team's situation room, where he'd be working. The walls were filled with photos and information she didn't have clearance to see.

He took the leftover food to put in the situation room refrigerator and ran into Brynn in the hallway.

"I was coming to find you." She gestured at the bag. "Smells good."

"It's yours if you want it." He held the door for her.

"You don't have to tell me twice." She grabbed a paper plate and utensils and took them to the table where Rick set the food.

"Anything new that I need to know about?" He sat at the table.

She started heaping rice, noodles, and spicy chicken onto her plate. "Nothing here in D.C. yet, but I processed the saliva found in Mobile. It matches the touch DNA lifted from Olivia's purse and the receipt."

"So the murders are officially connected, but without the DNA in the database there's not much we can do about it."

Brynn twirled noodles around her fork. "I've held off offering this option, but there are experimental things we could try, like using the DNA sample to extrapolate the person's age. It could give us our suspect's age with a margin of error of about four years."

"If the other sniper class members were born more than four years apart, that could narrow things down. Or it could tell us if we're wrong to suspect them at all. Why didn't you tell me about this sooner?"

"I didn't mention it because I'll need to ship a sample to the researcher pioneering this technique. Could take days to hear back, and then it could be a bust." She stabbed a chunk of chicken.

"You mentioned experimental *things*," Rick said before she could get the bite to her mouth. "Is there something else we can do?"

"Again, it would take special processing, but we can do a facial reconstruction, plus hair color, and racial ancestry from the DNA."

"Wait, what?" Rick sat forward. "You're telling me you could use the DNA to produce a sketch of the suspect?"

She nodded. "I'll have to send that off, too. We'll wait a long time for results. Weeks maybe."

Rick couldn't begin to imagine they wouldn't have the ordnance in hand before then. Still, he had to take every avenue presented until then. "A long wait or not, we don't have anything else to go on. So get the process started."

"It's pricey. Max will have to sign off."

"I'll make sure he goes for it."

"Then I'll ship the samples and let you know if and when I get anything back. What about you?" she asked, her attention back on her food. "Any new leads here?"

"All three victims have a five-millimeter scar on their wrists. It can't be coincidental, but I can't figure out what it could be." He took out his phone and opened the picture of the senator's wrist.

Brynn squinted at the screen. "Could it have to do with their sniping history? Maybe from shooting the same weapon?"

"Not that I can think of." Rick mentioned the senator's removed tattoo. "I was thinking maybe the little scar was also a tattoo, but there's no ink and the ME said it's not from a removal."

"It could be a tattoo, but you can't see it."

"We examined it under a high-powered light during the autopsy. If there was anything there we would have seen it."

"Maybe not." She took out her phone and tapped the screen a few times, then handed it to him. "Check this out."

She'd brought up an article about ultraviolet tattoos, and he quickly scanned it. "Tattoos you can only see under black light? Never heard of them."

"The FDA hasn't approved UV ink for tattoos, so it's not very common. But it could be the thing you're looking for here."

He eagerly grabbed his phone and dialed the ME's cell. Fortunately, he answered on the third ring.

"Agent Cannon here," Rick said. "Do you have a UV light at the morgue?"

"Yes, we use them for sexual assault cases."

"Would you mind shining it on that scar on the senator's wrist?"

"I don't see—"

"Please just do it, and you'll see why." Rick sat back to wait for a response.

The keypad lock on the door clunked, and the door swung in.

Kaci entered and crossed over to them. "I've got some information on Olivia's identity theft."

Rick held out his phone. "Can it wait until I get off my call with the ME?"

"You're gonna want to hear this, but if it has to wait..." She shrugged and fished a piece of chicken out of the takeout container, then stuffed it in her mouth as she dropped onto the chair.

"You won't believe it," the ME said. "It's a dinky tattoo of a number three."

"Three?" Rick muttered. "Can you capture it in a picture and e-mail it to me?"

"I'll do my best."

"Thanks. It's urgent." Rick hung up and faced Brynn. "You were right. It's a tattoo. The senator's is a number three."

"Why a number, I wonder?"

Rick took a moment to think about it. "Say it's related to the sniper class. Guys are ranked in sniper classes. Maybe he was third in his class and the men are being killed in order of their rank."

"Sounds like a—"

"No, wait. Scratch that. Levi was first in his class and only three guys have been murdered. I'll get the other MEs to check the tattoos, and hopefully, I'll hear from Levi soon, so there's no point in even speculating about it."

"Um, guys," Kaci said. "I was making some progress on the senator's hard drive and really need to get back to it, so..."

Rick stifled a sigh at her impatience, as she was only doing her job. "What do you have for me?"

She sat forward. "Olivia's brother emptied her accounts."

"Her brother. For real?" Rick's heart creased. "She's going to be devastated when she hears about this."

"I thought the same thing, so I double- and triple-checked," Kaci said. "I've got a concrete trail that you can show her. He took nearly thirty thousand dollars."

"Jerk," Rick said, wanting to meet the guy so he could do some serious damage to the guy's face.

"Some days our jobs just plain stink." Kaci got up. "I'll e-mail the file to you right now."

"Thanks, Kaci," he said, but his mind had already traveled to how he would tell Olivia about Harrison's betrayal.

When Rick's phone dinged with the e-mail, he read through the data.

"You think Olivia will press charges against her brother?" Brynn closed the empty containers.

"I honestly don't know." He sent the e-mail to the network printer in the corner.

"You could always bring him in."

"Me?"

"Bank fraud falls under our purview, and even if the dollar threshold isn't high enough for one of our typical cases, you could probably get Max to authorize the prosecution."

Rick pondered her idea while crossing the room to the printer.

"Well?" Brynn pushed.

He grabbed the papers and started for the door. "I won't be the guy who puts her brother in jail."

"A word of advice?" Brynn called after him.

He stopped to look at her. "Go ahead."

"Don't let Max see that smitten look on your face, or you'll be off this investigation at a speed faster than one of your sniper bullets."

She didn't seem too happy with his *supposed* look either, so he wouldn't discuss it with her. He stepped out the door and approached the conference room where Olivia sat obliviously reading the mystery.

A few pieces of paper were about to change her life forever. Just like the day his father had hit him. He knew the cost of the news he was about to unload on her, and he hated that she would have to deal with such a thing.

He motioned through the window for Agent Walden to join him in the hallway. She stepped out.

"I'll need a minute with Dr. Dobbs," he said.

She nodded, and he moved past her to enter the room.

Olivia looked up, and her ready smile disappeared. "Is everything okay?"

He shook his head and sat next to her. "It's about your identity theft investigation."

She closed the book and gave him her full attention. "What about it?"

"As I mentioned, Kaci was looking into the theft as part of your background investigation. She discovered the person who stole your money."

"Who?"

"I'm sorry, honey," he said, trying to soften the blow. "But it was Harrison."

"No." The color drained from her face, leaving her freckles more pronounced. "He wouldn't... He didn't... He would never."

Rick slid the report across the table. She scanned the pages, then jumped to her feet.

"How could he?" Her breath coming in rapid bursts, she marched across the room to her purse and dug inside. "My phone. I forgot I had to leave it in the locker at security."

"You should cool off before calling him anyway." Rick joined her and reached out to offer her a hug.

"No." She moved back. "I'm too mad to be hugged. I need to walk it off."

She stormed toward the door. He charged after her and rested a hand on her shoulder to stop her. "I'm sorry, honey, but you can't go running off in this building."

She stared over his shoulder for a long time. "You have your phone. Can I use it?"

"I wish you could, but it contains classified information, and I can't let you."

"But you'll be standing right here watching me."

"I'm sorry."

Her anger faded into disappointment. The look on her face that said she couldn't trust him to have her best interests at heart broke his heart. He recognized that look. He'd given it to his dad all the time, and now that he was on the receiving end, he didn't like it. Didn't like it one bit, but he *was* putting the investigation first. Otherwise he could call it a day and leave the office, and she could phone her brother.

Unable to see her disappointment any longer, he pulled his gaze away and saw Kaci jogging down the hallway. She frantically motioned for him to join her. He wanted to ignore her and help Olivia, but Kaci's expression said she had something urgent for him to deal with.

"Kaci needs to talk to me," he said. "Will you be okay if I leave?"

"I'll be fine." She turned her back on him and returned to the table.

On the way out, he squeezed her shoulder. His heart told him to stay, his brain said to go. Not only for the investigation, but also because he very much wanted to stay, and that scared him. His brain won out as usual, and he stepped out the door.

"Situation room, now!" Kaci spun to leave.

"Keep an eye on Dr. Dobbs," he said to Agent Walden, who stood waiting a few feet away. "She just got some hard news about her family, and she's upset."

Walden nodded, and Rick took one last look through the window before joining Kaci in the situation room.

"You won't believe this. I cracked the hidden drive on the senator's computer." She slapped a folder onto the table in front of him. "These are the files."

He opened the inch-thick folder. He wanted to delve in and learn about the lead, but his worry about Olivia left him unable to focus on pages and pages of data. "It'll take time to read through these, so how about a summary?"

"The sniper class members are involved in illegal sales of weapons."

Levi came to mind. "All of them?"

"All of them."

"Not Levi," Rick clarified.

"Yes, Levi, though there isn't as much info in the file on him. I've also located the group on the darknet."

"How can you be sure it's them?"

"Their log-in name is Chaos. Like the tattoo."

"Are they selling the smart-bullet technology, too?" he asked, suddenly feeling weary beyond his years.

She shook her head. "I haven't found any evidence to suggest that, but it wouldn't surprise me if they were involved."

"What exactly *have* you seen?"

"They're selling a variety of marine-issued weapons, but mostly M16s and 39s. Likely because they're so common and lifting them won't raise too many red flags."

He nodded. "Do they still have weapons for sale?"

"Yes."

"Then set up a buy, and we'll see what else they're trying to unload." Rick tried to sound confident, but in reality he was quaking inside. Levi hadn't been the guy behind the weapon that had taken out three of his classmates. He couldn't have been. He'd been deployed at the time. But was he really selling military weapons and betraying his country?

The thought was almost more than Rick could bear, and he felt sick to his stomach—wanted to hurl right there—but they finally had a strong lead, and he had a job to do.

Friend or not, if Levi was engaged in something illegal, Rick would bring him in.

CHAPTER

25

Quantico, Virginia
2:15 p.m.

Olivia sat in a stiff chair in a small waiting room at Turner Field. Rick had gone to find someone who could tell them if the team plane had landed so they could board for their trip back to Atlanta. She didn't know why they were leaving town so quickly, but it was clear that he was upset about something and wasn't willing to discuss it.

Which was odd to her. Not that he'd shared much without prodding, but in the conference room, he'd called her honey. Twice. That conveyed a connection that went beyond a professional relationship. Beyond being acquaintances. Beyond two people simply being attracted to each other.

So why would he keep whatever was troubling him to himself? His reaction seemed to be about something other than work. The expression that lingered on his face matched the one he got when he talked about his father.

Her phone rang and, seeing her mother's name, she grabbed the cell from her purse.

"Where's Harrison?" she asked right off the bat. "He's not answering my calls."

"I'm not really sure what he's up to. Is it urgent?"

"The FBI just told me he's the one who emptied my bank account." Olivia expected shock. Outrage even. She got dead silence. "Mom?"

"You can't trust the FBI. What do they know?"

Odd response. "I'm working with them, and they're very competent. Especially Agent Cannon, who's in charge of the investigation."

Her mother huffed a breath of air, and that's when it hit Olivia. "You're not surprised. You knew Harrison did it, didn't you?"

"I . . . I . . . Yes."

Olivia's anger evaporated, to be replaced by an ache knifing through her chest. That her brother had betrayed her was bad enough, but her mother? Unfathomable. "How could you not tell me?"

"He hasn't spent the money. He just wanted to teach you a lesson."

"A lesson. What kind of lesson?"

"You've been kind of stingy lately. He thought if you didn't have your nest egg to rely on you'd better understand what we're going through."

"Oh . . . my . . . gosh! You think I've been stingy. Unbelievable. Anytime either of you asks for money I give it to you."

"Yes, but honestly, you've been kind of cranky about it the last few months."

Olivia's anger returned with a vengeance. What should she say? Do? Nothing right now or she'd lose her cool, and saying something harsh would just exacerbate the situation.

"Besides, you know Harrison," her mother continued. "He's

not like the rest of us. He needs more grace, and we can't blame him."

"Oh, I can blame him all right."

"But you won't tell the police."

"The FBI *is* the police, Mom. They already know and, as far as I know, they'll prosecute him."

"No! My baby can't go to jail. He'll give the money back. Don't do this, Olivia. Just don't. It could tear our family apart. Exactly what I wanted to avoid. Why I didn't tell you."

Rick stepped into the room and signaled for her to join him. She was glad for the interruption so she could take the time to process her mother's news and not say something she'd regret later. "I have to go, Mom. I'll talk to you later."

"Don't press charges against him."

"I can't promise that."

"Just think about it. Please."

Olivia wanted to tell Rick about her mother, but something already weighed him down, and she didn't want to add to his burden. And truth be told, she was embarrassed over letting her family dupe her like this in spite of her professional expertise. If those weren't enough reasons to keep quiet, she'd come to rely on him too much, and she had to go back to standing on her own two feet.

She met him at the door, and they boarded the small jet together. The plane had eight luxury leather seats, two of them facing backward to form a small conversation grouping. In the middle row with two seats, computer monitors were mounted on swivel mechanisms affixed to the side walls. The entire team minus Brynn sat in the back. Olivia hadn't connected with Brynn, but she felt sorry for the woman for always being left behind to work crime scenes. Still, Olivia could tell Brynn loved her work, and Olivia also believed she was more at ease with her science than with people.

Olivia took a seat. Rick sat next to her. The engines rumbled, making conversation impossible as the plane rose into the sky. Her thoughts returned to her brother. She tried to take a deep breath, but the space felt airless and claustrophobic. Rick seemed to be experiencing the same thing, as he kept tugging on his shirt to loosen the collar.

"Want to tell me what's wrong?" she asked the minute it was quiet enough to hold a conversation without raising her voice and alerting the entire team to Rick's distress.

His eyebrow went up. "Is this Dr. Dobbs asking or Olivia?"

"I thought we were way past that." She tried to sound cheerful, but his words stung. "That you trusted me when I said I wasn't acting as your counselor."

"We are, but..." He shrugged.

"But what?"

"But I just had a blow, and I'm trying to work through it."

A blow? After the call from her mother, Olivia knew all about blows. She finally realized how much his parents' actions had hurt him, and sharing her pain wouldn't help him now. She needed to support him. Encourage him. She rested her hand on his, but said nothing and simply waited for him to continue.

"We learned that the sniper class is involved in illegal weapon sales."

"Everyone?" she asked, surprise settling in. "Ace. Cesar. All of them?"

He nodded, his face contorted. "Even Levi."

"Have you talked to him?"

Rick shook his head.

"Then don't jump to conclusions."

"You can read my mind now?"

"Your thoughts are written all over your face."

"Is that so?"

"You're thinking that if Levi's guilty, he's betrayed your trust just like your parents."

He pulled his hand free and rubbed it over his chin covered in dark whiskers. "Well, he has."

"He didn't do this to you. It's not personal. At least not like my brother," she added without thinking.

"Aw, honey, I'm sorry." Rick scrubbed his hand over his face. "Here I am thinking only about myself when you have to be hurting. Did you get a hold of Harrison?"

"We were talking about you," she replied to keep from adding to his burdens.

"It would do me good to focus on something else." A tight smile found his lips. "So about Harrison..."

"He didn't answer." Tears pricked at her eyes, but she wouldn't cry. Not now. Not in front of the team. After hearing about her rocky relationship with Harrison, they already had to think she wasn't much of a psychologist. She didn't want them to think she was weak, too.

"You must be eager to talk to him."

"Actually, no. I talked to my mom just now. She knew about the theft and—"

"She what?" His voice rose, drawing attention from the others. He leaned closer. "And she didn't tell you?"

Olivia told him about the conversation with her mother, and her tears continued to beg for release.

"What are you planning to do about it?"

"I guess it depends on what you all do. I mean, now that you know that he committed the crime, aren't you obligated to report it to the detective?"

He frowned. "There's no easy answer here. Bank fraud falls under the FBI's umbrella, but thirty thousand dollars doesn't meet the FBI's threshold for prosecution. Not that we don't want to take on every case, but it can cost a couple hundred thousand dollars to prosecute. At some point we have to say no."

"But I—"

He held up his hand. "That doesn't mean the local authorities can't handle this for you. I can pass the information on to them. It's up to you, though, to decide if you want to press charges."

How did she decide whether to send her brother to prison or not? She closed her eyes for a moment and took a deep breath. She looked at Rick. "If he pays the money back, I'm not sure what I'll do."

He nodded. "You should know that even if you don't press charges, the bank will likely want to."

"So what you're saying is that it looks like my brother will go to jail no matter what I do."

"Not necessarily. If you don't press charges, and he repays the money, then that could change the court's sentencing. And if you want, I can go to bat for him. Try to get the judge to be lenient."

She appreciated his help, but this was her problem to deal with. "I'll have to think about it. Part of me says it's high time Harrison faces up to his issues, and now is the perfect time to do so. But the other part of me says it's all my fault."

He stared at her. "How's that even possible?"

"As a psychologist I knew better when I kept making excuses for him no matter his actions." Her tears finally won the battle and rolled down her cheeks. "Still, I can't see ruining his life by branding him a criminal. How will that help him?"

Rick lifted a hand as if he planned to swipe away her tears, but then his arm dropped to the armrest. "We could go to the DA together. Ask them not to prosecute as long as he meets certain goals. That would hold him accountable, but not give him the criminal record."

"Do you think they'd go for that?"

He shrugged. "We can try."

"Thank you." She clutched his arm. "I don't think I could handle this without you."

He looked uneasy at her leaning on him, but his attention was soon pulled away by Kaci, who stepped down the narrow aisle.

She rested against the seat across the aisle. "I spoofed my messages on the darknet to look like one of the regular weapons buyers and set up a buy for as soon as we land."

"Good work."

"One thing you should know. The confirmation message said, 'No light, no deal.' I have no idea what that means, and it could blow the whole deal."

"Let's talk about that as a team to see if we can come up with a logical explanation." Rick got to his feet. "Any sign that Levi will be at the buy?"

"I'm not sure who I'll be meeting."

Rick clamped his hands on the empty seat in front of him and shook it. "What on earth was he thinking getting involved in something like this?"

Despite Rick's outburst, Olivia was impressed that Kaci's gaze didn't waver. "If he's the one who shows up at the meet, you can ask him yourself."

* * *

Atlanta, Georgia
5:20 p.m.

Rick had been sitting in the surveillance van with Cal and Shane for the last hour while Max escorted Olivia to the house. Max had volunteered to keep an eye on her while following up with the ME in Atlanta and Mobile to see if Griffin's and Santos's scars were UV tats of a number three as well.

Rick glassed the area with his binoculars and came to rest on Kaci, waiting in a rental car for their suspect to show up.

Rick received a text from Max. *Thought you'd want to know. Levi ditched his detail.*

Rick slammed a fist on the console.

"Problem?" Cal asked.

"Levi ditched the agent assigned to him."

"And you think that means he's coming here?"

"He might have done it just to mess with me, I suppose," Rick said, but he didn't really believe it.

He swallowed down the pain. He'd trusted Levi. Totally. Completely. With his life. He'd never been closer to another human being except Traci, and in some respects he was closer to Levi. Levi was like a brother. He didn't think brothers betrayed your trust. Fathers did. Mothers did. But now, thanks to Harrison Dobbs, he knew brothers did, too.

An older-model SUV pulled up behind Kaci's car. Rick offered a prayer that Levi didn't step out of the vehicle.

"Someone call Max to run the plates," Rick called out, not taking his eyes off the car as he waited for the driver to show himself.

"I've got it," Cal replied.

Kaci stepped from her rental car and approached the SUV. Rick didn't like putting her in harm's way and would have done the meet and greet himself, but if Levi was the buyer, he would take one look at Rick and hightail it out of there.

The SUV door opened. Rick held his breath. Booted feet dropped to the ground. Could still be any one of the men not in custody. The guy pushed out of the vehicle and came to his full height.

Rick's heart dropped to his stomach. "No."

"Levi?" Shane asked.

"Levi," Rick confirmed and started to get up. "I need to talk to him."

Cal grabbed Rick's arm. "You need to let Kaci make the buy first."

Protocol dictated that they allow money to change hands as proof of Levi's crimes. Rick knew that, but he could hardly stomach the thought of his best friend, the guy who'd saved his life countless times and vice versa, being arrested and rotting in prison.

"You brought the money?" Levi's voice came over Rick's earbud, and he thought he might hurl.

Kaci held out a tote bag. "It's yours as soon as I see the weapons."

"They're in the back." He made his way to the rear of the vehicle, keeping his eyes on Kaci at all times. "You're former military."

Kaci didn't speak at first. "What makes you think that?"

"Once a soldier, always a soldier. You're marked for life." He laughed.

The sound darted through Rick's brain. A sound he'd heard so many times in the past and couldn't reconcile hearing in conjunction with weapons theft. Levi. His buddy. Was a common thief.

Why, man?

Rick tried to push the thoughts from his brain, but as he

watched Levi, Rick couldn't let it go. He would soon be sending his best friend to prison. What would that do to Levi's wife?
Their kids? One of them Rick's godson?

Man oh man.

"Let's see the light," Levi demanded.

"About that," Kaci said, sounding uneasy.

"You don't have it?" Levi's tone was ice cold, threatening.

"I—"

Levi suddenly pitched forward and collapsed to the ground.
Rick's heart split, but he kept his binoculars on his buddy.

Kaci dropped to the ground and hovered over him. "He's
been shot. Large wound. Likely a .50."

"Take cover, Kaci," Rick commanded and forced himself to
forget that his friend couldn't have survived the shot.

"How?" she asked. "There's no way to take cover from a
smart bullet."

"Move to the far end of the vehicle," Rick said. "The bullet
will have to pass through the car to get to you."

"Roger that."

"I'm not leaving her out there alone." Shane lurched for the
back door.

Rick grabbed his arm. "I don't need two teammates as targets."

"We can't leave her," Shane snapped.

"Cal, get the van going and get us over to her," Rick ordered,
though if the shooter wanted to take them out, the bullet
would pass through the van like a knife through butter, and
from so far away they wouldn't even hear the rifle's report before
it ended a life.

Cal slid behind the wheel. It took what felt like an eternity
to move a few hundred feet. He swung the vehicle around and
backed up to the SUV.

Rick threw open the back door to find Kaci, wide-eyed and

looking up at them. He reached out a hand and pulled her inside the van, then slammed the door. Cal floored the gas and the van jerked into motion.

"What took you guys so long?" Kaci's face creased in a grin fueled by shock and panic.

Rick's heart began to beat again, but barely. They still weren't safe. No one was. Not with an unstoppable sniper on a killing spree.

* * *

Rick paced the road behind the yellow crime scene tape fluttering in the wind. Levi was dead. His buddy. Friend. Betrayer? Rick had confirmed it himself. Man oh man. The bullet. The damage. Rick had seen it before. In Iraq. Afghanistan. But other than losing Traci, nothing had ever been so difficult as witnessing the devastating injury to his best friend.

Shane crossed the road, his hands clenched. He was bringing bad news. Rick didn't want to hear it, but he stood waiting.

"So?" he asked.

"Levi has a tattoo on his wrist. It's a number three like the others."

Max had called to tell them Griffin and Santos both had tats matching Neal's wrist, too.

"Why a three?" Shane asked.

Why indeed? "Could be for the year they graduated from the Schoolhouse, but what's up with it being UV?"

Shane shrugged. "You should know the ME thinks Levi's tattoo is new."

"New as in he just got it?"

Shane nodded. "What do you make of that?"

"I don't know what to think." Rick stared across the road

to where the ME and her assistant had settled Levi's body in a black bag like the hundreds of bags Rick and Levi had managed to avoid on deployment.

He couldn't stand here any longer. "I need to take off."

"Of course," Shane said. "Take the van. We'll handle the scene and hitch a ride back to the house."

Rick trudged to the van and got it heading down the road. He tried to shake off the pain. He had to if he planned to find Levi's killer. So far they'd recovered the bullet, and Rick had located the hide. They'd cordoned it off, and Brynn was on her way back from D.C. to handle the forensics. But that was all he'd done to help with the investigation. He could do no more. The pain. Man, his gut was on fire with it. With the loss Levi's family was experiencing.

After confirming Levi hadn't survived, Rick had immediately driven over to Levi's parents' house to notify his wife that her husband had died. No way Rick would let April hear that from a stranger. He'd held her as she sobbed on his shoulder, then let his arms drop to his side as she beat on his chest, blaming him for not protecting Levi. She ended up kicking Rick out of the house. He didn't deserve that blame, but she was grieving, so he'd taken it. Shoot, maybe he *was* to blame for not being in Atlanta to protect Levi himself.

Rick sighed and parked in front of his parents' house, the anguish he was trying to contain riding on his breath. People could die in the briefest flash of time. He'd known that—experienced it, even—but Levi's death brought it all back. Reminded him that the sniper could get to Olivia, too.

Man, that was a kick to the gut. It didn't really matter how well he knew her or if he could trust her. She'd become important to him, and the thought of losing her felt like a tank crushing his chest.

He headed for the house. Olivia met him in the entryway.

"Do you want to talk about Levi?" Her soft tone should have comforted him, but it sounded like her shrink voice, and he snapped.

"Right. Dr. Dobbs reporting for duty."

She winced, but he wanted to lash out at someone, and unfortunately for her, she was the only one nearby.

"As much as you want to avoid it," she said quietly, "first and foremost, I'm your friend."

He bent his head and tried to clear the vision of Levi lying lifeless on the pavement. His guts spilled along with his blood. *God, why?*

Olivia approached him and gently raised his head with a finger under his chin. "I know you're hurting. I want to help."

He peered at her, and tears glistened in her eyes. Moisture pricked at his own eyes, and he bit the inside of his mouth, hoping the pain would take them away. No way he would cry. Not in front of Olivia.

"I'm sorry for snapping at you," he said once his emotions were under control. "I didn't mean it."

"It's okay. You're upset. I get it."

He took her hand. "But you don't deserve my anger. I do."

"You? Why?"

"If I'd been a better friend to Levi maybe I'd have seen what he was involved in and convinced him to stop. Or stayed here to protect him. Sure, he'd be in prison, but he'd be alive."

"Don't put this on yourself." She squeezed his hand. "You couldn't control Levi's actions."

"Just like you can't control your brother's or your mother's?" The words shot out before he could stop them, and the moment they hit her and her face paled, he wished he could take them back. "I didn't mean that either."

She took in a breath and let it out slowly, each second she didn't speak an hour to him. "It's okay. You're right. I've been taking responsibility for their happiness for years and enabling them. But I'm done with that. Not done with them, but I won't put up with their behavior any longer."

He got the message she'd not so subtly delivered. He'd written off his family, and she was telling him that he'd been too harsh. Reminding him to think about reconciling. Something he didn't want to hear right now, but he was thankful that she cared enough to keep after him.

She stood there in front of him, so fierce and yet irresistibly attractive at the same time. He couldn't resist tucking a stray strand of hair behind her ear.

She reached up and removed his hand. "Nothing has changed between us, you know?"

"Actually, it has. You know it and I do, too."

"You mean we've gotten even closer."

He nodded and rested his forehead against hers. "The question is, what do we plan to do about it?"

"I don't know." The words whispered out. "I honestly don't know."

CHAPTER

26

Rick couldn't quit thinking about Levi. Hours and hours of memories flooding his brain. Deployment together. Double dates with Traci and April. Levi's wedding. The birth of his children. Any joy Rick had in life outside the job had been connected to Levi and Yolanda. He couldn't sleep. Hadn't even tried. Just hit the gym and hoped he'd drop from exhaustion.

Hadn't worked. An hour on the treadmill and the sight of Levi's body remained etched in his brain. He needed more. To punish himself. He hopped off the treadmill and grabbed a bottle of water. He chugged most of it, then poured the remainder over his head and wiped it away with a clean white towel. He moved to the weightlifting bench and tossed down the towel. On his back, he grabbed the bar, clutching it with everything he was made of. Exactly the way he'd want to grab Levi and shake some sense into him if he were alive.

Agonizing pain swept through Rick's body. He jerked the weights free, dropped them down, and shoved them up. He'd thought he'd known Levi. Known the man, his character, but clearly he hadn't.

Could he really know anyone in life? Had he known Traci? The real Traci? Or had he ignored her issues because he didn't want them to be real?

He lowered the weights and held them there, feeling the burn in his muscles. From the day they'd met, he'd recognized her dependent personality. She always needed a man in her life. And he'd loved that. Loved that after living with such a controlling father, he had someone in his life who went with the flow and didn't try to tell him what to do. But she grew needier over time, and though he continued to love her, her growing dependence on him wasn't good for either of them.

Had he subconsciously stayed in the marines to deploy? To leave town and Traci behind? Guilt settled in, the weight heavy.

He shoved the bar up again. Held it. Relished the burn.

"Isn't it dangerous to be doing that without a spotter?" Olivia's voice came from the doorway.

"Probably." He settled the bar on the rack and sat up to grab the towel. "What brings you down here?"

She came and sat on the end of his bench. The sweet fragrance of her perfume drifted closer. "I wanted to see how you were doing with losing Levi."

"I'm moving along." He rubbed the towel over his neck.

"What does 'moving along' mean?"

"Right now I'm royally mad. At the killer. At God. At Levi. How could he be so stupid? He had so much to live for. His wife. Kids. How could he risk all of that? If I was him...No...No point in thinking that way. I'll never have what he had."

"Why not?"

He shrugged and draped the towel around his neck.

"C'mon, Rick. Tell me. I can help."

"I don't deserve it, all right?" He shot to his feet and paced to the small refrigerator in the corner for another bottle of water. He heard her soft footfalls as she followed. He turned, and though he could easily push past her, he felt trapped in the corner.

"Tell me why," she said softly.

He shook his head, but the words pushed at his tongue, and he couldn't hold them back any longer. "Traci died because of me. I shouldn't have trusted Dr. Fox to help her. I should have been here. I failed her big-time."

"But you couldn't be with her, could you? Even if you wanted to, you were deployed."

"Traci's unhappiness didn't spring up overnight. She couldn't deal with my frequent deployments. Got depressed when I left."

"Which is why you sought out Dr. Fox, right?"

"Right, but I should have sensed that the doctor wasn't helping. I could have gotten leave or even moved to civilian life."

She blinked a few times as if confused. "But you couldn't decide to leave the marines whenever you wanted."

"No, but I could have promised Traci I wouldn't re-up. Then she would've had something to hang on to."

"Did she ever ask you to leave the marines?"

He shook his head.

"Why do you think that is?"

"I don't know." He chugged more water as he pondered her question. "Maybe she knew how much being a marine meant to me, and she didn't want to take that away."

Olivia nodded. "That's how I would have felt if it was me. If you'd left your military career for her, she would know that and wonder if you resented her, adding to her unhappiness."

"I didn't think of it that way." He set the water on the counter and swiped the towel over his face. "Doesn't matter at this point. I can't change the past."

She grabbed his arm, stilling it. "But you can change the future and quit denying yourself the happiness you deserve."

"As long as our team gets called out for long periods of time, I won't have another relationship just to leave the person I love home alone and risk them not being able to handle it. So it doesn't much matter what I think, now does it?" He freed his arm.

Olivia pressed her lips together for a moment. "I didn't know Traci, but I can say not all women are strong enough to withstand being with a man who is gone and in danger all the time. But there are women with the strength to handle it. I see these women supporting their husbands every day in my practice."

"Traci wasn't the strongest of women, I'll grant you that. Probably why I fell for her in the first place. I didn't want another controlling person in my life."

"Strong and controlling aren't the same thing." Olivia eyed him, pinning him in place. "I like to think with God's help I'm strong enough to handle anything thrown my way, but I wouldn't say I'm controlling."

"You're right. You're not."

"Still, I hear the skepticism in your voice, and you're not willing to risk another relationship."

"Right again." He crossed his arms and widened his stance in hopes of ending the conversation. "Nothing you say or do will change that."

Her warm expression faded and her head dipped in a sad nod of acceptance. "If you want to talk more about Levi, I'll be at the guesthouse."

She marched out of the gym just like he wanted her to. Okay, fine, he didn't want her mad or disappointed, or even frustrated by him, but he had wanted the conversation to end. He just couldn't deal right now. Not with this. Not with Levi. His parents. None of it.

He headed up to his room to take a shower, then went in search of his teammates to find something he could work on to advance the investigation. He discovered Kaci in the library, staring at her laptop as usual.

She looked up and pushed up her glasses. "Good, I was just about to come looking for you. I finished reviewing the router logs from the coffee shop where the senator's ransomware originated."

He took the chair across from her. "And?"

"We've narrowed it down to one transmission, and I have a MAC number."

"I'm guessing that doesn't mean the guy used a Mac computer."

"Right. MAC stands for media access control. Without going into details, just know that a manufacturer assigns a unique number to every device that uses IP to access the Internet. Which means every device that used the coffee shop's wireless network to access the Internet is recorded, and we can narrow it down to a particular computer."

"Can we then use that number to find the owner of the computer?"

"Unfortunately, no. There's no centralized registry for MAC addresses."

"So what good is it to us?" He tried to keep his frustration out of his voice.

Her reaction told him he hadn't managed it. "We can actively monitor the router at the coffee shop to see if the device with this MAC address accesses the router again. If so, we know the guy is in the shop or at least nearby."

"You'll assign someone to do that, then?"

"I'm heading over there now. Cal will join me to help appre-hend the guy if he shows up. I've also arranged for local agents to man the router when we need a break."

"Thank you." He made sure his tone reflected his sincerity. "Sorry I was so short with you."

"Hey, I get it. You want to find this guy before he takes someone else out, and it's not going so well."

"Exactly," he replied.

"Maybe this will help. I also have video for the coffee shop during the time the malware was transmitted. I'll e-mail it to you so you can show it to Olivia, and maybe she'll see the guy who chased her."

"Then send it on, and I'll head over to the guesthouse right now."

She dipped her head and started typing. "On its way."

He went to his room to retrieve his laptop, then stepped outside to discover a fine mist falling over the property. As he approached the guesthouse window, he saw Olivia walking the floor with Natalie snuggled at her neck. She ran a soothing hand over the baby's back.

An aching longing ran through him, and his footsteps fal-tered. He'd known he wanted a family. But this pain? He clearly wanted it far more than he'd realized. Well, too bad. Just because he wanted something didn't matter. Life didn't work that way.

He continued on to the door and knocked softly in case Natalie was asleep on Olivia's shoulder. She opened the door and held a finger to her lips.

"Let me try putting her down." She went down the hallway and quickly returned without the baby.

"Success." A wide smile crossed her lips.

The sight sent his heart flip-flopping, and he was very thankful she didn't still seem upset with him. He held up his computer before he said something to take them back to their earlier discussion. "We have footage from the coffee shop where the senator's ransomware originated. I need you to look at it to see if you recognize anyone."

Her smile disappeared. "I should have known you didn't come to talk about anything but the investigation." She gestured at the small dining table. "Have a seat, and I'll take a look."

He wanted to tell her that despite the reason for his visit, he was happy to see her, but he wouldn't lead her on by making her believe there could ever be anything long-term between them. He brought up the video and set his computer in front of her.

His phone rang, and he jerked it from his pocket before the ringing woke Natalie. He spotted Max's icon as he lifted it to his ear. "What's up, Max?"

"There's been another shooting involving a self-steering bullet."

Rick almost hated to ask for details. "Where?"

"Here in Atlanta." Max rattled off the address in a less-than-desirable part of town.

"Marcus Floyd?" he asked, drawing Olivia's study.

"No. Floyd's still in the wind. James and Patton are in custody, though, so they're safe. The victim's name is Norm Mooney."

"What do we know about him?"

"Nothing yet. The team is getting ready to depart for the scene. You'll be needed to calculate the bullet trajectory."

"We can't leave Olivia alone."

"Already taken care of. Shane's volunteered to stay behind."

"Then I'll be at the house in a minute." Rick disconnected and met Olivia's curious gaze.

"Who died?" Olivia asked.

"His name is Norm Mooney. Know him?"

She shook her head, and a sigh of relief followed. "I hate that someone else has died, but I'm glad it's not someone I know."

Rick nodded his understanding. "I have to go. Shane will remain on the property for your protection."

"Okay," she said, but fear lingered in her eyes.

"Look." He took her hand. "Shane seems like this laid-back guy who might not be able to protect you, but he's as fierce as they come."

She stood, but didn't try to remove her hand. "It's not me that I'm worried about."

"Then who?"

"You." She took a step closer.

"Me? Why?"

"You've been distracted since Levi died. The shooter could still be out there, and I don't want you to let your guard down."

Despite his desire to keep things professional, her care and compassion had him cupping the side of her face. "Don't worry about me. I'll be okay."

The air between them crackled, and the look in her eyes held him captive.

She rose up on her tiptoes, inching closer. "Still, you won't mind a kiss for good luck, right?"

"No." The word choked its way out of his throat tight with emotion. "I wouldn't mind at all."

* * *

Olivia settled her lips against Rick's, the touch electrifying. What in the world had possessed her to kiss him? Something deep inside had spurred her on. But it was a mistake, wasn't it? She should pull back, but Rick's hand slid into her hair and drew her closer as he deepened the kiss.

Giving in, she snaked her arms around his neck and ignored the fact that less than an hour ago he'd told her didn't want a relationship, and she was only making things harder for herself. That she was opening herself for heartache. She'd live in the moment. Give herself to these feelings.

His phone chimed from his pocket. His head jerked up, and he looked bewildered until that iron control she'd come to associate with him slid into place and extinguished the warmth in his eyes.

"I have to go," he said, but didn't release her. "Promise me you won't leave the house for any reason."

"I'd like to promise, but I can't. Sometimes the only way to get Natalie to stop crying is to take her for a drive."

His eyes narrowed. "I don't like the thought of that."

"And I don't like the thought of Natalie crying when I have a way to stop it." She eased out of his arms. "Do you really think I'm in danger here?"

"There's no indication that our shooter knows your location. And right now he's likely too busy evading capture to pay any attention to you."

"So it should be safe for me to take Natalie on a drive."

"How about we compromise? If you have to go, bring Shane with you."

"But what if it's in the middle of the night? I don't want him to lose sleep."

"We're used to wake-up calls at all hours. Promise me you'll call him."

That was something she could do. "I promise, if you promise to stop in when you get back so I know you're all right."

"I could text you, then I won't have to wake you up."

"I won't be sleeping until I know you're safe."

Her comment brought a frown to his face. She searched for the reason, but before she could make sense of his expression, he placed a soft kiss on her forehead, grabbed his computer, and marched to the door.

"The video?" she called after him.

He glanced back. "I can't leave my computer. We'll look at it when I get back."

As soon as the door closed behind him, she felt the loss of his presence. *Craziness.* She'd come to depend on him. Totally depend on him, in less than a week, and her fear for his safety was very real. Traci had to have experienced these same feelings when he deployed. The loss all men and women experienced when their soldier spouses deployed.

She had to keep her mind occupied, so she started cleaning the kitchen. The staff kept the house immaculate, but she didn't care. She scrubbed counters and the sink and hand washed dirty dishes. Then she went to the main bathroom and, using a small brush, scoured each and every grout line in the tile.

Hours later, when Natalie woke up, Olivia was thankful to have the baby to concentrate on. But even after changing and feeding, the precious child continued to cry. Olivia found her pacifier and tried to plug it in. Natalie screwed up her face and spit it out, her screams intensifying. There was nothing to do but take that drive.

She didn't want to wake her sister or Wylie, so she grabbed her purse and Dianna's car keys and left to call Shane from outside. Rain fell softly, but the wind had picked up, and that could indicate a thunderstorm approaching. She strapped Natalie in her car seat and dialed as she settled behind the wheel.

"Wow, that kid has quite a set of lungs." Shane chuckled.

"Would you mind accompanying me on a drive to quiet her?"

"Glad to."

"Dianna's medicated so I also need someone to stay with Wiley, would—"

"I just saw Rick's mom in the family room, and as a mom, I'm sure she'd be glad to help. I'll grab her, and we'll be right down."

Olivia offered her thanks and hung up. Hoping for a distraction for Natalie, Olivia started the car running and turned on the wipers.

Natalie's crying wound down a bit but remained at a deafening level. Olivia turned and jostled her leg while cooing, but she kept screaming even when Shane opened the car door and slipped in.

Grace poked her head in. "Don't worry about Wiley. I'll take good care of him."

"Thank you," Olivia said, working hard to be heard over Natalie, whose screams ramped up into the ear-damaging range.

Grace hurried toward the house.

Shane pulled the door closed.

"Hang on," Olivia said over Natalie's noise. "I'll get us on the road as quickly as I can."

She raced down the driveway as fast as the rainy conditions allowed and swung onto the road, then made a few turns to get onto a four-lane road where they could pick up speed and drive for longer stretches without having to stop.

They'd traveled a mile or so when Natalie's cries started winding down and another few minutes before they turned to whimpers and finally ceased. Olivia braked at a stop light and held her breath. When no sound came from the backseat, Olivia let out a long sigh.

Shane peered over his shoulder. "It's crazy how well a drive works for her."

Olivia glanced in the rearview mirror to see the baby sound asleep. "I hate that we've come to rely on this method to get her to stop, but her pediatrician recommended it, so it must be okay."

"If you stop driving, will she stay asleep?"

"Usually. At least once we give her enough time to fall deeply asleep. I'll give her a few more minutes of solid movement, and then we should be able to head back to the house. If I bring her car seat into the house and leave her in it, she'll sleep for at least an hour."

"Only an hour?" Shane turned back around. "She's not a very good advertisement for parenthood."

"She might be a challenge, but she'll outgrow it, and this fussing is well worth having a precious child."

"Do you want to have kids?"

She nodded, but thoughts of Rick losing his child and saying he would never be a father tugged at her emotions. He had so much to overcome to be happy. To be the guy she knew he wanted to be. Could he do so? Of course, with God's help, but it would still be a struggle. Olivia offered a prayer for him and added one for his safety, too.

"We should be good to head back now." She found a place to do a U-turn.

The rain picked up, and she increased the wiper speed. The rhythmic sound and motion lulled her toward sleep, but when she approached a major intersection, she shook her head to improve her alertness. The speed limit dropped, and she slowed. The light turned green before she reached it, and she entered the intersection. Out of the corner of her eye, she noticed a large truck racing toward them at a collision pace.

"He not's stopping," she yelled, not caring if she woke Natalie.

Shane swung his face toward his window. His hand went up to the glass as if he could stop the truck. He couldn't. She couldn't. They were powerless in the lights bearing down on them.

In the blink of an eye, the truck slammed into the passenger side of the car. The large grille hit like an armored tank, and the car skidded wildly across the wet pavement.

CHAPTER

27

From the front seat of the SUV, Rick stared at Norm Mooney lying in his own blood under a hastily erected canopy in an industrial part of town. Max sat next to Rick, the windshield wipers groaning across the window to clear rain that had picked up in intensity. As Rick had worked to determine the bullet trajectory, a number of homeless men had lingered on the sidewalk that smelled like a public restroom, their lack of interest in the loss of life disheartening.

"I don't get the sudden change in MO." Rick tapped his thumb on the wheel. "According to the police, Mooney has no military connection at all."

"There has to be some connection to the shooter, who for all we know could still be Marcus Floyd."

"Maybe Mooney's connection is personal. A friend or family member that the shooter wants to pay back."

"Best way to figure that out is to get Kaci started on an in-depth background check on the guy."

"She's still at the coffee shop watching the wireless router. I'll give her a call." Rick dialed and put the call on speaker.

"Did our suspect show up at the shop?" Max asked.

"Not yet."

"Can you do a background check on Mooney while babysitting the router?" Rick asked.

"Not if you want us to apprehend the suspect if he shows up." Max frowned. "Not sure I understand that."

"The log I'm watching is real time. If I take my attention away to work on Mooney's background, our dude could show up, log in and out, and then disappear before I even see the entry."

"How about Cal?" Rick asked. "Can't he watch the log for you?"

"Um, yeah, but I...I want..."

"Want to be the one to save the day," Rick said, knowing how hard it was for her to be in the background all the time.

"I know it sounds lame, but it's not often that the geek is the hero, you know?"

"Hey, you always locate information that helps us bring in the bad guys," Rick said. "Makes you the hero in my book."

"But I'm never the one who sees the final bit of intel and can rush right out and make the arrest like I can here." She sighed. "But for the good of the investigation, I'll show Cal what to watch for and start the background check."

"Thanks, Kaci," Rick said, hoping that someday she got her wish and could be the hero she wanted to be.

* * *

The scream was long and tortured, and it took some time for Olivia to realize it came from her throat as the car bent to the truck's will. Time seemed to stand still. Glass shattered. Metal buckled and groaned under the pressure. She thought to turn and check on Shane and Natalie, but she couldn't find the strength to fight the momentum of the car's wild slide.

The rear of the vehicle came to a jarring rest against a tree. Olivia was tossed to the side, her seat belt cutting her and her head slamming into the window. Excruciating pain radiated through her head. Blackness threatened. She blinked. Swallowed hard.

Stay alert. You have to.

Natalie screamed in the backseat.

No, not the baby. Please, Father. No.

Olivia punched down the already-deflating airbag. Shane lay unmoving against the window.

"Shane," she said, "are you all right?"

He didn't answer.

"C'mon. Wake up." She touched his shoulder, her hand coming away covered in his blood. "No. No. No."

Her brain froze. Solid. Unthinking. Terrified. Natalie's shrill cries broke through. Olivia checked Shane's pulse at his neck. Found more blood, but also a solid thump under her fingers.

"Thank God." She sighed out a shaky breath. "Stay with us, Shane. I'll get help. Just let me check on Natalie."

Olivia twisted over the seat. Her muscles screamed in pain, as did her head. Blood dripped from her forehead, but she swiped it away.

"Shh," she cooed, and scanned Natalie for any signs of injury but found none. Fortunately for the baby, the truck had hit the front of the car. Shane wasn't as fortunate. Olivia turned back to him. He was still unmoving. She had to call 911.

She grabbed for her phone, but it had flown from the cup holder where she'd hastily stored it. Natalie's cries bit into

Olivia's aching head. "It's okay, sweetie. Give me a sec, and I'll come get you."

She searched the front of the car for her phone, each movement torture. The truck's lights shone into the car, but she couldn't find the phone. Maybe the truck driver had called 911 or at least had a phone.

"Be right back, Natalie." She wrenched her door open and climbed out, her body protesting and the pouring rain instantly soaking her.

The truck backed up and came alongside the car. Good. They wanted to help. She waved at the two men and mimed holding a phone to her ear. The passenger door opened. A short, burly man stepped out. He came around the car.

"My phone," she said, the panic in her tone evident even to her. "I can't find it and my friend is hurt. Did you call 911?"

He nodded.

"Good. Good. I have to check on my niece." She spun and almost lost her balance in the slick mud, but recovered with a hand to the roof of the car. She inched to the back door. Thick Georgia clay sucked at her heels, straining her muscles. She reached the door. Grabbed the handle. Wrenched the door open.

"Shh, it's okay. I'm here, sweetie."

Natalie's eyes widened, and her cries intensified.

"What is it, baby?"

An arm came around Olivia's throat, and her body was jerked back and out of the car.

She screamed.

The arm tightened, clamping down on her windpipe. Her oxygen was cut off. She clawed at the beefy muscles and tried to free herself. The man started backing away. She dug into his flesh with her nails. He swore and slammed a fist into the injured side of her head. Stars danced before her eyes.

No, don't let me pass out. Natalie. Shane. They need me.

She tried for a breath. Couldn't get one. The blackness beckoned. He dragged her through the mud toward the truck.

"Help," she yelled with her last breath as darkness took her.

* * *

Fatigue drained Rick's body, and he wanted to fall into his bed and crash for a few hours. But he'd promised to check in with Olivia, so he dropped Max at the main house and started back down the drive. He parked in front of the guesthouse and jumped out into the pelting rain. He took a quick glance in the family room window but didn't see Olivia. Hopefully, she'd forgotten all about waiting up for him and had gone to bed. The sun would be rising soon, and she could do with some sleep.

That's what he wanted. At least logically. But in reality he wanted to know she was awake and waiting for him. He wanted her to greet him at the door. Maybe wrap her arms around his neck again and welcome him home with a kiss. He liked the thought of that. Someone in his life again who cared if he made it home okay.

On the way up the drive, he noticed Dianna's car was missing. Okay, so maybe Olivia wasn't sleeping but had taken Natalie on a drive. Just in case she was asleep, he knocked softly. No one answered. The door was unlocked, triggering alarm bells in his head. He slipped quietly inside. Found his mother asleep on the sofa in the family room.

For a moment he gaped at her, but he soon recovered and gently shook her awake. "What are you doing here, Mom?"

"Olivia and Shane took Natalie for a drive to calm her down, and I'm here in case Wiley wakes up." She glanced at her watch and sat up. "That was four hours ago. I'm surprised they're not back."

A niggling of unease peppered him. "I'm going to check the bedrooms just to be sure she didn't come back and let you sleep."

With the car missing, he doubted she'd returned, but he had to be certain. He jogged down the hallway, throwing doors open on the way. Dianna was softly snoring in her room and Wiley curled up in a ball in another. He located the other bedroom, where Olivia had been staying, and found Natalie's portable crib empty.

Unease settled in, feeling like a rock in his gut, but he wouldn't panic yet. On the way back to the family room, he dialed Shane. With each unanswered ring, Rick's apprehension mounted. The call went to voice mail. He dialed Olivia. She didn't answer.

The rock in his gut turned into a boulder. He joined his mother. "Shane and Olivia aren't answering their phones. Can you wake Dianna up to see if she knows anything while I call Max?"

"Sure, but she was asleep when I got here."

"She may have woken up while you were sleeping and saw something."

"Right." His mom headed down the hallway.

He tapped Max's icon and got right to the point when he answered. "Can you check to see if Shane's in his room?"

"Something wrong?" Max asked as his footsteps sounded in the background.

Rick explained the situation, trying to remain calm, as his training dictated. He heard a knock on a door, then silence.

"He's not in his room," Max said. "Maybe you should try him again."

Rick hung up and dialed Shane again. No answer. With anyone other than a teammate, Rick would think the owner had
forgotten to charge the battery, but their phones were lifelines,
and they treated them as such.

He tried not to panic and called Olivia again. Still no answer.
Rubbing her eyes, Dianna entered the room, his mother
trailing behind.

"Did you find her?" Dianna asked, her tone as urgent as it
could be while she was under the influence of a sleep aid.

He shook his head. "Did you see or hear from them after they
left?"

"I didn't even know they'd gone." She twisted her hands.
"Please. You have to find them."

His gut clamped around the boulder, but he wouldn't let
himself give in to the panic.

"Do you have a way of tracking Shane?" His mother helped
Dianna sit on the sofa, then took her hand.

"Yes. Of course. I should have thought of that. Kaci can track
our phones." He dialed her number. It took a few rings before
she answered, her voice sleepy. He explained the situation. "Can
you pull up Shane's location?"

"Hang on." He heard her moving around, and then her fingers clicking on a keyboard. "He's down the road a few miles.
I'll text you the GPS coordinates."

"With the rain coming down out there, they might have had
an accident. Watch the signal for a few minutes to see if he's
moving."

"Gotcha."

Rick pulled up the text and tapped the GPS link. The
map opened, and he recognized the nearby location. Olivia was
close. Maybe needing him. No way he'd sit here and wait for
Kaci to respond again.

He relayed the information to his mother and Dianna. "I'm going down there. Call me if you hear from them."

He took off running. Into the rain. Into the darkness. Fighting his fear.

"Shane's signal's not moving," Kaci said.

Rick let terrible, horrible, mind-numbing thoughts take him for a moment. He saw Olivia's car crash. Her body trapped behind the wheel. Lying there hour after hour. No one coming to her aid at this time of night. Fighting for her life. Shane maybe injured, too. And the baby . . . not the baby.

No! his brain screamed, and he moved on to an even more terrible thought.

He'd failed to protect another helpless baby and the woman he had to admit he loved.

* * *

Forsyth County, Georgia
Tuesday, September 19
7:15 a.m.

Movement.

Olivia was moving. She tried to open her eyes to figure out where she was. Her lids felt like lead weights. She breathed deeply. Her neck ached. Her head. Her chest. What in the world?

The accident! She'd been in an accident. Then taken.

Oh God, Natalie. Shane. I have to help them.

Sleep beckoned, warm and comfortable. No worries. Just peace. She wanted to give in, but fought it off. Her thoughts went to Rick. Did he even know she was gone? Have any idea where she was located? Had he found Natalie and Shane?

God, please let him figure it out. Please let them both be okay.

She couldn't count on his rescue, though. She had to help herself. She listened. Heard tires hum and spit over the wet road. Heard breathing. Two men. A big truck. Her hands were bound behind her. Something plastic, cutting into her tender skin. Wet and moist. Bleeding.

Panic flooded her chest. She took a breath. Smelled body odor. Pungent. Thick. Nauseating. The men. Who were they?

She focused all her effort on her eyelids. Forced them open. Her gaze landed on the driver's hands planted on the wheel. His wrist. A tattoo. *Semper fi.*

The killer.

He had her.

* * *

Atlanta, Georgia
8:00 a.m.

Panic like Rick had never felt tried to swamp him. He swallowed hard, trying to get control. Took a breath. Then another and another until he could process.

"I'm heading out there," he told Kaci as he got the SUV running. "Send backup just in case."

He peeled down the driveway and got on the road as if in a foggy dream. His brain fixed on his request to Kaci. Backup meant danger. Meant Olivia, all of them, could be hurt. Meant he might lose her.

The SUV fishtailed on the slick road. He jerked his focus back to his driving. His heart told him to floor the gas pedal, but he slowed to make the turn onto the four-lane road. Then he pressed the gas hard. His wipers thumped across the window as he flew over the asphalt.

He approached the intersection where GPS placed Shane. He strained to see through the downpour. Spotted a car in a ditch, the rear end wedged against a massive tree. If he hadn't been looking in this exact spot, he would have missed it. He flipped on his bright lights. Didn't help. He couldn't see a few feet ahead, much less determine the car make or even color. He whipped the SUV to the side of the road and parked. He fumbled with the zipper on his go bag, but finally got a trembling hand on a flashlight and pushed open his door.

"Stay calm," he warned himself. "They could simply have spun out."

Maybe GPS was wrong and it wasn't even their car. No. He had to expect the worst. That's what would prepare him to act. He drew his weapon. Lifted it along with the light and set off. Rain pelted his face, but he fought the urge to race across the road and moved cautiously, paying attention to his surroundings. He was trained to handle a situation like this. Well trained. But no amount of tactical training would do any good if he didn't have the ability to recognize when to use it.

He ran the beam over the car. A VW logo and electric-blue paint confirmed that he was looking at Dianna's car. His heart sank. The passenger side was bashed in, and wide tire tracks showed that they'd been hit by a large vehicle. Had to be a truck. A big one. But it was gone.

Could be a hit-and-run. Could be, but a sinking feeling told Rick the collision was much more.

He aimed the light in the closest window, the beam highlighting Natalie in her car seat. Her eyes were closed, but her chest rose and fell. *Good. Good.*

He swung the light ahead. Caught sight of Shane in the passenger seat, slumped against the crushed door, blood caked on his head. Rick swallowed hard. Tried the door. The damage was too severe for him to open it. He studied Shane. Saw him breathing, too.

Rick drew in air and held it. His gut already aching over what he might find. He swung his light past Shane to the driver's seat.

Empty.

His throat closed.

Where is she? Father, please. Let her be alive. Please. Help me to do the right thing for her. For the baby and Shane.

He eased around the back of the car, swinging his light over the trees and thick understory, trying to cut through the rain to find any lurking danger. Satisfied it was safe, he bent in behind the steering wheel. Found blood smeared on the driver's side. His heart dropped lower, but he kept it together. Reached across the seat and felt for a pulse on Shane's neck and was glad to find a strong one. He didn't wait for additional confirmation, but dialed 911 and requested an ambulance while he moved to the back to check on Natalie.

She stirred, and her eyes opened. She blinked her thick lashes and screwed up her tiny face to cry. She didn't seem harmed, and a flash of happiness lit his heart. "It's okay, little one. You'll be all right."

He could barely walk away from her, but she was safe in her car seat and he had to find Olivia. He called Kaci and searched the ditch as the phone rang. He spotted blood and followed the trail to the road.

Olivia's spiky shoes lay discarded as if torn from her feet.

"No. No. No, no, no." He squatted. Found gouges in the red clay soil leading to her shoes. Two larger footprints marred the mud.

She'd been dragged. Olivia had been dragged. Unwilling. Abducted.

Kaci answered the call. "Did you find them?"

"She's gone," was all he could say. "Missing."

* * *

Forsythe County, Georgia
8:30 a.m.

Olivia wanted to hide in sleep. Ignore the miles sliding under the truck and ignore the panic that kept trying to wake her. If she was to have any hope of escaping, she had to know where these men sitting beside her in the cab were taking her. She opened her eyes. Spotted a US 19 road sign and trees grouped forest-close along the highway. They'd left the Atlanta metro area and traveled into the country.

Her heart sank. How would anyone find her out here?

She turned her head, the pain on movement excruciating. She blinked hard and waited for it to pass before she ran her gaze over the driver. The killer. Her heart thumped in her chest. He was muscular. Tall and not at all like the squat guy who'd grabbed her. The killer had an angular chin covered in stubble. Deep wrinkles next to his eyes. Unkempt hair, greasy and raggedly cut.

"She's awake," the burly guy said.

The driver looked at her. His face coming clear. She stifled a gasp. He was the man from the Chick-fil-A video. Not Marcus Floyd from the park. His eyes, mean and angry, sped up her pulse before he looked back at the road.

He had no qualms about killing her. She could feel it in his demeanor. After all, he'd murdered several men already, and if he was willing to let her see his face, there was only one possible outcome. He didn't plan on letting her go. Ever.

Terror lodged in her chest. She struggled to breathe. But she couldn't let the fear take her. Couldn't let it make her hyperventilate. She closed her eyes again until she could draw in regular breaths. When she opened them the killer was watching her.

"Welcome back." His voice, deep and rumbly, went with the size of his body.

If she knew who he was, she could figure out a way to best him and get free.

"Who are you?" she asked, hating how she let her fear sound through her words.

He quirked a brow at her. "You know who I am."

"A killer." She worked hard not to let him see her panic. "But what's your name?"

"So the FBI hasn't figured it out yet, huh?" He chuckled. "I could've taken you out, then, instead of going to all of this trouble to grab you."

Confused, she peered at him. "I don't understand. You tried to kill me before the accident, right? Why didn't you now?"

"The feds took the remaining targets in our sniper class into protection. Except Floyd. They're not gonna find him unless they go scrounging up here in the mountains." He laughed, a low deranged sound from deep in his chest. "I thought the feds knew about me, and I'd need some sort of leverage. Especially if I had to get out of the country fast. Then when the fed totally freaked out outside your office, I figured why kill you when you could be my ticket out?"

"You're lying," she said. "You didn't graduate in the '03 sniper class."

He bared his teeth at her like an angry dog. "I could kill you now, couldn't I?" She could easily imagine him salivating as he did it.

"They might still figure it out," his partner said.

The killer only glanced at him. He was mentally unstable. Meant unpredictable and he could snap at any moment. At any word.

Maybe she should shut up. No. She had to risk questioning him to glean information. But she'd obviously hit a sore spot and needed to shift his focus. Move on for now. She would circle back later.

"So you killed Floyd and the other snipers," she said. "Including Levi."

"Yeah, me and the trusty smart bullet," he replied. "Actually, the smart bullet did the work for me."

"Smart bullet?" she asked, wondering if this was the special weapon she'd suspected.

"A bullet with guidance inside. You know, like a missile, so it locks on anyone I fix the scope on and takes them down. Best day ever when we stole those bad boys."

"We're more powerful than God." The other guy grinned, revealing tobacco-stained teeth.

"You really think that?" Olivia asked, trying to get her head around the fact that a bullet like that actually existed.

"With the gun in my hand I do. We lock the scope on someone and fire. Poof, they die. Just like that." The killer snapped his fingers. "It's the perfect weapon system, and it's gonna make us rich."

"You're going to sell it?" Her stomach roiled.

"Gonna? Nah. We already did. Just need to deliver the bullets. At least the ones that are left." He grinned again.

No. They'd not only stolen these crazy bullets but already sold them? Who to, and how many?

She had to know. "How many?"

"Bullets, you mean?"

She nodded, her head swimming with pain.

"Let's see. Started with an even three dozen. Used five, so you do the math."

Thirty-one. A number far bigger than she'd expected.

She swallowed hard, but her mouth was cotton-ball dry. These men were going to deliver the remaining bullets to criminals. Maybe men even more dangerous. Men who could analyze the technology and reproduce it. Then this killer would take her out of the country and kill her, too.

Fear wrapped its tentacles around her. She couldn't let her emotions paralyze her.

She took deep breaths. In, out. In, out.

Calm down. Think. Stay alive.

She had to.

If she didn't act fast, these deadly bullets would end up in the hands of people even more dangerous than these killers holding her captive.

CHAPTER

28

The hospital ER's antiseptic odor left Rick feeling nauseated as they waited for word on Shane and Natalie. Right after calling 911, Rick had phoned his mother, who'd brought Dianna to the hospital to be with Natalie while the doctors gave her a thorough examination, even though she appeared to be unharmed. Yolanda was staying at the guesthouse with Wiley to spare him the turmoil of visiting a hospital. Rick had to admit he was thankful he'd decided to stay with his family, something he'd once doubted he'd ever say, but maybe...

No. Not the right time to go there, with Shane hurt and Olivia missing.

He paced the room, all of his teammates—except Brynn, who'd gone straight from the plane to the accident scene—doing the same thing. Brynn had wanted to come to the hospital, but it was more urgent for her to process the crash scene to find a way to locate Olivia. With Olivia's phone in the car and no traffic cams in the area that could have revealed the truck's departure route, Brynn's leads would give them the only chance of tracking Olivia.

"I've been thinking," Max said as Rick stepped past him. "We haven't yet asked how our suspect found Olivia. I asked Dianna, but she doesn't know a thing."

"He didn't follow me, if that's what you're getting at," Rick said.

"No, and I would expect that everyone else took the same precautions when leaving crime scenes and heading back to the house."

They all nodded.

"Then how?" Rick swallowed hard before his desperation got the best of him.

"Only one way I know to follow someone other than in a vehicle," Cal said. "From the air. Like with a drone."

"A drone? Maybe." Rick pondered the idea. "But it would have to be military quality or we'd hear it from the ground. Unless the guy flew above the legal ceiling."

"It wouldn't be surprising for a killer to ignore the law," Kaci said.

"Any way to track this drone?" Rick asked.

"Not with normal aircraft tracking systems."

"Why not?"

"Choppers and planes have transponders that squawk codes when in flight, and air traffic control tracks them via their squawk code. Even if they didn't squawk, their size guarantees they'll appear on radar." She paused for a moment. "On the other hand, both commercial and hobby drones are small. So small they look like birds on radar and can't be tracked. Anyone can fly a drone these days, and the only thing that's keeping them from interfering with other aircraft is that it's illegal to fly above that four hundred feet you mentioned. But even if someone breaks that law, no one is tracking them."

Rick clamped a hand on the back of his neck and massaged. "So we're out of luck."

"Not totally," she replied. "The government is interested in drones overseas. They especially want to track unknown and hostile drones in war zones, and they're working on a tracking system."

"So if our suspect flew a drone over the area, this system could track it?" Rick asked, a blip of hope on his radar.

"Likely."

"Then how do we access it?"

"I've been asked to review the software, so I have it on my computer."

Rick gestured at her laptop sitting on the table. "Then show us the program."

"It's not on this computer, but the one at your house."

Rick opened his mouth to tell her to head straight to the house to check for drones, but the doctor stepped into the waiting area, preempting him.

"Agent Erwin has regained consciousness," he said. "His eyes are open to stimulation, but he's lethargic. He has some brain swelling and bleeding causing sleepiness, but he's still arousable."

"Will he recover?" Max asked.

"Too early to tell. It all depends on the swelling. As it increases pressure within the head, it could potentially injure parts of the brain not initially affected."

"When will we know if he's in the clear?" Max asked.

"The swelling happens gradually and may occur for the next five days or so."

"What's your best guess on his prognosis?" Rick asked.

"I'd guardedly say he will fully recover, but again, time will tell."

"And what about Natalie?" Rick asked.

"She has bruises from the straps of her car seat, but otherwise she has no injuries, and we're releasing her now."

"Thank God for that," Rick said, and his teammates nodded.

"Can we see Shane?" Kaci asked.

"Maybe one of you. For a short visit."

Max shook hands with the doctor, then turned to the team and asked them to join him in prayer for Shane. Rick loved working with Christian men and women. Though, like him, some of them were struggling with their faith, they all believed in God.

Max offered a heartfelt prayer, then looked up. "I'll check in with Shane to see if he remembers anything from the accident. Cal, I want you to head back to the accident scene and bring me up to date on the locals' search for the suspect."

Cal nodded his understanding.

Max turned his attention to Rick. "And you—"

"Kaci and I," Rick interrupted, "have a date with her computer at my parents' house."

* * *

Lumpkin County, Georgia
9:25 a.m.

The sky opened up and a deluge of rain pummeled the truck. The killer clicked the wipers into high. Swishing blades cut fast and furious, but he still had to slow down. She'd caught sight of signs telling her they were approaching the foothills of the North Georgia mountains, but why? What could the jerk want in the mountains?

He flipped on his blinkers. The sight nearly made her burst out in laughter. Here sat a ruthless killer, and he obeyed traffic laws. Absurd.

He followed a main road for about a mile, but she couldn't make out the name of the road, and there were no landmarks to help. He soon turned onto a narrow lane. The truck bounced like a kangaroo over deep ruts, and pain screamed through her head.

She could close her eyes and rest. For just a moment, right?

No, she needed to know more about these men before they stopped so she would be ready to act if possible.

"You didn't tell me your name," she said to the driver.

"Guess it wouldn't hurt, seeing how you're not gonna live to talk about it. Name's Ike Zelner."

"I've never heard of you."

His focus remained on the windshield, where rivers of rain allowed them to see only a few feet in front of the vehicle. "Not surprising. I covered my tracks well."

"But you must be connected to the sniper class, so why hasn't your name come up?"

"Oh, we're connected all right. Guess the feds are too stupid to figure it out."

"Were you friends with the other snipers?"

"Friends. Ha!" The ice in his tone was colder than the air-conditioning pouring from the dash. "Jerks couldn't handle the competition. Bullied me until I failed and had to drop out of the Schoolhouse. They each had a bullet coming." He peered at her, his eyes daring her to question him, to push him and see what he was capable of.

Her training told her he was suffering from antisocial personality disorder. Aching for a battle. Aching to kill. He didn't care if it was someone he knew. He blamed others for his actions and didn't appear to feel any remorse for the deaths. She had to tread lightly and play into his overconfidence, another hallmark of the disorder.

"These guys didn't realize who they were messing with, though, did they?" She forced out a smile. "I can see that you're a powerful adversary."

He pulled a HOG's tooth from under his shirt, then another, and stared at them. "You better believe it. None of them could have come up with a plan to steal the smart bullets. Only I could do that."

Seeing Ace and Cesar's HOG's teeth in his hands tore her heart, and she wanted to rip them from around his neck, but she had to play along with him. "Of course. That's a given. How did you do it?"

"Planning and using my brain. Course, not many people can think the way I do, but it was simple for me. I made buddies with a couple of security guards at the bar. Guys if you bought them a few drinks it could loosen their lips. Figured there'd be some sort of score they'd tell me about. Didn't expect to hear about the smart bullets, though."

"So you got the guy guarding these bullets to tell you how to find them," she clarified.

"Nah, wasn't quite *that* easy. My guy heard about them from his buddy, who was sworn to secrecy. But he was no match for me. I got him to tell me when the company was going to transport the technology for a demo."

"That was some night," the other guy said. "You worked 'em good, Ike. Real good."

"Course I did." Charm and manipulation, additional indicators of his antisocial nature.

"And when you got your hands on the smart bullets you seized the opportunity to use the weapon to take care of inferior men."

"They didn't stand a chance." He laughed, the sound reverberating through the truck and grating on her nerves.

He slowed even more, the brakes squealing and mingling
with his laughter. He pulled off the road to park in a clearing
ringed by tall trees.

"You searched my office, too."

"Had to make sure your crazy clients didn't say anything
about me and you put it in your notes."

"Guess they didn't think you were worth mentioning." The
words slipped out before she could think.

He jerked back, his eyes narrowing into tiny slits. His breathing sped up, and he slammed the truck into park. She'd done it.
Made him mad, and now she was going to pay. She waited, breath
held, for him to hit her. Kill her. Respond in any way.

Instead he looked at the other guy. "Get the bikes unloaded
and the truck covered, Virgil. We'll wait here."

"But the rain," Virgil whined.

"Won't hurt you. Now move! We have a timetable to keep
and the rain has already slowed us down."

Virgil climbed out. Olivia didn't let a second pass before she
scooted away from Ike. The rain swirled like a hurricane into
the truck, drenching her. With her hands restrained behind her
back, she couldn't wipe the water from her face, so she blinked
hard through the drops.

"Not so smart now, are you?" Ike sneered.

"Why did we stop here?" she asked, hoping to move him on.

"You'll just have to wait to find out."

They sat there, time ticking by. The only sounds were his
nasal breathing and the rain pelting the roof. She couldn't believe she was sitting here next to a killer. He'd ended so many
lives and seemed happy to end more. *Wait.* She hadn't asked
him about the last man.

She faced him. "What did Norm Mooney do to you?"

A look of confusion crossed his face. "Do to me? I don't even know a guy named Mooney."

"Then why kill him?"

"Oh, I get it." He grinned. "You must be talking about the homeless dude I offed to get the feds away from protecting you. Didn't even know his name."

Olivia's stomach roiled over his callous disregard for life. She had to get away from him soon.

Virgil jerked open the door. He was drenched and angry looking. "We're good to go."

"Before you get out"—Ike met her gaze, locking on and holding—"you should know that I'm more than willing to plug you with a bullet. Especially since it looks like I may not need you to get to Mexico."

Why had she told him the FBI didn't know his name? Why oh why?

"You try anything foolish, and I mean *anything*, and you'll find this." He drew his gun and pressed the cold barrel against her forehead. "Exploding in your face."

Fear almost paralyzing her, she forced herself to move. Her bare feet hit the slippery soil, and she had to rock back and forth to stand upright. Thankfully, the rain had let up a fraction. In the morning light trying to break through the clouds, she made out a narrow path ahead.

Virgil shoved her forward. With her hands tied, she lost her footing and landed on the drenched soil. Her head screamed, but she bit her lip to stay quiet, the taste of thick clay mud filling her mouth.

"Clumsy much?" He laughed and jerked her up by the zip ties, the hard plastic cutting like razors.

He dragged her to a pair of motorcycles. The mowed-down

shrubs and plants stabbed her tender feet, but he kept pushing her after Ike, so she couldn't take her time to pick her way through the spiky vegetation. She found Ike already mounted on a motorcycle. He started it up, and given the size of the bike, she expected a powerful rumble resembling Rick's Harley, but it barely hummed.

"What's with the motorcycle?" she asked. "It sounds weird."

"This baby?" He patted the side. "The military's stealth prototype. Lets me sneak up on unsuspecting enemies."

"There it was. Right in the van with the smart bullets and ours for the taking." Virgil chuckled.

"Now quit wasting time." Ike waved his gun at her. "You'll ride behind Virg, and I'll be right on your tail with my gun at the ready. Cut her ties, Virg, and then get her on your bike."

Virgil freed her hands. She flexed her fingers to start the blood flowing and briefly considered taking off, but Ike's gun kept her following directions, and she climbed on the bike behind Virgil. She didn't want to touch him, but other than ending up on the ground, she had no choice but to grab hold. He drove them through a narrow path cut in the trees. As they rumbled along a wide ditch, she listened for Ike's motorcycle behind them. She didn't hear it, but she sensed him following. They traveled a short distance when Virgil stopped the bike.

"Get off," he demanded.

Gladly. After she'd stepped away, she swiped moisture from her face and gulped in the cooler mountain air. Ike parked behind them, and she watched him dig out a headlamp from a saddlebag and put it on. He handed a second one to her.

"Let's go." Ike shoved her ahead of him.

She turned to snap at him, but he pointed the gun at her face, so she continued on, climbing the hill in front of her.

She counted her footsteps. She'd gotten to a hundred when he stepped toward a round opening in another hill.

"Get in the tunnel," he said.

"In that dinky hole?" She shot him a look. "You're kidding, right?"

"Nope. We're going to the mine. You first."

"But I..." She didn't know what to say. What could she say? A hole gaping in the hillside. Black and tiny. She wasn't even sure she'd fit unless she lay down. Not to mention the rain rushing into the opening. Water and a tunnel did not mix in her mind.

Who in their right mind would climb in there?

"Turn on your headlamp and get moving," Ike commanded. "I don't have all day."

God, please, she begged. *Don't let him take me underground, please!*

Atlanta, Georgia
9:50 a.m.

Barely able to stand still, Rick forced himself to remain behind Kaci and her computer in her bedroom at his parents' house. She brought up a screen holding several columns of data.

"These are the listings for drones that flew in the area last night." She ran a finger down the list and clicked an entry dated the prior evening. Another window opened to display a flight path that led from Levi's murder scene to where Levi's parents lived.

"He tracked me when I went to notify April of Levi's death." He slammed a fist into the desk.

Kaci jumped but didn't speak. She clicked a few additional links showing the drone following Rick home from there and hovering for hours over the house, then disappearing and not returning.

He punched the wall. "I led him to her."

Kaci shoved her computer away. "You couldn't have known."

"I know, but—"

"Stop wasting time on feeling bad. We have a killer to catch. What else can we do to find him?"

Rick resumed pacing. "Wait, my parents' security footage. If the suspect ever approached the house he'll be on the feed."

"Hold on." Kaci clicked a few keys on her laptop. "I can see the security system log-in on the network. If you get me the password, I can download the files."

"I'll be right back." Rick charged down the hall and pounded on his parents' bedroom door. "Mom. Dad. I need your help."

His mother opened the door, still dressed from caring for Natalie and visiting the hospital. "What is it? Is it Natalie? Olivia?"

"Olivia," Rick said. "I need the password for your security system so I can look at the gate footage."

"It's 'Rick' with a capital *R* plus your date of birth."

With Olivia missing, Rick doubted he could feel more pain, but he did. Deep inside. His mother could be using his name as a password because it was easy to remember, but her angst said that she was still suffering after all the years they'd spent apart and the password was a connection she'd made to him. A sad one. Desperately sad and all his fault.

He grabbed her in a hug. "Thank you."

"You care for Olivia, don't you?" his mother whispered.

"Yes."

"I like her, too."

He released her, and she gazed up at him, her eyes hopeful.

"I'm sorry, Mom, for not getting in contact sooner." The words slipped out. Surprised him as much as they appeared to surprise her. "I have to go. We can talk after I find Olivia."

"Stay safe," his mother called out as he dashed down the hallway.

The moment he reached his bedroom door, he rattled off the password to Kaci, and she typed it in. "Okay, I see the gate camera files. I'll rewind slowly as we watch."

Rick moved behind her to see the footage roll past. Nerves frayed, Rick tapped a finger on the desk to keep from losing it.

Kaci planted her hand on his finger to still it. "You're making me nervous." She pointed at the screen. "There. Olivia and Shane are leaving the property."

Rick's mind drifted to Olivia. To what she must have been thinking at that time. *Get moving. Get Natalie quiet. Get back home.* She hadn't a clue what was awaiting her. He hadn't had a clue when he'd left her either, or he wouldn't have gone.

Dark emotions grabbed him. Emotions like those he experienced the night he'd learned of Traci's death. He hadn't been there for her when she needed him. He hadn't been there for Olivia in her time of need either. At least in this case she and the baby were alive. Or he thought Olivia was alive, anyway. He couldn't consider anything else at this point and stay upright.

Kaci stopped the video. "Nothing."

"Back it up to when Olivia and I first arrived here," he demanded.

She cringed, but pressed the button again. She had to know continuing with the recording was a long shot. He knew it, too, but he couldn't miss any chance to locate Olivia.

Where are you? Are you all right?

The file whizzed by until Kaci had backed up beyond the day they'd arrived at the house. "We should stop wasting time and head over to the accident scene," she said. "Maybe Brynn has a lead."

If Rick had been thinking with his brain instead of his heart, he wouldn't have needed Kaci to tell him. "Let's roll."

He took off and expected Kaci to keep up. He got the siren going in the SUV and made good time, pulling up to the side of the road near Dianna's car in minutes. Large klieg lights cut through gloomy skies, a fine mist falling now.

He reached the car and got his first clear view of the damage. Of the blood left in the driver's seat. On the door. On the wheel. His knees buckled. He planted his hands on the roof to steady himself. With the amount of blood and Shane's extensive injuries, Rick wouldn't be surprised if Olivia's injuries were severe as well.

Are you even alive? He hated the thoughts taking over his brain.

Brynn joined him. "We'll find her."

He felt like someone was strangling him, and he focused on not hyperventilating. "Tell me you located something to back up that claim."

"Three things, actually. White paint transferred from the truck to Dianna's car, plus several male footprints, and tire treads holding very interesting particulates."

Hope started to flourish in his heart. "So the paint can help us find a vehicle, but the particulates? What will they do for us?"

"My analysis could help us figure out where the suspect was before coming here and could lead us to him."

"How long will that take?"

"If I leave right now, I could have it done in a few hours."

"A few hours! No way. No. We can't wait that long to find Olivia."

"I can't get the results any faster." Brynn frowned. "Didn't you say the guy from Chick-fil-A drove a white truck?"

He nodded. "But there weren't any plates in that video. No plates. No registration and no driver ID. And there aren't any traffic cams around here, so we have no idea the direction he headed. It could take days to view the closest cams."

"Then you and the team can figure something else out while I process the particulates. I arranged to use the lab again. I'll do the particulates first, then the paint, which I have to warn you will also take time."

"Time we don't have."

"They've also reserved a conference room for the team, so you all can work on locating another lead."

Rick appreciated her help, but they were fresh out of leads unless her particulates or the paint gave them something. He could do nothing—nothing!—to find Olivia any sooner. He was helpless. Exactly as he'd been when Traci died. When his father hit him. When Levi died.

He struggled to breathe.

Time to face facts. Everything was out of his control. Only God could fix this, and Rick didn't even know if God wanted to hear from him, much less come to his aid.

* * *

Lumpkin County, Georgia
10:15 a.m.

Ike started toward Olivia, his gaze mean, ugly, and as focused as a honed knife. She didn't want to incur his wrath. No telling what he might do. She sat down at the tunnel opening, put on the headlamp, and slid her legs inside. The ground dropped away.

Reality hit. They'd be going down. *Down.* Into the ground. Her fear ratcheted up.

"I can't..."

"Just feel for the large rocks with your feet and hold on to the walls."

She found a cold, rough boulder to settle her feet on. She slid into the darkness. The minuscule space smelled of mold and raw, earthy scents. She swung her head around, the light illuminating yellow stone walls and a narrow tunnel that felt like a prison.

She forced herself to move a few more feet. A cool breeze wafted up from below.

Good. She could breathe, at least. Plus she was out of the rain. *Okay.* She could do this.

"These tunnels aren't safe," Ike called from behind her. "Keep your hands off the ceiling. You don't want to cause a collapse."

Her confidence evaporated. She hunched down. Put out a foot. Felt around. Stepped ahead. One painstaking step at a time.

Halting thumps sounded behind her. Ike. Likely Virgil, too, finding their way over the rocks. She moved through the seemingly endless tunnel. Suddenly it widened into a small room. She hurried ahead. Turned in a circle, her lamp displaying sparkly flakes of dust dancing in the air.

The room smelled foul. A mixture of marijuana and rotting food. She spotted a mound of garbage in the corner, mostly McDonald's bags. A long wooden box marked with stenciled letters and seemingly random numbers sat nearby. Could it contain the rifle used to fire the smart bullets?

Footsteps sounded in the room. She turned to see Ike. Watched the tunnel and waited for Virgil to emerge from the dark. He didn't.

"Where's your buddy?" she asked.

"Now that he helped me get you down here just fine, he has some business to attend to."

She wasn't fond of Virgil, but being alone with Ike underground? Alone. With a killer. Not good.

"Might as well take a load off," Ike said. "You're gonna be here for a while."

"How long?"

"Until Virg confirms our meet is on to deliver the weapon and bullets."

"And how long will that take?"

"Eager to get rid of me?" He snickered.

"Just curious."

"Round-trip, I'd say he'll be back in less than four hours. Then I'll deliver the package and reevaluate my need for you."

Four hours. The exact time it would take for this killer to decide if she would go with him to Mexico or if she would die in a hole in the ground, never to be found.

* * *

Atlanta, Georgia
2:00 p.m.

"You won't believe what I discovered." Brynn sat back from the petri dishes lined up on the lab countertop and lifted her safety glasses.

"Just tell us," Rick demanded then felt bad for pushing her. "Sorry."

"The boot print had gold in a tread. Not refined gold like in jewelry, but raw gold."

Rick's mouth fell open, but his mind flew over the implications. "The north Georgia Mountains are known for the eighteen-hundreds gold rush. There are quite a few abandoned mines in the area."

"You think our suspect has been hiding out in an abandoned mine?" Kaci asked.

"No one would think to look there," Cal replied.

"Means we now have a direction he might have headed and we can review traffic cams for his truck," Rick said. "The most direct and fastest route to the mountains is US 19."

"*If* he took the main road," Cal said. "He might have gone the back way to avoid police."

Rick wouldn't even consider that now. "We'll start with the main road. If that doesn't pan out, we'll regroup."

"I can't give you a make or model of the truck until I analyze the paint," Brynn warned.

"I'm not waiting for that. With the extensive damage to Dianna's car, the truck has to be bigger than a pickup."

"Tire tracks we cast at the scene confirm that," Brynn said. "But I can't give you the exact size without sending the casts to Quantico for analysis."

Rick didn't care about proof right now. "We know the truck's white. Maybe a two-ton vehicle like the guy drove in the Chick-fil-A video. That should be easy to spot in traffic cams at this time of night."

Kaci jumped off her stool. "I'll get started obtaining access to cameras on that route."

"And I'll process the paint," Brynn said. "The test requires special light sources, so head back to the conference room, and I'll come find you when I'm done."

Kaci started for the door. Rick and Cal followed. In the conference room she went straight for her computer on the long table. Cal sat next to her. Her fingers flew across the keyboard, giving Rick some comfort that they'd soon be tracking the truck and locating Olivia.

Her fingers stilled, and she sat back. "There. Now we wait."

"Wait? Why?" Rick asked.

"I've texted my contact at GDOT for access to the files. He's been great so far at getting back to me quickly."

"No!" he shouted, and she cringed. He lowered his voice. "We can't wait. Every minute could be the difference between life and death."

She peered up at him, her face a mass of frustration, too. "The only other choice I have is to hack the feeds. I'll get started on it just in case he doesn't get back to me."

"How long will it take?"

She shrugged. "Won't know till I get started."

"Then go for it."

Waiting to see the videos would feel like an eternity. Rick had to keep busy. But how, when all he could think about was Olivia bound, maybe gagged, in an abandoned mine? Terrified. Panicked. Maybe crying. Wondering where he was. Why he didn't come for her.

God, please. You proved your point. I'm helpless. Don't punish Olivia because I was too dumb to see that I needed You. Show me what to do.

He resumed pacing. Thought about jumping into his truck and driving up to the foothills. But if she was in a mine, she was underground. Sure, they might be able to follow the killer's truck, but these mines were well off the beaten path. If their suspect wasn't there right now, how would they know which mine he'd put her in? Know where to begin to look for her?

He charged over to Cal. "We're going to need a way to locate Olivia underground."

"Ground-penetrating radar?" Cal suggested. "But it's known to return a lot of false positives, so it could take some time."

"We don't have time. We need something better, but what?" Rick racked his brain trying to come up with something. He had to find her. "That's it. FINDER."

"What?" Cal asked.

"Remember that demonstration we had of FINDER a few months back? FINDER, the acronym for Finding Individuals for Disaster and Emergency Response equipment developed by NASA and the Department of Homeland Security."

"The equipment that can locate heartbeats under rubble," Kaci clarified. "But what if she's d— No. I'm sorry, Rick. I shouldn't even think that way. We'll find her alive."

Rick ignored the comment to keep them focused. Maybe to keep himself from thinking that FINDER wouldn't help if there was no heartbeat to pick up. "I have a contact on a local search-and-rescue team who tested a FINDER prototype in exchange for keeping the equipment. I'll give him a call, but we should locate a source for ground-penetrating radar, too."

"I can do that," Cal offered. "We'll want the best machine, so I'll look for archaeologists in the area first."

Law enforcement agencies sometimes owned GPR, but their equipment wasn't of the quality that an archaeologist's would be.

"FYI, Rick," Kaci said, her focus still on her laptop, "FINDER is computer controlled. We'll need your friend to give us a quick tutorial when he drops it off."

"I'll arrange it." Rick got his contact on the phone and explained the situation. "We need the equipment ASAP."

"No problem," his contact said. "But you know this equipment isn't easily replaced, and my boss will require me to keep it in sight at all times."

"We can work that out when you get here," Rick replied, though he didn't intend to take a search-and-rescue guy along just to expose him to a .50-caliber bullet to the gut.

*   *   *

Lumpkin County, Georgia
4:20 p.m.

A battery-powered lantern visually warmed the mine, but
dampness from the cold floor seeped into Olivia's body. Her
bones, her head, her chest all ached. To get warm she'd need
to move. She'd tried. Once. Gotten up only to have Ike
shove her back to the ground. There she'd been for hours.
Knees tucked up. Time ticking slowly by. No idea how to
escape.

She rested her chin on her knees.

Think, Olivia. Think.

She closed her eyes, but grogginess tried to take her. She
snapped her head up. Heard footsteps thumping from the tunnel. A beam of light spilled through the entrance, growing
larger and larger.

Ike shot to his feet and pointed his handgun at the tunnel.
Virgil emerged, a frown on his face.

Ike sagged against the wall and shoved his gun into his belt.
"Where have you been?"

"Chill. Rain caused an accident and closed the road for a
while. I couldn't get back here."

"Any law enforcement people sniffing around up top?" Ike
asked.

"None, but the meet's up in the air. They said for you to get
your butt on a video call or the deal's off."

Ike swore, and his eyes narrowed into dark slits.

Perfect. This setback would buy her more time. Maybe even
cancel the sale of the weapon.

"No Wi-Fi here." Ike seemed to be thinking through his
problem aloud. "I'll have to head into town to make the call."

His gaze moved to her, appraising her for a long moment before turning back to Virgil. "I'll go. You stay with her."

"You know I can hardly breathe down here," Virgil whined. "You promised I wouldn't have to stay for long. I'm sure as shootin' not sittin' here for hours."

Ike ran a hand over his oily hair, then scrubbed his palm down his jeans. "We'll secure her to the bolts. You can hang outside."

"In the rain?"

"Do you always have to be such a big baby?"

"Maybe," Virgil sneered. "But you need me."

"Fine. Let me get her secured, and you can come with me." Ike stomped to his backpack and pulled out the dreaded zip ties.

Olivia's wrists were still raw, and she couldn't imagine the hard plastic digging into the open wounds. "You don't have to use those."

Ike rolled his eyes. "Face me and move against the wall."

She ignored him. He slammed a boot into her side, ground in the steel toe. A scream sounded in her mind, but she kept it from reaching her mouth. Creeps like him took pleasure in hurting others, and she wouldn't give him the satisfaction.

"Right," he said. "You're such a tough girl. Let's see if you can handle another one without crying out."

"Wait," she said. "I'm moving." She couldn't let him continue to hurt her. She had to protect herself so she was physically able to escape. She scooted to the wall.

"Move closer to me," he demanded.

She slid ahead, stopping at a metal eyebolt protruding from the rock wall and a mound of shards and dust lying below. He'd obviously installed the bolt for such an occasion.

"Hands behind your back," he commanded. "Unless, of course, you want to feel my other boot."

She leaned forward and clasped her hands together as directed. He snapped the rigid plastic around one wrist. Pain sizzled up her arm. His fingers fumbled to slip the tie through the bolt and fix it to her other wrist. He dropped it, and his curses echoed through the space.

"C'mon. Quit messing around." Virgil tugged at his collar.

"Zip tie's too short," Ike said. "You'll have to stay."

"No way, man." He shot across the space. "Cuff her in the front. That way her hands can be closer to the wall."

"You're not so dumb when fear motivates you to think." Ike grinned at his buddy, then glared down on her. "Do as he said."

She gladly shifted, putting her body parallel to the wall and holding out her hands before Ike realized he could connect two ties together and still bind her hands behind her back. This angle would be more comfortable and would give her a better chance to escape.

He secured her wrists to the eyebolt, then bound her ankles, jerking the tie tight enough to dig into her skin and cut off circulation.

She bit down on her lip so she didn't cry out.

He withdrew a nasty bandanna from his backpack and tossed the pack to the ground by her feet. "Can't have you screaming for help."

"I won't." She gagged looking at the soiled rag. "Please don't put that thing on me."

"Have to," he said.

She clamped her lips down tight.

"Don't fight me, or I won't leave you with the headlamp. Then you'll be in the dark."

She'd rather have a nasty gag than sit underground in the dark, so she opened her mouth. He tied the filthy rag around her head, pulling hard and tearing at the sensitive corners of her mouth, adding to the throbbing in her head that was making her nauseous.

She breathed in and out through her nose until the feeling passed.

"Now don't go trying to pull on your zip ties. It won't do any good. And I've already told you these walls aren't stable. The wrong kind of movement could start a cave-in." He ripped off her headlamp and patted her on the head. "That's a good girl."

What? If she didn't have the stupid gag in her mouth, she would spew anger at him. Okay, fine. She was angrier with herself than with him. She should have known better than to trust a thief and killer.

He strapped the light on his head and switched off the lantern. Steeped in darkness, the space seemed to shrink in size, like a dark coffin. Her pulse kicked up.

"Be back in a few hours," he said. "Don't go anywhere."

He laughed, the sound reverberating off the walls, then trailing him down the corridor. The light from their headlamps soon evaporated. Darkness settled in like a black cloak covering her head. The eerie quiet was deafening. Claustrophobic.

What if they were killed in a car accident and didn't make it back? Or what if they just decided to leave her here?

No one knew she was buried deep in the earth.

No one. No one at all.

CHAPTER

30

Rick slammed a fist into the wall of Ike Zelner's dilapidated house, catching the attention of his teammates. He didn't care. They'd struck out again. The traffic cam had revealed a large white truck, and they'd caught Zelner's license plate. So they'd rushed to his house, but he wasn't home. They'd turned the house upside down for a lead. Discovered nothing other than that he was a former marine. Sure, that could potentially connect him to the investigation, but it wasn't concrete proof that he was the killer who'd taken Olivia.

Still, Rick's gut screamed they were on the right track. Zelner's DMV picture came to mind, and Rick could just imagine the narrow-eyed guy holding Olivia. He punched the wall again, relishing the pain in his knuckles.

Cal stepped over to him. "Hey, man. Take it from me. That won't help."

A year ago Cal had been in a similar situation when a crazed bomber had taken his wife hostage. Back then, Rick had told

Cal to calm down. Now he needed to take his own advice. "I guess the shoe's on the other foot."

"So you *are* in love with Olivia." Brynn stepped across the room. "It looked like it, but then—"

"We never know with you," Kaci said from the other side of the room, where she sat at the table with her computer. "And none of us was about to ask."

Rick didn't take offense at her statement. For years he'd made sure that they understood his private life was off limits, but now the personal had mixed with work, and he needed their help. "We've got to find her."

"We will," Cal said. "If we stay calm and think this through like any other investigation."

"Let's run what we know," Brynn said. "Make a plan."

Rick nodded, but took a moment to clear his anguish so he could think clearly. "Okay. So we know the truck headed up US 19. Perhaps to an abandoned mine. It was last seen at the intersection camera fifteen miles south of Dahlonega. But didn't appear on the first Dahlonega camera. So it had to have turned off or stopped somewhere in that fifteen-mile stretch."

Rick's phone rang.

"It's Max," he said, and answered. "Got you on speaker, Max."

"First, I wanted to let you know Shane's more alert, and the doctor's very optimistic about a full recovery."

"That's great news," Brynn said, and the others murmured their agreement.

"Second, it looks like Zelner is indeed our guy."

"How do you know?" Rick asked, hope making a comeback.

"Now that I have a contact at the marines, I got him to rush me Zelner's SRB. He was in the '03 sniper class, but washed out. The file said he had ongoing difficulties in playing nice with others and let his attitude sink him."

"He could blame the other class members for his failure," Rick said. "And the murders are payback."

Cal shook his head. "If Shane was here, he'd tell us that wasn't enough of a reason to commit murder. That there has to be more to it. Like Zelner was already mentally unstable."

"His SRB hints at that," Max said. "But my question is why wait years to start killing when he possessed enough training to take them out sooner?"

"Maybe we're wrong, and it's not about the past," Cal suggested. "He could be part of the group selling weapons. If they stole the smart bullet, he could be trying to keep all the money for himself."

"No," Rick said. "I refuse to believe that Levi would be a part of selling such a deadly weapon."

"That seems odd to me, too." Kaci looked up from her computer. "Zelner's name wasn't mentioned in the senator's information, so maybe there's no connection between the smart-bullet theft and the sniper group selling other weapons."

"We have James and Patton in custody and can question them," Max said. "But so far they've been uncooperative."

"And Floyd?" Cal asked. "We any closer to finding him?"

"No," Max said. "With the number of agents looking for him, I'm starting to think he's dead, too."

"Yes!" Kaci pumped her fist. "I just located a cell phone for Zelner. Max, can you get the phone company to ping it?"

"Do you think the guy would be dumb enough to continue using his cell instead of buying a throwaway?" Rick asked. "I mean, if he's the one who deployed the ransomware, he has to be knowledgeable enough to get a burner, right?"

"I just looked at the coffee shop video, and Zelner isn't in it," Kaci said. "So we have no proof he deployed it. The ransomware might not be related to these shootings either."

"Plus if he *is* using his cell, he wouldn't be the first suspect we've tracked to miss the obvious," Max said. "I'll give the phone company a call. Our exigent circumstances should get them to release the data with a promise of a warrant to follow."

"Call back the second you know anything, Max." Rick disconnected. "Since we last saw Zelner's vehicle near Dahlonega, we have to think that's where his phone will ping. I'll head that direction, and Kaci will come with me. Brynn and Cal, I want you to stay here in case he returns home."

Rick received a surprised look from Kaci. He didn't waste time explaining that he wanted to give her a chance to be in on the bust so she could feel like the hero for once, but jogged to the car. He got them on the road and drove as fast as the rainy conditions allowed.

"I have Zelner's online phone account." Kaci opened her laptop. "And I'll try to hack it in case Max isn't successful with the phone company."

Rick left her to do her thing until they approached the intersection where the traffic cam had last recorded Zelner's truck. Sunset was still an hour or so away, but the skies were gray with dark clouds, making it hard to see.

He grabbed his binoculars and handed them to Kaci. "This is our intersection, so look alive."

She glassed the area, and Rick kept his head on a swivel. With each passing mile and no sign of the truck, his hopes dwindled. No. He had to stay positive. They had the tools needed and would locate her. Cal had secured GPR, and the FINDER unit had been delivered before they'd set out for Zelner's house. It had taken a few minutes of fast talking to get his contact to hand it over, but he'd finally agreed, and the unit sat in the back of Rick's SUV along with the GPR.

Rick's phone rang with Max's tone. Rick hit the speaker button.

"Phone company came through, and I have Zelner's GPS co-ordinates. He's just off US 19."

"Text them to me," Kaci said. "And I'll get directions."

"Send Brynn and Cal as backup to that location." Rick hung up and waited for Kaci's phone to ding. When it did, he almost came off the seat.

Calm down, he warned himself as she tapped her screen.

"He's nearby," she said. "But we passed the turnoff. Hang a U-turn at the next exit, and I'll give you directions."

Rick's gut clenched. Sure, they now knew Zelner's location, but it could also mean they were about to find out that they were too late to stop him from killing Olivia.

* * *

Lumpkin County, Georgia
6:30 p.m.

Olivia ignored the dark, the panic, and assessed her situation. She had little range of movement, but she could curl forward enough to jerk the dirty bandanna from her mouth. She tried to gather enough saliva to spit out the sour taste, but her mouth was too dry. She turned her attention to the eyebolt. Too bad she couldn't see it, but she knew Ike had secured each hand individually to the bolt, giving her more flexibility.

She grasped the cold steel and twisted. No movement.

"Try harder."

She gripped the bolt tighter. Turned. Movement? Maybe a fraction of an inch. She tried again. Felt it budge. Kept at it. Turn after turn. No real movement. She couldn't get the right leverage, so her hands were sliding over the metal.

"So now what?" she asked to stave off panic.

She closed her eyes to think. If anyone could see her sitting in the dark with her eyes closed, they'd think she was nuts, but choosing her own darkness rather than letting the actual darkness choose her was the only thing keeping her from giving in to the panic. She ran through the hours she'd spent in the tunnel, trying to come up with anything that could help.

A flash of Ike dropping the backpack by her feet came to mind.

"That's it!" It could contain tools. If she scooted forward, she could hook the pack with her feet, then move it up to her hands. Never had her daily yoga been more important. It gave her the core and leg strength to succeed.

She slid forward until her feet touched the canvas. Twisting on her side, she scooped with her feet and drew her knees closer until the rough canvas lay beneath her fingers.

"Please let this backpack hold something I can use. Please."

* * *

"There." Rick pointed ahead at a cleared area near the road. "It's recently been mowed. Tire tracks in the mud."

"This's our location all right, but there's no sign of Zelner's vehicle."

"Let's circle around to make a stealth approach." Rick continued down the narrow road until he found a spot wide enough for a three-point turn.

He stopped shy of the clearing, and they got out to retrieve their gear from the back. They still wore body armor from the raid on Zelner's house, but even their type-IV vests wouldn't do much good against a smart bullet. They grabbed assault rifles and extra ammo, and Rick strapped his sniper rifle over his back. No way would he go against a lethal smart bullet without a long-range option of his own.

Rick signaled for Kaci to follow him and set off. His rifle to his shoulder, he kept his body low and his gaze sweeping the area. He noted motorcycle tracks near the tire ruts and a pile of discarded branches. He pointed at the items for Kaci, who nodded, displaying her understanding that Zelner had once camouflaged something there, likely his truck.

Rick moved on, discovering scrub that had been trampled by large boots. In bare patches he also spotted smaller, female footprints in the mud. The delicate prints nearly swamped him. On the one hand, he was thrilled to see Olivia had reached this location alive. On the other hand, her bare feet in the mud reminded him of her vulnerability.

He forced himself to continue forward and slip through a narrow opening in the trees where motorcycles had decimated the soil. About twenty feet later, the path opened to a clearing where a ditch ran alongside a creek. He ran his binoculars over the area.

"Motorcycle tracks in the ditch on the right," he whispered. "Two different tire treads."

"Two bikers, then," Kaci replied. "Zelner has help."

"With no truck at the road, it's likely Zelner isn't here."

"He could have been dropped off and is in the mine. No, wait. That doesn't work. The odds of a signal pinging from underground are slim."

"Maybe the GPS was wrong."

Kaci shook her head. "Maybe he was on site when the phone company pinged his cell, and then he left. He'd have to depart to the south, or we would have seen his truck on the road. I'll text Max to issue an alert."

While she sent the text, Rick ran the latest development

through his brain and boiled things down to one option. "If there's even the slightest possibility that Olivia is here, we go forward."

Kaci nodded.

"We'll track the bikes," he said. "I'll head out first."

Together, they bounded from one covered position to the next. When the motorcycle tracks ended, Rick signaled a break and a search of the nearby area. Kaci soon waved him over to where she bent over boot prints, her phone out. "Same prints as the ones Brynn lifted at the crash scene. We might not find Zelner at the end of the trail, but at least we know he's been here."

* * *

Hysteria threatening, Olivia plunged her hands into the backpack. Her fingers landed on a headlamp. She laughed with joy, a nutty, wild laugh scaring her almost as much as her surroundings. She turned it on. Nothing happened.

"No! It can't be dead." She shook it. Got a flicker of light, but then it went dark. Tears pricked at her eyes, but she wouldn't cry. She swallowed hard and frantically clawed through the bag until her fingers landed on the coolness of a switchblade.

"Yes! Yes!" She started maneuvering the knife out of the bag, but dropped it.

"Calm down." She thought of escaping and being reunited with Rick to calm her nerves and located the switchblade to prop the handle between her knees so she could cut off her cuffs. She sawed at the ties. Wrists first, then ankles. When the last one broke, she crawled toward where she'd last seen the lantern, her body stiff and clumsy and her feet numb.

Her fingers touched the hard plastic. "Yes!"

She flipped on the switch and light, blessed, wonderful light, flooded the space. She blinked hard until her vision cleared. She spotted a six-pack of bottled water and rinsed out her mouth, then chugged a whole bottle and planned her next move.

She would have to flee, but which way did she go? Ike and Virgil had entered on one side but departed in the other direction. She had to assume they knew the best way to enter and exit the mine, and she would follow their lead. But in case they came back through the exit, she needed to be armed.

Her feet tingling, she crawled back to the pack to take inventory. The bag contained first aid supplies, more of the confounded zip ties, and another headlamp, this one in its original packaging. She unpackaged the lamp, confirmed it worked, and fixed it on her head. She then searched for a weapon other than the knife, which she had no confidence in her ability to defend herself with. She came up empty-handed.

She glanced around the space again. The box. Rifle. Yes! She crawled over to it. Found a large—no, monstrously big rifle and giant bullets. She held one in her hand. It ran nearly the full length from her wrist to the tip of her middle finger.

She couldn't possibly handle the large weapon that shot these monster bullets, but if they were the self-steering ones, she couldn't leave the box behind for Ike. She stood, testing her feet. Found them able to hold her. She tried to grab the handles to lift the box, but she couldn't reach both ends. Still, she could drag it behind her. She only had to hope that she found a flat tunnel and equally flat terrain outside.

She secured the lid again, then took another long drink of the water. Having no idea what she might face ahead, she put another bottle into the backpack and slipped it on her back. It would be nice to take the big lantern for better lighting as she moved, but she needed both hands free to get the box out of the mine.

"Okay. You can do this." She grabbed the nearest box handle and backed toward the opening.

A quick shine of her light down the tunnel, and she was happy to discover a smooth, level floor, but the ceiling wasn't very high. She bent low, placed one hand on the wall behind her to help stay in the middle of the tunnel, and then started backing out. She dragged the box through the dirt, the rasping from the wood sliding over rough ground comforting as she achieved a rhythm.

The tunnel soon turned right. Her head throbbed with the exertion, and she stopped to catch her breath. She shone her light down the new route. The passageway was taller and a bit wider here. She maneuvered safely around the corner and picked up speed in the larger space. The box hit a rock in the floor and bounced to the side, striking a timber. The rotting wood gave way with a sharp crack. The rock above her groaned.

A wide crack split the ceiling. The earth opened up. Dirt and debris hissed through the gap. Filtered to the ground.

A loud rumbling reverberated above. The sound built, resembling a freight train. The ground shook. She teetered.

"No. Oh. No."

She dropped the box.

Ran under the collapsing ceiling. Begging, with each step she took, for her life to be spared.

CHAPTER
31

A rumble sounded to the east and shook the ground beneath Rick's feet. He knew the feeling. Had experienced it when caves collapsed in Afghanistan.

Olivia!

He threw caution to the wind and charged up the hill, then ran until he stood in front of a narrow mine opening. Clouds of lung-clogging dirt and dust whooshed out and mingled with the rain.

Kaci rushed up behind him. "You think Olivia's in there?"

"Yes." He was surprised he could form a word.

"Stay here. I'll go back to get FINDER and the other equipment," she offered.

Shovels. She meant FINDER *and* shovels to dig for Olivia. For a moment his brain refused to comprehend the situation, then reality hit him with the earth-shattering force of the tunnel collapse.

"Rick?" Kaci asked.

"Be careful," he managed to get out.

He heard her bolt in the other direction, but he couldn't take his eyes from the opening. Should he go in after Olivia, or would that put both of their lives at risk? He knew nothing of the inside of this mine. Had no idea of the depth, the length, the stability. Based on the small opening, he doubted it was much of a mine, and guessed that whoever had dug it likely hadn't shored up the walls, as safety standards hadn't existed back then.

What could he do? Could he even call out to her, or would Zelner come slinking out of the woods and put a .50 in Rick's back?

"What next, God? What?" He waited for a moment, hoping for some crazy sign in response, but God didn't work that way. Rick had to take action. If he failed to have peace about his decision, that would be his indicator that he was doing the wrong thing.

He covered his mouth and nose to keep the dust out and moved closer to the opening. Peered inside. Haze and blackness greeted him. He skirted to the side, scrambling up the hill. Dirt filtered into the air ahead from what he believed to be an exit. Could he move over the ground without risking another collapse?

"Think, man." His brain seized up. He was frozen in time. Unable to move forward. Backward. The stakes were too high for him to make a mistake.

He had to try. He moved ahead, judging the soundness of the earth one step at a time. Expecting it to collapse at any moment. He kept going. Traveled the distance. Saw the exit with rocks piled high.

His heart fell. If Olivia was inside, could she possibly be alive? Kaci would soon be back with FINDER. Then he'd know.

He heard a muffled noise from behind. Kaci? He whirled to check.

A gunshot sounded from the trees. A bullet rasped across his forehead. He lifted his rifle. Another slug slammed into his chest. Hitting his vest. Knocked the breath from his body, and he dropped his rifle as he doubled over in pain. He scrambled to grab it.

A third bullet hit him from the side. Sliced into the unprotected area by his armpit. Razor-sharp pain cut through him and brought him to his knees. Blackness colored his vision. He fought it off. Tried to move. Couldn't.

He collapsed to the soggy soil. Rain pelted his face. He tried to get up. Failed. He was powerless to save his own life, much less save Olivia's.

A man walked past him. Zelner.

Rick reached for his handgun, but Zelner bolted over the hill ahead before Rick could lift the gun into firing position. Was the creep heading for the other tunnel entrance? Going for Olivia?

Rick swiped at blood streaming down his forehead. He rolled to retrieve his rifle. Stars danced in front of his eyes. He blinked hard and waited for the wooziness to pass, then he belly-crawled.

Stay low. Dig deep. Just like you learned in the marines.

Blades of fire knifed through his chest and blood oozed out. Blackness threatened. Beckoned, offering relief from the pain. He was weak, but he only needed one shot. Perfectly aimed. He had to keep moving.

He gritted his teeth. Swiped the blood from his eyes again. Moved forward. Every few inches he had to rest. Breathe. Pray he didn't black out.

At the crest of the hill he saw the tunnel opening. Saw

Zelner step inside. Olivia's face came to mind. Her soft smile trained on him, beckoning and encouraging him to keep going. He had to do this. For her.

He gripped the rifle to his chest and rolled down the hill. Every time his shoulder hit, he nearly retched. He reached the bottom, breathless and weak. He dug for strength and practiced deep breathing to gain control and move into position.

Slowly, painstakingly, he unfolded the rifle bipod. Planted his left forearm on the ground, the pain excruciating. He dialed in his scope. Searched the tunnel for Olivia. Didn't see her. Good. She wasn't in the line of fire. He dialed in on Zelner. Rick didn't relish propping the rifle stock near the gaping bullet wound, but he had no choice. The recoil would intensify his pain. Take him out. Meant he had only one shot before blacking out.

He exhaled. Dropped his finger to the trigger. Planted the rifle butt on his shoulder. Blood left his head. Darkness swirled like a fog.

He dug deeper. Aimed. Fired.

The recoil took his breath, and the blackness came.

* * *

Zelner dropped to the ground. Olivia screamed, then clamped her hand over her mouth. Had Ike's buyer trailed him back here to kill him and steal the weapon? If so, she was a sitting duck, and he would kill her, too.

She clawed at the rocks that were trapping her foot. Frantic. Panicked. They didn't move. Of course not. They were too big, and she'd already tried and failed to move them.

Was she going to die here? Near enough to the entrance to

see the daylight? To reach out and almost touch the fresh air, yet unable to move into it?

She heard a noise outside. Footsteps coming down the hill. A low voice. Female? Maybe. She couldn't be sure, but who said the buyer couldn't be a woman?

The footsteps closed in on the entrance.

Olivia looked for a way to hide. She couldn't.

A shadow moved over the opening. The person was holding a rifle. Olivia held her breath. Waited.

Father, if I'm to die, please watch over Rick. Over my family.

A rifle swung around the corner. The person darted back.

"Olivia, is that you?"

Kaci? Dear God, is it Kaci?

"Kaci," Olivia called out.

"Are you in danger? Zelner?"

"He's dead. Someone shot him."

"Rick," Kaci replied, and swung into the space.

"Rick? Where is he?"

"He's been shot."

"No! Is he—"

"He's alive. Barely. I packed the worst wound. Medevac helicopter is on the way." She set down her rifle and grabbed a board.

"Zelner had a partner," Olivia warned. "Virgil."

"No worries. He's cuffed to his truck." A quick grin flashed on Kaci's face as she shoved the board under the largest rock. "When I lift this top boulder, pull your leg free."

She pressed down on the end. Her face contorted with the strain. The rock rose. A sharp ache cut through Olivia's ankle, but she bit down and pulled it free. She stood and pain nearly took her down, but she had to see Rick.

Kaci came to support her, and they hobbled outside together.

Rick lay on his back. His face deathly pale. A blood-soaked bandage at his chest. Olivia picked up speed. Dropped to the ground beside him.

"Rick," she said as she cupped his face, tears falling like the rain around them. "Wake up, Rick. Please."

His eyes opened.

"You're safe," he whispered.

She smiled at him. "I love you. Don't you dare leave me."

His eyelids closed. She took his hand. Prayed. Begged.

Brynn and Cal sidestepped down the hill, their faces filled with worry, but Olivia wouldn't budge from Rick's side. When the medics arrived, the others dragged her away from him.

Medics worked on Rick. Put him on a backboard and declared his loss of blood the greatest danger to his life. They headed up the hill.

She started after them. Her gimpy ankle took her down, and she struggled to get back up. Brynn and Kaci came to her rescue and helped her up the steep incline to where the whirring sound of a helicopter's rotors made talking difficult. Medics loaded Rick into the helicopter. She tried to go after him.

Brynn held her back. Tears poured down Olivia's face, and she could barely see the helicopter spiral up into the sky.

"I have to be with him," she said between her sobs.

"Don't worry," Brynn said. "We have a chopper on standby to pick us up."

Olivia faced the woman who'd been so reserved thus far. "I don't care what you say. I'm going with you."

"Of course you are." Brynn smiled. "Look. I know I was the last one on board with believing in your innocence, but it's my job to watch out for my teammates. I didn't want Rick getting involved with a woman we hadn't cleared."

"And I'm cleared now?"

Brynn nodded. "Zelner might have died before we could question him, but Virgil filled us in on the operation. He even laughed when I mentioned that you might be involved."

The sound of the next chopper approaching took Olivia's attention, and everything was a blur until she was in the hospital waiting for Rick to get out of surgery.

"You look pale," Kaci said as she dropped into a nearby chair. "You shouldn't have refused to let a doctor check you out. You clearly have a head injury, not to mention your ankle. You can't ignore them."

"I'm fine for now."

"At a minimum you're in shock." Max came to stand over her. "Maybe not the medical definition of it, but in shock nonetheless."

"Like I said, I'm fine, and I won't be sitting in some exam room when Rick wakes up."

"That could take hours." Kaci rested her hand on Olivia's.

"Then I'll sit here for hours. Days, if that's what it takes."

Kaci's phone dinged, and she took her hand back to tap the screen. "Got a text from one of the agents watching the coffee shop. They caught the guy who deployed the ransomware on the senator's machine."

"Any relation to our case?" Max asked.

She shook her head and turned her attention back to her phone.

The team settled in to wait with Olivia, offering to get coffee and snacks, but she couldn't eat until she knew Rick was okay. Three hours passed before he was out of surgery and recovery, and Olivia hobbled to his bed, each step nearly taking her down. A bandage covered his forehead, and she saw the outline of a much larger one under his hospital gown. His color had returned, and the doctor said he would make a full recovery. She studied his face, so peaceful in sleep. The peace she wanted for him, but not this way.

The door opened, and she spun, nearly toppling as she watched Max pushing Shane in a wheelchair. Max stopped near the bed. Olivia wanted to tell them to go away. She didn't want to share Rick with anyone. She had to let him know how she felt, and she wouldn't do that with an audience.

"Thought it might do Rick some good to see Shane's recovering," Max said.

He was right. She was being selfish. Rick would recover, and she had plenty of time to share her feelings. She smiled at Shane. "I'm happy to see you up and about."

"Thanks." A weak smile crossed his face, but Rick stirring behind her quickly took her attention. He opened his eyes and blinked a few times.

"I didn't dream it. You're alive." He latched on to her hand with a viselike grip. "Your head. Are you okay?"

"I'm fine," she said, but now that she knew he was going to be all right, her injuries started throbbing.

He sighed and trained one of his heart-melting smiles on her.

"Dude," Shane said, taking Rick's attention. "You always have to be the center of attention."

"You know me. The prima donna of the group." Rick laughed, but a flash of pain lit on his face and he stopped. "Good to see you on the mend."

"Likewise." Shane gave a mock punch to Rick's forearm.

"We won't stay long, but I wanted you to see Shane," Max said. "And I have some news on Levi."

Rick's eyes narrowed. "What?"

"He was working undercover for the marines to bring the guys in his class who were selling weapons to justice."

"For real?" Rick asked.

"For real. And before you think he or the other snipers on his team were involved with Zelner in stealing the smart bullets, they weren't. Zelner had a partner. A Virgil Kunkle, and he's explaining everything. Including that Zelner killed Levi and the others because they made his life hell in sniper school. Once he stole the smart bullets, he figured it was the perfect chance to get back at them."

Rick sighed. "I'm glad the guys on the team didn't stoop low enough to take the self-steering bullets."

Max gave a solemn nod. "About these guys. We've also learned that the UV tattoos were used to prove to the buyers that they'd hooked up with the right seller. So when Kaci was told to bring the light, if she'd been the actual buyer she would have known to bring a UV light with her."

"And the three?"

"Pretty simple. It's for the year they graduated. They never got Levi involved in the past because he was a Christian and wouldn't go for it."

"That's why his tattoo was new."

Max nodded. "He'd gotten it on deployment so when he hit the States he could swing into action and join the team. The buy with Kaci was supposed to be his initiation."

"But he didn't have any backup."

Max shook his head. "They didn't want to bust this buyer, but have Levi make a connection. So his handler decided it was too risky to have anyone in the area. Unfortunately, Zelner followed Levi after his plane touched down, and when he broke off from our agent, Zelner took the chance to kill Levi."

"Levi shouldn't have taken a risk like that," Rick said. "But that was Levi. The guy who would do the right thing no matter the risk."

"Just like you all," Olivia said.

Rick opened his mouth as if he planned to speak, but his face contorted in pain and his eyes closed. "Maybe a quick nap."

Olivia didn't know if he really was tired, or if the loss of Levi was hitting him hard again and he didn't want to lose it in front of his buddies.

"We'll take off, then," Max said.

"Get well, man." Shane squeezed Rick's arm.

After they departed, Olivia waited until Rick's hand fell away before she dropped onto a bedside chair. She sat by his side and prayed. She ignored the increasing pain in her ankle and head and watched him until his eyes opened again and locked on hers. She hobbled to his side and sat on the bed. She found a mixture of emotions deep in his eyes. Longing, caring, worry. It was the last one that had her concerned.

"Hey." His voice was low and sleepy.

"Hey back atcha," she said, suddenly feeling tongue tied.

He reached out and snagged her hand before bringing her fingers to his lips. "I hate that I let you down. I shouldn't have let that creep get the drop on me. Still don't know how he snuck up on me like that."

"Ike stole a prototype motorcycle being built for the military."

"A stealth bike?"

She nodded. "He said he stole it when he took the smart bullets."

"Makes sense. We knew another technology had been stolen but didn't know what it was." He sighed. "I'm sorry I blacked out. Did that creep hurt you?"

That was the Rick she'd come to know—apologizing for blacking out when he'd sustained multiple gunshot wounds. He was typical of the strong men and women in the military and law enforcement. When things got out of their control, and they couldn't be there for those they loved, they took it harder than most.

"He didn't hurt me. I'm fine."

His gaze drifted off. "I need to ask you something important."

Her stomach clenched. "What's that?"

"Do you think you could you refer me to someone in D.C.? I think it's time I see a counselor. I need to find a way to meet my parents in the middle so I can get on with a relationship with someone special again." He twined his fingers in hers. "A Christian counselor would be a good idea."

She nodded eagerly. "I'm so happy, Rick."

"Don't get ahead of me here, honey," he said softly. "I want to change. Know I need to, but *if* I can do it still remains to be seen."

"Just so you know, I'm putting on my doctor's hat here. I've worked with a lot of clients over the years, and some people aren't able to overcome their obstacles, but you, mister..." She lifted his hand to her lips and kissed it. "You have an iron will, and I know when you set your mind to succeeding you'll do so." She grinned at him and tried to strike a flirty pose. "Besides, look at what you'll be missing if you don't succeed."

He growled, jerked her to him, and wrapped strong arms around her to cradle her tightly against his body.

"But your chest," she said as pain pulsed through her head.

"Trust me, Doc. I'd never let physical pain come between me and something I want. When I thought I'd lost you, it became very clear that I want you in my life."

"And I want you, too." She raised her head, ignored the pain, and smiled at him. "To kiss me right now."

"Happy to serve, ma'am." He saluted, then lifted his head, his lips inches from hers. "Before I do, you should know there's no one as gung ho as a marine. We fight to the finish, and I'm planning to fight for us." He settled his lips on hers, and a shock wave of emotion raced through her body.

He suddenly fell back on his pillow, a grin on his face. "Fight to the finish."

CHAPTER

32

Atlanta, Georgia
Friday, September 22
9:30 a.m.

Olivia had made no progress. None. Her brother and mother sat across the conference room table alternating their glares between her and Rick. The assistant district attorney had just departed after reviewing the agreement that, if Harrison signed and obeyed it, would keep him out of jail. He would be on probation for two years, and he had to comply with all those regulations. He also had to get a job and maintain regular employment during this time and pay compensatory damages to the bank.

"You can stop this, you know." Her mother shoved the agreement back across the table. "Harrison gave back your money."

"But he still committed a crime," Rick said, earning a glare from her and Harrison.

"I'm sorry, Olivia," Harrison said. "I've learned my lesson. Please don't do this."

Surprised at hearing him apologize, she hurried to him and gave him a hug.

"And," he continued, "if you would reinstate our allowance,

maybe increase it, I won't be forced to take such drastic action again."

Feeling as if he'd knifed her, Olivia stepped back. He hadn't learned his lesson. Not at all. Her heart breaking, she reached for the court agreement and put it in front of him. "Sign it or don't sign it, it's up to you. I've done everything I can."

She tried to march out of the room, but her walking cast wouldn't let her move as fast as she wanted. Still she kept going before her breaking heart caused her to give in to Harrison. She heard Rick's footsteps, and he caught up to her in the hallway.

"That didn't go so well," she muttered.

He slid his arm around her shoulders, the warmth easing out a bit of her angst. "I'm sorry, honey, but as you've told me all week, things have a way of working out for the best."

"I'm not going to think about it anymore," she said. "We have more important things to do today."

She continued out of the building to Rick's car. As they drove to her house, her thoughts went to Ace's funeral, scheduled to begin in an hour. Levi had been buried the day before in a lovely service that paid tribute to a wonderful man who would be missed. She doubted Rick had recovered from seeing his best friend lowered into the ground, but he'd insisted on accompanying her to Ace's funeral to support her. He really was an amazing man.

Rick parked in front of the house, and Olivia climbed out of the car. Natalie had a doctor's appointment that morning, so Olivia wasn't surprised to see her sister's car missing. Olivia didn't feel like talking about what had happened with Harrison just yet, so it was just as well that Dianna wasn't home.

In the family room, Rick kissed her on the forehead. "I'll get changed."

She'd already dressed for the service, but Rick would wear

his military uniform, and he chose not to go dressed that way to the DA's office. He headed down the hallway, and she went to the window to stare at the sun trickling through tall trees and dancing over the yard. She lost track of time trying to process all that had happened over the last few days, so when she heard Rick walk into the living room it caught her off guard.

Not for long, though, as she turned and got her first look at him wearing his dress blues. Her heart took a tumble at the sight. The navy jacket with red trim fit him like it had been tailored for his body. The white belt accentuated his trim waist and made his chest and shoulders appear even broader. He was a poster-worthy example of a marine.

It hit her then, really hit her, that he'd been a soldier. Had seen the same horrific action as the soldiers she counseled. Had gone through hell and returned as whole as could be expected.

Tears of gratitude stung her eyes, and she rushed over to throw her arms around his neck and hug him hard.

"Hey," he said. "What's that for?"

"If you hadn't made it back from your deployments, I might never have met you."

"But I did."

She leaned back. "Thank you from the bottom of my heart for all you endured for our country."

A quizzical look claimed his face. "You've already thanked me."

"Did I?"

"At the memorial in Mobile."

"Seeing you in uniform really brought home your sacrifice."

"And here I thought you'd take one look at my uniform, swoon, and fall into my arms." He grinned.

She loved how he'd lightened up the last few days. She was pleased to learn he had a great sense of humor.

"Is that what other women do when they get a look at you in uniform?" she asked, playing along.

"Maybe not fall into my arms, but yeah...there are women who can appreciate the uniform." His lips quirked in a playful smile.

She pressed the back of her hand against her forehead. "Oh, sir. You're right. I think I might faint."

"Can't have that." His deep Southern drawl left her feeling like Scarlett O'Hara. He drew her close and kissed her hard.

She did swoon then, but only in her emotions, as she was caught unaware by the incredible power her love for him gave him.

When he looked up, the grin returned. "Hope I was able to resuscitate you, ma'am."

She laughed and hugged him again, but she caught a look at the clock over his shoulder, and her laughter died away. "We should get going."

He tucked his cap under his arm and escorted her to the car. As the familiar scenery flew past, her mind went to the future, and she pondered her options. She didn't know for sure what she wanted to do, but she wanted Rick in her life. How to make that happen with him living in D.C. was the challenge. She'd no more ask him to leave his job than Traci had been willing to ask him to leave the marines. She'd be the one to make the change, and she was ready for it anyway. *If* he wanted her to, that was. Right now, she thought that was a big if.

She faced him. "For the last year or so, I've been struggling with my work. Burning out from the intensity of working with PTSD sufferers, you know?"

"When someone cares as much as you do, it has to be emotionally taxing," he replied. "But it would be a real shame if you quit. Our soldiers need you."

"I was thinking more like taking a sabbatical for a year."

"And what would you do to keep busy for a whole year?" He glanced at her.

"Write a book." She held up a hand. "Before you laugh, it would be nonfiction where I interview PTSD clients and have them talk about the struggle from their point of view. I'm hoping it will help other sufferers who are hesitant to seek counseling see the benefits of it."

"Sounds like a great idea."

"I also think a year of focusing on the positives will be cathartic for me."

He was silent for a moment. She wanted to will him to speak, but he peered at her for long moments before asking, "Would you close your practice?"

She nodded. "After I find someone to work with any clients. I can wrap things up within a month or two."

"And then? When the book is finished?"

"Then I find a job at a hospital or other organization so I don't have the added responsibilities of billing and paperwork and the job doesn't consume me."

He nodded, but before they could continue the discussion, he turned onto the driveway of the cemetery where Ace's graveside service would be held.

Mixed emotions fought for her attention. "I still can't believe Ace and Cesar were involved in stealing weapons. They loved our country, and I could never imagine them doing something like that."

"Technically they didn't steal the weapons. And they might have had the tattoos, but we don't yet have proof that they were actually selling. Just Patton's word."

"He has no reason to lie, right? I mean, he could have tried to blame everything on Ace and Cesar."

"Once he was shown the evidence that we have on him, he had to tell the truth or be labeled uncooperative and likely receive a harsher sentence."

"Makes sense, I guess. But what I still don't get is what possessed Ace and Cesar to participate in something like this. I know soldiers aren't well paid, but they had to realize the stolen weapons could be used against them and their fellow marines."

"Patton said to prevent that they only sold them to drug dealers. Figured the druggies would use the guns to kill each other and that would be a good thing."

She shook her head. "I guess I'll have to accept that as an explanation for Ace and Cesar, too, or drive myself crazy wondering."

Rick parked in the lot, and when they got out, he took her hand. She looked for Ace's mother among the few mourners. A uniformed marine detail and a chaplain stood by the casket. Violet Griffin sat in the front row of chairs, staring up at the men.

Olivia turned her focus to Rick. "Does it bother you that Ace participated in the weapons theft, and he's being given a military burial?"

"Bother me?" he asked. "In one respect he served his country, so he deserves the funeral. But no matter what we discovered about him, the marines wouldn't act fast enough to stop the funeral. So yeah, I guess I'm conflicted over it. What about you?"

"I'm glad for Violet's sake, but I think it dishonors others who served honorably." She shifted her gaze to the grave site. "Still, I'll make the best of it for Violet."

"I will, too," Rick said.

Olivia removed her hand from his and joined Violet. "I'm so sorry for your loss, Violet."

"Dr. Dobbs. Thank you for caring enough to come today."

She clutched Olivia's hand and drew her onto the seat next to her. "Sit with me. Please."

"Of course." Olivia continued to hold Violet's hand. Rick quietly sat next to her.

They remained in place without speaking. Letting grief and pain have their way. Absorbing the moment until the chaplain began the service.

Violet held up through his touching message, the gun salute, and the forlorn sound of taps ringing from a trumpet. The marines handed her the folded flag. She stoically placed it on her lap, but her shoulders shook, and her sobs cut through Olivia's heart. She gripped Violet's hand tighter and vowed to keep her own composure to help her. After the service concluded, Olivia helped the older woman to her feet and gave her a hug.

Violet soon pulled back and held out the flag. "I want you to have this."

"No," Olivia protested. "I couldn't possibly take it."

"Please," Violet said. "You cared so much for my son. Any quality of life he had these last few years was due to your kindness. He would want you to have it."

Olivia didn't want to take the flag when Violet was likely letting her grief take over. But she graciously accepted it and would check back with Violet in the next few weeks to see if she'd changed her mind.

Violet's gaze shifted to Rick, her eyebrow rising in question.

"This is Rick Cannon," Olivia said. "The FBI agent who located the shooter."

"Thank you." She clutched his hand. "And I see you served in the military, too."

Rick nodded, but said nothing, likely because he couldn't lie about how he felt about the military funeral.

When others stepped up to talk to Violet, Olivia said good-bye and promised to check in with her. Rick took Olivia's hand, and they headed for the parking lot. Olivia made sure she was out of Violet's earshot when she finally let her tears go.

Rick put an arm around her and without a word escorted her to the car, where he stopped to hold her in his arms. She clutched the flag between them and rested her cheek on Rick's chest.

"Violet was right," he said. "You helped Ace, and it would be great if you could continue to help others."

She peered up at him. "I hope that's what the break will allow me to do."

He nodded. "Now would be a good time for me to mention that we have hospitals in D.C. And you can write a book anywhere, right?"

"I can at that," she said, hoping this was headed where she thought it was headed.

He gnawed on his lip for a moment. "Maybe you'd consider moving to D.C."

"I'll do more than consider it if you want." Her heart pounded in her chest as she waited for his response.

"Oh, I want, honey," he said, his lips lifting in a heart-melting smile. "I want."

EPILOGUE

Washington, D.C.
Tuesday, November 22
6:20 p.m.

With one kick of the starter, the Harley's powerful motor thrummed to life below Rick. He exited the airport hangar and couldn't wait to get to his house to see Olivia. She'd flown in that afternoon for the annual Thanksgiving party held by Tara's Aunt June.

He motored to the state-of-the-art security gate and flipped up his face shield.

The night guard, who looked like he could bench-press four hundred, poked his head out the door. "Evening, Agent Cannon."

"Steve."

"Heading home?"

"I am at that."

Steve opened the gate. "Stay vertical, man."

Rick smiled at the common parting expression between bikers. Steve had once been an avid biker, but after he married and had his first child, his wife had urged him to sell his bike. Rick couldn't do the same thing. He'd been through two months of counseling and had made progress with his issues. He'd reconciled with his mom and spent time with her and Yolanda when he'd visited Olivia. And he'd even made an uneasy truce with his father, though they had a long way to go. But giving up his bike? That he couldn't do.

Or could he? If Olivia asked, he would. The thing was, she knew the joy he took from his bike, and he doubted she would ask, so he might never know.

On the road he hammered down and let his mind drift to the conversation he planned to have with her. Conversation, shoot. He was going to propose. Wouldn't be a surprise to her. They'd talked about their future over the last couple of months as she'd worked to finalize things with her clients. Still, Rick was more nervous than he'd ever been.

Relax. Enjoy the ride. He settled in and let the rushing wind and hum of the motor calm his nerves while he thought about taking Olivia out on the new Harley for the hour-long ride to June's farm. Sharing his love of riding would be sweet. *If* she was willing to try it after expressing her fear of motorcycles.

He took the last corner to his house low, balancing nearly horizontally in the sweet spot between optimum speed and eating asphalt. He rolled past Olivia's rental car and into the garage. The inside door was suddenly flung wide. He put down the kickstand, and Olivia came flying out to the garage. She wore pants that fit her like a glove and sent his senses reeling. She catapulted into his arms. Touching her fired off the few senses that hadn't already awoken.

She kissed him hard, and he deepened it until they were both breathless. She lifted her head and smiled. "Hi."

"Hi back atcha." Happiness, still so foreign to him, made him smile.

She poked a finger into his cheek. "I love your dimples."

"I don't have dimples."

"You do when you smile, and you've been doing a lot of that lately."

"You, too."

She leaned back farther. "I have a lot to be happy about. If you don't count my mother and Harrison still not talking to me."

"They'll get over it," he said and hoped he was right. "Speaking from experience, you're a hard person to stay unhappy with."

She tapped her watch. "We should get going. We can take my rental car."

"There's one thing I need to do before we go." He reached behind her to a blue blanket and whipped it into the air to reveal the new Harley he'd bought a few weeks ago. The bright-red paint and polished chrome begged for him to take a ride, but he'd held off riding the beauty this long so he could take the maiden voyage with Olivia. What was a few more minutes?

"Ooh." She ran a hand over the seat. "You bought a pretty new bike."

He faked an angry look. "Okay, first of all, no 'pretty' remarks."

She saluted, but her grin said she had no intention of complying. "And second?"

"Second, it's not just any bike."

She stared at it. "No?"

"No. It's totally different from my other Harley."

She shot her gaze between the two. "Okay, I give up. They look the same, other than one is an older restored model and this one looks brand new."

"Hop on and maybe you'll figure it out."

Her eyes cleared. "Oh, I get it. There's room for two people on the new bike."

"Exactly." He held his breath in anticipation of her response.

She sidled up to him. "Are you telling me something here?"

"No, asking." He opened a saddlebag and drew out the ring box he'd stashed inside it before his latest trip.

She clamped her hand over her mouth, her eyes shining with joy and giving him courage to get down on one knee and leave himself open for the possibility of great hurt.

"I trust you and love you with my whole heart, Olivia." He gazed up at her and flipped open the box to reveal the solitaire diamond his mother had helped him pick out. "Will you marry me?"

"Yes. Of course. There's no one I'd rather be with for the rest of my life."

He slipped the ring on her finger and got to his feet to kiss her, but before he could, she climbed on the back of the new bike.

"Guess if you trust me enough to ask me to marry you, I have to return the favor." She reached for the helmet.

He settled on the bike facing her, taking her hands and stopping her from retrieving the helmet.

"I bought the bike as a symbol of us being together. You don't have to ride with me if you don't want to. I'm pretty sure we can have a wonderful life even if you don't like motorcycles."

"Ah, but I love you, Rick Cannon, and I'd take any opportunity to put my arms around you. So fire up this bad boy, and let's take a spin."

He clutched her to him, and happiness invaded his soul. "June's house, here we come."

"No need to rush things," Olivia whispered in his ear. "Let's start with a short trip to the end of the block and back. I have years with you to work up to a long country drive."

ACKNOWLEDGMENTS

Thanks to:

My family for making so many sacrifices so I can continue to follow my dreams.

My agent, Chip MacGregor. Your talent and skills have blessed my writing career, and when I panic over the little things you are always there to talk me off the ledge.

My editor, Christina Boys. I continue to be in awe of your insight and suggestions, and I thank you for walking this journey with me and making the White Knights series so much better.

The talented marketing staff at Hachette/FaithWords—Sara Beth Haring, Sarah Falter, and Katie Connors. I have been so blessed by your support.

Ron Norris, who continues to give of his time and knowledge of police and military procedures, weaponry details, and information technology. As a retired police officer with the La Verne Police Department and a certified information systems security professional, your experience and knowledge are priceless. I can't thank you enough!

Vance Nebling, criminalist in the Portland Police Bureau Forensic Evidence Division. Thank you for the tour of your department and for answering my forensic questions. Your willingness to share your expertise and even suggest unique plot twists is greatly appreciated!

Any errors in or liberties taken with the technical details Ron or Vance so patiently explained to me are all my doing.

And most importantly, thanks to God for giving me the opportunity to share stories of hope and for giving us strong men and women in law enforcement and the military who risk their lives every day for our safety.

READING GROUP GUIDE

1. Rick closes his mind to indicators that he bears some responsibility in the loss of his wife and child. Have you ever blamed someone for something that you had a part in causing? If so, what did you do about it?

2. Rick badly wants to get married and have children, but he denies himself that dream. Is there anything in your life that you are denying yourself that might actually be possible for you? If so, how can you overcome that?

3. Olivia decides that she has been putting limitations on God and she needs to let go of her wishes and trust Him. But it's not long before we see her wanting to take her life back and questioning God's ability to do the right thing by her. Do you ever resolve to act one way then find yourself not doing so? Have you found a way to stop or curtail that behavior in your life?

4. Rick has a huge issue with trust in his life. The people he trusted in his adolescence let him down. Has anyone ever let you down, and you haven't trusted them since then? Do you want to change that? If so, can you now see a way to make the change?

5. Both Rick and Olivia have been betrayed by their families. Has anyone in your family or even a close friend betrayed you? Are you happy with the way you handled it, or do you wish you could change how you behaved? Is it too late to change, or can you still do so? How?

6. Olivia is warm and caring, and her job as a psychologist fits her personality perfectly. She also lets it affect how she deals with her mother and brother. If you're like me, you probably wished she wouldn't let them take advantage of her so often. As a counselor, she recognizes her behavior is wrong and knows she needs to change, but it's hard to do so. Is there an area in your life where you need to change, but are putting it off? After reading *Kill Shot*, can you find a way to make those changes? If so, what might you do?

7. Olivia talks about how people tell themselves lies and can't reach their full potential until they let go of these lies. Are you lying to yourself about something? Is it affecting your life, and would you like to change it? If so, how can you make the change? How might God fit in this decision and in finding a way to make that change?

8. When Rick's wife and unborn child die, he stops praying because he doesn't think prayer does any good. Has a situation in your life ever caused you to stop praying? Have you resumed your prayer life, or are you still not talking to God? Should that change?

9. Olivia is hurt by Rick several times in this story. At first she responds with anger or disappointment, but we soon

see her giving those up in favor of helping Rick with the areas he struggles in, only to have him disappoint her again. How do you think she is able to let go of the hurt so quickly? Do you think she was foolish to do so, or do you admire the way she was able to put Rick first so much of the time?

10. At one point Olivia tells Rick to love people like Jesus, because love always expects the best in others. Do you agree with this statement? If so, why? If not, why not?

ABOUT THE AUTHOR

SUSAN SLEEMAN is a bestselling and award-winning author of more than thirty inspirational/Christian and clean read romantic suspense and mystery novels. With three-quarters of a million books in print, readers love her romantic suspense series for the well-drawn characters and edge-of-your-seat action. She graduated from the FBI and local police citizen academies, so her research is spot on and her characters are real. In addition to writing, Susan also hosts thesuspensezone.com. She has lived in nine states but now calls Oregon home. Her husband is a retired church music director, and they have two beautiful daughters, a very special son-in-law, and an adorable grandson.

Look for the first book in the White Knight series
FATAL MISTAKE

Tara Parrish is the only person ever to survive an attack by the Lone Wolf bomber. Scared and emotionally scarred by her near death, she goes into hiding with only one plan—to stay alive for another day. She knows he's coming after her, and if he finds her, he will finish what he started.

Agent Cal Riggins has had only one goal for the past six months—to save lives by ending the Lone Wolf's bombing spree. To succeed, he needs the help of Tara Parrish, the one person who can lead them to the bomber. Cal puts his all into finding Tara, but once he locates her, he realizes that if he can find her, the Lone Wolf can, too. He must protect Tara at all costs, and they'll both need to resist the attraction growing between them to focus on hunting down the bomber, because one wrong move could be fatal.

"A must-read action-packed romantic suspense."
—Elizabeth Goddard, author of *Targeted for Murder*

Available now from FaithWords wherever books are sold.